THE
KING
OF THE
DAMNED

NORTHERN LIGHT PRESS

TORONTO

ISBN: 978-1-7389631-7-1 (e-book edition)
ISBN: 978-1-7389631-6-4 (print edition)

Northern Light Press
Toronto, Ontario

I

The Carpathian Mountains, Wallachia

The snow drifted menacingly around them, cloaking them in a blanket of white. Yara waited for the shivers to wrack her body, for the tips of her fingers to turn a pearly blue from frostbite, but her hardened skin endured. It was like a yolk had grown across her flesh, protecting her from the cutting bite of winter.

In the dark she found herself haunted by the tales once told to her by her nursemaid of creatures that were cast away from God's light and existed in the dark. Strange how the stories that had once frightened her were now her reality.

She was a vampir.

Prince Mircea and his sired vampir Zuri ran on either side of her. Their footsteps were soft as a whisper. Yara's old mortal eyes would have seen nothing but a mass of twisted fabric and hair drifting hauntingly behind them like capes, but her vampir eyes could trace their every move. Like the shadows that had once shrouded her vision had been lifted. The world was brighter and more vibrant. She could hear the rushing flow of a stream several miles away and the tingling song of a goldcrest bird. Sometimes she'd be so focused on all the sounds around her that she'd forget to look ahead and crash into a sycamore tree. She had crashed into three in the last hour. And from the tight line that pulled Mircea's lips, she could tell he was getting annoyed by her untried limbs.

It had been three days since they had escaped the Court of the Undead. Since she had escaped the new Undying King, Eldar Demirci. Since her world had crumbled to ashes around her.

Her blood spiked in anger to think of all that he had robbed her of. He had ripped Aylin and Ilyas away from her, taken her very life, and imprisoned her. Without Volkan by her side, the pain of transitioning into a vampir had returned. Her eyes hurt and her gums felt stiff and painful to the touch. Zuri promised it would fade in a few weeks or so, but Yara could see no end to this torment. Perhaps, if she were resting and not fleeing for her life, she could endure the changes that were assaulting her body.

They traveled in the depths of the Carpathian Mountains, surrounded by trees that stood like frightful sentries and a horizon that was nothing more than a line of white. The animals feared them and gave them a wide berth, and it often felt as though they were the only souls to exist in this barren wasteland. During the day they'd bury themselves beneath the snow to escape the sunlight, and Yara would spent most of those hours crying. It was so lonesome and felt so much like being buried alive that she couldn't bear it. While she did not require air, the feeling of snow filling her nose was both ticklish and uncomfortable.

"Let us rest," Mircea said.

Yara tried to stop running, but before her legs could receive the message, she collided with a juniper tree. Snow rustled down from the branches and covered her head. She slumped to the floor, rubbing her aching bones.

"I hate this," she huffed. "I hate all of it."

Mircea chuckled. "You will run smoothly enough in time, child. You cannot master a way of life that you've been introduced to only three days ago."

Zuri offered her a hand with an amused smile. Her braids swung under the cape of her hood, creating flickering shadows on the pile of snow beneath them. Zuri was Prince Mircea's loyal right hand. During their time at court, she had managed Mircea's network of spies, and when he had been imprisoned alongside Yara, it had been her who had come to their rescue.

"Stop laughing at me," she grumbled. "Both of you."

"We would cover more distance if your legs weren't so slippery," Mircea said. "If we don't laugh about it, the alternative is to complain."

"You may thank Eldar Demirci for that," Yara said. Her anger wrapped around her throat like a fist. "If it were not for him, I wouldn't be running in the Carpathian Mountains in the middle of winter drinking filthy wildcat blood."

Even though blood tasted delicious, a part of her was still disgusted that she was guzzling the lifeblood of a poor animal. It wasn't half as sweet as human blood. It was duller, and she hated that she noticed. She hated that it bothered her.

"Pitying your situation won't help," Zuri said gently. "You must accept who you are. You will shine brighter for it."

"Do you think Volkan will find me?" Yara whispered. "I know I will be better if he comes. Can we go back for him, please?"

A day hadn't passed where she didn't think about him. A part of her feared that this deep need for him was their sire bond and not what her heart *truly* felt.

Zuri gave her a tight smile and patted her shoulder and returned to the log that Mircea sat on. Her words were a hushed whisper when she spoke. Zuri must have forgotten that her hearing was better now. And Yara felt some shame about eavesdropping, but not enough to stop.

"Have you known of any sired vampir who transitioned without their sire nearby?" Zuri asked.

"In the old days, the trueborn would lock their transitioning sired in a cellar. It made them needy and desperate for them. And once they were unshackled, they would serve them more efficiently, desperate to never know the punishment of an existence without them," Mircea said. "She will survive, but it may strengthen her attachment to him. When they are reunited, they may forge an unbreakable bond."

"He may have aided his brother in this coup. We must assume that Volkan is our enemy as well," she said. "Can we trust her?"

Mircea sighed. "Her loyalty is first and foremost to her sire. It is not ideal, but at least she was not sired by Eldar."

"Thank God for small mercies," Zuri said. "But we cannot let Volkan Demirci live. We cannot let any of them live. The Demirci line must fall."

Yara felt her bones shake. Her teeth lengthened and her claws unsheathed. The pointed tips sharp enough to shear the skin from one's flesh. A rumble sounded in her chest, and their heads snapped up. It took Yara a minute to realize it came from her, a sound so strange and animalistic, it was as if it were drawn from the darkest recesses of her soul.

"We are only strategizing, Yara," Zuri said, palms raised in defense.

But Yara had stood up with the single mission: to eradicate the threat against Volkan. He would not be safe until Zuri was gone.

"Tell her, Mircea."

"We won't kill Volkan," Mircea said in a placating tone, as if she were an unruly child throwing a tantrum. "Not now, at least."

"Swear it," she hissed. "Swear that you won't touch a hair on his head. *Ever*."

Mircea blinked his bright red eyes. All trueborn vampirs had eyes red as his—a mark of their transition. When they fed, the color changed into an obsidian shade that reflected an abyss. And, while sired vampirs kept their natural eye color, their eyes also turned crimson when they were hungry.

Their eyes hadn't darkened once during their travels.

"The Demirci line deserves to fall," Mircea said, echoing Zuri. "Do you think we can rid the world of Eldar and his brother won't come for our throats? They have been inseparable since birth and they are young, their bond not yet tainted by the rot of immortality. I won't risk another Demirci coming for my throne in the name of vengeance."

"I won't let you hurt him," Yara said. "He saved me. He's the reason I live."

"We will discuss this when the time comes," Mircea said. "We are not far from her."

"From whom?" she asked.

"Lady Lugrezia Carrara," he said. "She owes me a favor and will aid our cause."

He said the name as if it were supposed to mean something to her. Yara blinked, awaiting further information. He sighed before patting the spot to his left. Yara sat by him, staring forlornly into the distance. He uncapped the tin of blood he carried, and Yara grimaced before she took a sip. It tasted slightly sour, like it had gone bad, but it was just the taste of animal blood. Not as refreshing and heady as human blood. It was strange to long for something that she knew was wrong for her. Something unholy.

"Lugrezia Carrara. She's from the Carrara trueborn line," he said. "They pay tithes to Dracul, but they keep away from court except for rare circumstances and occasions."

"You said she owes you a favor?" Yara asked.

He nodded. "When I first met her, her brother had her wed to a mortal man. A demeaning betrothal intended to lessen her in the eyes of his family. She was set to be the head of the family, but when she was wed at fifteen, she hadn't transitioned and couldn't escape her brutish husband."

"That's terrible," she said. "Are all vampir so cruel? I have yet to meet any to be admired."

"Not even your precious Volkan?" Zuri teased.

"He was cruel when I first arrived," Yara said thoughtfully. "I haven't forgotten his true nature. Not even when he uses his smile to cover it."

"Smart girl," Mircea said ruffling her hair. It was already a tangled mess, so she didn't bother scolding him for it. It was not exactly the place for frivolity, but she would do anything to take a bath along with a fresh pair of clothes and a little kohl on her eyes and perhaps some lip paint--oh, who was she kidding? There was always a time and a place for some thoughtless meandering-- she hadn't felt this kind of hardship in a long time. Not since she and Aylin were little girls waiting for their father to come home and save them.

"Lugrezia, will she help us?" Yara asked. "Will she help us dethrone Eldar?"

He didn't deserve power.

He didn't deserve the title of the *Undying King*.

He didn't deserve to live.

Her fist clenched tight at the thought of him. Nothing hurt worse than his false promises that night on his throne, dangling the possibility of power before her like a carrot to a horse. Only to snatch it away and imprison her in return. She had been so foolish to think he would ever make her his equal. How could he when he enjoyed tormenting her so much?

"The Carrara hail from Florence and are the trueborn family that controls most of the trade and wealth in Italy. I took Lugrezia from a hard life not too long ago and helped her kill her brother and regain her rightful seat as the leader of the Carrara family. She has a residence she keeps close to court in the winter in case she is ever summoned by Vlad," Mircea said. "You'll like her. She's like you. She's a fighter."

Yara blinked into the distance. All she saw were tree. The forest was cloaked in an eerie silence that made her skin itch. The darkness was unending, and shadows crept along the ground like wolves.

"How much farther?" she asked.

"If you don't run into any trees, we could get there in as little as three days," he said.

"So, four days in total," Zuri said with a twitch of her lips. She had been in far better spirits since they left the confines of the fortress, as if the rules and stiff posture of the court had been erased from her. Yara liked this side of her, even if she had to endure most of her playful ribbing, since Zuri wouldn't *dare* poke fun at Mircea.

"I can barely stand another day of this misery," Yara said.

She wondered if Aylin had made it back to the hunters and if Ilyas had survived the attack. It hurt that she hadn't had a chance to speak to her sister, and she worried that Aylin was upset with her. That she would see her as a monster now. That she wouldn't recognize her anymore. The thought of it made her sick.

She hadn't had a single moment to process everything that had occurred, all she had lost during the battle. Her innocence, her mortality, her dreams and hopes. From where she sat, her future looked bleak and filled to the brim with uncertainty. The only thought that kept her pushing was the war she would wage against the Undying King and the pain she would bring him for everyone whom he had hurt: Mircea, Aylin, Ilyas.

She would not stop until Eldar Demirci was nothing but ashes.

II

Wallachia was drenched in the cold grasp of frost. It was almost the end of December. The month when weak things died. And while the cold didn't touch Volkan's skin, the ever-present chatter of his blood slave's teeth was enough to set him on edge. Thaddeus thought bringing along two of his blood slaves was excessive, but Volkan despised animal blood. He couldn't risk one of them succumbing to the cold and leaving him without a spare.

His hand tightened on the reins and his leather gloves stretched across his long fingers. It had been three days since he left. Three days without Eldar. It was strange to not see his scowling face or hear his blunt voice or clever insults.

"Stop thinking about him," Thaddeus said.

It wasn't the first time he had thought about his brother. Thaddeus knew as well as Volkan did that it would not be the last time.

"You don't know what it's like," Volkan said. Nobody knew what it was like. To be born with someone. Eldar was more than merely his brother. He was a piece of his soul. They had never fought like they did that night. He had never seen Eldar look so lost. Volkan could admit that it had felt a little nice to know he was just as dependent on Volkan as he was on Eldar. It was his brother's name he had whispered in a loop on all those miserable nights he spent in captivity, left to the whims of Titus and Pomona Maleinos. Curled and broken, all he could think about was Eldar saving him. For so long he had relied on Eldar; he had never thought that perhaps Eldar relied on him as well.

"He's too far gone," Thaddeus said. "Blinded by power."

"Undying King," Pariza said with a thoughtful look. "Do you think he is looking for a consort?"

Pariza was another one of his sired vampir. Besides Thaddeus, she was his closest friend. She had arrived recently from the Demirci home in Angora. Volkan had summoned her a few weeks ago. He had sensed that Eldar was up to something the night Pomona had died and he had caught sight of his altered brother. Feeding on a vampir had been outlawed a very long time ago, but Eldar had never been one for rules.

"Your desperation for Eldar is getting old," Thaddeus said, shooting Pariza a disgusted look.

"I'm sure he only needs time to warm up to me," Pariza said with a toss of her dark hair.

Many men would fall on their blades for Pariza. Volkan had a taste for surrounding himself with beautiful people. All his sired were either renowned for their artistic talent or beauty. He had a great appreciation for the arts and an even greater appreciation for God's creations.

"His type isn't a loudmouthed girl with few manners," Thaddeus said.

"I'm upset he gave you your heart back," Pariza said with a sniff. "I wish he had burned it."

"You told her that?" Thaddeus said, looking at Volkan accusingly.

Before he could respond, Thaddeus had turned back to Pariza. "I wish Volkan had let you die of the plague instead of turning you."

"I wish your mother died on the birthing bed."

"I wish your father became impotent before he bedded your mother."

"I wish your grandmother—"

"Enough," Volkan said. "You both will give me a headache."

"When Eldar makes me his consort my first verdict shall be your execution," she said, glaring at Thaddeus.

Pariza and Thaddeus got along much like oil and water. Before Eldar and Volkan had returned to court, Eldar had warned Volkan he could only bring one of them along. It was a never-ending ring of insults and biting remarks anytime they were around each other. Like two children desperate for the attention of a parent, they fought for Volkan's goodwill and always sought to outdo the other. And while Volkan usually enjoyed stoking their competitive spirit, he was too worried about Yara to play along. She must have been so afraid and lonely, and the thought made his chest hurt.

"Eldar would sooner make *me* his consort than you," Thaddeus said. "At least he and I have had a conversation before."

"We've had a conversation," she said with a sniff of her nose. It was her tell that she was lying. Volkan wondered if Thaddeus knew that. "A meaningful one."

Thaddeus snorted. "You wishing him good morning and him not acknowledging you isn't a conversation."

"Silence. Both of you," Volkan said sharply. "If Eldar had trouble tracking us before, he'll have no issue with your shouting. You may as well light a smoke signal."

Eldar had his men combing the nearby village and mountain for Yara and the last thing Volkan wanted to do was to lure his soldiers straight to her.

He didn't trust Eldar around Yara.

Pariza sighed and trotted her stallion to the opposite side of Volkan, far away from Thaddeus.

"Do *you* think I have a chance with your dashing brother?" she asked.

"No," he said. "Eldar only ever liked my toys."

"So, what you're saying is if he sees me flirting with you, he'll chase me to the ends of the earth?" Pariza asked, her eyes alight with interest.

"Being wanted by my brother is not a pleasurable experience," Volkan said. "You should ask Yara. He turned her to a vampir against her will, imprisoned her, fatally injured her friend, and sent her sister away all in the span of one night."

Volkan knew his brother better than anyone. Eldar did not hate Yara. If he had, she would have been dead a long time ago. He had turned her because he wanted her, and in his twisted mind a mortal wasn't worthy of being with him, but a vampir certainly was.

"It is impressive, the work he can do in a single night," Pariza said. "You know I want someone vicious, Volkan. Someone ambitious and headstrong. That's why he has always appealed to me."

"I'll put in a good word the next time we see him," Volkan said.

Perhaps Pariza could distract him from Yara. Perhaps she could break this obsession before it festered and consumed them all.

Eldar had always focused on tasks with enviable focus. If he ever put aside his fear of being in love and pursued Yara, it would ruin them all, especially Volkan, because he wanted Yara for himself. She was the first person who made him doubt everything he had ever known and who made him feel like his demons wouldn't drown him.

In a sea of mayhem and destruction, she was his anchor.

She was his calm.

———

"There is someone following us," Thaddeus whispered.

It would be dawn in a few hours, and they had to pitch their tents before the sun arose and blackened them to ashes. Volkan despised their weakness to the sun. He hated that he had to waste precious hours asleep while Yara's trail grew cold. The footprints of Mircea and Yara and the third person they traveled with were growing faint with every snowfall. It was only his bond with Yara as her sire that made her scent easy to trace.

"We have to find whoever it is before first light," Volkan said. "We cannot set camp if there is someone who could be a threat."

Thaddeus nodded.

"We'll find them," Pariza said, her teeth lengthening. The dark rope of her braid swung behind her shoulder as they both tore off into the distance.

Volkan curled his finger at the boy, the blood slave. He dutifully offered his wrist, and Volkan fed. He watched as the boy's eyes dimmed with pleasure, and it reminded him of Yara. Of her soft brown eyes and the way she looked at him when he fed from her, as if she would let him do anything to her if he only asked. He missed her. More than he cared to admit.

It was hours later when Thaddeus returned. By then his blood slaves had braided his hair and bathed him with melted ice and soap. His eyes were hooded with sleep when the tent flaps were drawn open, and he sat up in alert.

"I found a rat," Thaddeus announced.

He drew in two sentries. Their faces were covered by scarves. It wasn't surprising that Eldar's army had caught up to them. Thaddeus kicked out their legs from under them, and they both fell to their knees.

"It's been a long day," Volkan said. "I will give you the pleasure of a quick death."

He unsheathed his claw to tear out their throats.

"Yara will be upset if I die," a familiar feminine voice said.

Volkan ripped the scarf from the small frame, unsurprised to find Yara's demonic sister. He found it hard to believe they were both conceived in the same womb. This one was feral, while Yara was poised and delicate. Yara was his little flower while this one was the thorns that grew on the side.

"*You*," he said with a slight curl to his lip.

"Volkan the idiot," she spat.

"That's not his moniker," Thaddeus said with a swift kick to her ribs. "Volkan the beautiful will suffice, or Volkan the clever."

The man beside her growled and attempted to charge at Thaddeus, but Pariza grabbed him by the neck and peeled back his scarf. Volkan tilted his head curiously; he wasn't her Transylvanian beast, but another man. One with cropped blond hair and hard green eyes. There was something rabid about him. As if he would attack anyone at the slightest provocation.

"You've found a new lover?" Volkan asked. "Did you tire of the old one?"

A flash of pain crossed her eyes. A hint that she wasn't as cold as she pretended to be.

"Did you tire of being your brother's shadow?" she asked. "He's the more cunning and beautiful one. I learned all that from the five minutes I spent in your company."

Volkan smiled a sharp smile that always brought shivers to the mortals. "I could say the same about your sister. She is superior to you in every way that counts."

"Nice try," she said with a smile that mimicked his own. One as sharp as blades. "Do you think that'll make me cry tonight? That I will soak my pillow with tears because you insulted me?"

"Don't listen to a word he says," her companion said. His lips were tight, as if he were picturing crushing Volkan's skull beneath his boots.

"Why are you following us?" Volkan asked.

"We left the hunters to save Yara. After everything your cursed brother did, I knew she wasn't safe. Domenico and I overheard a pair of soldiers on our way to Poenari. They were looking for my sister and said she escaped," she said. "We killed them, stole their uniforms, and joined the search party."

"Clever," Pariza said, waggling her finger at her. "I like this one."

"What do you want with Yara?" the girl demanded. "Do you want to take her back to him?"

He couldn't recall her name for the life of him.

"No," Volkan said. "I sired her. She belongs with me."

"She belongs with herself," Yara's sister said sharply. "You vicious men don't own her. Release us."

"Tie them both to the beam," Volkan said. "Until she learns some manners and whatever demon is possessing that one is expelled." He pointed at the boy. "I want eyes on them both."

They both dove in opposite directions to catch Pariza and Thaddeus off guard. But, as well trained as they were, their strength did not compare to a vampir's. They were quickly subdued and tied to the wooden beam that held their tent upright.

"We should strip them of their clothes," Thaddeus said. "Humiliate them for their disrespect."

Volkan's lips curled. "She may look like an underfed boy, but she is still a woman, and we will treat her as such."

"Idiot," Pariza murmured under her breath.

"It was just a suggestion," Thaddeus grumbled.

"I didn't know you were so chivalrous," the girl said with a sarcastic bite.

"I'll decide your fate at nightfall," Volkan said.

"You can't kill me," she said, raising her chin. "Yara would never forgive you."

"I never said anything about killing you. But him"—he looked at the boy, who glared at him like he could kill him with his stare alone—"he is fair game."

Volkan was pleased to find his statement shocked her into silence. No clever retort, no smirk, not even a blink of her eyes.

He would try to keep her intact for Yara, but Volkan had a bad habit of killing things that irritated him. It would be a challenge.

He only hoped she didn't tempt him into a temper.

III

Yara didn't think she'd survive another day of this torturous journey. It was a miracle she had made it this far. But as the days progressed, her transition into a creature of the night worsened. It was like her body was rebelling against the very idea of this metamorphosis. Her muscles shook and everywhere ached. She also seemed to be the only one sweating. She didn't even think a vampir *could* sweat. The heightened sight and hearing often made her head pound and her gums ached terribly that even speaking hurt.

Mircea said it took days if not weeks for a vampir to fully transition. Until then her body would be torn between its old mortal form and her new vampir form.

"She has a fever," Zuri said, wiping the sweat from Yara's brow. "Her transition isn't going well. She needs to be near Volkan. Or she will suffer needlessly."

"We can't afford to stop," Mircea said. "And he is not here, so she must endure."

"What do we do?" Zuri asked. "She cannot go forward."

"We'll carry her," he said.

Yara groaned when he picked her up. She just wanted to rest. She just wanted enough time for the pain to dim. She'd be fine if she could just rest for a bit. She said as much, but Mircea gently shushed her. And then they were running again, the wind scraping her cheek with idle fingers.

Her vision flickered, swaying like a lost ship caught among the tides. She saw a woman in the distance with dark skin and a bright smile. With pretty, dark hair that coiled in a knot above her head. Yara reached out a hand to touch her, to feel her, to embrace her. An ache spread through her chest.

"Mama," she whispered.

It had been so long since she'd seen her face. Since she'd felt the gentleness of her touch and heard the beauty of her voice as she sang old folk songs around the fire. Yara walked toward her. Tears slipped down her face, sliding down her chin and into the collar of her dress. The closer she approached her the more her smile dimmed, and her eyes grew wide with fright. Each step Yara took towards her was mimicked by a step back. Her mother's limbs shook, quivering like a fallen leaf, her teeth clicking in a broken rhythm.

"You're a monster," she whispered. "Stay away from me, and stay away from Aylin."

"No, no, Mama," she said desperately, struggling to grasp ahold of her. "It's me, it's Yara."

"Stay away from me," she hissed. Her lips were pulled back in a snarl that she had never witnessed before. Her mother was afraid of her. She was disgusted by her.

Yara stumbled back, falling on a lump of snow beneath her. The cold did not make her flinch. It matched the temperature of her skin. Matched her soulless, cursed body.

When she blinked, she saw Aylin beside her mother. It was the old Aylin with her beautiful dark hair spun like woven silk, clasping their mother's hand.

"Aylin," she said with relief.

A small sob escaped her. Aylin loved her. Aylin would never turn away from her.

"Aylin, I miss you."

"My sister is dead," Aylin said. Her eyes were empty and devoid of feeling. "I watched her die. You are nothing but a demon pretending to be her. My sister is dead."

"No," she whimpered. "No, Aylin. It's me. I'm alive."

"I would rather you had died than become a monster," Aylin said, lips curled in disgust. "As far as I am concerned, my beautiful, sweet Yara is dead."

Beside them was their father, his arm wrapped around their mother and Aylin as if he sought to protect them from her. His eyes were cold and hard, as though they were fashioned from steel. She knew he would shun her; she could see it in his eyes.

I didn't choose this.

I didn't want this.

She pressed her fists as hard as she could into her eyes to erase this terrible vision. When she lowered her hand, the vision was gone, and she sighed in relief. In the place of her family was Volkan, and she couldn't help but run to him, let him protect her from their accusatory eyes and vicious tongues. She came to a screeching halt before him when she caught sight of his eyes; he did not look at her with any affection, but rather horror.

"You are tainted," he said. "Look at you."

Yara stared down at her hands. Black veins drifted beneath her skin like lace gloves. They climbed upward, toward her shoulder in a grotesque mimic of a *henna* design. She dug her nails into her skin as if she could peel off the taint. As if she could wipe the disgust from his face if she were only less monstrous.

She covered her face with her hands. She couldn't handle the disappointment and hatred.

It was too much.

It was drowning her.

Leather-clad hands drew her fingers away from her face. Her eyes rose slowly to look at *his* face. His dark hair billowed in the breeze and his pale face blended into the landscape. He looked beautiful in the dark. She didn't even find the black veins that began beneath his neck gruesome, nor did she flinch at the black mass that was his eyes or his sharp teeth that now descended past his lips. Far sharper than any vampir she had seen before.

"They will never understand you," he whispered. "They will never want you."

A jolt of fear slipped down her spine at the sight of him.

The Undying King.

Eldar tilted her head back. "All this time I had thought I had failed you. I thought I was broken, and that the cost of power was for me to never sire another immortal."

"You didn't sire me," she whispered. "Volkan did."

She knew it. She knew in her heart that she was sired by Volkan. She had felt it that night when she was curled in his bed. When it had felt like for a moment that everything would be fine. That she would be safe.

"No," he said. "We both did."

Yara stiffened. "That is not true."

More importantly, it was not possible. From what she knew during her time at court, only the trueborn could turn mortals. A single trueborn vampir could sire multiple mortals, but multiple trueborn vampir could not sire a single mortal.

"Then how are we here?" He spread his arms to gesture at the empty white landscape. "Why do we have a sire bond? Why can we speak to each other?"

"That is not true," she repeated. "I feel strongly for Volkan. I want to protect him. All I want to do now is to claw your eyes out."

"Do it," he said.

He stepped forward till their chests were pressed against each other. Till she could feel the icy graze of his breath along her cheekbones.

Yara raised her hand. She had seen the vampir dig their claws into their enemy's chest to yank out their hearts. If they could do it, so could she. She aimed for his chest, but her fingers froze just before they grazed his silky black kaftan with the silver clasps.

"What did you do?" She glared at him. "I can't touch you."

"No, you can't *hurt* me," he said. "Because you are sired by me. We are bonded by blood. I am inside you. Here." The gloves were gone, vanishing into thin air. And when he raised his hand to skirt those ink-tipped claws up her sternum, she could feel the sharp drag of it along the fabric of her dress. It traveled lazily up her collarbone until his long fingers performed their favorite gesture and wrapped around her throat.

"I don't believe you," she said, swatting his hand away. He withdrew it with a sharp grin. "I don't believe anything that comes out of your mouth."

"I've never lied to you," Eldar said. "I never pretended to be anything less than who I am."

"Who you *are* is the problem," she spat. "I will never forgive you for everything. I will not stop until you are dead. If your words are true and I can't strike the killing blow, then I will find someone who can."

His face hardened and his hand fell abruptly. "I advise you against the 'who can hurt the other best' game, little mouse. It won't work out well for you. It never did the first time around."

"I'm not scared of you," Yara said. "I have nothing left to lose."

"We will see about that," Eldar said. "Return home in a fortnight, or I won't be held responsible for what I do next."

Yara raised her chin. If she had to become a monster to defeat him, she would. If she had to lose every last trace of the person she had once been to ruin him, she would. There was no line too far to cross. No battle too large to wage. He had stolen her mortality, hurt her friends and family, and imprisoned her. He would pay for his crimes against her. He would pay for *everything*.

"Do your best," she said. "I only hope Volkan forgives me for your death. He is all I have to share this miserable life with. You took Aylin and you took Ilyas, but he will never leave me. You can paint me these twisted visions all you please. You do not frighten me."

Eldar smiled a gruesome smile that only made him look more monstrous.

"He doesn't care about you. There have been dozens before you and there will be twice as many after you," he said in his darkly enchanting voice. "You are nothing to him but a pretty distraction. A trinket. A *pet*."

"As if I am anything more to you," she said. "Tell me, Eldar, why I should return to you when all you've ever done was hurt me."

"Because I am not Vlad. I will not hide in castles and rule over the undead," he said. "I will start with your precious Constantinople and expand to the east, the west, and everything in between."

"You are lying," she whispered.

"Don't test me, little mouse," he said. "I will burn your world if it means you return to me on your hands and knees."

Yara woke up suddenly to find her head on Mircea's lap. His lips were tightened in a scowl and his eyes were latched on to her hands.

"Look," he said gruffly.

Yara followed his gaze down to her hands. Behind her brown skin was a mapwork of stark black veins that matched *his*. Its poisonous arms climbed higher with each minute that passed. Her heart clenched.

It hadn't been a nightmare.

"I'm sired by them both," she said, slowly tracing the dark veins on her left arm with her thumb. It felt strange and unholy. A marker to prove she was *other*. A threat to both mortals and vampir. When she looked across at Zuri, she looked frightened by this development. Yara turned her gaze to Mircea to see if it was reflected in his eyes, but he only looked uneasy, as if he were contemplating a heavy decision. It felt as though she had awakened in the middle of an important conversation.

"It's unheard of," Mircea said. "But I suppose it makes sense. They are twinned, after all. Their blood must be near identical, and you said Eldar tried to revive you before Volkan arrived."

"She has his power, Mircea. His strength and speed and lord knows what else," Zuri said tightly. She did not speak it as if it were a good thing. Zuri spoke as if Yara could not be trusted, as if this brought her loyalty into question.

"I know," Mircea said.

"If she sides with him, we will have no chance of survival," Zuri said. Before Yara could blink, Zuri was by her side with a blade to her heart. It pricked her skin, and she stilled. "We must get rid of her now, my prince, while she is weak and transitioning. We won't stand a chance after."

Mircea was silent, and Yara stared at him, eyes marked with uncertainty.

"Mircea?" she asked softly. "Do you think I am a monster as well?"

Even though she knew what she had seen had been one of Eldar's twisted mind games, she could not help but think of everyone she cared for turning against her. Especially now that she looked at Mircea with equal parts sadness and hope, and it felt as though the terrible vision Eldar painted was manifesting before her.

"Her loyalty belongs to the Demircis," Zuri continued. "She will always put them first. Just as I put you first."

"I would never hurt you, Mircea," Yara said. "You are like a father to me. I love you."

His brows crinkled in pain.

"My prince, think with your head, not your heart," Zuri said. "If she sides with Eldar, your throne will be lost to you. Your home will be out of your reach. Your life will be at risk."

"I hate Eldar," Yara insisted. "I hate him more than I ever thought possible. I would never stand with him."

"My Prin—"

"Lower your blade," Mircea said.

"But—"

"You've never doubted an order before. Do not let this be the first," he said in his regal voice, cold and dismissive. It silenced Zuri, and she swiftly withdrew her blade, tucking it into her sheath with a loud snap. She disappeared into the thicket, braids swinging furiously behind her.

Yara lifted her weak frame long enough to wrap her arms around Mircea.

"Thank you," she whispered.

"You won't ever turn against me, will you?" he asked.

Yara shook her head. "Never."

"You are my child, yes?" he asked. "Will you always obey me?"

Yara nodded. He had saved her from that wretched cellar. He had pulled her through a half-frozen river and carried her when her legs were weak. Mircea had taken care of her without ever expecting anything in return. Only family ever took care of you so selflessly.

"I will, Mircea," she said. "I promise."

She was not the innocent girl she had once been, and she would never dare come before her old family again as she was. Both because she feared their reaction to her and because her old life was gone. The need to return to Constantinople had fizzled to embers when she died. Mircea was all she had left. He was the closest thing to family that she had.

A part of her was frightened of Aylin rejecting her. It hadn't been long ago when she hunted the vampir. She hoped that Aylin would return home to Baba, so she never had to live with what her sister had become. In the coming months, their father would need her by his side. It was time that he properly mourned Yara and moved on with his life. His little girl was dead, and it would do Aylin well to mourn her as well.

Mircea's face softened as if he could sense her turmoil and anguish. He patted her head gently which for Mircea was a gesture equivalent to a passionate speech.

"Do you feel better?" he asked. "Can you walk?"

Yara nodded, standing up to stretch her limbs.

She struggled not to think of Eldar Demirci standing in the snow. The trail of his cold hand. Even now in death, she could feel his otherness, feel the biting cruelty of his eyes.

A man more fearsome than Vlad Dracul.

A man who hungered for her demise.

He was wrong if he thought she would sit and cower until he found her. Yara was done grieving the girl she had once been. The old Yara had died on the stone floor of the castle. She was a vampir now. One that intended to strike fear in the hearts of her enemies. One who had the power and strength of the Undying King flowing through her veins and who would use it to destroy him.

And Eldar Demirci, King of the Damned, would never see it coming.

IV

Aylin tested the knots of her bond, but it held against the pressure. They had tied her and Domenico together, their wrists conjoined in twin knots, forcing them to lean on each other. It had been a week and a half since they arrived in Wallachia with the goal of erasing all the vampir at Poenari Castle. It had been a few days since they had left Salvatore Di Mazi and the hunters of the Silver Cross in Arefu and just as long since she had last seen her sister. All Yara and Aylin had shared was their brief reunion before the Undying King orchestrated their painful separation. Aylin was tired of having her sister ripped away from her. It felt as though fate conspired against them.

Guilt twisted her gut at the thought of Ilyas on that cot, unconscious and broken. Blood had been leaking from his scalp when she had last seen him. She didn't know if he lived or if he had succumbed to his injury. His words haunted her every time she closed her eyes.

You are all I have, Aylin. You are all I've ever had.

Why did it feel as if she had betrayed him? As if she'd turned her back on him? It was worse now that she was accompanied by Domenico Zancherelli, their worst enemy. There had been a time when they had been at each other's throats. When all she had wanted was to feel his blood soak her hands and the scar of his death to mark her consciousness. But ever since the battle, all she felt was hollow.

It was strange to be far from Ilyas. To exist without him.

"Why are you helping me?" she asked Domenico one cold night when the shadows flickered ominously in the snow and the only way to fight against the biting cold was to entangle herself in his embrace. To let his cursed arms wrap around her waist. It was made worse so by the fact that he had cleaned the wound on her stomach a few hours earlier. That she had raised her tunic for his inspection and felt the cold graze of his hand skirting the wound before he cleaned it and wrapped it.

"Maybe I simply wanted an excuse to do this," he said, tightening his arms around her waist. "And this." She felt the slide of his thigh shift between her own. She hated that her muscles tightened, and her skin burned. She hated that she reacted to him at all.

"Behave," she said sharply. "This is merely a survival tactic. It means *nothing*."

"To you," he said. "To me it is everything."

"I don't want you, Domenico," she said. "And now that we are far from Salvatore you have nothing to lord over my head. No more dirty secrets. Nothing to force me to be with you."

"I don't need to blackmail you to keep you," he said. "You are mine. You have always been mine. You are simply too blind to notice."

Aylin sighed. "You must have hit your head in battle. Nothing you say is coherent at all."

"Think about it," he said. "That idiot—"

"You mean yourself?" she bit back. "Because Ilyas is the cleverest person I know."

"If I were *not* clever, you would be back in Salvatore's camp rather than here in my arms." His arms tightened just hard enough to make her breath hitch. She would rather succumb to the cold than have him hold her.

"What is it that you even like about me?" she asked. "Name three things."

Domenico tilted her till she faced him.

"Your eyes, your mouth, your tongue," he said, striking off a finger for each absurd comment.

"Your words threaten to make me swoon," she said dryly. "So masterful and romantic."

Aylin turned away from him. He was so close that even looking into his eyes felt unbearably intimate.

"I like it when you flirt with me," he said. Her back was turned to him, but she could feel his smug smile even with her eyes closed.

"There is nothing flirtatious about wanting to slit your throat," she said.

"Careful," he warned. "Or I might think you want me to propose."

———

Volkan had set a rotation of guards around them. It was either the boy with the mismatched eyes or the pretty raven-haired girl who watched over them during the long hours of the day, while Volkan slept like a corpse with his palms folded neatly on his chest and his glossy white lashes as still as a frightened canary. It almost looked like he was dead. Aylin had to remind herself several times that he technically *was* dead.

Two humans traveled with Volkan and his entourage, which were no doubt their food. They didn't speak. From their similar features and hair, they were likely related. Aylin suspected they were siblings.

"When we escape, we should cut his hair," Aylin whispered, knowing full well Pariza could hear her. They were both so protective of Volkan that she couldn't help but goad her. "He is so vain he won't know what to make of himself."

"I want the other one's eye," Domenico said, eyeing Thaddeus. "I like keepsakes."

"And her?" Aylin asked, pleased that he was playing along with her. Ilyas would have scolded her and warned her not to provoke their captors. Her heart clenched at the thought of Ilyas. She prayed that he recovered and that he waited for her. Aylin would return for him. There was no force in this world strong enough to keep her away.

Domenico studied Pariza thoughtfully, like she was an animal he had every intention of cutting to pieces. He neither let himself be distracted by her beauty nor paid it any mind. Her skin was pale as milk and her hair dark as night. A striking contrast. Aylin had never seen anyone as beautiful as Pariza, except for Yara, of course.

"Her skin," Domenico said at last. "I want to carve it off."

Aylin turned to him, underestimating how close he was to her. The brush of his stubble scratched her cheek, leaving behind little pinpricks on her flesh.

"How?" she whispered.

"I'd slide the blade under the seam of her mouth, begin with her face, and then work downwards. It would make a nice carpet for our future home," he said.

"I don't see a future with you," Aylin said. "But I like the picture you paint."

"If she doesn't want you, then I don't mind taking her place," Pariza purred. "I like a man with a taste for violence."

It was clear from her sharp grin that she wanted to provoke them both. Aylin hated that her chest tightened and that when Pariza's claw reached to stroke Domenico's throat, she itched to break it in half.

"Don't touch me," Domenico said. His words were a mere rumble in his chest.

Pariza leaned away from him as if she could sense the beast inside him. The one that would tear and claw at her till nothing remained but shreds. Domenico was vibrating beside her, and she watched the ropes strain against his chest.

"Easy," she said softly.

It was instinct when she wrapped her smallest finger around his thumb. The tension leaked from his body, and his breathing turned even.

"Interesting," Pariza mused.

Aylin had no interest in looking at her any longer. She closed her eyes to get some rest. She had to preserve her energy for the journey ahead. They would set out in a few hours, once night fell. Assuming, of course, that Volkan did not kill them. He had already threatened to kill Domenico.

"Rest your head on my shoulder," Domenico said.

Aylin hesitated. Her back was stiff, and it would be difficult to sleep in this upright position.

"Are you sure?"

"Have I ever said anything I didn't mean?" he asked.

Aylin tilted her head till it rested on his broad shoulder. She could feel every breath he took. Her eyes grew heavy, and she could barely make out the whisper of his next words.

"I'll look after you," he promised.

And then there was only darkness.

———

"Don't you dare," a deep voice growled.

Aylin had barely opened her eyes when she felt a bucket of cold water drench her from the top of her head to the tips of her toes. Her eyes opened to find Thaddeus smiling smugly above her. He crouched down, staring at her with glee.

"You look like a wet rat," he said.

He had only woken her up so rudely and Domenico was spared this treatment. Thaddeus was probably still upset that she had called Volkan an idiot and was punishing her for it.

"I will kill you," Aylin promised. "It will be a slow and miserable death, and I will wear that pretty blue eye of yours on a silver chain when it is all said and done. Oh, also, Domenico will eat the other one."

"Did you hear that?" Thaddeus asked Domenico, with a lazy grin. "She thinks my eyes are pretty."

"Pretty enough to rip out," Domenico said. "I happen to share her sentiment."

"Do you want her to catch her death?" Volkan asked from where he lazily slouched on his throne of pillows as they awaited sunset. "Dry her. *Now.*"

He frowned. "Pariza, dry her. I don't want to touch her."

"Clean up your own mess," Pariza replied.

He found a rag and roughly scrubbed Aylin's face and neck. It felt as though he were flaying the skin off her bones. It was a small mercy that she wore her stolen breastplate armor. If she were only protected by cloth, her skin would have scabbed from his harsh treatment.

"Saddle the horses," Volkan said. "You will each ride with one of them. I want them separated."

"She doesn't leave my side," Domenico said.

Volkan didn't bother with a response, and the way Domenico stared at the white-haired vampir chilled her. It was a raging violence that begged to be unleashed. Yara might not be pleased if Domenico killed him. Aylin would have to find a way to prevent him from killing Volkan, and vice versa.

"Great," Thaddeus murmured. "A feral girl and her wild dog. Excellent company."

"Play nice, children," Volkan said. "We are far from Yara, and I don't wish to spend the whole journey listening to you bicker."

"Just as I did not wish to spend the day watching you primp yourself while my sister could be dead."

Aylin had never seen anyone take so long to get dressed. He had spent twenty minutes having his hair detangled by the servant boy and another ten minutes spreading some cream into his face and drawing kohl on his eyes with a small compact mirror, before patting his lips with a glossy red lip paint. Who would think to pack such a thing? He clearly was not worried about Yara, to think of such frivolous items.

"Unlike you, I don't want Yara to cringe at the sight of me when we are reunited," he said. His nose wrinkled. "When did you last bathe?"

"I don't know. I seem to have forgotten to pamper myself after everything that happened," she snarled. "You are unworthy of her, and I'll tell her *exactly* what I think of you the moment we see each other."

"Bitter words from a bitter girl," Volkan said with a cold smile.

"You are worse than him, the Undying King," she spat. Perhaps it was a bit of an exaggeration, but at that moment she truly did hate him. Standing above her so high and mighty and certain that he was deserving of her sister. In truth, he did not deserve her. None of those creatures deserved her sweet Yara. Even if Yara had become one of them, she knew her sister would never lose her soul. She would always be *her* Yara.

"Your sister thought that once too," Volkan said. "She was convinced that I was the worse of the Demirci brothers. First impressions can be deceiving."

"Or perhaps you simply hide it better."

V

THE CARRARA FAMILY HOME, BORDER OF WALLACHIA

They were in Oltenia, also known by some as Little Wallachia and were not far from Olt River, the namesake of the province. Yara let out a breath of relief when Mircea announced that they had reached their destination. The residence of Lugrezia Carrara wasn't as big as Poenari, but while Poenari had been grim and frightful, Lugrezia's home had once been a monastery. Something about it felt soothing, like the calm hands of a favored prayer.

Its design held elements of typical Roman architecture with ornate arabesques. The Moorish elements were a nice contrast to the traditional Wallachian spires that cut through the silver fir with their gabled roofs. The windows were stuffed with brick trapped behind barbed wire, as most vampir residences were. It was common practice even at court to seal the windows to protect the vampir from the sunlight that poisoned their skin. The gates were decorative, not intended to protect a stronghold. Nothing like the gates that protected the New Palace in Constantinople from the potential of a siege or the great big walls that surrounded Poenari like the arms of a loved one.

"Your friend needs to look into improving the security of her castle," Yara said. "An amateur could breach her home."

"Would anybody dare such a thing?" a soft, feminine voice said.

A woman rode toward them on horseback. Her spine was straight and regal. Her fair hair fell in controlled waves down her back, and she had a sword with a gold-trimmed handle strapped to her back. She twisted a hand, and two guards who wore camouflaged white fatigues rose from the thick quilt of snow. They stepped forward at her command. Yara hadn't even noticed them. She *was* a bit impressed by that.

"Lugrezia," Mircea said with a wide grin. "Still the huntress I remember."

Yara noticed a boar being dragged behind her on another horse. It was bigger than any she had seen before, and Yara was further impressed by her skill.

"My prince," Lugrezia said. "What a surprise!"

She hopped off her horse and bowed regally.

"Rise," Mircea said.

He didn't hesitate when he embraced her. It was a tad emotional, more so from Lugrezia, who looked at him like he was a hero. She seemed to be around Mircea's age, perhaps thirty-five or so, and possessed a youthful spirit. One that Yara found warm and welcoming.

"Have you heard any word from court?" he asked.

Lugrezia shook her head. "I sent my advisor on my behalf. You know I've never been one for politics. His letter was due a few days ago. Is there something to be aware of? Does Lord Dracul require my return?"

"Dracul is dead," Mircea said with little emotion. "The throne has been usurped by Eldar Demirci."

"Eldar the child?" she asked incredulously. "The boy who would hide under the table at court functions?"

"It was Volkan who hid under the table," Mircea said.

"Yes, Volkan was the shy one," she said with a snap of her finger. "Eldar was the one with the sharp stare and polite demeanor. He was always cold and distant, much like Cetin, his father."

Mircea's lips tightened. He didn't respond.

"It makes sense," she said offhandedly. "His father was called Cetin the Ruthless, and Eldar possessed an uncanny resemblance to him. Not physically—God knows he was the spitting image of Izabela Danesti."

"He has broken the sacred rule of cannibalism. He has devoured the flesh of our kin," Mircea said. "He was stronger than my brother when I saw him last, and Vlad was the strongest of us all. I will need an army to reclaim my throne."

"I would love to help, but my resources are thin," Lugrezia said. "As your lovely companion pointed out, this is not a stronghold. It can easily be breached by an enemy party."

"We don't intend to face the usurper here," Mircea said. "But we do require a safe place to plot our next move, and Yara, my child, is in the middle of her transition. She needs to rest."

Yara's chest warmed when he called her his child, and she stared at him with all the gratitude she could muster. She would still be locked in that cellar. At the whim and mercy of Eldar.

Lugrezia stared at her with gentle eyes. "My home is yours."

And then her gaze returned to Mircea, eyes burning with a fierce display of loyalty.

"I owe you a life debt, Mircea. Anything within my power that you need to secure your throne is at your disposal," Lugrezia vowed.

Lugrezia led them up the stone stairs and through the arched doorway that funneled into the foyer like the fingers of a river. The foyer was wide and spacious. Pointed archways led into separate hallways, and faded tapestries hung from the wall. She could tell the reformed monastery had survived much. It evoked a sense of history and solemnity. A staircase with grim iron railings led them to the second floor.

"You may rest here, Yara," Lugrezia said.

Her bedroom was small and intimate, with a miniature

dressing table and matching dresser. A lone bed sat in the center, and her muscles grew lax at the thought of resting and recovering both from the journey and her arduous transition.

"I shall have the servants bring you some clothes," she said. "And a blood slave shortly after when you're settled."

"No," Yara blurted. "May it be served in a cup?"

"Newborn," Mircea whispered to Lugrezia. "Still adjusting."

Lugrezia smiled faintly. "A cup shall do just fine."

The door clicked shut behind her, and Yara collapsed on the bed, sinking into the heavy padding. One of the bed legs cracked and she sighed in frustration when it fell forward. She was strong. Far stronger than most vampir. Or so Mircea said. It made sense now that she knew the source of her making.

She stared at the frescoed ceiling, at the saints and angels painted with delicate brushstrokes. It was both marvelous and breathtaking. It reminded her of the splendor of the Ottoman courts. It had been a long time since she'd thought about *home*. The word brought a hollow, empty feeling to her chest. Strange that what had once made her feel alive now made her feel dead. Even her fondest memories of celebrating feasts during the birth of the new prince and the sighting of the moon for Ramadan could not warm the chill in her bones. Yara could not resist the temptation of falling into the gentle caress of the memory, letting it unspool in her mind like a thread.

She thought of the last Ramadan she'd had with her family. She remembered sitting with Aylin and subtly pointing out which men would make the finest husbands based on their social standing, reputation and wealth.

"I think he could be a perfect match for you," Yara said. "He is shrewd and cunning, just like you."

"Yara, I tire of these marriage talks. You are worse than Aunt Sevda." Aylin flung her arms dramatically. Her cup of *hoşaf* sloshed, and the twinkling particles of the fruity drink stained the cuff of her *entari*. "Has Aunt Sevda put you to this task?"

"No," Yara said, casting her gaze away.

She had been a terrible liar then. Or perhaps it was simply that her sister could read her like a book. It was as if the pages of her soul were written in a language that only Aylin could understand.

"You little rascal, she did!" Aylin said, her voice bringing them several stray gazes from the noble courtiers.

"Shh," Yara said. "You are embarrassing us."

"Then cover for me while I sneak away," Aylin said. She leaned forward, her brown eyes glittering. "I overheard father with his men the other day. A military engineer is visiting, and he has designed a canon that is capable of mass destruction. They are calling it 'The Ottoman Bombard.' It has been built with wrought-iron bars and shall change the course of siege warfare as we know it!"

"Does Father know that you are spying on him?" Yara asked.

"I could ask you the same thing," Aylin fired back.

"Aunt Sevda said that I will be punished if I condone and support your actions," Yara said. "I cannot in good conscience—"

"Very well, I shall go make a fool of myself," Aylin said, dusting the pastry crumbs from her skirt to rise. "Ruin all my potential marriage prospects *and* yours."

"Stop." Yara grabbed her wrist while Aylin simply smirked. She had Yara in a trap, and she knew it. All that Yara cared about then was securing a marriage that would propel her into the highest of ranks. She intended to flirt and see if the imperial prince paid her any mind tonight. He was her mark, and she intended to capture his attention.

Yara sighed deeply.

"One hour," she said sternly. "I will cover for you for one hour *only*."

"Three hours," Aylin said. "And you have a deal."

"Two."

"Two and a half."

"Fine."

Aylin bent down swiftly and kissed her cheek.

And then she was gone, quick as lightning.

Yara would do anything now to have spent more time learning her sister's interests. She wished she had embraced her the night before her kidnapping and told her that she loved her. Because God, did she love her. More than anyone in this world.

For so long, Yara had been repulsed by the vampir, by their behavior and cruelty. When she had first arrived, Volkan had treated her abhorrently, and Eldar had volleyed cruel threats and poisonous barbs at her at every turn. It had never crossed her mind that one day she would become the very monsters she despised.

Yara knew then that if she didn't accept her fate, she would fall into a melancholy so deep that only God would be able to pull her from the grasp of darkness. She had fought for so long to return home, to be safe with her family, and all she felt now was this vengeance that threatened to undo her. It wrapped its immoral hands around her heart and whispered its dark vow that she was now tasked with killing the Undying King and that failure was not an option.

If vengeance was all she had, if retribution was the only melody that soothed her, Yara would hold on to it, until it fixed all that had been broken.

Until this ache inside her vanished.

And there was only the imprint of an infinite, comforting silence left behind.

It had been a few days since they arrived at Lugrezia's home. Most of her days were spent sweating and floating in a wave of fog. It was a miracle that *he* did not reach out to her again. Yara knew it was only a matter of time before she was caught in his dark presence once more. The next time it happened, she would be ready.

They dined in the Main Hall that night. Yara sat on the dais alongside Lugrezia and Mircea, cutting into a slab of bloody meat. Under normal circumstances, she would be put off by how raw the meat was, but with her new diet, she enjoyed the thick blood that clung to the half-cooked flesh. Though they were in Oltenia, the court of Lugrezia all wore the Italian clothes of their ancestry. Yara wore an extravagant dress of gold-brocaded voided velvet. The sleeves were long and flowing. On top, she wore a *pellanda*, a grand robe with the sleeves cut out in the Florentine style to reveal the design of the dress underneath. It was lined with white fur, which served as a stark reminder that she was no longer susceptible to the cold. The cuff of her sleeve was embroidered with the motif of a swan, which was the Carrara family crest.

There were blood slaves in Lugrezia's court, but they were not dressed as vulgarly as the ones in the Court of the Undead. These blood slaves were dressed in a similar manner to the servants. They wore bland grey garb with red sashes in the middle to identify their station as blood slaves. Mircea plucked the pale wrist of one of them, sinking his teeth into her flesh. Yara could make out the outline of his teeth under her delicate skin, woven between her indigo veins like a serpent. She turned away from the sight, studying the tapestry that hung on the wall. It was the sigil of the Carrara family, a blue shield with a white swan with its arms spread prepared to take flight.

All the trueborn families had their own coats of arms. During court, she had often seen a flag by each family's table to represent their house. She intended to learn more about the trueborn families and their political alliances during her time here. She needed to learn everything about this world that had become her own, so she would be able to survive its cruel machinations.

She refused to drink from the blood slaves, but their blood called to her. It smelled like a nectar that belonged to the heavens and highlighted how subpar her current meal was, how it lacked in flavor. She found herself lured by the trail of fresh blood around her. Yara let her fork drop in dissatisfaction.

"You know you'd be happier if you fed from the blood slaves," Mircea said.

"I can't," she said, glaring at him. "You forget I was one not too long ago."

"That was then. This is now," he said evenly.

Yara did not bother to dignify that comment with a response.

The doors were pulled open, and the guards marched in, clutching several intruders in their punishing grip. Yara smelled him before she saw him. She knew his scent as well as she knew her mother's favorite lullaby. He smelled of wildflowers and green apples, and the intoxicating scent awakened her like a rush of cold water sweeping over her soul.

Yara stood up so fast the table rattled. She ran toward him with a singular focus. Cups and plates fell to the floor in a loud crash. Broken pieces of porcelain covered the floor, spreading like an outstretched rug. All the guards raised their swords in unison and pointed them at the doorway. Mircea attempted to catch her, but she was too quick. The walls were a faded blur, as were the tapestries that hung like curtains from the hooks.

She saw nothing but him. He was restrained by two guards, his lips turned up in that infernal smile that had once angered her, but that now filled her with delight. The guards released him in alarm at the sight of her approach. She collided into him, and Volkan fell to his back with a soft grunt. The floor cracked beneath the force of their bodies. A dark line ran beneath the feet of the guards, and they jumped back to evade the damage. Yara would have laughed at the panicked alarm that crossed their faces if she had not been so distracted by the presence of Volkan Demirci.

"My beautiful pet," he whispered. "How I longed for you."

Yara tucked her chin into the crook of his neck, inhaling his scent. And there it was, wildflowers and green apples, like traipsing through a beautiful meadow. It soothed her, and she felt her limbs slacken. It was strange that his blood ran through her veins and that it had forged such an unbreakable bond. It felt as though she had been reunited with a lost limb. As though she was whole once more.

"You came for me," Yara whispered.

"Did you think I would stay at that despicable place without you?" Volkan asked. He pulled back, swiping her dark hair behind her ear. "You are as beautiful as I remember."

"It's only been a few days."

"For you," he said, flicking her nose. "For me it has been an eternity."

"Does that line usually work for you?" she asked.

"Like magic," he said.

A startled laugh escaped her. It felt strange to laugh. She hadn't had much to celebrate since the attack at court. His hand slid up and down her spine, soft and lulling. The graze of his claws teased her through the cloth of her robes. Her skin burned when his hand slithered up her nape. His long fingers held her in a gesture that was somehow both intimate and rough. Yara knew that she should listen to her senses and rise from the floor. They *were* still lying in the Main Hall of Lugrezia's home, embracing each other as if they were not in a room with dozens of people. But in that moment the very thought of parting from him frightened her, making her limbs shake and a soft whimper escape her.

"I'm here now," Volkan whispered. "I promised that I would be your hand in the dark and that I would never let you go. Do you remember that?"

"Yes," she said softly.

"I am here now," he said. "And I will never let you go."

Her arms tightened around him. It wasn't until he cleared his throat that she realized she might be hurting him.

"Sorry," Yara said.

"You're stronger than me," Volkan said. "How delightful!"

"I missed you," Yara said.

"And what of me, Yara?" a familiar, dainty voice called. Yara looked up to find Aylin caught in the arms of a guard, effectively restraining her. Yara's eyes widened in surprise. In her single-minded focus on Volkan, she hadn't even realized that he had not come alone. "Shouldn't you greet your sister first?"

Aylin's lips tilted in that arrogant smirk she had longed to see. God, she'd missed her sister.

"Aylin!" she shrieked. "Release her. *Now!*"

When the guards weren't quick enough to follow her orders, Yara hissed, revealing her sharp teeth. Their eyes widened in surprise, and she realized that the dark veins had appeared beneath her skin. The marker that proved she was sired by Eldar Demirci. That his poisoned blood now ran beneath her skin like a curse. She had forgotten that Volkan and Aylin did not know that she was sired by Eldar. She hadn't expected to reveal it so soon. She'd been very careful about not going full vampir––which was when one revealed their true form, with the lengthened claws and teeth. Since she did not feed publicly, she had been keeping it hidden.

Yara watched as her sister's eyes widened at the sight of her, and Volkan tilted his head with a look of confusion. His gaze locked on the dark veins beneath her skin. As far as she knew, no vampir besides her and Eldar had these midnight veins beneath their skin. So, it would not take him long to suspect the truth.

Tension bracketed his mouth when he asked. "What is this?"

His gaze was locked on her hands. It was fading away, since she'd retracted her claws and teeth. She could tell that Volkan had pieced it together but simply waited on her confirmation.

"A gift from your brother," Yara said. "Mircea says I am sired by you both."

"I see," he said darkly.

He folded his arms across his chest, not pleased with her explanation.

"Aylin?" she asked nervously. "May I embrace you?"

What if her sister was frightened of her? What if she pushed her away now that she was a vampir? Her heart tightened at the thought, and she felt as though she would break in half if she did. Aylin's reaction had not been too terrible during the battle at Poenari, but then Yara had just been a vampir. Now she was a vampir *and* she was sired by the boy who had ruined their lives. A piece of him existed inside her, and if she could carve it out, she would.

Aylin frowned. "If you don't, I will."

Yara exhaled in relief and wrapped her arms around her sister. She had missed her so much. It had felt like winter had settled in her bones, and now that she was here, the warmth of summer had finally returned. It was like everything suddenly made sense again, and that fear and pain and wretchedness she'd felt since she awakened into a creature of the night had vanished. A strangled sob escaped her, and Aylin soothingly stroked her hair, holding her while she came undone. Yara felt safe for the first time in months, knowing that her big sister was here. That she was not disgusted or afraid of her and had welcomed her with open arms. She could feel her acceptance in the way her small hands gripped her shoulders, in the biting press of her nails into her flesh. Yara greedily absorbed her love, clinging to it like an anchor caught amidst the burgeoning waves.

"I missed you, my little one," Aylin said between clenched teeth. "But you must lessen your hold, it hurts."

Yara released her abruptly. "I'm sorry!"

"Don't be. Now that you're strong, perhaps you can beat him," she said, pointing an accusing finger at Volkan.

"She jests, my darling pet," Volkan said, coming swiftly to her side. He peeled back a stray curl from her hair. "She is tired from the journey and short-tempered."

"He refused to let me—"

"Will you introduce us to our hosts?" he asked.

Yara narrowed her eyes at him. "I'll get the full story from her later."

"She will no doubt add a storyteller's flair to it," Volkan said with a smile that could charm the coldest of hearts. "You mustn't trust a word she says."

He stared at her with those pitch-black eyes, such a startling contrast to his snow-white hair, reminding her all too well of the white wolf she had met the day she was brought shackled to the

Court of the Undead. Volkan enjoyed tormenting the innocent and despised mortals, and Yara would not let anybody hurt her sister. Not even the boy she cared for.

"We will discuss this later," she said tightly. There were far too many eyes on them both, and she didn't want anyone overhearing their squabble.

Yara was trying to change how she presented herself among the vampir. She didn't intend to be the little mortal girl anymore. She didn't want to be afraid of her own shadow or tormented by the stronger vampir. She didn't want to cry herself to sleep because she'd been cut open by the harsh words of a cruel man. She wanted to be different. She wanted to be *more*.

"These are my guests," Yara said, raising her chin as she turned to face the dais. "I hope you will treat them as graciously as you did me."

"The pale-haired beauty with the mischievous eyes," Lugrezia said absently. "Pomona spoke fondly of you, Volkan Demirci."

"We don't speak *her* name," Yara snapped. "She is burning in hell as we speak. It is the least of what she deserves. If she lived, I would tear out her heart with my own hands."

Volkan gently stroked her head in an attempt to rein in her temper. But nothing would silence her when she recalled how Pomona and Titus Maleinos had hurt Volkan.

"Be that as it may, we don't allow people from House Demirci here," Lugrezia said. "It is a conflict of interest."

"We will have to imprison him before he runs to his usurper brother and tells him our location," Mircea said from his place beside Lugrezia on the dais. Fury danced behind his eyes, as if he did not see Volkan but rather Eldar. "Or better yet, let us send him his heart."

"Mircea," Volkan drawled. "Poverty and desperation ill suits you."

Mircea rose from his seat, chair scraping behind him in a harsh screech and brows thundering down like a scythe. He had crossed the room before she could blink. Yara intercepted him, pressing a placating hand to his chest.

"He does not think before he speaks, Mircea," Yara said. "Forgive him."

"Release him, Yara," Volkan said. "We will see who the better prince is."

"You are no prince," Mircea spat. "You are *nothing*."

"I am Prince Volkan Demirci, Brother of the Undying King, Eldar Demirci, and second in line to the Blood Throne."

"Volkan," Yara said, twisting her neck to glare at him. "Silence, please."

It was not the time to boast.

"I will not be silenced," Volkan said. "I am pleased that your worthless line has fallen and that you are hiding in the wild because my brother bested the mighty Draculesti. It brings warmth to my dead heart knowing that you suffer. I only wish that I was still at court to watch the vultures eat Radu's entrails, but it is fine I took a token from Vlad before I left." He dug his hand in his pocket and pulled out a sharp bone that looked like a rib. "I intend to have an ivory necklace forged of it."

Mircea's face twisted in a blind rage, and before she could scold Volkan, Mircea was gone, slipping beneath her hand to charge at him. Thaddeus and a dark-haired girl stepped forward to shield Volkan, but Mircea made quick work of them both, shoving them back until they fell upon opposite walls. A crack outlined the stone where their bodies collided. Mircea wrapped his hand around Volkan's neck, pinning him in place. Volkan got in a good swipe of his claws, slashing his skin open, but it was clear to see he was a far better wordsmith than he was a fighter. Mircea's claws sunk into the flesh of his neck, and blood trickled out his lips. The pain did not wipe that arrogant smile from his face. If anything, he grinned wider, no doubt pleased to be the center of attention.

"Mircea, release him, please," Yara said.

She hated the desperation that coated her voice. She hated

that she didn't know if this was because he was her sire or because of her own feelings for him. "He is in pain."

"We will send a message to Eldar Demirci," Mircea said. "Bits and pieces of his weakling brother until he steps down. We will start with his eye." He raised his hand, and Yara didn't think when she screamed.

"*Stop!*" Her voice echoed along the walls.

Mircea paused his assault, hand outstretched in the air as if his muscles had frozen. Yara released a sigh of relief that he had listened to her. But his hand did not relax, it remained there as if he had forgotten how to use his limbs. It brought back an image of when Eldar had made Aylin and Ilyas freeze in place like a pair of statues. She had felt a force in her voice when she'd spoken, one that had made her bones tremble. It thrummed with pure, raw power, much like a wolf that had forced the pack into submission. As if she had crawled up this hierarchy of monsters and found that she was the most corrupt of them all.

"Yara, release me," Mircea said through clenched teeth. Volkan pried his limp hand from his throat and barked out a startled laugh.

"She has the voice of command," Volkan said with a delighted clap. "Oh, this is simply splendid. Make him dance for us, or better yet, undress! Command him to undress. Do it now, for me, Yara."

"Mircea?" Yara whispered.

"Now, Yara," Mircea said. His eyes darted around as if he were afraid someone would attack him. It must have been Volkan who unnerved him. He was circling him as if he were prey, far too close for comfort.

"You are released," she said, speaking in a high, clear tone trying to bring about that sense of certainty and demand she'd infused into her voice when Volkan had been in danger.

"Volkan, come here," she said before Mircea lunged for him again.

Everybody was staring at her with fear in their eyes. Even

Thaddeus looked appalled from the corner where he rubbed his injured head. Aylin was silent, her eyes distant, as if she was trapped in a faded memory, most likely the time when Eldar had controlled her and Ilyas. Mircea looked angry and Lugrezia was wary. For a moment, Yara wanted to flinch under the weight of their stares, but she reminded herself that she was different now. She was a *vampir*. She was untouchable.

She straightened her shoulder just as Volkan wrapped his arm around her waist, drawing her to his side. She let herself settle in his arms. For a moment, she thought he would be frightened by her as well, but he looked pleased to be by her side, honored to have her in his arms.

"My little savior," Volkan whispered in her ear. "How the tables have turned."

"Don't distract me," she said. "You've been here for less than five minutes, and you've spoiled everything."

"I've enlivened this dreary place," Volkan said, looking around at his handiwork. At the room of chaos and doubt that reeked of a fear so strong it made her flinch. "You should thank me."

"We will have a private conversation in the council room," Lugrezia said. "Yara and Mircea, please join me."

Lugrezia arose from her chair, the trim of her blue gown scraping the marble steps. Her eyes focused on the boy who stood by Aylin. He was so close to her that a feather wouldn't fit between them. His face was stern, almost as if it were marked with cruelty. His hair was short and cropped close to his scalp. And he had vicious green eyes.

"Domenico?" Lugrezia asked, mouth parting in shock.

"You are not dead," he said in a clipped tone. "Who is in the wooden box we laid in the plot behind our home?"

Lugrezia looked speechless. For the short time that Yara had known her, she had learned that she was not a woman who was ever short of words.

"I was never human, Domenico," she said slowly, gently. "To prevent the birth of a mortal child, our kind rarely couples with mortals before our transition. It is considered demeaning to birth a lesser person."

"I'd much rather you were dead than hear you spew these vile words," Domenico said with a snarl. "You've tainted every last memory I had of you."

"That did not come out right. There is much for us to discuss," she said, folding her shaking hands atop each other. "Once we've decided upon the fate of our guests, I will summon you. I'm glad you are well, Domenico. Truly."

"I wish I could say the same," he snapped. He had a wild look in his eyes that made Yara want to pull Aylin far from him. She couldn't put her finger on it, but she didn't quite like him.

Lugrezia flinched, but then she raised her chin and stepped out the door with Mircea not far behind her.

"Behave," Yara said to Volkan.

"Or what?" he asked with a lazy grin. "Will you punish me?"

"No," Yara said. "You are a deviant who would enjoy that."

"You know me so well."

Yara stepped out of the room. It didn't take her long to catch up to Mircea and to be met by his furious stare. He had a rather menacing face, all hollow lines and sharp turns. The dark patch that covered his eye was made of the same black velvet fabric as his robe. And his dark hair was drawn back sternly from his cheeks.

"I'm sorry," Yara whispered the moment they were far from the desperate ears of Lugrezia's courtiers. "It was unintentional, I promise you."

"You humiliated me," Mircea said through clenched teeth. "Worse, you left me vulnerable."

"I didn't know that would happen," she said. "I was just so upset you were hurting him. I lashed out. I had no control over it."

"If you cannot control yourself, you are a liability," Lugrezia said sharply. "And if you turn on us, that makes you an enemy."

The door clicked shut behind them. The council room was a spacious, dimly lit chamber, and the three members of Lugrezia's private council trailed behind them. She had introduced them to her yesterday; Magno and Tobias were her military strategists and Stefano Boldù was her advisor. Stefano tended to do most of the talking during these meetings. Magno and Tobias contributed more to their war discussions, namely how Mircea should proceed with reclaiming his throne. Magno was a thin man with bone-white spectacles hanging from his nose. Tobias was the utter opposite with a heavy frame, thick fists, and a long black beard.

"We will put it to the vote," Lugrezia said. "All in favor of hosting the brother of our enemy as our guest, raise your hand."

"That is unfair," Yara said. "Your advisors will vote as you do."

"Perhaps, one day when you have your own home, you may hold a majority vote over what guests reside there," she said in a severe tone. It was clear to see she was not pleased with Volkan's antics. Nor was she amused by Yara's unwavering defense of him.

"It is in our favor to have Volkan here. Eldar cares about him he can be our leverage," Yara said. "It also means he is not working with Eldar."

"Nobody fears Volkan Demirci," Mircea spat. "He is a child who runs his mouth and is in desperate need of discipline. Even Eldar is not foolish enough to require his council. He is no threat. He never has been."

"If that's the case, then we have nothing to fear and he can stay," Yara said, lips peeling in a smile. "You have proven my point. He is harmless."

"He is a liability," Lugrezia said. "He could be a spy sent by his brother. We simply cannot risk it. He must go."

"I trust him," Yara said. "I trust him more than anyone."

"As you are sired to do," Mircea said. "A sired vampir is always loyal to their master or mistress. We do not blame you for being his advocate, but we need to imprison him. Since you are so fond of him, we will let him leave with his life when this ends. But until then he must be kept under close watch."

"He will not survive imprisonment," Yara said. "I refuse it."

Yara stared at them, at Mircea's hard eyes and Lugrezia's open sympathy, as if she understood what it was like to care for someone. Or perhaps she thought of the boy outside who had provoked such a strong reaction from her. While Lugrezia's advisors looked at Yara as if she were a foolish girl who was inviting the wolf to dine with them.

"I am not a mortal. I am not the weak girl I was," she said with a raise of her chin. "I am the only one strong enough to stop Eldar. The only one who possesses his power. I hold the voice of command. I can lead armies and destroy them."

"What are you implying?" Lugrezia asked warily.

"Do you think that I will allow Volkan to be captured like a bird in a cage?" Yara asked. "Do you think your unprotected castle and measly foot soldiers will take on the army at Poenari when the Undying King comes to strike without my help?"

"Careful," Mircea growled. "You toe the line of disrespect."

"I speak the truth and you both know it," she said. She stared at them with iron in her veins. For so long she had hidden behind her sister, behind men stronger than her, and she had blindly trusted and foolishly fallen for their wicked lies. She was prepared to protect Volkan. Not because he sired her but because he'd saved her more times than she could count. He had saved her from Pomona. He had saved her on that marble floor in Poenari when she had died, and his blood had awakened her. She remembered the fear that had soaked his eyes when she had awoken. The fear that had marked *both* their eyes. She didn't know why Eldar had cared if she died, but he had. She had seen the proof with her own eyes, and it was a thought she was desperate to erase from her mind.

But among all the chaos, Volkan had been her calm.

It was silent as her words filled the room. She averted her gaze from Mircea, who was both surprised and upset by her stance. She didn't want to leave Mircea, nor did she want to forfeit her only chance of defeating Eldar. But she would do anything to keep Volkan safe. And to watch as he was forced to relive the brutal treatment of his imprisonment was not something she would *ever* stand for.

It worried her that she felt so strongly for him. She didn't want to feel *anything*. She had lived her entire life feeling far too much, and now she simply wanted the silence. But her wretched emotions were doomed to follow her in death as they had in life.

"You hated him not too long ago," Mircea said. "Have you forgotten how he chained you? How he humiliated you before the court? How he dressed you in those rags he called clothes?"

Yara hated that he had brought back those horrid memories. Especially before these people who had never known her shame. It felt like a betrayal. It was a reminder that there were strings attached to Mircea's love. Strings that relied on her loyalty to him first and foremost.

"I was the one who saved you, Yara," Mircea continued. "I was the one who led you to Dracul to gain his mark. I was the one who trained you to defend yourself, clothed you, and sheltered you. It was *not* Volkan Demirci."

"He's changed," she said. "You don't know what we've been through."

Nothing had been the same since the day she had been kidnapped by Pomona. Volkan had saved her, and she liked to think that she had gifted him Titus's death in return. An act that had lightened the torment in his eyes and the shadows that darkened his mind. They had both saved each other. And bonds like that were impossible to sever.

Mircea's claw clicked on the table. She could feel the displeasure rolling off him in waves, and Lugrezia frowned as if all this information was rather off-putting. Yara wondered if she regretted inviting them into her home. It was clear that her peace had been disrupted by their presence.

"There will be conditions to his stay," Yara said. To soothe both parties. "I'll make sure he doesn't break your rules. We will not involve him in politics, and if he is caught spying or is discovered to be in allegiance with Eldar, we will discuss next steps. I won't be betrayed again."

It was silent for a long moment while they contemplated her words.

"Very well," Mircea said at last. "But if he betrays us, he is not getting a slap on the wrist. I will end him."

His words were a promise, and Yara knew she could not push him on this matter. Not after defying him in public. They both looked at Lugrezia to see if she was aligned with their proposal.

"Very well," Lugrezia said. "So long as he accepts our rules."

The screech of Lugrezia's chair sounded as she rose to return to the main hall.

"What is the boy to you?" Yara asked, just before she left. "The one beside my sister."

Lugrezia's eyes were distant. It was a long while before she spoke.

"He is my son," she said.

VI

Yara stared across the room at Volkan. It was strange to think that he was here in the flesh, and when her eyes turned to the left and saw Aylin, it felt like she was looking at a phantom. It felt far too good to be true. After all the horrible things that had happened to her, she had not for a single moment believed that anything good could follow. But the people across the room were proof that God was watching over her and that her desperate prayers had been answered.

Lugrezia and Mircea took their seats while Yara stood at the front of the dais, prepared to pass their verdict.

"Volkan Demirci, you will be provided temporary shelter with House Carrara on the basis that you respect the rules set by our host, Lugrezia," Yara said. Volkan's shoulder was perched against the wall, and his eyes sparkled in delight, as if this were a grand performance. "If you are suspected of being a spy or a saboteur, you will be sentenced to death. You will also not voice any support of the usurper. Neither in private nor in public."

"That seems rather dramatic," he said, pushing out his bottom lip. "I cannot speak of my brother?"

"This is not a matter to take lightly," she said. "Do you accept?"

He stroked his chin as if he were truly pondering her offer. Several long minutes passed, and the silence had gone from cold to simply disrespectful.

"Volkan," she said in a strained voice. "We do not have all night."

"I won't interfere in your politics," Volkan said. "Politics bore me. Like now I can scarcely keep my eyes open."

"So, you accept," she said. "Be straightforward, please."

"I accept, but only for you," he said. "If you had not left, I would have stood by my brother and watched the last of the Dracul burn for their sins."

His gaze was locked on Mircea, whose fists were curled, as if he contemplated racing across the room and killing him.

"That settles it," Lugrezia said. "We shall act in a cordial manner from this moment forth."

Yara left the dais to go help Aylin. She looked worn and tired. It dawned on her that she looked a lot rougher than Volkan and his party. Her eyes narrowed as she passed him. Had he forced her to sleep with the wild animals? She slipped her hand into Aylin's and was instantly soothed by the touch of her rough palm. Her callouses stroked her flesh and reminded her distinctly of home. It dawned on her then that perhaps her *home* had never been a place or a country. It had always been Aylin.

"What did you do to her?" Yara snarled. "Did you have her dragged behind your horse?"

"Do you think he is capable of such a thing?" Thaddeus asked with a shocked gasp. His curly blond hair was in desperate need of a cut. It sprung forth from his head in pretty ringlets. "He has been nothing but gracious and honorable."

"As if she would take your word for it," the dark-haired girl who accompanied them said. "You would lick Volkan's boot if he asked it of you."

"Any good sired would," Volkan said. "I'm offended, Pariza, that you would not do the same."

Yara stared at her, feeling a strange twist in her chest. They spoke with ease, and she was terribly beautiful. With dark brown eyes and luscious black hair. *Pariza.* Even her name was beautiful.

"Yara, that hurts," Aylin said.

Yara stiffened; she'd forgotten she still had Aylin's hand clasped in hers. She had trouble controlling her speed, and now it seemed she would have to learn how to handle her strength.

"I'm sorry," Yara said. "Maybe I shouldn't touch you for now."

"It is fine," Aylin said, recapturing her hand when Yara slowly pulled away.

Aylin turned to her companion, Domenico.

"Will you speak to her?" she asked, jutting her chin at Lugrezia.

"I suppose," he said reluctantly. "Get some rest. I'll find you later."

Yara led her down the hallway to her bedroom. She wanted her close by in case she needed her. They'd always shared a bed when they were young, especially after their nursemaid Sevda Ghulam had told them one of her twisted tales. Often at the request of her sister.

The walls were decorated with all types of artifacts and weapons. Aylin lingered to admire the wall of weaponry: lances, maces, and swords. Some were old, the bronze faded, while others were recent, bearing markers of the curved style the Ottoman Empire preferred.

"You can admire these later," Yara said. "You must rest."

Aylin grinned sheepishly as Yara tugged her from the wall of weapons and back in the direction of her bedroom. She had just opened the door when she felt a gust of air behind her.

"May we speak?" Volkan asked.

His hands were clasped politely behind his back. A paragon of civility and innocence. It was a weak façade, considering all the chaos he had unleashed. He nodded to Pariza and Thaddeus, who hovered behind him like a pair of twin shadows, to go ahead without him.

Yara was still a bit peeved by everything that had occurred since his arrival. Firstly, there had been his need to provoke Mircea and put her in a terrible position, then there was his harsh treatment toward Aylin, and lastly, his beautiful, mysterious companion, who seemed to dote on his every whim. It was childish, but Yara simply decided to ignore him rather than face him when all this turmoil existed inside her. She took a step to follow Aylin when he caught her wrist, spinning her around to face him.

"Aylin, give us a moment, please," Yara said.

His dark eyes were hooked on her. Frosty lashes scraped his high cheekbones with each blink.

"Don't let him slip back into your good graces," Aylin warned. "He doesn't deserve you."

The door clicked shut behind her, and Yara tapped her foot impatiently. He placed his hands on either side of her hip, long fingers spanning the width of her sides. Shivers raced down her spine at his familiar touch. Her skin would have burned if she were still mortal. And her heart would have beat as loud as a drum.

"Is this the cold reception I deserve?" Volkan asked. "I left Eldar behind and traveled through these abhorrent mountain lands where the dry air sucked the moisture from my hair and skin, for *you*. Have I not suffered enough?"

"You poor thing," she cooed. "You must be so tired."

"Very," he said, not grasping her sarcasm. "It doesn't help that we'll be squalling in this tasteless place. The blood slaves look worn and dull, and I have yet to spot a musician or entertainer. Will we sit in silence during dinner, or worse, indulge in polite chatter?"

"You attacked Mircea's character senselessly, and you've hurt my sister," she said. "And all you can think of is how *you* are suffering."

"No, I care about you as well. How has your transition been?" His eyes grazed down her form. His hand drifted along her hand. The veins were gone now, since she felt neither angry nor threatened to go full vampir. But if he continued this line of questioning without acknowledging his wrongs, she would snap.

"Are you truly sired by us both?" he asked with a grim look. "I don't like sharing."

"Well, you won't have to worry about that," Yara said. "I want neither of you."

She slipped out of his arms and disappeared into her bedroom.

She could sense his frustration from the small growl that escaped him.

"Yara," he said. "Unlock this door."

There was no lock. She merely leaned against the door, and her strength prevented him from opening it.

"All I could think about when I left was you," she whispered, knowing that he heard her. "When I was in pain, all I wanted was you. But I don't know if what I feel is because of our sire bond or if it is genuine. I don't know what is true and what is false. I don't want to be a mindless sheep who follows you because you made me. I don't want to confuse servitude with love."

"Do you feel this way towards Eldar?" he asked. "Do you want him as well?"

"No," she said.

It felt easier talking from behind a door. She couldn't think straight when he touched her.

"Then you have your answer," he said. "I'm sorry that I hurt you. I'll be more cordial to your sister. I won't cause so much trouble."

"He's lying," Aylin whispered.

"I can hear you, mortal," Volkan snapped. "And don't interfere in business that does not concern you."

"See?" Aylin pointed out. "He just said he'd be cordial!"

"We will talk later," Yara said. "My sister needs me."

"Fine," he said. "But we *will* talk."

Yara waited until she heard the fading sound of his footsteps before she turned to Aylin with a wide smile.

"My beautiful sister," she said, wrapping her arms around her in a gentle embrace, afraid that she would unintentionally hurt her.

Aylin scoffed. "Don't lie. I look like an underfed boy."

"The prettiest and sweetest underfed boy I've ever seen," Yara teased.

"That's more accurate," she said with a light chuckle before her eyes grew serious. "How are you, Yara? Truly?"

Aylin led her to the edge of the bed. With their hands clasped, it felt like they were children again, and her big sister was leading her along as she always had. She felt safe for the first time in a long while, both because Aylin was here and because Volkan was close by. Even if she was quite annoyed with him at the moment.

"I was scared at first of becoming like them. They have been the monsters of my story for so long, I never thought someday I'd become one of them," she said. "I don't think Eldar expected me to have as much power as him. He made a mistake turning me, and he will suffer for it. I'm going to destroy him."

It felt like she was humanizing him every time she uttered his name. And she knew firsthand just how monstrous and wretched the Undying King was.

"*We* will destroy him," Aylin corrected. "He took much from me as well."

Yara straightened, realizing that she hadn't seen Ilyas. Fear tightened her chest, and her thoughts drifted to the unthinkable.

"Where is Ilyas?" Yara whispered.

"I left him back at the camp with the rest of the hunters," Aylin said, looking down at the carpet, eyes heavy with guilt. "He needed a healer, but you needed me."

"I didn't want you to choose between us," she said. "Ilyas is your world."

"You are my world, Yara," Aylin said. "You'll always come first, before any man."

"Likewise," Yara said, leaning her head on her shoulder.

She stiffened at the scent of her blood. It smelled like warm honey. Her stomach tightened with hunger, and she could feel her teeth slide free from her gums. She stumbled back from Aylin, ashamed of her reaction. She folded her arms across her torso, hiding the inky veins beneath the layers of her dress and pressing her lips together to conceal her elongated teeth.

"Are you hungry?" Aylin asked with furrowed brows. "Here. Come drink." She held out her wrist as if it were a regular occurrence between sisters. As if Yara was still the same girl she had grown up with and not someone who was barely recognizable. Someone who defied everything they had always believed in.

"I can't," she said. "Mircea will find me sustenance. He knows I don't like drinking from people. I prefer cups. It feels normal, or rather, normal to me."

"Just this once," Aylin said. "I don't want you to be in pain."

"I just need some distance for a bit. It will settle. Promise."

Aylin didn't seem convinced. "Are you certain?"

"Yes," Yara said. "I don't want anything to change between us."

Aylin's brown eyes softened. "You know this changes nothing. You are still my sister, Yara. You will *always* be my sister."

Yara felt her heart swell. She loved Aylin so much.

VII

Poenari Castle, The Fortress of the
Undying King

Eldar was learning to coexist with the anger that often seized him. He had learned to let it soak his veins and infect his bloodstream until it finally softened into a dull, meaningless throb.

He couldn't erase it. The lingering echo of the betrayal tended to strike him at the moments he least expected it. And attempting to rid himself of it was futile, like a pesky thorn he could not reach, stinging his flesh until he felt as though he would cut his entire hand off to spite the pain. He couldn't pretend to be unaffected by the reality that his brother had abandoned him. That the boy whom he had spent his entire life protecting had left him when he needed him most.

And then there was *her*.

The girl who haunted his mind.

The girl whose very existence threatened everything he had ever thought he knew about himself.

"My lord."

The head of the Danesti family kneeled before him. All the lords and ladies of the eight trueborn families were bowing before him and accepting him as their leader. Some were far more willing than others, but fear kept them in line. It helped that he looked monstrous. It helped that he had cut out Radu's lying tongue before them, gouged out his eyes, and burned him alive. It helped that he'd returned to his throne when it was all over and licked the blood off his fingers.

Fear kept them in line. Fear was a powerful motivator.

There was a line to the dais. Eldar's hand dangled lazily from the armchair of his throne, and he stared at the sea of faces. None of them were the people he wanted to see. He hated Volkan. He hated him for leaving him when Eldar had sacrificed everything for him. Volkan had known that he was in the middle of a power shift. He knew that the Dracul were proclaimed to be the First Vampir. Some said they descended from the loins of the Devil himself. The type of loyalty those legends birthed could not be erased so easily. He needed his brother. He needed someone he trusted wholeheartedly. Not a flock of vultures who smiled at him from behind barbed teeth.

And in his greatest moment of need, Volkan had abandoned him. He had chosen *her* over him.

Eldar heard the screeching sound of his claws tearing through the polished black enamel that coated the armrest. It wasn't just Volkan who had betrayed him. It was her. She stood with the false prince Mircea. She stood with the traitor.

You had her. You pushed her away.

"My lord," a sultry voice called. Eldar resisted the urge to sigh. All manner of women had flocked to him in the past few days. Some were desperate to warm his bed and seduce their way into his favor, and a cunning few sought to wed him in the hopes that he'd make them his Undying Queen. The betrothal between him and Akila was broken. The whispers of it had spun through the court like wildfire, and shortly after was when the parade of women had begun.

"You don't have my permission to speak," Eldar said.

"I can be her, my lord," she whispered. "The girl who plagues your mind."

Eldar wondered if he could have her put to death for her insolence. The thought was tempting, but angering another trueborn family would not help his cause.

"You haven't spared a glance at any woman. No desire burns in your chest except the one you feel for her," she said. "I know what that is like, to want what you cannot have."

"Are you calling me desperate?" Eldar snapped. "Are you calling me a fool?"

His gaze snapped up to stare at her. His breath caught in his throat. Perhaps, if he was drunk, he would have believed it was her. But Eldar never drank. He refused to let any substance impair his judgment. He was *always* in control.

She looked like her. But only at first glance. She had her long dark hair and those little dimples on her cheeks. Her eyes were blue. A cold glass blue that reminded him of a frozen lake. Nothing like her warm brown eyes. And she was no trueborn, which made her offer downright blasphemy. The girl before him was not his equal in any manner. But neither was *she*, and he had still wanted her. In the dark, damp, rotten corners of his soul, his hunger for her had rivaled his desire for power.

"I find it offensive that you'd think I'd ever be interested in you," he said.

"I saw you watching her. You and Volkan. Similar taste between similar brothers," she said. "I can be *her*."

"Perhaps my brother could entertain an imposter, but not me," he said harshly. "Leave before I kill you and everyone you care for."

Eldar's eyes drifted away. Nobody knew this, including Volkan, but Eldar had never been attracted to a person before. He had wondered often why he didn't feel a wave of desire like other men. Volkan had told him once that he could have no less than three lovers in any given week. Eldar had been both disgusted and repulsed by the thought of multiple partners, let alone handling them all at once, as his brother often did.

Before *her*, he had never allowed anyone to touch him, to kiss him, to sink beneath his skin. She made him feel foreign emotions he could not begin to describe. It was why he hated her so much. He wanted to rip out every piece of himself infected by her. He would be lying if he said he wasn't drawn to her eyes that always turned cold when he looked at her, and to the pinching feeling of her nails scraping his wrist anytime he grasped her neck. All because he enjoyed the feel of her pulse beneath his fingertips. His reminder that she was alive.

"My lord."

Eldar's head snapped up at the sound of his commander's voice. Rahim was a member of the Demirci household, and while Eldar had efficiently slaughtered every man and woman who was sired by his father, he had left Rahim untouched. Volkan had always been fond of him. So, he'd lived, and now he served him faithfully.

"Any word?" Eldar asked, swirling the tangy berry drink mixed with mortal blood in his palm.

"No, my lord," he said. "We followed their tracks, but the snow got thicker, and their trail has gone faint. I have three legions of my best men scouring the Carpathians."

"All I hear is excuses," Eldar said coldly. "And incompetence."

"We are doin—"

"It is not enough," Eldar said bitterly.

She was far from his reach, and she had taken Volkan with her. It was worse now that he knew that she was sired by them both. It meant that she was as strong as him. That there was a possibility that she had his ability to take down twice as many men as a regular vampir without breaking a sweat and perhaps even the voice of command. It meant that she was a formidable opponent, and if he didn't find her soon, she would discover just how much power coursed through her veins. And her gifts would lie in the hands of his enemies.

"Join me in the war room in ten minutes," Eldar said.

"Yes, my lord."

Eldar slid his eyes shut. The first time he had found her, it had been unintentional. He had felt her reaching for him for comfort.

She had been in pain; transitioning without your master or mistress nearby was an unpleasant experience. Even Eldar, who had no love for those he turned, tended to stick around them for days afterward so they could gain some measure of comfort from his proximity. It was a primal thing, that they yearned for the one who made them. So, he'd caught on to their sire bond and showed her what she was without him, using her memories to poison her against her old family. To draw her closer to him.

But he couldn't sense her anymore, and a growl of frustration escaped him. Volkan must have found her. She had his brother by her, so she didn't need him anymore. She didn't call for him. It was a confounding thing to think they had both sired her. It was unheard of. Or perhaps nobody had ever been desperate enough to try. Eldar tried hard not to think of what he'd felt when he held her limp body in his arms. But the images assaulted his mind: the blankness in her open eyes, the deadness of her heart, the color that had drained from her deep skin. The frightening thought that he had killed her. That he had erased her from this world because of his selfish need to make her strong enough for him. To make her his equal in every meaning of the word.

Rahim and four of his closest advisors were waiting for him around the map on the circular table when he arrived. Wooden pawns sat around regions that indicated which vampir clan ran those parts. Countries, cities, and provinces were sprawled before him. Eldar intended to punish the families who had stood against him; all the families who had stood with Vlad Dracul would suffer. It wasn't enough that the Maleinos family, the most loyal of Vlad's nobles, still lived at their family home in Greece.

"How much land do they own?" Eldar asked. "We will begin with the Draculs. I want every home they own to be burned to the ground, and once there are only charred remains behind, we will rebuild on the plot of land."

"Alexandru, Vlad's favored child, owns half of the Draculesti empire. Mircea and Radu owned the other half. Mihnea, his heir, was intended to have Poenari Castle upon his transition, along with their birthright home in Tărgovişte," Rahim said. "And of course the throne."

Eldar hesitated at the mention of Alexandru. Alexandru had been something of a friend during his boyhood. And Eldar used the term *friend* loosely. They had an understanding. It was the silent knowledge that they would someday be considered the strongest men in any room they walked into. Alexandru was much like him: ruthless and manipulative. Eldar admired cruelty. In a world filled with weak-minded souls, it was rare to find someone like himself.

"May I advise that attacking Alexandru would be a risky endeavor? He has a private army hired to protect his compound. We would have to deplete almost all our resources to wage a war against him," Rahim said. Worry creased his thick brows, and his lips tightened in disapproval. "And we cannot cut ourselves thin knowing Mircea plots against us."

"Tell Alexandru, Son of Dracul, that he is required at court to bend the knee to his Undying King," Eldar said. "With a reminder that refusal to do so will be considered an act of treason."

"Understood."

"My lord, if it comes down to it, should we prioritize the capture of Mircea or the girl?" Irfan, his second commander, asked.

"I want the girl," Eldar said. "She is to be returned to me unharmed. She is our priority. She is *everything*."

She wasn't the wide-eyed girl brought to him on her hands and knees. She was powerful now. His equal in every way that counted.

A worthy opponent.

He would find her.

Even if he had to burn the world down to do it.

VIII

Aylin woke up at dawn. She lay in bed for a few minutes, staring at the window. The outer glass had been packed with brick, but from the inside it was beautiful. The glass was stained and decorated with ornamental roses separated by traceries.

She enjoyed the simple feeling of just being near her sister. It had been a long time since she last shared a bed with her, and while Yara's skin was now cold and her flesh hardened, she was still her sister. Dimples still pierced her cheeks when she smiled, and she looked at Aylin like she would protect her from the dark, even though Yara had always been the one afraid of the dark. She was stronger now, both physically and mentally, as if the trials she had suffered had honed her into a fine blade. It saddened Aylin to think that Yara's innocence had been robbed from her.

After a quick rinse and prayer, Aylin descended the stairs into the dark foyer. They all slept during the day. Their bodies were still and unmoving. She had shuddered at the sight of Yara, whose chest hadn't shifted and whose palms were folded flat on her chest like a corpse. For a long time, she had looked at her. At a face as familiar as her own. Her beauty had taken on a cold, almost ethereal look. The bones were somewhat sharper, erasing her softness.

And her touch made chills slip down Aylin's back. It was as cold and desolate as a Turkish winter. Yara was her sister, but she was also becoming something she could not fully understand.

"I have been meaning to speak with you," Pariza said.

Her dark hair was coiled in its signature braid and her twin daggers were strapped to her hips. Much like Aylin, she did not bother with dresses and frills, but quite unlike Aylin, her trousers were designed to fit her, and her fancy top was covered in an embroidered bodice. Nothing like Aylin's ill-fitting trousers and the tunic she'd stolen from Ilyas. It still smelled like him, like woodsmoke and mint leaves and boyish sweat. It felt safe.

"Come to insult me on behalf of Volkan?" Aylin asked, folding her arms across her chest.

"No," she said almost sheepishly. "To apologize."

"I suppose Yara had a word with your lord," Aylin said.

"Volkan isn't forcing me to do this," she said. "I thought you were a threat to him, and my job is to protect him, as it is the duty of all his sired."

"Including my sister," Aylin said bitterly. She didn't like that he had an unseen hold on her. That as his sired, Yara was *made* to do his bidding. She didn't trust him to not abuse his power.

"Volkan cares for her," Pariza said. "I know he won't hurt her."

"And if he does?"

"You will be the first to know," she promised.

That brought her a small measure of relief.

"I truly am sorry for my behavior," Pariza said. "It was unacceptable, and I promise you I don't make it a habit to hurt the innocent."

"Well, in that case, I forgive you," she said.

"Thank you," Pariza said, reaching for her hand to squeeze her flesh. Her brown eyes were sincere, and Aylin decided she was not the worst person in this place. "I would like us to start afresh."

Aylin nodded.

If Yara was serious about Volkan, she might as well become

cordial with his best friends. While she did not think she would ever see eye to eye with Thaddeus, Pariza she would give a second chance to.

———

Aylin left Pariza to continue her perusal of their temporary home. She made her way to the main hall, studying the tapestries that hung from the great walls. She may have also spent some time admiring the wall of displayed weaponry, before making her path to the hall.

"Yara's sister."

Her head snapped up to find the older man Yara seemed attached to. The one she trusted.

Mircea.

His hair fell to his shoulder and an eye patch covered his eye. The one that remained was black and eerie.

"What do you want?" she asked. Her hackles were raised; she didn't trust any of them, and she still hadn't heard the full tale of her sister's capture.

"Vicious," he murmured. "It seems they turned the wrong sister into a vampir."

"I'm taking Yara, and we are leaving," she said. "Whatever issue you have with that monstrous king is between you and him. Yara has suffered enough at the hands of your kind."

As much as she wanted to stay behind and kill him for hurting her sister and Ilyas, it was foolish to underestimate him. She remembered the cold gaze of the Undying King's eyes, almost as if he possessed no soul. A chill slipped down her spine at the thought.

"Yara is hungry for revenge," Mircea said. "And she is different now. *Powerful.* We don't know the full extent of her strengths, but she may be the only one who can tip the scale in our favor."

"She is not a weapon for you to use in your quest for power,"

Aylin said sharply, fists curled by her sides. She had an unbearable urge to punch him.

His dark eyes drifted past her. "Perhaps we should ask her ourselves."

Aylin turned to find Yara dressed and polished. She wore a black gown designed in the Venetian style with a fitted bodice with floral red embroidery and a heavy skirt. She hadn't even heard her approach, and she was so still it was almost as if she were a statue. Her hands were folded neatly in front of her. Yara had always had such an expressive face, but Aylin found that she was rather difficult to read now. As if she had learned to mask her true feelings. Once again, she felt an unbearable sadness that her sister had been forced to carve away her softness. The brightness that had once shone in her eyes was impossible to see.

"I don't want to run, Aylin," Yara said gently. "Not from this."

"He bested us, Yara. As much as I want to kill the Undying King, he is too powerful, and it is better to take our losses now and move on," she said. She looked at Mircea sharply. "This is not our war."

And she had lost far too much. She had abandoned the only boy she'd ever truly cared for. Nobody could ever replace Ilyas. She dreaded the thought of speaking to Domenico, of telling him the truth: that she was in love with Ilyas. That she had been in love with him for as long as she remembered. But Aylin had never been good at talking about her feelings, and the thought of revealing that to Domenico sickened her. She could barely admit that she loved Ilyas to herself, and she was not yet ready to share it with anyone else. So, she buried it deep inside herself to pick at it again at a later time.

"I owe Mircea, but more importantly, I owe myself," Yara said. "I swore to myself that I would end him. I need this, Aylin. I don't think I can recover from all of it knowing that he lives."

"And what of the fair-haired one?" Aylin asked. "Is he comfortable with you killing his brother?"

"Volkan does not care for politics," she said. "He will not get involved."

"You don't think he'll try to sabotage you?" Aylin asked. "You don't think he'll betray you?"

"Your sister speaks sense," Mircea said in that even-toned voice. "You should listen to her."

"Gossiping about me?"

Volkan slid into the room like the serpent he was. He was dressed in an elaborate kaftan that would put the sultan to shame. Royal blue with silver trimming and pearlescent beads that looked hand-crafted. His pale hair was combed and fell to his waist in a sheet of white.

Disgust curled in Aylin's stomach at the sight of him. She didn't like the way he stared at Yara as if she belonged to him. And she hadn't forgiven him for tying her up and letting his idiot friends torment her.

"Are they trying to cause a rift between us, my dear?" he asked, curling his arm around her sister's waist.

"Do not taunt him, Volkan," Yara said, with a warning stare. She easily stepped out of his embrace, and Aylin felt a spark of warmth in her chest when Yara held out her hand for her. "Come, I know you're eager to see the training yard."

Aylin grabbed her hand. It wasn't until they were several corridors away from the main hall that Yara spoke.

"I was thinking perhaps you could train with Lugrezia's men. It will help keep you active," she said.

"You want me to fight in this war with this vampir lord?" Aylin asked. It sounded ludicrous simply saying the sentence. A year ago, she wouldn't have fathomed the existence of their kind, but now her sister was one of them. Her sweet, darling Yara was plotting a war, and Aylin wasn't sure if she could protect her anymore. It made her feel useless.

"No, of course not," Yara said. "You are human, and they are strong and immortal." She shook her head as if remembering she was one of them. "*We* are strong and immortal. But there is no harm in staying sharp. I'd hate for you to get bored."

"I've killed far more of them than you have," Aylin said, abruptly coming to a halt. "I can hold my own, Yara."

"I don't want you to fight, Aylin," she said in that soothing tone of hers. "Eldar will use any weakness he can against me. I won't let him use you as a pawn to force my hand."

Aylin hated every word that came out of her mouth. She was the protector. She was the warrior. She was older than Yara. Aylin had sacrificed everything to bring her back home, yet all Yara saw was a weak creature in need of protection.

"Is that what you think of me? That I am some frail mortal who needs to be protected? A *weakness*?" Aylin asked, the words poison on her tongue. She pulled her hand away, fingers tightening into a fist.

"You're being unreasonable," Yara said.

She mumbled something under her breath far too soft to hear.

Aylin glared at her. "What was that?"

"As always," Yara said a bit sharply. "You are being unreasonable as always."

"I am unreasonable?" Aylin demanded.

"I don't wish to quarrel," Yara said. Always the pacifier. She reached for her hand, squeezing it tight. It was meant to be a soft gesture, but Aylin winced when she gripped her too tight.

"Sorry," she whispered, instantly releasing her.

"I do not think we should fight this war, but I can see you are set on it," Aylin said. "If there is a war, I am fighting in it. As I fought at the palace."

"If that is what you want," Yara said. "I never had much luck talking you into changing your mind."

"Nor I you," Aylin said. "I suppose we get our stubbornness from father."

"How is he?" Yara asked. "I miss him terribly."

"He was devastated by your disappearance," Aylin said. "I doubt he is taking my absence any better."

"I'm surprised he let you come after me," Yara said.

"He didn't," Aylin said sheepishly.

Yara chuckled. "Of course not."

A door creaked open, and Aylin looked up to see Domenico step outside a room followed by Lugrezia.

"What do you think it will mean?" Yara asked. "Now that he is her son."

"Nothing good," Aylin said. "I don't trust him."

Lugrezia seemed desperate to mend their broken relationship, and she wouldn't put it past him to capitalize on that desperation. Domenico was a viper.

"Good morning, ladies," he said.

"Yara, please join me in the council room. We have much to discuss," Lugrezia said.

"Are you able to find your way to the training yard?" Yara asked.

Aylin nodded. She had never been a fan of politics. Her weapon of choice had always been a blade, while Yara's had been her tongue. She'd rather train till her limbs gave out than sit in a room with the vampir and attempt to understand their machinations.

Aylin looked at Domenico, but he stood firmly by his mother's side.

"I think I'd much rather join the conversation about killing the vampir king," Domenico said.

Aylin narrowed her eyes. He was definitely up to something.

"Walk me to the training yard first," Aylin insisted. "I'd hate to get lost on the way."

"Very well," he said.

"What are you up to?" she whispered, the moment they were out of earshot.

"What makes you think I'm up to something?" he asked. His lips rose in a crooked smile that gave away his devious intentions.

"I would be surprised if you *weren't* up to something," she said. "You and your mother seem close."

Aylin paused to look into his eyes. She couldn't read him very well while they were walking. Now that she thought about it, she couldn't read him well regardless. If his secret plans somehow harmed her sister, she would never forgive herself.

"Your mother is a vampir and your father is a vampir hunter," she said.

His father, Cristifano Zancherelli, had led the Silver Cross before Salvatore. He had a high position in the brotherhood, and she had always assumed Domenico would follow in his footsteps and remain with the brotherhood for life. "Who is your allegiance with?"

"My allegiance is to us," he said. Aylin was not surprised when his big palm rested on her cheek. He touched her as if she belonged to him. Sometimes it frightened her, but other times, such as this, it soothed her. It was foolish of her to seek comfort from him, especially knowing whom her heart belonged to, but she couldn't resist resting her cheek for a split second before her senses crawled back in and she smacked his hand away.

"What does that mean?" she asked.

"It means I need to secure our future," he said. "I don't want to return to Venice, and I doubt you want to return to the Ottoman Empire."

"Maybe I do," she said. "Ilyas wanted to return home to Constantinople."

"He could be dead for all we know," Domenico said.

A sharp stab tugged at her gut. The thought was unbearable. Of course, it had crossed her mind several times that perhaps his injuries were worse than she thought. Perhaps he had been buried in some empty plot in a foreign country surrounded by Christian men who didn't have a single idea who he truly was. That he had sacrificed everything for her and her sister, and she hadn't been there for him in his weakest state. Or by his side during his final moments.

A lump built in her throat, and when she spoke her voice was hoarse. "Don't say that."

He tugged her chin up, staring at her with those deep green eyes the color of a murky lake.

"Nobody has ever taken care of you the way that you deserve," he said. "I would kill for you, Aylin."

It would be so easy to stop fighting and accept his twisted brand of love. For so long, Aylin had been alone. Not in the physical sense—there had always been people around her—but emotionally. Yara had always been the sensitive one, so people had always coddled her, whereas Aylin had been the fighter, the survivor. She was not allowed to be weak. She was not allowed to need anyone.

"I know you're tired of fighting alone," he whispered as if he could read her mind. "Let me take care of you."

He wrapped his arms around her, and Aylin listened to the sound of his heart. The steady rhythm tricked her into falling deeper into his embrace. She could feel the weight of his chin on her head.

It was easy to get lost in the comfort he provided.

But even when her mind had softened to a quiet purr, all she could think about was Ilyas.

IX

He awoke to a pounding headache radiating from the back of his head to just behind his eyes. He didn't know where he was and couldn't remember anything that had occurred before this moment. Panic tightened his chest when he realized that darkness cloaked his left eye.

A young man sat beside him with pale hair and warm brown eyes.

"Elijah," he said with relief. "You are awake."

His throat was dry, and the man gave him a cup of water. He drank it greedily and when he lowered it, he felt a terrible sense of absence. He felt too big for his body, as if his skin would tear at any moment and he wasn't quite certain what to do with his hands. He felt lightheaded, and the shadow that darkened his vision refused to leave. His finger rose to touch it, wondering if some damage had happened to it.

Elijah.

Was that his name?

"Who are you?" he asked. He looked around the room, searching for the number of exits and entrances. He had to turn his head farther because there was something wrong with his left eye. He couldn't see from it.

"I'm Salvatore," the young man said. "You must have hit your head pretty hard if you don't remember me."

He turned back to the stranger, Salvatore to gauge his strength. Salvatore had less muscle mass than him, which was a relief. He would likely win a fight against him. It was an odd thing to think, but it felt natural.

There was an elderly man in the corner writing at a short table, wrinkled fingers making looping scrawls.

Salvatore summoned the elderly man with a curl of his finger. Salvatore exuded a natural-born grace and command that spoke of a higher education and noble upbringing. He wore scarlet robes and had a silver crucifix dangling from his tan throat.

"Is there something wrong with him?" Salvatore asked, concerned.

"What is your name, young man?" the old man asked. He reached forward to peel back his eyelids. "Name and age."

"I don't know," he said. "My eye. Something is wrong."

The old man pursed his wrinkled lips.

There was a fog that clouded his mind. He couldn't remember anything. That familiar panic that had chocked him earlier returned, and his hand desperately reached for someone. Someone who *should* have been there. Someone he relied on. But there was nobody there. Nobody but Salvatore and this old man. The panic built, and he felt as though he could not breathe. His hand reached for his chest, and he saw Salvatore shoot up from his chair.

"What is the matter?" Salvatore asked.

"I need...I need..." he gasped.

But the words evaded him; he didn't know what he needed.

Salvatore gripped his hands tight between his own, resuming his seat once he realized it was a fit of nerves rather than an attack of his heart. "Take a deep breath first."

He struggled to suck air through his mouth and when he did,

it didn't soothe the fear in his chest that something was amiss. It didn't bring him relief. Just a new wave of misery.

"He has sustained much damage to his head," the old man murmured. "I'm afraid it has affected his vision and memories. Do you remember anything?"

He flexed his hand, staring at it oddly. Someone was missing. He could feel it, someone that should have been here.

"Do I have a wife?" he asked.

"No, you are celibate," Salvatore said. "You do have a brother and a sister."

"Oh," he said.

The words didn't bring him much relief. They were not the person he needed. His heart beat fast at the thought of this person. He loved this person. He knew that much.

The old man pulled Salvatore aside. He whispered, but the room was far too small for privacy, and every word they spoke floated toward him, painting a bleak, terrible picture.

"I am afraid that the vision from his left eye is gone," he whispered. "He still understands questions and is aware, but I believe all his memories are lost."

"Can he be treated, Vincenzo?" he whispered. "Can he be treated for both?"

"Only time will tell," Vincenzo said. "It is in God's hands now."

Elijah, he had called him. Even his name felt strange and heavy on his tongue. As if it didn't quite fit.

Salvatore returned to his side and crouched by him. His voice was gentle when he spoke, as if he were a frightened child.

"We will start anew, brother," he said. "You will have a place with the Silver Cross for as long as you need, and if you are not fit to fight, we will find you some other role. We will not abandon you."

"Will you tell me who I am?" he asked.

He nodded. "You are Elijah. Born in Transylvania. I assume

you are either nineteen or twenty. You have a brother named Aydin, and a sister who was captured by the vampir."

Elijah recalled the vampir. A flash of sharp teeth and mad eyes played across his mind, and he shuddered.

"You recall them, then?" Salvatore asked.

"I know things, but not anything that matters," he said. "I know that I am missing someone. Someone that I love more than life. I know that I can trust you. I know that there are monsters."

He didn't know who he was or what his purpose was. He felt untethered and alone. But these basic facts gave him some measure of comfort.

"You can trust me," Salvatore said. "And you can trust my men."

"Where are my brother and sister?" Elijah asked.

It brought some relief to know that he had a family. That he was not alone in this world.

"Your brother left to go after your sister. He was accompanied by Domenico, one of my men," he said. "They are both brash and reckless, and I do not understand their friendship, but Domenico will look after the boy."

Elijah nodded. He hoped the boy survived and found their sister. He tried to picture them, but nothing came to mind.

"Rest," Salvatore said. "We are home now."

Elijah liked the sound of that word.

But it didn't fill the void in his chest.

It didn't make him feel complete.

X

"Well, this is splendid," Thaddeus said, collapsing on Volkan's bed. It was a large feather bed with a splendidly carved wooden frame. "I presume you want to take the left side?"

"You presume correctly," Volkan said, staring at the small intimate bedroom. There was no sitting room or dining room. It was a mere bedroom, far smaller than the one he'd had in his childhood. Lugrezia's home lacked the opulence of the Demirci household and the spaciousness of their quarters at Poenari. In comparison, it was incredibly lackluster.

"Is it not to your taste, my lord?" Pariza asked with a teasing smile. She sat on the wardrobe, perched atop the smooth frame like a kitten. Long legs folded beneath her to support her balance.

"It is adequate," he said. All that mattered was that he was near Yara. They hadn't had the reunion he expected. But he had a plan to amend that.

His mind raced ahead of him, concocting various gestures that would make her forgive him. A part of him was excited to court Yara. He had never courted a girl before. It had never appealed to him. After he had been imprisoned by Pomona, he had sworn that he'd never let another woman touch him, and for a few weeks he had stuck by it. It had taken him months before he could stomach lying with a woman. He had vomited the first few times, but then he'd learned to anchor his mind in the moment, and it had stuck. It had been important for him to heal. To not let her win.

And he also enjoyed lying with beautiful women too much to stop.

Yara was not a girl who would ever be satisfied with a physical relationship, nor would she allow it. She was elegant and beautiful and faithful, and he couldn't be his usual scoundrel self with her. He had to do better. He had to *be* better.

Volkan collapsed on the bed, resting his head on Thaddeus's chest. His mind filled with thoughts of Yara, and he felt a strange sense of giddiness.

"I will leave you two to your bonding or whatever it is you do in the privacy of your own company," Pariza said.

"Quick, Thaddeus, undress the moment her back is turned," Volkan whispered loudly.

"Help me with my belt buckle," Thaddeus said, playing along with his game. "You know I like it when you use your teeth."

Pariza sighed. "You two are children pretending to be men."

Volkan's lips rose in a partial smile. "Jealous you can't join us?"

Volkan knew he shouldn't pick sides in their rivalry. He could tell from Thaddeus's bright smile that he was pleased he was goading her. Pariza and Thaddeus had despised each other for as long as he could recall. Everything was a competition between them, which somehow both amused and annoyed Volkan.

"You wish," she said, wrinkling her nose in disgust. "I can't think of anything worse."

She flipped her dark hair over her shoulder and disappeared out the door. Volkan sealed his eyes shut with a deep sigh.

"She's mad at me," Volkan said.

"Pariza?" Thaddeus asked. "Who cares about that old hag?"

"She is younger than you," he said. "Besides, I'm talking about Yara."

"Oh," he said. "Is it because we mistreated her sister?"

"Yes, and my altercation with Mircea," he said.

"That is what happens when you chase a girl who was mortal for most of her life. Her morals will always get in the way of the fun," Thaddeus said. "Why don't you give her a few years to mature? Her self-righteousness might tire you if you pursue her now."

"Have you seen her?" Volkan asked, tilting his head to look up at him. "She is the most beautiful and remarkable girl I've ever met. She won't be available for long. I must have her. *Now*. While her attention is yet unclaimed."

Volkan had initially been struck by her beauty. He had felt a strange, possessive need to keep her. To tuck her away somewhere far and dark to be admired by him alone. He'd been shocked by the intensity of his need. But that night Pomona had kidnapped her, something had changed: his obsession had morphed into something more tender. He hadn't wanted anyone to hurt her. It had brought out a different side of him that ached to protect her.

For so long, all he'd wanted was to hurt others. To hurt the courtiers who had watched him be dragged away by the Maleinos, to hurt the Maleinos who had set him up, to hurt the Draculs for sentencing him. But when he saw Pomona's filthy hands on her, he would have done anything to save her, anything to pull her away from the demons of his past.

"You truly care for her?" Thaddeus asked. He seemed a bit surprised, as if he hadn't thought Volkan capable of such a thing.

"Why else would I leave? Why would I turn my back on my brother?" he asked. Nobody but her could ever pull him from his brother's side.

"He didn't look stable," Thaddeus said, concern lacing his voice. "He seemed unhinged. Both by her departure and yours."

Volkan waved a hand. "Eldar will be annoyed for a few days, but he will get over it. He never laughs at my jokes and thinks you and I are both dreadfully immature. And perhaps he is attracted to Yara, but her absence won't destroy him."

"I don't know," Thaddeus said uneasily. "Something in his eyes made me nervous."

"I won't let him hurt you," Volkan said. "I've done an excellent job protecting you thus far."

Thaddeus had a terrible habit of angering the wrong people. There had been many drunken fights where Volkan had saved the little poet, always pulling him far from danger, which was a feat because Volkan himself was not a fighter. He preferred to spar with his tongue and trade barbed insults rather than fold his sleeves and tighten his fists. While he was a vampir who enjoyed blood, he didn't quite like the sight of his *own*.

"It's not me I'm worried about," he said. "It's everyone else."

"Eldar will forget about us soon," Volkan said.

His eyes slid closed, and he clasped his palms to his chest. Within seconds he could feel his mind submerged in the dark.

His senses were high, but his mind was sinking into the shadows of sleep. Before he knew it, he was lost to the world.

———

Volkan straightened when Yara entered the main hall, lifting his slender frame from the slouch he'd been in while he awaited her arrival. He could feel the room shift, necks twisting to face her, whispers flooding the air. Everyone had witnessed her power the other night when she'd revealed that she could command vampir, and the fear in their eyes at her presence aroused him. It filled him with a strange, unnamed pride to know that everyone in the room feared *his* girl. She wore a long black gown embroidered with silver hummingbirds in the Italian style that the Carrara court favored. Her sister walked beside her in a pair of ill-fitting trousers and a black tunic with the sleeves rolled up to her bony elbows.

"She's magnificent," he whispered.

"You are so lovesick," Thaddeus said with a good dose of disgust. "It is making me nauseous."

"I prefer this side of him more than when he's a whore," Pariza said. "Much more tolerable."

Volkan tossed an almond from his plate at her head. She threw her spoon at him, but with his reflexes, she stood no chance. He caught it with ease and smiled smugly at her. Pariza huffed, but her lips pulled up in a reluctant smile. She never could be angry at him for long.

He turned away from her to look at Yara, who returned his gaze with a strangely hurt look on her face. He frowned.

"Oh," Thaddeus said, sitting upright. "Is little Yara jealous?"

He watched Yara stiffen, her mouth tightening in annoyance.

"She can hear better, you little shit," Volkan said.

"I know," he said. He winked at her, and Volkan kicked him hard under the table.

Volkan looked back at her, but she was standing by Mircea near the dais. There was a boy beside them with tan skin and copper hair.

"Is that..."

"That cursed Dante," Thaddeus said, sitting upright. "What is he doing here?"

Volkan didn't want to call him a rival or a nemesis; the words were too strong for the petty squabbles they'd had in their youth. Dante Carrara thought he was God's gift on Earth, which was strange because if God had made a person to symbolize perfection, it would be Volkan.

He was the nephew of Lugrezia Carrara and it was rumored he would take her place as leader of the family when she stepped down.

Volkan had always gotten some perverse enjoyment from getting under Dante's skin. He'd always stolen the girls he was interested in and thrown far better revels. Their feud had begun when Volkan had bedded a girl whom Dante had been obsessed with. In truth, he didn't even remember the girl, but Dante had never forgiven him for the slight.

"Looks like Mircea is introducing her," Thaddeus said. "Can you hear them?"

Volkan shushed him, concentrating so he could cut through all the sounds around them and listen.

"This is the girl I told you about, Dante," Mircea said. "Lugrezia says you are looking for a wife."

"Mircea," Yara said with a nervous chuckle.

Volkan stood up, fists curling in anger. How dare the Dracul bastard present her as an option? As if someone as perfect as her would look twice at Dante. He was so utterly beneath her it was laughable.

"Your reputation precedes you," Dante said. "You must be the girl with the voice of command."

"I go by just Yara," she said.

Volkan was by them in mere seconds, using his vampir speed to cross the room in the blink of an eye. He wrapped his arms around her waist, glaring at Dante.

"I didn't know they let rats into the dining area," Volkan said.

Yara gasped, and Mircea's brows descended in anger.

"Volkan, still as immature as I remember," Dante said, taking a shallow sip from his chalice.

"It is Prince Volkan to you," he said. "My brother is the Undying King now, haven't you heard?"

"You are a title-less bastard," Mircea spat.

Volkan felt a thrill seep down his spine at the fact that he'd spoiled both of their good spirits. Eldar always said it was a talent that Volkan could make enemies so quickly, but he was one to talk. Eldar seemed to be the most despised man among the vampir as of late.

"As are you, Mircea the worthless," Volkan said.

Yara stood between them as if she knew Mircea would lunge at him. He placed his hands on her hips, pulling her back so her body was flush against his. It was charming how she was so little yet so fierce. She barely came up to the middle of his chest, but Mircea halted at the sight of her as if he had come upon a giant. Now that they knew how powerful she was, nobody seemed interested in going against her.

He rested his chin on her head. "How nice it is that I have my girl to protect me."

"Hiding behind a woman." Mircea shook his head in disgust. "How pathetic."

His words barely touched Volkan. He loved that Yara was so strong and that grown men were afraid of her. It pleased him that she was so frighteningly powerful.

Volkan turned back to Dante, a few clever insults dancing on his tongue. He didn't know which to say first; he had far too many to count.

"Save it," Dante said. "I've outgrown these childish retorts."

"Have you?" Volkan tilted his head. "Or am I simply so perfect that your mind fails you?"

Dante rolled his eyes, turning back to Yara. "Would you like to go on a walk with me?"

"No, she would not," Volkan said. "She is taken."

Yara lifted her head to look at him. She didn't seem to like that response.

"I'd love to go on a walk," she said. Her next words were sharp and directed at Volkan. "Maybe you should return to your *friend*."

"Pariza?" he asked, surprised. "She is—"

Yara slipped out of his arms, and he gritted his teeth.

"She is a friend," he finished. "Like Thaddeus."

"Have you ever been with her?" Yara asked.

"God, no," he said. His stomach churned at the thought. Pariza was a beautiful girl, but he had never seen her in that light.

Her eyes narrowed as if she did not quite believe him.

"You've never kissed her?"

He was silent. He'd kissed her one night when he'd been incredibly drunk, but he regretted it almost immediately. It had felt like nothing. Tasted like nothing. He hardly remembered it, and he was more ashamed of it than not. Not one of his finer moments.

"It meant nothing," he said.

Pain flashed across her eyes for a second before they grew so cold, he flinched.

"I see," Yara said. She turned to Dante. "I think some fresh air will do me good."

"Yara, be sensible," Volkan said, reaching for her, but she was gone before he could touch her. Quicker than he expected—he still tended to forget she was a vampir. But she was, and she'd left him behind. Her dress was a faint whisper through the crowd as she stepped out the doors with Dante, the hungry dog, heavy on her heels.

"Smart girl," Mircea said. "I warned her earlier of the importance of marriage and how uniting herself with Dante would be in her best interest. I thought I'd have to do more to convince her, but you did half the work."

"Nonsense," he said. But his words weren't as confident as it usually sounded. In fact, he sounded a bit uncertain.

"The trueborn don't wed sired vampir," Volkan said.

Betrothals were often made between trueborn children of powerful families for many reasons, the most important of which was that only trueborn vampir could have children. Since all sired vampir were incapable of having children, a child between a trueborn and a mortal was always mortal. Trueborn marriage was necessary to continue their family lines.

But because there were only nine families to choose from, betrothals were insanely competitive.

"She's different," Mircea said. "Many men will be interested in her. She is a weapon now. It increases her value."

Volkan's lips tightened in a frown. He did not like the sound of that.

Mircea's lips peeled back in a satisfied smile, as if he knew that he'd struck a nerve.

Volkan left him behind. He stepped outside into the gardens, following the sound of her soft voice. If she thought he would wait for her while she went off with that vulture, she was mistaken.

He found her walking with Dante. Volkan was behind them in moments, and before they could notice his arrival, he wrapped his long fingers around Dante's neck and cracked it, letting his limp body fall to the ground. He bent down to wipe his fingers on Dante's coat, staring at him with a satisfied look.

"That should buy us some time," Volkan said, offering her his elbow.

Her mouth was slack in horror as she stared at Dante.

"He's not dead," he said. "Unfortunately."

"You can't just do that," she said. "You can't hurt people."

He tilted his head. "But I just did."

Her mouth twisted in anger, and if he had a heart, it would have skipped a beat, because she was marvelous when she was angry. Like a dark angel who'd come to cut out the hearts of all those who stood before her, and he was completely at her mercy.

"You are so maddeningly beautiful," he whispered.

"Don't try to soften me with your honeyed words," Yara said with a sharp tone. "It won't work. I thought you changed. After everything, I thought you changed, but you didn't."

"I am coldhearted," he said, taking a step forward. And then another when she backed away.

He didn't stop until her back was against the garden wall, caught between the vines that curled like fingers around the trellis. He caught her wrists and pinned them high above her head, enjoying how it drew her bodice a little lower than was appropriate. He lost his focus for a split second, distracted by the sight of her flesh.

He leaned down to whisper in her ear. "I am cruel."

Her body trembled, and his lips rose in a smile as he trailed his tongue along the shell of her ear.

"I am wicked," he breathed.

He wished he could hear her heartbeat thundering in her chest or those little gasping sounds she used to make. She was terribly still just then, eyes wide open, mouth slightly parted. Her tongue ran along her lips nervously, and he couldn't resist bending down to taste her. He held her face with his hand while tightening his fingers around her wrist, reminding her that he controlled her and, despite all her protests, she *enjoyed* being controlled. He ran his tongue along the seam of her lips before he bit her. *Hard.* He was rewarded with a small whimper, feeling her body melt against him.

He pulled away far too soon. "You don't walk away from me. *Ever.*"

"I'll do whatever—"

"I please," he cut her off. "You will do whatever *I* please because I am yours and you are mine."

"You hurt my sister. You injured Dante. You riled up Mircea for your own amusement, and...and..." Her next words caught in her throat before she softly added. "And you kissed *her.*"

He hated that she was hurt by that meaningless kiss that had happened years ago. He'd been so desperate to feel something, anything when he was freed, as if the right person could wash away his demons and the pain that plagued him. He drank every night and lost himself in far too many bodies to count. But none of them meant anything to him.

"I was drunk. I was always drunk then," he said. "It takes a lot of work to get drunk as a vampir, so that must tell you how terribly I wanted to get out of my head. To forget that I was Volkan Demirci. To forget that I was empty inside and nothing and no one could fill the void. I kissed far more people than I ever expected in the months after it happened. It didn't change anything. It didn't make a difference. It didn't fix me."

"She's beautiful," she whispered. "She makes sense."

"I would rather shove a blade in my heart than be with Pariza," he said. "I'd rather be with Thaddeus than her. We have far more in common, and he laughs at my jokes."

Her lips twitched, and he rested his forehead on hers.

He released her wrists, feeling the words he wanted to say weigh heavy on his chest. They caught in his mouth like a spider trapped in its own web. His hand was gentle when he cupped her face, like she would crumble to powder if he exerted any force. When he spoke, the words were pathetic and not the ones he wanted to say. But he said it, nonetheless.

"I've never felt this way before," he said softly.

"What do you feel?" she asked. Her big, brown eyes stared at him, and he was glad that sired vampir kept their eye color. It was too beautiful to disappear; he would have mourned them if it had.

"*Everything*," he said. "Will you have dinner with me, tomorrow night?" Volkan asked. Half-hopeful, half-nervous.

"I don't know," she said. "Will you behave?"

"For you, my darling pet?" he asked. "Anything."

He would win her over. It was what he had come here to do.

And he would not stop till she was his.

XI

"Lord Alexandru Dracul has arrived, your grace," a servant boy said.

Eldar stared at the procession of nobles lamenting their woes and slights to him. He listened with one ear and passed his judgment swiftly after. One thing about the vampir was that they could hold a grudge. Some of these feuds were decades or even centuries old. Yet they spoke of them as if they had occurred just yesterday.

"Dismissed," Eldar called, and they all returned to their dinner tables. There was a distinct lack of excitement in gaining everything he had hungered after for so long. An emptiness that he could not quite pinpoint.

"Invite Alexandru to a private dinner once he's rested," Eldar said to the servant.

The families respected and feared Alexandru Dracul. To have Alexandru's support would strengthen his claim, but Eldar did not trust him enough to receive him in the Grand Hall. Alexandru was prideful and hadn't bent the knee to his own father. Vlad had loved him too much to care, but Eldar did not share his sentiment.

Alexandru could not be threatened; there was nothing and no

one that he loved. So, Eldar would have to make sure he had something to lose. Vlad had never personally gotten involved in betrothals and alliances. He let the trueborn do as they pleased, but Eldar would not sit back and let them pretend they had an ounce of free will. Alliances would not be made unless they benefited him.

And Eldar knew *exactly* whom to pair Alexandru with.

———

It had been years since Alexandru and Nikolina Osakwe had seen each other.

"He won't like you forcing his hand," Rahim warned. "And the Osakwe already made a match with her and Maxim Kuznetsov when she was a little girl."

Eldar had sent for Nikolina shortly after he had sent for Alexandru. Alexandru despised Nikolina now, but there had been a time when he had loved her.

Eldar would also not have any great difficulty convincing Nikolina to keep an eye on him.

Nikolina would be his spy *and* Alexandru's weakness.

"I recall," Eldar said.

Alexandru's mother, Nazia Laghari, who had been the last surviving member of the Laghari trueborn family, had put Alexandru forward for Nikolina's hand when he was just a boy of twelve. Many families did the same; even Eldar's father had put him and Volkan forward. Their father had thought he would have better luck snagging the girl if he put two boys forward rather than one.

Eldar had never understood what was so special about Nikolina.

"You will make enemies," Rahim said. "You will be despised."

"This new alliance will benefit me greatly. It will give Alexandru a weakness, and weaknesses can be exploited. It will show all the trueborn that only I have the final say on matches," he said. "I am not Vlad. I will not turn a blind eye to their plotting."

Eldar was wiser and harsher than Dracul. His subjects had learned that when he had hung Radu out in the bone garden. For twelve nights, he had been left there with his gut cut and the crows feeding on his entrails, then promptly returned inside just before sunrise so he could heal. On the thirteenth day, Eldar had mutilated him and killed him. But for those first twelve nights, they had dined outside, feasting on the echo of his screams.

Eldar had relished the fear that hung in the air. The way they could barely meet his gaze. It was exhilarating.

"Have you found her?" Eldar demanded.

"The men still search," Rahim said. "The weather has grown worse, and any traces of footprints have long since been swallowed by the winter storm."

Eldar rubbed his chin, fury slipping under his skin. Every day that she remained away from him was a day longer that this rift between them grew. It was more time that Volkan spent with her and used his stubborn will to build something unbreakable with her. Something that Eldar would have little hope of undoing. The concept of them growing closer disturbed him, but Eldar refused to touch that poisonous thought with a ten-foot pole. He would let it languish in the recesses of his mind and hope that it didn't come back to haunt him.

He recalled faintly when his father had told him once that Volkan was his heir and Eldar the unwanted spare. He had reminded him every day that he was a mistake, and that they had planned for one, not two children.

He is everything and you are nothing.

Even his mother had been gentler with Volkan, treating him like a precious vase, combing his pale hair while he slept on her lap. She had always been wary around Eldar and told him often that she did not like his stare. His father's words and his mother's attention toward Volkan had never caused a rift between the brothers, and neither had Yara. But for a small moment, he wondered if anyone would ever choose him first. If he would ever be anything more than second-best.

Eldar sat down at the dinner table. They had prepared a small feast for Alexandru and Nikolina, who would join them shortly. He hadn't exactly told her she was to be engaged tonight.

Eldar supposed that would be the fun of it all.

"Eldar Demirci," Alexandru drawled. "Or shall I say, King Eldar."

Eldar's lips lifted in a faint smile. Alexandru wore his signature black kaftan with the fur-covered shoulders. His short dark hair curled above his eyes.

"I don't suppose you are going to bow."

"I bow to no man," he said. "But if it is evidence of my support that you require, you have my approval. I never thought Mircea or Radu would make particularly good kings."

He was not surprised that Alexandru refused to bend the knee. If he'd been lesser man, Eldar would have cut his legs out from under him, but he respected Alexandru.

"And you think I will?" Eldar asked.

"That is yet to be seen," Alexandru said, sitting down on the chair drawn out for him.

"Do you know where your uncle is?" Eldar asked.

"I presume he's gathering an army or enough desperate men to help him overthrow you," he replied, cutting neatly into a slab of bloody deer meat.

"I find it odd that he didn't reach out to you, considering I burned and killed every other person with significant power under the Draculesti banner," Eldar said. "He has no allies, so it would make the most sense."

It would be arrogant of Eldar to not be suspicious of him. Alexandru was an impossible man to read.

"Like I said, you are a better fit," he said. He eyed the table setting before him, noticing the extra plate and cutlery. "Are we expecting someone?"

"Yes," Eldar said. He nodded at the servant, and the doors

were pulled back. Nikolina walked in, carrying the confidence she had so desperately lacked when they were young. She had been quiet and soft then, but he could see she had grown a few thorns of her own. She was no longer the naive little girl who was poked fun at by all the trueborn children at the behest of Alexandru. Her bone-white hair swept down her back with a few sparse braids intertwined, and she wore a white dress that left very little to the imagination.

"My lord," she said, bowing deeply before him. She arose and turned to Alexandru, the smile falling off her face. Alexandru stiffened, and his eyes shot to Eldar with a suspicious look.

Nikolina's mother was a Danesti just like Eldar's own mother, and she had the unnaturally white hair his brother did, which, coupled with her tan skin, was both shocking and bewitching to people.

"Alexandru," she said with a good layer of disgust. "I was praying that some harm befell you as it did your kin. We watched your uncle burn not too long ago. I had hoped you'd be next."

"I see you've grown a backbone," Alexandru said. He stared at her as if she were no better than the dust on his shoes. "Broken from your father's tight leash, have you?"

Eldar leaned back in his chair, sipping his chalice of blood in mild amusement.

"I at least have a father," she snapped. "Yours was cut down not too long ago. He suffered the fate that will come for all of your bloodline."

Alexandru's tattooed fingers tightened around the stem of his chalice as if he pictured her delicate neck beneath his hands.

"A bit harsh," Eldar said with a wide smile. "Do you not think, Nikolina?"

"I am not afraid of him anymore," she said, raising her chin. "The Draculesti are nothing. He is merely the child of a dead king."

Alexandru tore out of his chair, long fingers coiling around her neck. Her back was pressed against the wall, and a sharp inhale escaped her. She hadn't yet transitioned to a trueborn vampir and was still painfully mortal, but Alexandru was a vampir. So, perhaps she had miscalculated his power.

"Do you think that because you have not seen me in years that I've grown softer?" he whispered harshly. "That I have changed from the boy who would make you crawl on your pretty knees to me and whose every command you obeyed because you were weak and pathetic?"

"You forget yourself," Nikolina said. "I am not one of your blood slaves. I am a trueborn. You don't own me."

"I do not *want* to own you," Alexandru spat. "You've lost your charm. And as far as I'm concerned, you deserve that sniveling boy you are set to wed."

"Speaking of marriages," Eldar said. "Please be seated, we have much to discuss."

Eldar could slice the tension with a blade. And while it was enjoyable, he did not have the time to sit around and wait for their argument to boil over.

Alexandru returned to his seat, and Nikolina sat stiffly across from him.

"I did not invite you both here to bicker," Eldar said. "I came to propose an alliance between the Osakwe and the Dracul."

Nikolina frowned. "We hate them."

"In this case, I agree with the girl," Alexandru said, as if he had conveniently forgotten her name. "There is bad blood between us."

"Vlad is gone, and the court is to run differently now that I am your leader," Eldar said. "Any betrothals made under Dracul's rule are void. I will be overseeing all betrothals from this moment forth, and in rare circumstances, I will put together a new betrothal."

"Is he to wed my cousin Amara?" she asked. "They would be a terrible match. He will make her miserable. We must reconsider, my lord."

"Alexandru will wed *you*," Eldar said.

Silence echoed for one blissful second before they both began to speak at once.

"I will not wed *her*," Alexandru said.

At the same time, Nikolina said, "I will kill myself before I tie myself to him."

"You will do as I command," Eldar said, "or you will die as traitors."

That silenced her, but he had no such luck with Alexandru.

"Whom does this alliance benefit?" Alexandru demanded. "Besides angering the Osakwe and the Danesti, you will do more harm than good."

On the contrary, Eldar expected this to work out in his favor. The Osakwe could be soothed, and the Danesti were of no importance to him.

Alexandru stood up, fury marking his face, and was gone before he could say another word. Eldar could hear the satisfying sound of him breaking a vase in the distance.

"Well?" he asked, staring at Nikolina, who seemed to be suffering from some form of shock. "Are you secretly pleased?"

Her head snapped up as if she'd just noticed he was present in the room. From the horrified look in her eyes, he could tell she intended to pretend like it had never happened, like she hadn't once been in love with Alexandru. Before things had soured between Alexandru and her, they had been so entangled with each other, it was difficult to tell where one ended and the other began. And if they were apart from each other, Alexandru would simply stare at her. Sometimes they'd be sitting together between lessons in the Hall to dine, and Alexandru would simply tilt his chair, place his elbows on his knees, lean forward and just *stare* at her.

Eldar had never understood how he could stomach existing while it seemed his heart belonged in the body of another. Perhaps he understood it a bit now. He hadn't been himself since *she* left. It was as if he had been robbed blind, but he couldn't exactly tell what the thief had taken.

"What could possibly please me?" she asked. "Anybody else and I could stomach it, but *him*. He is a monster, my lord."

Eldar stood up and was not shocked that she grabbed his hand with desperate fingers.

It was pure insolence.

"You overstep, Nikolina," he said tightly. "Release me."

"Do not trap me with him," she said. Her hands fell back to her sides. "Please, my lord. Any price you name, my father will pay."

"Do you want to break this betrothal?" he asked.

"More than anything."

"Prove to me that he is a traitor," Eldar said. "If you do, I will kill him, and you can keep all his possessions and estates."

He watched her eyes spark with interest.

"I can be free," she said.

"You have my word," Eldar said.

Nikolina would be his eyes and ears on what Alexandru was up to. And if Alexandru betrayed him, he would erase him from this world.

Dinner had begun as it usually did, with the blood slaves making their rounds and servicing the trueborn. Each family had a table with their family flag above it. On the right side were the Osakwe, the silver-haired Danesti, the Ramose, and the Dracul tables. As much as he wanted to destroy the Dracul table, he didn't want to deal with the awkwardness of where Alexandru Dracul and his entourage or other members of the Dracul family who were now loyal to him would all sit. He had spared a few of them who had bent the knee and offered their allegiance to him.

So, he let Alexandru and his household have the former Dracul table, which had often hosted Mircea and Radu before their fall. On his left side were the Kuznetsov, the Maleinos—

those who'd survived his slaughter and vowed to serve him—the Yamazaki, the Carrara, and the Demirci tables.

It wasn't until they had reached the midway point of their night that Eldar heard the commotion. He let out a heavy sigh at the sight of Nikolina's brother, Tiberius, also known by all as Tiger because he was rather unpredictable. He'd torn out a blood slave's eye when they were children. It had been rather gruesome, and Eldar could still hear the echo of the mortal boy's cries as he fell to his knees. Nobody had punished Tiger for it. Nobody ever punished him for anything. And now he was up in Alexandru's face while the latter simply had his hands folded across his chest. Tiger possessed a larger physique and was more menacing, but Alexandru possessed a lethal brutality that only a fool would underestimate. Behind him was Maxim Kuznetsov, whom Nikolina had been betrothed to before Eldar had ended it in favor of Alexandru, and behind him was his cunning older brother, Vissarion Kuznetsov.

"My lord," Rahim said. His face was tight, lips pursed in distaste, "I am afraid there is about to be an altercation."

"Regarding?" Eldar asked. Even though he could see what was happening, the little Osakwe brat hadn't swayed Eldar to end her new betrothal, so she brought her wild dog brother along with his friends to handle Alexandru.

"Lord Dracul demands that Nikolina sit at the Dracul table, but she insists on sitting with Maxim," he said. "The young Lord Osakwe says that she has free will and the papers are not yet signed, but Lord Dracul insists. Shall we send the guards?"

"No," Eldar said. "They all need to learn some conflict resolution. They will handle it themselves."

Rahim frowned but he stayed put, hands folded behind his back.

Vlad would have put an end to it, but Eldar was in desperate need of some entertainment, and he sat back and took a shallow sip from his cup of blood, tuning in to their feud.

"I won't ask you twice, Alexandru," Tiger said darkly. He had his mother's fair complexion, but his father's dark hair cropped close to his scalp. A faint pink scar ran down the right side of his face from temple to jaw. His eyes were cold and unwelcoming when he looked at Alexandru.

"She doesn't want you," Maxim said almost childishly.

"I don't," Nikolina echoed. "So just leave."

"I tire of this petty squabble," Alexandru said. His hand swiftly caught Nikolina and, just as the boys lunged, he wrapped his leather-clad fingers around her throat. "If you make a move, I'll snap her pretty neck."

He could see Tiger shaking with anger, claws and teeth descending in rage. Maxim turned full vampir while Vissarion simply stared at Alexandru blankly. Vissarion was Tiger's best friend. He was the blistering winter to Tiger's burning rage. The terrible duo struck fear in the hearts of all their prey. Vissarion placed his pale hand on Tiger's shoulder and his little brother's, reining them back in like feral horses.

"You can enjoy Nikolina's company *tonight*," Vissarion said, fluidly speaking in Russian so they were not overheard by the courtiers or, at the very least, those who did not speak the tongue. But Eldar's Russian, while poor, was not so poor that he could not understand them. "But until the papers are signed, she is still betrothed to my brother."

"We will see about that," Alexandru said, lowering his hand from her throat. "I must leave on urgent business in a few hours, but my men are under strict orders to watch her until my return. And to ensure she sits with her new family. Isn't that right, Nikolina Draculeste?"

"I am not yours," Nikolina spat, struggling in his arms. Her hand reached to tear away his forearms, but he did not budge.

"I swear on everything, Nikolina, if you do not behave..." Alexandru whispered harshly in her ear.

"You'll what?" she dared.

He tilted her chin so she looked at him, and he didn't say a word. Only stared at her with a blank look that made her shiver.

The fight bled out of her, and he half-dragged, half-carried her to his table. When he sat down, he held her on his hip, her fists clenched tight to her side.

Vissarion whispered harshly to Tiger and Maxim, and they disappeared into the shadows with murderous looks on their faces.

"See?" Eldar said with a satisfied smile. "Conflict resolution."

"Her family and the Kuznetsovs have asked for a formal meeting to understand the new betrothal," Rahim said. "They are all upset about this turn of events."

"We will hold off the discussion until Alexandru returns," Eldar said.

It would be a lie if he said he was looking forward to it. But he could put it off for a little while longer under the guise of Alexandru's absence. Give them time to settle into their animosity and despair. They were so busy hating each other that nobody seemed to hate him anymore, which was a miracle. He had ruined their weak alliances, and by the time he made a few more betrothals amongst the trueborn, the line between friend and foe would be so twisted it would be impossible to tell them apart.

The only true ally they'd all share would be him.

Their Undying King.

XII

Yara sat in the council room, refusing to meet Dante's eyes. Dante was not exactly pleased that he'd awoken alone in the garden with a stiff neck. She'd apologized earlier that evening, but he had barely cast her a glance. Yara had no interest in Dante, and she'd only entertained it to get a reaction from Volkan. To see his eyes flare so beautifully with silent rage, with that same jealousy that had twisted her gut when she saw Pariza beside him.

"How much longer shall we wait for the boy?" Stefano asked gruffly.

Lugrezia wanted Domenico here. Yara didn't know what had occurred when they'd spoken, but it was clear to see Lugrezia was attempting to forge him a position at her court, much to the displeasure of Dante. Mircea said Dante was her heir and would lead the family when she stepped down. Since she had no vampir children naturally, it would all go to her chosen kin, and Dante seemed to be her favored.

"Easy," Lugrezia said sharply, baring her fangs. "That is my son."

Stefano lowered his head, as if he could evade her temper by disappearing into the ground.

"I don't trust the boy," Mircea said. "There is something unnerving about him that I can't quite pinpoint."

Yara sighed. "Eldar is probably fortifying his castle and assembling his troops, and you are all bickering about the wrong issue."

Domenico arrived then, unsurprisingly nonchalant and carefree.

He walked toward Stefano and said rather curtly, "*Move.*"

Stefano glared at him, prepared to argue, but one sharp look from Lugrezia, and he had risen from his chair for the little golden boy. There was a feral quality to Domenico. Fair-haired and green-eyed, he looked like a rabid woodland creature. He could almost be considered pretty if he didn't appear so harsh. Yara had noticed that he was different around Aylin, more watchful and less cutting, but to the rest of them, he was indifferent.

Stefano cleared his throat. "How many men do you reckon Eldar commands, my prince?"

Mircea's brows crinkled. "All of Vlad's sired would serve him. They are unbound from Vlad's will and, I presume, fearful for their lives. I'd say around one hundred thousand soldiers. Not including the Demirci vampir, which I reckon are around thirty thousand."

"I have twenty thousand men, little more than half the number of the Demirci foot soldiers," Lugrezia said. "He must have fortified the walls by now."

"And secured all the hidden passageways," Yara added.

"Not all," Mircea said. "The tunnel we escaped from is one of many. I lived with Vlad for many years. I know the castle. Both its strengths and weaknesses."

"That doesn't rectify the numbers," Magno said. "We are terribly short."

And from Tobias's displeased look, she could tell he shared the sentiment.

"We've written to my nephew," Mircea said. "Lugrezia dispatched the letter late this evening to his residence."

"The child?" Stefano asked incredulously. "Vlad's son?"

"No," Mircea said, looking annoyed that he'd even suggest such a thing. "The child is most likely dead. Eldar would have considered him a threat to his rule and killed him along with Radu."

Yara gasped. To kill a child was an unbearable thought. She remembered Little Mihnea sitting with his stout nursemaid during dinners. He couldn't have been older than seven.

"You need to quit those mortal gestures, Yara," Mircea said with a frown. "It is unbecoming."

"He would kill a child?" she whispered.

"He is capable of anything," he replied.

Eldar was cruel. She had watched him transform into a monster before her very eyes. She hated that his blood coursed through her veins. That a piece of her would always be tied to him. If she could cut it out, she would, but he was tangled so deep inside her she couldn't remove him without killing herself in the process.

"I have reached out to Alexandru Dracul," Mircea said. "Vlad was fond of him. He had gifted him with many trained soldiers to protect his strongholds from human invaders a few years ago. Alexandru has the numbers. He's heavily involved in various business ventures, including the selling of mercenaries and weapons. He would be a powerful ally and could turn this war in our favor."

"And will he accept your invitation?" Stefano asked.

Yara could see why Lugrezia had him on her council: he never seemed to run out of questions and had a permanently skeptical look on his face. His main objective was ensuring the safety of Lugrezia's home and court. He didn't seem to like the idea of waging this war against Eldar. But Lugrezia owed Mircea a blood debt and was determined to pay it back.

"He was close to his father," Mircea said. "He will avenge him."

"What if he makes a bid for the throne?" Yara asked.

If Vlad's heir, Mihnea, was dead, as was Radu, the second

contender for the throne, Yara couldn't understand why Alexandru would help Mircea rather than reclaim the throne for himself.

"Alexandru keeps away from court for a reason. He despises politics," Mircea said. "He will help us."

"We will await his response," Lugrezia said. "And pray that it is a good one."

———

Yara had spent three hours preparing herself for dinner with Volkan. To say she was excited was an understatement. Aylin watched her from their bed, a book in her hand about war strategy and torture tactics. She'd said Domenico had recommended it, which did not surprise Yara.

Of course, Lugrezia's cold-eyed son read books about torture for leisure.

"How do you stand all those pins in your head?" Aylin asked, twisting her body so her head hung from the bed. Her short dark hair fluttered down, and Yara felt a spike of guilt that she had cut her luscious locks for her. They had caught each other up on the months they had been apart. Aylin had sacrificed much to save her. Yara regretted that Aylin had been too late, that the sister she remembered had died, and all that was left was Yara the vampir. It felt like everything she had risked had been for nothing.

Aylin had the most splendid hair Yara had ever seen. She had always been envious of it. It rarely got tangled or knotted. It simply existed, swaying and tilting like the branches of a tree caught in the breeze.

"Does your head not hurt?" Aylin pressed.

Yara laughed softly. "No."

"You look pretty," Aylin said. "Not that I think he deserves it. Or deserves you, for that matter."

"This is not for Volkan," she said.

Her dress was the color of pomegranate seeds. It made her

brown skin look vibrant and golden under the light. She'd pinned her hair up to reveal the expanse of her collarbones, leaving two tendrils to grace the sides of her face.

"So you say," Aylin said with narrowed eyes.

"Are you adjusting to Lugrezia's court?" Yara asked, swiftly changing the topic. Aylin would warm up to Volkan eventually. He would win her over as he had Yara. She just needed to give it some time.

A part of her was worried that Aylin was spending far too much time alone. She'd catch her lying in the yard some days after training, half-coated in sweat, just staring at the sky with this sadness about her that made Yara's chest ache.

While Domenico seemed interested in the vampir war, Aylin had retreated to the library and the training field. There was this hollow look in her eyes that worried Yara, and she'd also lost a bit of weight.

"It's not the worst place," she said. "Preferable to Salvatore's little camp." Aylin sat up. "I keep dreaming about it. That night when *he* attacked Ilyas. The night when you died."

Yara put down her pot of lip tint and sat on the edge of their bed, clasping her sister's fingers. It was no secret whom she spoke of. Her lips curled when she said *he*. She spoke of the Undying King.

"Do you know what I keep thinking about?" she asked. "The way he looked at you when you died. For a split second, I could believe..."

"Believe what?" Yara asked. Her skin felt tight and prickly, and for a moment she wanted to stop her sister from speaking any more. To place her hand on her mouth so her words would not torment her.

"That he loved you," Aylin whispered.

Her stomach dropped. "Why would you say that?"

"He looked at you like his world had come to an end," Aylin said. "I must know if there was something between you both. If you will hesitate when it is time to cut out his worthless heart."

How could she think she would ever fall for his tricks a second time? She had seen who he was. He had revealed his truth. No honeyed words could erase how terribly he had ruined her. How he had turned against those she loved so swiftly and cruelly, and worse, how he had turned against her. Because for all his horrid nature, somehow Yara had believed that there was some invisible line that Eldar would not cross when it came to her. But she was not spared from his tyranny, she was just as much a victim as anyone else.

"He killed me, Aylin," she said. Her voice trembled when she spoke. "And I swore that I would do the same to him."

Aylin looked uncertain, and she hated that she doubted her. That somehow, even now, he controlled her in his own way. Tainted her before the people she loved.

"I will prove it to you," she promised. "I will bring you his heart."

———

Yara was surprised to find the lean, gangly form of Thaddeus slouching outside her door that evening.

"Hello, Yara," Thaddeus said with an almost friendly smile.

"You're being nice now?" she asked. "Funny how nobody is wretched to me anymore now that I can hurt them twice as hard as they did me." She raised her hand, letting her sharp white claws flicker under the candlelight.

"Well, the world is filled with prey and predators," he said. "You just happen to be the latter now."

Yara was pleased by his words. She *was* a predator, and she would never let them forget it.

Thaddeus fell into a dramatic bow. "I am here to lead you to our most gracious sire, Volkan Demirci."

"How much did he pay you to say that?" She raised a brow.

Thaddeus sighed. "Not enough."

Pariza appeared by their side in mere seconds. Her dark hair trailed behind her like a cape. "Yara, Volkan would like you to join him for a private dinner."

"Volkan sent me to fetch her," Thaddeus said, annoyed. "Leave."

"Well, he thought you'd ruin her night before it started, so he sent me," she said.

Yara was surprised when Pariza knotted their arms together, turning her around. Thaddeus grumbled under his breath about "infuriating girls" but followed close behind them.

"You are very beautiful, you know," she said. "Like a lovely little doll. I see why Volkan is so obsessed with you."

"Thank you," Yara said. "I will admit I was worried when I saw you with Volkan. You were so effortlessly elegant, it would be a lie if I said I wasn't envious."

Pariza laughed, a charming little sound. "You need not worry. I find Volkan rather repulsive. I've always been more drawn to his brother. I like a man who is a bit mean-spirited. It keeps the spark alive."

"Eldar?" Yara asked, wrinkling her nose. "He is terrible."

"I think ambition requires cruelty. Every man in power has done something heinous to gain his status. The only difference is if they hide it behind a smile or are up front about it," she said. "I prefer the latter."

"Well, you can have him," Yara said. "At least until I kill him."

Pariza chuckled. "If anyone can kill him, it would be you." Pariza's eyes softened. "Volkan truly does care for you. I've never seen him this way about anyone before."

Yara couldn't resist the smile that tugged at her lips. It was impossible to hide how much Pariza's words pleased her. She had been worried when Volkan had told her that he and Pariza had kissed in the past, but speaking to her now, she could see that Pariza was uninterested in him.

Pariza led her to the balcony door and wished her well.

"Give him a kiss for me," Thaddeus added, making her chuckle.

Yara tugged the curled iron handle and stared at the snow-covered floor. There were candles lit on either end of the small table and two chalices filled with blood. She could smell the delicious scent of fresh human blood, and her gums tightened as her teeth elongated. Volkan leaned against the banister and turned at the sound of her entrance.

"My darling angel," Volkan whispered, the words almost reverent.

"My presence doesn't mean that I've forgiven you," Yara said. "I love Aylin, and anybody who hurts her does not deserve to be in our lives. You haven't apologized yet for mistreating her."

"I'm sorry," he said. "It is difficult to see mortals as worthy of my kindness, but that is not an excuse. You love her, and I should have been more understanding. Forgive me?"

"Do you mean that?" Yara asked. "Or are you simply saying what I wish to hear?"

"A bit of both," he said.

Yara sighed. "I suppose I can admire your honesty."

He withdrew her chair for her, and Yara sat down, feeling the fluttering graze of his fingers on her shoulders as he pulled her chair in. A shiver ran down her spine, and Volkan did little to hide his smirk when he sat across from her. He stretched his unbearably long legs till they slipped between her own, tangling in the fabric of her gown. He wore a loose white tunic; the drawstrings were undone at the top, and the slit sank so low she could make out the narrow lines of his ribs and breastbone. His pale skin and white hair looked hauntingly beautiful in the dark.

"How did he let you go?" Yara asked.

Eldar was possessive of Volkan. She couldn't imagine him accepting that his brother had chosen her.

"We got into an argument before I left. I didn't agree with how he handled things that night. He had no right to turn you against your will," he said.

Yara remembered how angry Volkan had been that night when he held her. And that had made her like him so much more.

"I may be a monster, but I have my limits," Volkan said.

"You're not a monster, Volkan," she said softly. "Not to me."

"Come here," he said, reaching for her hand. He pulled her onto his lap, and Yara didn't know why, but she suddenly felt the horrors of the past two weeks catch up to her. Dying and becoming a vampir, fleeing into the cold night while her body morphed into something she could not control, abandoning the hope of ever returning to Constantinople and her father.

She hadn't had a chance to mourn who she'd been.

The girl who had died that night.

Her throat tightened, and she felt a sob escape her lips. It meant something that she could be vulnerable around him. That being in his arms made her want to unburden herself of the pain in her chest. She hid her face in the crook of his neck while the tears slipped down her cheek, soaking his collar.

"Shh, you're safe now," Volkan said. "Nothing bad will happen to you ever again."

It was an impossible promise to make, considering they were preparing for war, but she clung to the illusion with desperate fingers. Volkan's hand tightened around her, and it was so easy to let him comfort her. To lose herself to his words and touch.

"I'm trying so hard to be strong. For Mircea, for Aylin, for you, for myself, but I'm scared. I'm scared of *him*. I'm scared that he'll hurt the people I love."

"I know, my dearest," he said. "You have a right to be angry and scared and sad. You were mortal not too long ago. You knew exactly who you were, and now everything has changed for you overnight. You haven't had a chance to process that."

His claw slipped beneath her chin, tilting her head back.

"I won't let him lay a finger on you," he promised. "I swear it."

"I'm sorry," she said, wiping the tears from her eyes. "I didn't mean to spoil our night."

Volkan brushed aside her finger and wiped her tears.

"This is not the end of your life, Yara," he said. "It is the beginning of a beautiful one."

"It doesn't feel that way," she said.

"It will. Someday, you will learn to appreciate who and what you are, and you will shine brighter for it," he said. "I am going to teach you how to be a vampir. Thaddeus wants to help as well."

"I'm not sure the thought of you two teaching me fills me with much confidence," she teased. "You are both rather corrupt."

Volkan grinned. "We will behave." After a brief pause, he added, "For the most part."

"I want to learn how to use my voice of command," she said. "But I don't know how."

"I'm not sure I know how either. We can control mortals with our bite, but to control a vampir is almost unheard of. Eldar's power is rather blasphemous among vampir. The trueborn are considered kin. To devour your kin is considered sinful. To control them is downright heresy," he said. "First, you shall learn the basics of being a vampir, and then we will build up to that."

"Thank you," she said, leaning her head on his chest.

She felt a safety in his arms that she hadn't experienced in a *very* long time.

"Must you play this game of power with my brother?" Volkan asked. "Can we not leave and travel the world?"

"After Mircea is rightfully crowned again, we will go anywhere you please," she promised.

"I don't want him to die," Volkan said. There was a sadness to his words. One that nearly undid her. But there were no words to reassure him. Nothing that wouldn't be a lie. "He is my brother. We are twinned."

Yara was silent.

"Tell me that this is only about the throne and not his life you seek," he said. "Eldar cannot die. I won't allow it."

"He does not deserve to live," she whispered. "I'll never be safe so long as he exists."

"You will," he said. "I'll protect you."

His thumb stroked her chin, and she felt a strange desperation to change this subject. She didn't want to make him promises she couldn't keep. She didn't want to lie to him. And she didn't want to lose him either.

Her eyes trailed down his face, lingering on his lips. His eyes darkened, and she placed her palm on his cheek to capture his attention. She leaned forward and kissed him. A small, soft kiss before she pulled away.

"I want to move slowly," she said. "Whatever this is between us, I want it to be more. More than what I've seen you give other women before. I don't think I saw you with the same person twice at Vlad's court. I don't want to be another distraction. Or simply a pretty trinket on your arm."

Volkan pulled away from her. His eyes were shuttered, and she couldn't quite tell what he was thinking.

"I don't know what I am doing, Yara," he said softly. "I've never courted anyone before. I've never wanted to settle down. I haven't been with someone for longer than a few days. I'm afraid that I will ruin it. Ruin *us*."

"I know," she said. "And I don't want you to force yourself into this relationship if you are not ready. I don't want you to think you have no choice with me. You will *always* have a choice when you are with me."

Her words meant something to him. She could tell by the way he leaned his forehead on hers, and how, for a small moment, it felt as though she carried the weight of him. Her fingers delicately traced his back, feeling the slim lines of his spine.

She knew that after everything that happened with Pomona, he would have some difficulty being in a relationship. Pomona had broken him, and his trust in women had most likely fractured not long after. She didn't want him to feel overwhelmed by her attention. She did not want to frighten him. And she *never* wanted him to feel trapped with her.

"How about you sleep on it?" Yara said. "See if this is what you want. When you left Poenari, emotions were high. We had survived a battle, and your brother had seized the throne. You haven't had a moment to gather your thoughts."

Yara stood up to return to her chair and put some distance between them. She didn't want to lose herself in him if he was uncertain about what he wanted. He had this strange, lost look in his eyes that frightened her. It made her want to cry, but she could not do so. Not now. Not in front of him.

"If you are near me, I want you to sit on my lap," he said, yanking her wrist till she fell back into his arms. "*Always.*"

He was silent for what felt like hours.

"I want to try," he said. "I want to try being with you. Even if I'm scared you will see what my father saw in me, and what Pomona saw in me. That I am not fit to be loved."

"That is not true," she said, brushing back the silvery strands of his hair. "They did not deserve you, Volkan. And I will do everything in my power to prove to you that you are worthy of love."

She wished that he could see inside her. See what his pain did to her, how it twisted her from the inside out, like someone had torn their fist into her chest and squeezed as hard as they could. It left her wrung out and half-undone. He wrapped his arms around her waist and pressed his face against her collarbone. She stroked the silky strands of his hair. She wanted nothing more than to love him. To erase all the pain and torment he had experienced in his short life. To prove that he was worthy. That he was perfect.

She had come a long way from the girl whose heart had been filled with so much hatred. The truth was that she had forgiven him that night that Pomona had kidnapped them.

But a part of her was scared that he would hurt her.

He was a Demirci after all.

And they were made for destruction.

———

"You look happy," Aylin said when she returned to their bedroom.

Yara jumped on the bed, tackling her in a hug.

Aylin chuckled. "Is this about a certain fair-haired vampir?"

"No," Yara said defensively.

"It's fine. I'm not mad at him anymore," Aylin said. "At least you are not interested in his brother."

"In that case, yes, it is about Volkan," Yara said. "He apologized for being so dreadful to you, you know. I think he pushes people away when he first meets them to protect himself, but once he opens up to you, you will adore him."

"I will tolerate him," Aylin corrected. "And you deserve every ounce of happiness in this world. I hope you know that."

"I've missed you so much."

"Me too," Aylin said.

It was silent for a bit, in that comfortable way that she could only ever share with her sister.

"I want to go after Ilyas," Aylin said. "I think they've gone back to Venice."

"I don't think that's safe," Yara said. "If that's true, then he is safer there than here. At least until this war ends."

"I feel as though I betrayed him. And I know the choice was between him and you. I don't regret that, but I feel wretched. He's done so much for me, for *us*. I don't want him to think I abandoned him. I didn't even leave a note."

"Perhaps we can have a messenger send a letter," Yara said. "I'll speak to Mircea."

She could see in her sister's eyes that she wanted to go after him. She wanted to save him because she loved him. Aylin had always loved Ilyas. Yara didn't know when she realized it, but now that she did, it made perfect sense. Ilyas had always found Yara annoying, while he merely *pretended* to find Aylin annoying. In truth, his eyes had always brightened when Aylin visited the barracks and when she played her silly jests on the other Janissaries.

"It's not enough," Aylin said.

Yara knew her sister like the back of her hand. She knew that if she did not dissuade her, Aylin would run headfirst into danger. It was not what Yara wanted, and it was not what Ilyas would want either.

"I need you here, Aylin," she said, feeling a flutter of guilt at her words. Aylin would never leave her side if she felt needed. "I don't know who to trust, and I'm scared."

Her sister's shoulders slumped. And her smile was faint when she looked up at her.

"Of course," she said. "I would never leave your side."

"Good," Yara said. "Because I need my big sister."

She could not lose her. She had lost far too much.

Yara kissed her forehead. "I'll speak to Mircea tomorrow. We can send Ilyas a letter to let him know you're safe, and perhaps instructions on a safe place to meet. How does that sound?"

"The messenger will have to be a mortal," Aylin said. "The hunters will kill and torture any vampir who finds them."

"I'll pass that along to Mircea," Yara said. "You know, I don't believe a world exists where Ilyas would not find you."

"I know," Aylin whispered. "I just hope he doesn't hate me when he does."

Guilt sunk deep into Yara's chest, and she worried that maybe Aylin had lost far more than she had, that maybe Ilyas had not survived, and she would not recover from the loss of him.

That maybe she'd ruined her sister's life.

XIII

Elijah rested until he could rest no more. It was on the third day of being an invalid, doted on by a shy girl named Leandra, that he'd had enough. He grabbed his blade and swung his arm in an arc. The blade was of a unique make unlike the Venetian weapons his comrades possessed. The end was curved, and the handle looped in a secure hilt. His muscles were stiff, but it felt perfect in his grip.

He had debated covering his blind eye with a cloth, but he didn't want to reveal his weakness. It looked the same as the other: a piercing blue that was filled with rage. A reflection of his dark thoughts. But he didn't mourn the loss of half his vision. He had felt utterly numb the past few days besides the fleeting anger that struck him at odd times, an anger that increased each time he tried to recall his past.

"Do you miss *Don* Aydin?" Leandra asked, picking up the silver tray that held his old plates.

"It's hard to miss someone I do not remember," he said.

"You were very attached to him. I could see how much you loved him," she said. "He was so kind. Always wished me a good day and complimented Mother's cooking."

He swung his arm against his invisible foe. It would take him some time to learn to navigate his blind spot.

As the days passed, Elijah had grown strangely cold inside. His brother had left him wounded and injured to save a sister who could, for all they knew, be dead. Days of staring at the ceiling and feeling the world spin around him anytime he stood, along with the sharp, blinding pain that occasionally traveled through the left side of his head, had filled him with a strange bitterness for this *family* of his.

He hated them all.

"I don't wish to speak of him," he snapped.

She flinched, the tray rattling in her nerve-stricken fingers. Elijah opened his mouth to apologize, but she was long gone before he could speak.

Anger rushed over him like a surge of cold water, and he threw his blade at the wall. Everything felt wrong. His name tasted like ash on his tongue. He had prayed in the chapel yesterday, and the words had been stilted and clunky on his tongue as he flipped through the pages of the Bible. He had found the braided hair of a woman in his pocket, and he knew it belonged to the woman who haunted him.

A woman who remained out of his touch.

———

He left his bedroom, stepping out of the estate. It was late, and the sun had long since set. Elijah didn't stop until he was in the thick of the forest. He sat on a broken log and wondered what was next. Salvatore had told him all about his crusade, about his lofty plans to eradicate all vampir from the world. First, they would cleanse Wallachia, and then move East until all the continents were pure.

Elijah took out the braid in his pocket and coiled it around his bruised fist. He wished she was here, his mystery woman, so that she could guide him. He wondered if she was the same woman who was written on his paperwork. He had found an old identification paper intended for traveling and the name of a woman who had been listed as his wife. *Aylin*. Which was quite similar to his brother's name, but his head hurt when he thought too hard about it.

He felt lost and untethered. Salvatore's passionate speeches did not move him, but he didn't know what other purpose he had in life. He barely had enough coin to pay for a meal, and nothing but the clothes on his back and an old travel document. It all felt too familiar, as if he had once before been alone in the world and pulled away from the people he loved.

As if his loneliness were an old friend.

The crunch of leaves sounded behind him, and he spun around just in time to face his attacker. The man leaped from the trees; teeth descended for battle. They were sharper than any mortal man's and several inches longer than what was considered normal.

Elijah had just enough time to turn around before it bit him. He held the vampir away from him, but it was far too strong to contain. He didn't have a weapon on him, but the vampir did.

He swiped the blade strapped to the creature's hip and plunged it deep into its chest. A snarl sounded behind him, and he felt the wet slide of claws sliding down his jaw. It stung, and he could feel the blood drip down his chin. The woman was stronger than the man had been, and he struggled to keep away from her claws. She was also faster, which concerned him. He parried with his blade, attempting to sever her hands.

His blade fell to the ground during their fight, and he cursed.

He kicked her legs out from under her and choked her, digging his fingers in as deep as he could as he grappled for his fallen blade. Once he felt the cold touch of metal, he used the end of the blade to slit her throat open. It was enough to shock her. He slipped his hand beneath her neck and twisted hard until she died. But it was not a true death. Nothing but tearing out their hearts would kill them permanently.

Elijah grabbed her hand and dragged her to the estate.

"How did this one find us" Borza asked, surprised.

Borza was a giant of a man with a good temper and sage advice to share. He'd sat down Elijah one night and told him of a man whom he'd fought alongside who'd lost both legs. To lose the sight of one eye, he said, was not so terrible as that. It was a grim tale, but Borza had spoken it as if it were the speech that would renew his will to live.

"You were no chatterbox before," Borza had said. "Lord knows you didn't have a chance to get a word in with Aydin around. The boy spoke like he was paid to keep yapping. I'd be lying if I said I didn't miss the unruly thing. But you've barely said two words since you returned with Salvatore."

Elijah had not responded to that. He never knew quite what to say when people spoke to him about this brother he did not remember. Pietro spoke about him often too.

"I don't think they were here for the hunters," Elijah said. They had not come with the intention to attack a large group. Their numbers were small, and they didn't fight like soldiers but trained assassins.

He wiped the blood from his chin. "Have a few men on rotation and do a full sweep of the estate."

Someone had intended to send him a message, and he would find out who. He dragged the vampir to Salvatore's office.

Salvatore was in the middle of a conversation with Cristifano and Antonio when he barged in.

"Elijah." He stood up abruptly. "Where did you find it?"

"In the woods," he said.

"How did it find us?" Salvatore asked with a frown.

"Not certain. They were waiting in the woods. If we intend to grow the brotherhood, we need to relocate to a more secure compound," Elijah said. "A place with gates and guards around the clock."

Salvatore looked at Cristifano, exchanging a set of silent words.

"You may take her to the prison," Salvatore said.

Salvatore lifted the decorative mask behind his desk to unlock his secret tunnel to the chamber where they tortured the captured vampir. Elijah chained her to the bed and returned to the study.

"Sit, son," Antonio said. "We have much to discuss."

Elijah sat down across from them, uncertain what they would demand from him now. Without much purpose to his life, he felt as though he had no other option but to pick up the torch of their crusade.

"I am going to Rome, to the Holy Church," Salvatore said. "We have underestimated our enemy. They surpass us in wealth, strength and numbers. I intend to work with the Pope to build a bigger army. We have decided that you are the best person to lead the Silver Cross in my absence. And you are correct: this estate is no stronghold. Now that we have struck first, we must relocate to a stronger outpost. What do you think about Wallachia? It is the home of their court. We would be within striking distance."

"You want me to lead?" he asked incredulously. It had been a week since he woke up. He was still teaching himself to swing a blade with one working eye. "I just learned my name."

"Vincenzo said only your memories were affected, not your intelligence or mobility. You still think as a strategist and carry your blade like a seasoned warrior," Antonio said. "It is a fresh start."

He was silent as he contemplated this offer.

"You will be paid a generous stipend," Cristifano said, as if he were annoyed that he hadn't jumped on the offer yet. "Perhaps, when it is all over, you can retire to the countryside and build a life."

"I will not become a priest," he said. It didn't feel right, though he could not pinpoint exactly why. From what Salvatore said, he'd been born a Christian, but it did not call to him.

Nothing truly called to him anymore. Some days he wondered why he even bothered to get off the bed.

Antonio sighed. "We do not want a priest. We need a warrior."

Elijah nodded.

"Then I accept."

XIV

Alexandru arrived a fortnight after they had mailed their letter, with a retinue of almost one hundred sentries and servants. His soldiers wore the livery of the Draculesti clan: black breastplates with a silver dragon swallowing its tail painted on the front. They arrived with warhorses twice the size of regular steeds and a carriage made of pure gold and trimmed with onyx.

The servants were orderly in matching grey uniforms, and the blood slaves wore red robes that looked almost cultlike. Their young, pale faces stared at them with glazed eyes. Their necks were marked with puncture wounds. They stared at the vampir around them with dark devotion, and the sight sickened Yara. It reminded her far too much of when she had been lost to the poison of their bite. Sometimes it struck her how she had been powerless once, and the fear of being that doe-eyed girl again made her skin break out in goosebumps.

"Do you think he will accept Mircea's proposal?" Yara asked. She stood behind the window in the hallway. There was a small crack where the bricks that had been caked to the front had loosened.

"He is so handsome," Pariza whispered.

"He looks frightening," Aylin said.

The three of them were crowded by the small crack in the window, their noses pressed to the glass as they stared at their new visitor like a trio of little girls.

"What are you girls looking at?" Thaddeus asked, hovering over Aylin to get a good look at their new guest. "Oh, he's handsome."

"Handsome?" Volkan asked. "Should I be jealous?"

Yara felt him coil his hands around her waist, and she smiled to herself, both at his remark and his touch.

"Very, very handsome," Yara said.

Mircea and Lugrezia had gone down to greet Alexandru Dracul and were blocking her view as she spoke. Even though she hadn't gotten a good look at him, she couldn't resist taunting Volkan. His fingers on her hip tightened ever so slightly, and a small rush of air escaped her. A human gesture that Mircea despised but Yara still clung to. It was impossible to shake off her habits.

"Is that so?" Volkan whispered. "I suppose I'll have to cut off his head then."

"Are you *that* jealous?" she asked.

"Murderously so," Volkan replied.

"You two make me nauseous," Aylin grumbled.

Yara poked her in the ribs, and Aylin swatted her hand away.

"Alexandru always liked Eldar," Volkan said. "Truth be told, I was always a little jealous of their friendship. I didn't like to share Eldar."

"I suppose knowing that Eldar killed Alexandru's father will break the ties of that friendship," Yara said. "Eldar is an abominable person."

"He is not as terrible as you make him seem," Volkan said.

Yara spun around to face him. "How do you continue to defend him?"

"Simple," he replied. "I love him."

"I love you too, Volkan," Thaddeus replied, cutting into their conversation with the clear intent to dissolve their tension. He draped his arms across both their shoulders. "I don't quite like it when my parents quarrel."

"You are an idiot," Yara said, staring up at the ceiling as she asked God for the patience to deal with them both.

"This idiot is going to teach you your first lesson in being a vampir," Thaddeus said. "You may refer to me as *master* during our lessons. Any mention of my name shall be handled with swift discipline.

Yara laughed. "There is nothing to be learned from you because there is nothing inside your pretty head."

"I can see why Eldar likes you. You are as cruel as him," Thaddeus said. "Also, you think I'm pretty?"

Volkan shoved him hard. "Don't flirt with her."

Yara stiffened. She had tried so hard to forget that night on his throne. When he had promised her power and for one small, desperate second, she had reached for it. He hadn't looked at her like she was beneath him or that she was simply a weak mortal, but rather his equal. And she had been drunk on the thought of becoming his Undying Queen.

Yara had craved power from a young age, and had spent most of her days eavesdropping on her father's meetings with men of rank. She had always struggled to carve a future of worth for herself. In the Ottoman Empire, women could not carry power, nor could they pass it on to their daughters. But in this vicious world of vampir, anything was possible.

Yet the thought that there was something inside her that called to *him* frightened her.

"You've upset her," Volkan said.

"It was a joke, Yara," Thaddeus said. "Eldar only likes his reflection. I think if he could wed himself, he would."

Yara felt her lips tilt slightly. "You are forgiven."

Pariza gripped her arm. "Come, let's go introduce ourselves to Alexandru."

Yara giggled at the sight of horror in Aylin's eyes when Pariza pulled her along as well. His party had just entered the doorway, and Yara got her first good look at the man that would change the fortune of their army. He looked to be a few years older than them, and had olive skin and dark hair that fell into his eyes in luscious waves. His hands were covered in an inky pigment design that reminded her of the henna she would have painted on her hand before wedding celebrations. But his ink was black, a tattoo of some sort. It crawled along his throat like a collar. He was handsome, with long lashes and a firm mouth that did not shift in amusement or pleasantry.

She could see why he had gotten along with Eldar. He was just as serious and dull as him.

"Lord Alexandru," Pariza purred.

His dark eyes drifted to her, before turning away dismissively. He gave Aylin the same uninterested look, and Yara was surprised when she was given the same treatment. It was odd that his eyes did not linger on her. She could not recall the last time a man had looked at her with no form of appreciation in his gaze.

"Where are my chambers?" he demanded during Mircea's welcome speech. "We shall discuss more at dinner."

Lugrezia quickly called for her servants, looking unnerved by his cold manners. Even Mircea looked ill at ease. It was easy to tell Alexandru Dracul had a commanding presence, and a frightening one at that.

"What a dreadful man," Aylin whispered under her breath.

He turned around, slowly, deliberately, and a dark silence filled the hallway.

"Your servants are untrained," he said. "If she served my house, I'd cut off her tongue."

"I'm no servant, you fool," Aylin snapped.

He raised a brow at Lugrezia. "What action shall you take to discipline her?"

Lugrezia cleared her throat. "The girl is a guest, and she forgets herself."

"See to it that your guests do not address me unless spoken

to," he said sharply.

He turned on his heel and disappeared around the corner. A hoard of his own servants tripped over themselves to follow him.

"I think I am in love," Pariza whispered.

Yara exchanged a look with Aylin that confirmed that their new friend was a terrible judge of character.

"Well?" Yara asked Mircea. "Do you think he is inclined to join us?"

"He was summoned to Eldar's court to swear fealty," Mircea said in a bitter tone. "He claims his loyalty is, as of yet, undecided."

"Which way do you think he'll sway?" she asked.

"He is impossible to read," he said. "But he was not as pleased with Eldar as expected. I reckon they had some altercation. It may sway him in our favor."

"We will convince him," Yara said. "We must make him an offer, to be claimed once you've secured your throne. Perhaps land, or a higher title, or a position in court."

"Alexandru does not care for court squabbles. He thinks himself above such pettiness," he said. "That will not work. Besides, he is richer than the throne."

"I presume he does not care that Eldar killed his father?" she asked.

"No," he said. "Alexandru has always had difficulty *feeling*. He reckons Vlad had always been curious about the afterlife and now he gets to experience it firsthand."

"Why did you think he'd help us to begin with?" Yara asked.

"I was hoping he'd be bored enough to try," Mircea said.

That was not reassuring at all.

"We'll convince him," she said. And then added a bit more forcefully. "*I'll* convince him."

"Do not expect him to be taken by your charm," he said. "He finds almost everyone utterly lacking."

Yara shook her head. "I'm hoping I can show him my strength and prove that we can overpower Eldar once we defeat his army."

Mircea frowned. "Have you done it since that day? Used the voice of command?"

"No," she said. "But I intend to learn."

———

"Oh, this is such a bore," Thaddeus drawled. "Your commands don't work."

Yara frowned. She had tried to make Volkan do her bidding, but it hadn't worked. She assumed that she couldn't control him because she was sired by him. So, she had tried Thaddeus.

"It should work on you," she said. She turned to Pariza. "*Pick up that candle.*"

"No, my darling," she said, toying with her dagger by balancing it precariously on the tip of her finger. "Perhaps a bit more practice will do."

It should have worked.

Volkan stared at her in amusement from where he lounged on the velvet settee. His bedroom was far superior to hers, and she knew with little doubt that he had put in a request for such accommodations. It seemed they had moved him to a bigger room. His blood slaves sat on either side of him on the chair, a young girl and boy who looked related. Volkan lifted both their wrists and bit into each one in turn.

"Come, perhaps some fresh blood will help," he said, offering the girl's wrist to her. Yara stiffened; she had made it clear that she would only ever drink from a chalice. It seemed cruel to drink from a human. To treat them like cattle when she had once been abused herself.

"I can't," she said.

But her teeth still lengthened, and her claws unsheathed. She could control them, retracting her teeth and claws as she pleased. She realized that while some did it to appear more human, other vampir enjoyed showing their true nature. They simply did not hide.

But at that moment, she *could* not hide her nature. It demanded to be seen, to be fed. Her throat burned like someone had lit a fire beneath her skin. And her limbs shook as she struggled to stay where she was and not run toward the delicious scent.

"We said we would make you stronger," Volkan said in his musical voice. "That means feeding directly from the source. It is far better than that stale blood you drink. More potent. More delicious. It will only whet your appetite. Come, my pretty darling. Just one sip."

She felt a hand grip her elbow and lead her to him. She was so focused on the dripping blood, she could not speak or focus. It smelled divine. Like the richest nectar one could ever imagine. Saliva pooled in her mouth, and she felt Volkan guide her down till she sat devotedly on her knees before the girl, and before him as well. His eyes were dark when he looked at her, filled with unmasked desire.

"She is here to serve you, Yara," he whispered. "Think of her as your maid."

He raised her wrist to Yara's mouth, and she plunged her teeth into the bite he had made for her. Blood slipped down her throat, and she hummed in delight. It was as delicious as he had said. It eased the burning in her throat, soothing it like a cold glass of milk.

"Good girl," Volkan purred. "Isn't she perfect?"

"Simply marvelous," Thaddeus said. He had been the one who'd brought her to him. And his hand was heavy on her shoulder, as if she would escape.

"I'm going to leave before you all start undressing," Pariza said.

Yara heard the door slide shut, dand she closed her eyes, drinking from the fountain. It tasted so much better than the stale blood served in a cup.

Mircea said that the blood served was usually a few hours or sometimes a few days old. It was taken from blood slaves and was kept on hand for guests who preferred a cleaner method of feeding during formal dinners. But it was by no means made to replace the natural way vampir were made to feed, which was directly from the source.

"That is enough," Volkan said, prying the girl's hand away from her. "We do not want the poor thing to faint."

Yara was horrified to see the young girl's ashen face. She stumbled away from her, her back hitting Thaddeus's knees. He placed his hands under her arms and carried her to Volkan's lap.

"How could you?" she asked harshly. "How could you tempt me?"

"It is better you learn now to control yourself and stop when you've had your fill," he said, "rather than suck them dry and kill them. That would hurt you more."

He placed one hand firmly on her waist and raised the other to catch a drop of blood that trickled from her lips. She felt his thumb glide across her skin and then slip between her gaping lips and stroke her tongue.

"I told you I'd make you stronger," he whispered. "You are stronger once you drink fresh blood. You cannot exist as a vampir with a conscience. It makes you weak."

"I don't want to compromise my morals," she said.

"Then that makes you weak," Thaddeus said.

Yara turned to look at him and the dazed blood slaves.

"May we speak in private?" she asked. Thaddeus merely echoed Volkan. She could not win an argument against Volkan when he was there.

The door clicked shut behind them.

"You are angry," Volkan said.

"You tempted me," she said, "without asking if I wanted to do that. I am not your blood slave anymore, Volkan. And I do not care if I am sired by you; that does not mean I belong to you."

"You said that I was to teach you to be a vampir. Not that I was to coddle you," he said. "This is how I taught Thaddeus and Pariza, and how they've taught my other sired. To be a vampir, you must be cruel. You must be heartless. And you must be fast."

"I am not yet hardened," she said. "I cannot kill and maim and hurt so easily. I want to be strong to protect myself, not to hurt others."

"I know, my little pet," he whispered. "But we must carve out that softness or it will get you killed. You've been betrayed and hurt and broken before. I don't want to see that happen to you again."

"I'm afraid," she said. "I'm afraid that I won't recognize myself one day. That I will look in the mirror and see a monster and not a girl."

"You won't," he said. "You are still that girl who fought tooth and nail to survive a vicious vampir court. You are still that girl who gained the mark of Dracul and forged a strong allegiance that threatened my brother. You are still that girl who saved me time and time again, even when I didn't deserve it. You are still Yara. You are still *you*. Nothing can change that. Not even becoming a vampir."

"And what if I change, Volkan?" she whispered. "What if I lose myself?"

Deep inside her chest, she nursed a small kernel that ached for more. She had seen the way they had all looked at *him*, after the defeat of Dracul. With respect and with fear. Yara craved that, and she was afraid to speak of it aloud, as if it would give life to it. Volkan would not understand. He did not care for power. He did not care to rule.

Only *he* would understand.

"I will bring you back to me," Volkan said. "*Always.*"

Yara leaned her head on his chest, listening to his still heart. He knew exactly what to say to ease her worries.

"I will take care of you, Yara," he said. "Nothing that I ask of you will compromise your soul. All I ask is that you be open-minded. We are predators. We are monsters. We are the shadows that haunt the night. But you are one of us now, and you must either live like us or be devoured by us."

"I will be like you," she said.

She had been weak once. She could not afford to be weak again.

He kissed her jaw, unable to hide how pleased he was by her acceptance.

"Then let us start our lessons."

———

Alexandru was late to dinner.

It surprised no one that he was not taken to being early. His hand was curled around a hound that came to his hip, a big, monstrous beast no different than his master, with a wide jaw and sharp teeth. He walked to the dais as if it were the most natural thing in the world to bring a *hound* to dinner. He passed it to a servant before he climbed up the steps to the walnut table. Lugrezia's humble hall had been transformed that night. Candles adorned with crystals were lit along the sconces, and tapestries that depicted old Venetian folk tales were hung up on the walls. Glorious depictions of foxes and elephants and lush greenery spread along the right wall. Several Christian motifs were painted on gilded frames, including a few of Jesus and his disciples.

Yara sat on the dais with Lugrezia, Domenico, Mircea, and Aylin. Lugrezia drew the line at Volkan sitting beside them.

Everyone in the hall did a meager rise from their seat out of respect, as if Alexandru were the Undying King himself.

"Kerberos is starved," Alexandru said curtly to the servant. "Have him fed some raw meat."

"What a fitting name," Domenico murmured. "A Grecian dog that belonged to the god of death."

"What do you think of him?" Aylin asked.

Domenico shrugged. "Not much to think. He seems painfully boring. Kind of reminds me of your *brother.*"

Yara frowned. "We don't have a brother."

"He speaks of Ilyas," Aylin said, glaring at him.

Aylin had briefed her about her time with Silver Cross and her disguise of being Ilyas' brother.

"Oh, right," Yara said.

Alexandru was offered the middle seat between Lugrezia and Mircea as the guest of honor. Yara sat by Mircea so she could pitch int o the conversation when required. She had not yet mastered her voice of command to impress him, but she intended to mention it just the same. Perhaps it would sway him to their cause.

"Good evening, Lord Alexandru," she said. "My name is Yara." She hesitated to say her surname. It had died with her in the stone walls of Wallachia. Volkan had once asked her to take his name, and she had refused him because she didn't *want* his name. But surnames mattered in this court. It showed who you were allied with, and whether you were tied to a powerful family. Eldar was the Undying King, which made his family the most powerful family in the vampir hierarchy.

"Yara Demirci," she said.

She couldn't help but look out on the floor to see Volkan. He had a wide grin on his face, and it did not surprise her in the least that he was eavesdropping.

"You are sired by Eldar?" Alexandru said.

"Volkan," she corrected. "We are together."

"Oh," he said, sounding terribly unimpressed. "I see."

"We require your aid, nephew," Mircea said. "We will need about one hundred thousand men to seize Poenari and unseat the usurper."

"I never made a public claim during my visit to Poenari. If I give him my vote, then the trueborn will follow. They respect the Draculesti. They respect the Dragon. I do not like Eldar, but I do not see how aligning myself with you benefits me," Alexandru said.

"You would betray your family so easily," Mircea spat. "Why did you accept my invitation?"

"Mircea," Yara said sharply. It would do them no good to pick a fight. From the way Alexandru behaved he knew that the power lay in his hands. He was aware that he could sway the war in their favor.

Alexandru picked up his chalice of blood, revealing his ink-covered fingers.

"You appeal to my sense of familial duty as if I have any, Uncle," Alexandru said. He leaned toward Mircea and asked in an almost mocking tone, "*Why* should I help you?"

"It is a risk, but it will be worth it," Yara said. "Eldar is not as powerful as you may have heard. I can kill him."

"A sired vampir can kill a trueborn?" he asked dryly. "Has the world come to an end?"

"I have his power," she said.

While she couldn't do the voice of command yet, she could do the little parlor trick of revealing her inky veins and shadowy eyes. Yara felt her claws and teeth lengthen. She dug deeper. She felt the darkness inside her that was all him. She felt the tingle beneath her skin, and she knew that those cursed veins had shown up beneath her skin. She opened her eyes to hear a spoon clatter beside her, and she knew then that her eyes were mere pools of shadow. It was abominable. It was unnatural. Even for the vampir.

"I have not yet learned the extent of my power, but I know that I can stop him," Yara said.

Alexandru looked interested, but only mildly.

"How are you sired by him?" he asked.

"I am sired by both of them," she said. "But my loyalty is tied to Volkan as my sire. If they were both in danger, I would save Volkan without a second thought. And if I stood before Eldar at this very moment, I would kill him with no hesitation."

"I've never heard of anyone being sired by *two* vampir," he said with narrowed eyes. "And certainly, never heard of one who can kill their sire."

"It happened. I was there. She was turned by them both," Aylin said. "And if her case is so unique, isn't it possible that she can kill him for precisely that reason?"

"What a resounding vote of confidence," Alexsandru said.

"But I don't exactly trust your frail mortal judgment."

"You don't need to be so impolite," Yara said.

"I can be whatever I please," he said, folding his arms across his chest. "Last, I recall I have an *actual* army. Not some pathetic sentries and a weird assortment of mortals who dine among vampir." At this, he looked pointedly at Aylin and Domenico. "And the brother of the king you intend to kill, who is probably a spy." This was directed at Volkan. "And an anomaly." This was directed at her.

"And yet you accepted our invitation," Yara said. "To what? Look down your nose at us?"

"I can give you the funds you require to hire men and a contact you may reach out to who sells mercenaries at a fair price. I'll expect to be repaid with interest once you've reclaimed the throne," he said. "I do not want my name nor my reputation associated with this war, and will not spare any men under my banner."

He stood up, fixing the folds of his black kaftan. "I think it'll be interesting to see who wins and loses. War is always good for business."

Yara slumped back in her chair, it wasn't their direct terms, but it was a step in the right direction.. It wasn't until Alexandru left, with a servant on his heels leading along that hound of his, that she felt Lugrezia's hand pat her shoulder.

"I didn't think he'd give," Lugrezia said. "Excellent job, Yara."

"Yes, good work, child," Mircea said fondly. "He clearly thinks you are an asset."

"I wasn't sure if I could prove it without the voice of command," she said.

Yara looked down at the dark veins; she hadn't quite learned how to make them go away, though they did tend to fade away in their own time. Sometimes they disappeared when she retracted her fangs and claws. But sometimes they lingered.

"You took his name," Aylin said. She seemed saddened by the thought, and she toyed with the tablecloth when she spoke.

"I needed it," Yara said. "It is the way things are done here. Sired vampir take their master's or mistress's surname."

"You don't belong to anyone, Yara," she said. "I don't want you to ever forget that."

"I know," she said. "But nobody cares who you are if you are not a trueborn or tied to one. It doesn't mean that I am not your sister. It is just politics."

"You love it, don't you?" Aylin said. "The politics, the war, the life at court. If you cannot live in Constantinople, I think this is the next best thing for you."

"I've always loved it like you love that blade," Yara said, jutting her chin at the *kilij* strapped to her hip. It was a long, curved Turkish blade. "I'm surprised you have it after all these years. It's the one Ilyas gave you, right?"

Yara regretted mentioning his name when Aylin's face fell.

"Why did you bring him up?" Domenico asked her with an accusing look. She hadn't even realized that he was listening to them. "He is dead, and if not that, then perhaps he still sleeps. You know my father told me when I was young that some people whose heads are wounded may sleep for *years*."

"Now why did you bring *that* up?" Yara snapped.

Aylin looked stricken. She never saw her sister cry, but when her lips trembled, she knew she was about to break down.

"Excuse me," Aylin whispered.

Yara turned to Domenico the second Aylin disappeared.

"I know what you're doing," Yara snapped.

"And what's that?" he asked uninterestedly, picking beneath his nails.

"You think if she assumes he's dead then she'll move on, and it will give you a chance to slither your way into her life," Yara said. "But you do not know how much she loves him. That kind of love never dies."

His eyes were sharp when he turned to her. It was almost wolflike.

"We'll see about that."

XV

Yara knew something was wrong the moment she closed her eyes that night. The dream unspooled like a weaver's yarn, and she found herself standing in the Grand Hall amidst the dark columns and shadowed corners. She knew the stone walls, the vaulted ceiling, the stretched oak wood tables, the bleak throne with the iron wings fanning the back that had caused so much anguish.

It was the room she had been brought to a long time ago as a wide-eyed girl with nothing but scraps to clothe her and left to the mercy of monsters she had only ever read about in fairytales. It was strange to look upon the face of a predator, reflected to her on the marble floor. Her dark hair was unspooled, falling to her hip. It grew incredibly fast, faster than it had as a mortal. She still had the same face with her piercing dimples, brown eyes, and small nose. But there was something about her beauty that was less sweet and more deadly. As if it had been honed into a fine blade.

She was barefoot, wearing the same nightgown she had worn her last night there. Black and lacy and equal parts beautiful and macabre. Yara walked to the throne, admiring the dark materials assorted to make the gruesome seat. She remembered the slithering tail of the dragon in the center of the metalwork from when

Dracul ruled. Her eyes narrowed; there was something off about the tail. Upon closer inspection, she noticed it had been carved into a scorpion's tail.

The sigil of House Demirci.

She stepped away, feeling dread crawl up her spine. She bumped into a hard surface, and she spun around abruptly.

"I knew you'd find me," he said. His words slithered up her skin as if a serpent crawled along her flesh, and a shudder rolled down her back.

Yara pinched her skin. Hard. She had to wake up. Aunt Sevda had always said to pinch herself if she was ever ensnared in a dream spun by the wicked fingers of the *jinn*. And Eldar Demirci was worse than any demon that walked this earth.

She couldn't face him. She wasn't ready yet. She'd said she would be ready, but she was not. Especially when she did not understand the rules of this world or the strength of this bond.

Fear crawled up her throat, and she stumbled away from him until her back hit the pillar behind her. His steps were slow and confident as he approached her, trapping her in a cocoon of darkness. His pale hands lifted high, resting on either side of her head. His familiar iron ring sat comfortably on his finger.

She wondered if he'd always been that tall. And had he always been this frightening? He didn't even pretend to hide his monstrosity. Black veins climbed up the column of his pale neck. They were worse than she remembered, lingering beneath his beautiful face like cracks, and his black eyes were mere pools of darkness. There was no evidence that there had ever been a pupil. No hint that he had once been a boy and not a monster.

"What is this place?" she asked.

"Sometimes when a vampir and a sired vampir form a bond, they can converse in each other's minds. They can create a space shared between them both. A world of their own."

"We don't have a bond," she snapped. "We have nothing."

"Our sire bond says otherwise," Eldar said. His gaze was locked on her eyes, but it fell, looking at her body. He'd never looked at her like *that* before. Like he wanted to swallow her whole. "Do you know how rare and special it is that we have this bond, Yara?"

"I don't want to speak to you. Not until the day I shove a blade in your miserable, rotten heart," Yara said.

His lips tilted in amusement. "I've missed this. Our banter."

"You jest, but when you are dead with nothing but my blade in your chest, you will regret your words and actions."

His hand rose, resting on her face. His thumb stroked her cheekbone slowly and sensuously, up and down. And then back up again.

"Come home," he said. "And I will give you all I promised you."

"What? A corner in your prison chambers below?" she asked with a harsh laugh. "Threats and cruelty? Or better yet, will you whisper all your false promises to me again?"

"Perhaps, I overreacted, and you didn't deserve to be with that traitor. Your crimes were not as severe as his," Eldar said. "I can admit that."

"You have nothing, and you have no one," she said, raising her chin. "And you intended to make me as miserable as you. You sought to tear my sister and Ilyas away from me, but you failed. I have my sister and I have Volkan. He is everything to me, and you are *nothing*."

His hand dropped. His expression growing cold. For a small moment, he looked hurt. As if her words had truly affected him.

"I thought to try a different approach," he said coldly, "to appeal to your weak mortal need for kindness. But I can see you intend to be cruel, so I will be cruel as well."

"Perfect," she said. "I'd hate for you to strain a muscle with all that effort."

He was silent, probably thinking of which threats would strike the hardest. But he surprised her when he next spoke.

"You were going to accept," he said. "That night when you sat on my lap, and you kissed me so sweetly, you would have forgiven me for everything for a taste of power. You would have ruled by my side. You would have been *my* Undying Queen."

"I would have stayed," she whispered. "And maybe I would have killed you, or maybe I would have grown to forgive you in time. Maybe you would change for the better, or I would change for the worse. We could have been villains or heroes, but you pushed me away. You chose yourself. You didn't choose *me*."

Yara didn't know why she spoke the truth. Perhaps because it was easier to confess in the dark. Perhaps it was the fluidity and dark charm of his voice. Perhaps it was this world that was not a world that loosened her tongue.

"And if I made a mistake?" he asked. "If I asked you to return home and start afresh?"

Even in the dark, Eldar could not say what he wanted aloud. He spoke with vague questions and an indifferent tone. Yara knew that he did not love her, and she knew that he never would, but he *was* obsessed with her. And to be the object of someone's obsession could be as overwhelming and suffocating as love itself.

"It is too late for us to be anything less than enemies," she said.

Eldar's lips twisted in a strange mimicry of a smile.

"You won't win against me," Eldar said. "I will have you on your knees before me."

Yara awoke with a gasp, jolting upright.

Aylin stirred beside her, mumbling at her to keep it down.

She rubbed her face, shocked to find her cheek cold from his touch. Sire bonds were rare. He did not lie when he said that. It often took years, if not centuries, until a sired vampir built one with their sire. Nobody would suspect that she shared one with Eldar, but if anyone ever discovered the truth, they would think she was in league with him. They would question her loyalty. And with so many eyes on her, she could not risk the truth. Not after she had worked so tirelessly to gain rank in Mircea's court. Once his throne was secured, she would have a place in his court and hopefully a position on his council. She would have power and respect.

Yara would have to keep this secret tucked close to her chest.

Nobody could ever know that they shared a sire bond.

———

Yara sat outside, her body exhausted from a long day of training. She'd asked Volkan for a moment alone. She was rarely ever alone these days. And the silence felt nice and welcoming. A part of her was deeply shaken by her conversation with Eldar. She felt tainted almost as if his dark touch had seeped into her flesh like poison.

She didn't sense his approach. Not until she felt the weight of his heavy hand on her shoulder. She looked up to see Mircea and her lips pulled in a smile at the sight of him.

"You rarely smile you know," she said when he didn't return her grin.

"Only weaklings smile," Mircea said. "And idiots."

"*I* smile." She pointed out.

"You're the exception," he said.

Yara chuckled.

"How has your transition been going?" he asked, brows furrowed. "I worry about leaving you in the care of the Demirci child."

"He's a wonderful instructor," Yara said. "You know I would love it if you two would get along. You are both so important to me."

He sighed, sinking his fingers into his beard absently.

"The reason I care so much is because I would not want him for my daughter," Mircea said. "And you are the closest thing to a child that I have."

Yara's throat tightened. Mircea was not an affectionate person besides the few times he patted her head. So, she could feel him stiffen when she reached for his hand, feeling his claws pinch her wrist.

"You remind me so much of my father," she said softly.

"He must have been a powerful man to raise a girl so strong and fearless," Mircea said with admiration in his tone. He could not hide how proud of her he was. "You had the heart of a vampir before you even turned. I saw it in you, and it was the same thing those terrible twins saw in you. It is why they claimed you before anyone else. They knew someday you would be greater than them all."

"Do you truly think I am strong enough to take down Eldar?"

Yara still nursed the guilt of her sire bond with Eldar. She needed to know that Mircea believed in her. Even now when everything was veiled in so much uncertainty.

"I think you can take down anyone you set your mind to," he said, standing up. His hand slipped out of her own. And she wasn't surprised when he patted her head. "There is nothing a child of mine cannot do and that is what you are Yara, my child."

He left before she could tell him how much those words meant to her. How it had soothed something inside her to know that he cared. He had proved it many times. He had given her the chance to gain Dracul's mark of protection and had saved her from Eldar's prison.

Yara would not fail him. Not now. Not ever.

XVI

"I want to go," Aylin said.

Aylin knew that she had to go the moment Yara told her that they needed a few people to go to Hungary to hire the mercenaries paid for by Alexandru. In truth, she had begun to feel suffocated lately, as if the walls were closing in on her. She knew a big part of this was that she missed Ilyas and was worried about him. She tried to laugh and eat and banter with Volkan's friends, but she felt empty. As much as she loved Yara, this was her world, not Aylin's. She was not made for political dinners and gossip. She was made to be on the road with a blade in her hand.

"It will be dangerous," Yara said. "I want you to be safe."

Aylin felt a rush of excitement at the thought of *danger*. God, she missed it. She missed the thrill of not knowing if she would live or die.

"I can see that the mere mention of danger has only excited you," Yara said with a sigh. "I cannot come along; I have duties to attend to here. Zuri and a few of Lugrezia's men will accompany you."

Zuri was a shadow who was rarely seen. Yara said she was Mircea's spy and even here among allies she was gathering secrets for him. She was often gone for hours at a time.

"Accompany you where?" Domenico asked.

"Hungary," Aylin said. "I'm going to hire some mercenaries for Yara's war."

"Mircea's war," her sister corrected. "And I will leave you to it."

"You're leaving?" Domenico asked, staring at her with his green eyes. "I'm coming with you."

"No," she said. "I need time to myself. It's been a lot, Domenico. Leaving my country, searching for my sister, losing my best friend. I haven't had a moment to catch my breath. I need to do this by myself, *for* myself."

"Why didn't you tell me you felt this way?" He frowned.

"Because you didn't ask," she said.

Ilyas would have asked. Ilyas would have noticed.

"When will you be back?" he asked.

"In a few weeks," she said.

"Safe travels, then," he said. "We will see each other upon your return."

Aylin nodded, surprised that he hadn't put up more of a fight. She could see he was uncomfortable with the words she said, as if it were unlike her to be so weak. He didn't say it, but she could see the disappointment in his eyes.

Ilyas would not have judged me.

"Aylin," he called.

She turned to face him, taken aback by the hard look in his eyes.

"He is dead," Domenico said. "But I'm here, don't forget that."

"He's not dead," she said sharply. "Stop saying that."

"Mourn him and be done with it," Domenico said. "I won't wait forever."

He walked away from her before she could curse him. She'd never asked him to wait around.

And until she saw his corpse, Ilyas was alive. She had to

believe it. Or she would crumble into a million pieces too small for anyone to put her back together again.

———

They prepared to leave at sunset. It would take them around eight or nine days to reach Buda, the capital. Aylin was surprised to find Pariza coming down the stairs with an elegantly carved oak trunk that rivaled a princess's belongings.

"Don't tell me Volkan is joining us," Aylin said.

"No, he'd never leave Yara's side," Pariza said. "But he did ask me to join you because Yara was worried about you. I am your personal guard until we return."

"We have Lugrezia's men for that, and Zuri is quite fearsome," Aylin said.

"Not as fearsome as I," Pariza said. "Do not let my pretty face fool you. I have killed men three times my size and never broken a nail."

"I would have thought you'd stick around to charm Alexandru before he leaves," she teased.

"Oh, that old bore," she said. "I hardly recall why I liked him."

Just as she spoke it, Alexandru came down the stairs with his procession of servants, blood slaves and guards.

"Good evening, Lord Alexandru," Pariza said with such zeal that Alexandru flinched.

Aylin snickered. "So much for saying you are done with him."

Pariza elbowed her, and Aylin bit her lip to control her laughter.

"Off to torture some children?" Aylin asked him because she could not resist.

"And infants," he said dryly.

"You have a sense of humor," she said.

"And you have an inflated sense of self-worth," he said. "You offend me by looking at me, let alone speaking to me."

"I hope we never cross paths again," Aylin said.

Alexandru nodded to that.

And then he was gone, disappearing into the confines of his carriage.

The carts were stacked with their provisions, and the men had mounted their stallions.

"We are all ready to go," Zuri said.

Zuri was one of Yara's trusted friends, a woman who looked to be either thirty or thirty-five and of East African descent. She coiled her hair in the most splendid braids. It made Aylin miss her own long hair. It was difficult to style her hair, which had grown to chin length and was far too short to tie back. So, it just framed her face in soft curls.

Yara stood nervously at the top of the stairs, entangled in Volkan's arms. Sometimes they felt like one person rather than two separate individuals. He was never far from her, and Yara tended to grow anxious without him. Aylin had once thought about asking her if it was healthy to be so attached to him. If this were all heightened by her new role as a sired, whom Aylin heard were made to loyally serve the ones they called the trueborn, but she hadn't wanted to upset her.

Yara waved a shaky hand.

I love you, she mouthed.

Love you more, Aylin whispered.

Aylin thought of embracing her, but she feared she might stay behind if she did.

After all she had done to be reunited with her sister, it felt foolish to leave her when they'd only been together for four short weeks. But the thought of the open road filled her with an ease that erased the tension that had gripped her ever since she arrived.

She settled into the carriage, draping the velvet curtains closed. Her *kilij* was strapped to her hip, and she touched the handle fondly.

For the first time in weeks, she felt as though she could breathe.

They made camp during the day so the vampir could hide from the sun. Tents were perched beneath fir trees, and a blockade of rolled ice was used to protect the flaps from intruders. If the snow even shifted, the vampir would awaken and slay whomever dared cross their path. Aylin shared a tent with Pariza, who regaled her with fascinating Persian ghost stories.

"And beneath the women's skirt, there were no human legs," she said with a dramatic pause. "But the hooves of a goat."

"What a splendid tale." Aylin clapped.

Pariza grinned and bowed dramatically.

"How long have you been a vampir?" Aylin asked.

"Not long," she said. "A year. All of Volkan's sired vampir are only a year or so old. He is fairly young, so he hasn't had years to build a horde."

"Is that what you wanted, or did he force you?" she asked.

It was impossible to not think the worst of him. And while she told Yara she'd try to be open-minded, she couldn't resist pushing for more information.

"He promised to take me out of poverty. I lived in a small village in Persia, and my family was suffering. Volkan changed their lives and mine. I love being a vampir. It is a better fate for a woman than to be confined in a home, birthing seven babies and cooking till your fingers are worn. As a vampir I get to go on adventures and travel the world with my friends."

"I suppose I can understand that aspect," Aylin said. "It wasn't any different in the Ottoman court. It sounds terrible, but these past few months were the first time in a long time where I felt like myself."

Of course, if she could go back in time, she would never wish for her sister to endure what she had. But if Yara had never been kidnapped, she'd still be trapped there. Stuck behind the gilded bars of her cage. Forced to mold herself into a dutiful wife and a mother. It reminded her of a time when she had snuck away to the village for the celebration of Eid al-Fitr.

She had been sixteen and so pleased with her efforts at evading the guards, she had felt as though she were on top of the world. Hours passed her as she filled her stomach with sweets and sang hoarsely during the parade. Yara had told her father and Aunt Sevda that she'd come down with a fever. It hadn't been easy convincing her sister, but Aylin was nothing if not persuasive (she had stolen Yara's favorite necklace and refused to return it unless she lied on her behalf).

Aylin had sat down to rest her aching feet when someone had pulled her hood down, and she jumped upright. Within moments she was on her feet, staring into a pair of frigid blue eyes.

"Ilyas!" she said surprised.

"Little thief," he said.

"I didn't steal anything," Aylin said defensively. "I simply escaped that dreadful palace."

"This is a servant's cloak," he said. His long fingers stroked the rough, woolen fabric of her hood. "It is nearly midnight."

"And the night is still young. I know the palace is still celebrating," she said. "You are off tonight. Why would you spend your holiday looking for me?"

"Why would you risk your life by leaving without any guards?" he demanded. "Any harm could befall you."

He looked odd walking around without his soldier's uniform. It was strange to see him in a simple kaftan, his brown hair swaying in the breeze. He looked oddly boyish. Like a prince from one of those fairy tales Yara was so obsessed with.

"Unlikely," she retorted. "I have a wicked blade, remember."

She pulled out the *kilij* he had given her. Aylin used it to tilt his chin up, watching his dark hair fall backward. It was a heady feeling to toy with him. She had always enjoyed getting under his skin.

"Don't test me, Aylin," he said gruffly. "I can disarm you before you blink."

"But you won't," she said.

"But I won't." He sighed.

Aylin grinned widely. "You are a fool."

Aylin sat back down, and Ilyas wrinkled his nose before he reluctantly sat beside her. He despised uncleanliness. A strange trait for a soldier. His nails were always short and well kept. And his hair was nice and groomed.

"It is strange to see everyone celebrating with their families," he said. He had a somber look in his eyes.

It struck her then that she hadn't thought about how hard it would be for him. He always refused to come celebrate at court when she invited him. And she knew he turned down similar invitations from his comrades. She had never asked how he spent his Eid.

"I miss them on days like this," he said. "Far more than others."

He didn't have to say the words for her to know that he was thinking about his family in Transylvania. Her heart ached. She always felt his pain most acutely. Ever since that day she had found him crying alone, a fresh-eyed Transylvanian boy brought to serve the empire, Aylin knew he had stolen a piece of her, and she would never be strong enough to take it back.

"I'm sorry," she whispered.

"I thought about running away when I first came," he said.

"Why didn't you?" she asked.

He looked at her. His gaze was heavy and filled with so many unsaid words, it threatened to drown her. Ilyas lifted a finger, tucking a strand of her dark hair behind her ear. He stared at her with a strange mixture of longing and sadness.

"Aunt Sevda was talking about finding you a match this week," Ilyas said.

Aylin rolled her eyes. "Good luck to her."

"Have you ever thought about the future?" he asked.

"I don't know what I am doing tomorrow, let alone anything past that," Aylin said. She had a few nutshells in her pocket, and she pelted them at him. "Besides, you think enough for the both of us. You are like an old woman, filled with caution and turmoil."

A small chuckle escaped him, and he caught her wrist in his long fingers, halting her attack.

"You would walk into the ocean if I wasn't there to pull you back," he said.

"I would walk into the ocean *because* I know you would always be there to pull me back," Aylin said.

His smile dropped, and he released her wrist. And then she saw it again, that overwhelming sadness that filled his eyes. She wondered if it had ever truly left.

"You are going to leave someday," he said, gazing ahead as if he could not bear to look at her. "You will wed and start a family."

Aylin wrinkled her nose. "Not if I can help it."

Ilyas did not speak, and neither did she. She could feel something weighed on him, but she did not know how to shoulder the burden.

So, she did not speak.

"Yara is in good hands," Pariza said softly, drawing her back to their conversation. "I think Volkan may be in love with her."

"I just don't want to see her hurt," Aylin said. "I know he can be cruel, but I hope he is not cruel to her."

"He is not," she said. "One thing about Volkan, and perhaps even Eldar, is that they are fiercely protective of the people they love."

Aylin nodded. "That is all I ask for."

———

It was on their sixth day of travel when they were attacked. A single arrow pierced the throat of Dmitri, one of the guards, and his body crumpled to the floor while his blank eyes stared ahead into the distance.

"Take cover," Zuri bellowed outside the carriage.

Aylin looked around her at the wide-eyed blood slaves. All the humans traveled in the carriage whereas the vampir took the horses and a few even ran ahead on their feet, a mere blur of cloth and hair as they raced in the wild like predators.

Aylin withdrew her blade and looked past the curtain. There were men in the treetops, mere shadows in the dark, carrying weighted crossbows. She heard the startled neigh of the horse that led their carriage before it came to a screeching halt, and the passengers all fell upon one another, limbs tangling like vines.

"Surrender," a voice bellowed.

It was silent outside, and she reached for the handle.

"No!" A girl grabbed her wrist, nails digging into her flesh. It was one of the blood slaves. "Do not open the door."

"Better to face the danger than wait for it to come to us."

Aylin opened the door. The first thing she saw was their breastplates, made of forged steel with the symbol of the cross. These men were not raiders. They were hunters.

Borza held the slumped form of Zuri. Her neck was at a strange angle, a clear sign that it had been broken. The others had surrendered at the sight of her defeat. Pariza had a blade in her chest, one that was dangerously close to her heart, and anytime the hunter twisted it, she'd flinch in pain.

Aylin's gaze traced the familiar faces, desperately searching for any sign of *him*. Even though her heart fluttered with hope she didn't think she'd see him.

Aylin felt her breath catch in her throat.

Ilyas sat proudly on his horse. He looked different, and it was not the shadow of facial hair that covered his strong jaw. His eyes were empty and cold. His beautiful, harsh face looked around, taking stock of his new prisoners. The relief she felt nearly knocked her down to her knees. Her heart thumped painfully in her chest, banging against her ribs like a fist against a door, seeking, demanding that she run to him and fling herself into his arms.

He was alive. He was whole. He was here.

"Ilyas," she whispered, his name a gust of air from her lips. It was far too low for him to hear her. Far too soft for it to carry any real weight.

He did not look at her. His gaze simply assessed the vampir they'd managed to capture with their sly maneuver. Of course, she was impressed by his tactics. He was the cleverest person she knew.

"Tie them to the trees," Ilyas commanded. "The sun shall rise in a few hours. We will let God burn the skin from their flesh."

"And the humans?" Borza asked. He turned to look at her, and his eyes widened. "Why if it isn't the work of God! Aydin, that you, my boy?"

"Hi, Borza," she said weakly. "Can you release her? Can you release all of them, please? They are in pain."

He looked to Ilyas. When Ilyas looked at her, he didn't react, as if she were a stranger. She wondered if he was angry at her for leaving. So angry that he could barely stand the sight of her. She took a step forward. A pleading look in her eyes. She hadn't meant to leave him on that cot alone with people who did not care for him half as much as she did.

Regret made her chest tighten. She should have put him on a horse and forced Vincenzo the healer to accompany them. She should have done something that did not include running away from the boy who was prepared to die for her when faced with the choice of his life versus hers.

"I'm sorry," she whispered.

His gaze was empty. Blue eyes cold with indifference.

He hated her for leaving. She knew it. She could *feel* it.

"Il--" She cleared her throat. "Elijah, may we speak?"

He didn't respond to her.

"Please," she added desperately.

She took a step forward, walking at first and then running to embrace him, to touch him, to kiss him. Even if the latter thought was simply that—a thought. She was not brave enough to do it. She would not survive his rejection.

His voice brought her to a crashing stop. And the breath was knocked from her lungs.

"On second thought, tie up the humans inside," he said as if she hadn't just spoken. As if none of the words she said mattered. "We will question them all."

Aylin frowned. "Elijah, did you hear what I said? Free them. They are my friends."

"Tie him up too. We do not deal with vampir sympathizers," he continued, pointing directly at her.

Aylin was so shocked that she barely reacted when her blade was stripped from her fingers, and she was shoved forward with the others. She looked up at Ilyas with a betrayed expression. He didn't even bother to look at her while she was dragged away from him. He didn't seem to care that the men gripped her so tightly it made her wince. He didn't care that she was pleading with her eyes for him to save her companions.

To Ilyas, she may as well have been a ghost.

XVII

Elijah hopped off his stallion, flexing his gloved fingers. It had been fortuitous that they'd come upon the very creatures they hunted. Pure luck indeed. They were traveling to their new stronghold in Wallachia. And it seemed the vampir were traveling *away* from Wallachia. The hunter's camp was not far from them. Borza was quick on his heels as Elijah made his way toward his tent, where his horse could rest and feed.

"You may not remember much, but that boy is your brother," Borza said. "The men have grown to respect him and don't want to see him punished."

That boy was not his brother. Anyone with two eyes could see that. They looked *nothing* alike. He was short with soft eyes and a sharp face. His hair was long enough to graze his chin in a manner that looked distinctly feminine. And he did not share Elijah's pale complexion and light eyes.

"Put him in my tent," Elijah said. "And have the other humans put in another tent."

By the time he had tied up his horse and pulled open the flaps to his tent, the boy had been brought in. His small wrists were secured by a length of rope, and his arms dangled from one of the wooden posts they'd used to pitch his tent.

"Ilyas," he whispered.

The name struck him in the chest, and Elijah crouched in front of him. He had beautiful brown eyes that were easy to get lost in. But he was not his brother, which meant he was an imposter. He wrapped his hand around the boy's slim neck, feeling his pulse jump beneath his fingers. He tightened his hold, watching those sharp eyes of his widen in shock.

"What are you doing?" the boy gasped.

"I ask the questions, not you," he said. "Who are you?"

"Is this a trick? Is someone watching us?" he asked. "Or are you upset at me for leaving? I do not understand what is going on. Why are you treating me this way? I'm sorry! I'm sorry that I left."

"Answer me," he said. "Or I will string you up naked from this post until you do."

He blinked at him in shock, as if he could not believe his words. The boy looked around like someone would come out to provide answers, but nobody came to save him. Just as nobody had come to save Elijah.

All he had when he'd woken up had been an unknown priest. No friends or family or lovers. Just emptiness. It had made him question a lot of the life choices he had made to find himself in a cramped room with nothing but his miserable thoughts for comfort. If this boy was a relative, then that meant he had abandoned him. And he wanted him to hurt. He wanted to see those soft eyes filled with the same pain he had felt when he had awoken to nothing and no one.

When he did not respond, Elijah raised him roughly to his feet and grasped the button of his trousers. If he thought he'd been bluffing, he was mistaken. He would strip him down and torture him if necessary.

"I...I didn't know you wanted to see me naked so bad," the boy said under the guise of humor. But his voice shook, hinting at his fear.

"A few hours without clothes and food and water should improve your disposition," he said.

He clutched the hem of his shirt and raised it to his neckline. Or rather *her* neckline.

He froze, staring at her delicate ribs and small breasts. She was breathing hard, her chest rising and falling like the tides of the wave. His fingers shook when he pulled the cloth back down and tucked it hastily into the folds of her trousers. He buttoned her trousers a bit more roughly than expected and she jolted, her hips colliding with his. He placed his hands on her waist to steady himself when he was done and felt her shiver under his touch.

His mind spun with this revelation. He didn't know what to make of it. Only that he wouldn't be as callous as he had been to a girl. This changed *everything*.

"I don't remember," he said through gritted teeth. He didn't want to confess that he was broken. Not to this strange girl. "After the battle, I sustained a head injury. I lost the vision in my left eye along with my memories. I didn't know my name, my history, my life. All I had was this bone-deep anger that has haunted me ever since I woke up that I am missing something vital, but I don't know what."

His face dropped, but she was short, so he could not avoid the sight of her eyes filling with tears. He didn't like that he had upset her. Somehow her reaction hurt more than he expected it to.

"Ilyas, I'm so sorry," she said. "My name is Aylin. I'm not your brother, as you have so clearly seen. We grew up in Constantinople together and are the best of friends."

He reached for her chin, tilting her head right and left. Her face was small and narrow with big, brown eyes that were almost doe-like. She had coltish limbs and a sharp smile. Something stirred in his chest as he looked at her, and he instinctively reached for his pocket, drawing out the severed braid. He held it to her head. It was made up of the same raven strands as the ones that sprung from her head. The same wavy texture and color.

"I didn't know you still had that," she said, surprised.

He didn't say anything, but he didn't release her chin. He liked it. This small bit of contact reassured him.

"It must have been terrifying waking up alone," she said. "I wish that I'd stayed, but my sister was in trouble. Her name is Yara, and you and I had left Constantinople to save her from the vampir."

"Is my name not Elijah?" he asked.

"It was when you were born, but then you came to Constantinople and converted to Islam, and you were renamed Ilyas."

Ilyas. The name fit. Far better than Elijah. But something was still missing.

"You said we were friends," he said. "Were we ever anything more?"

It didn't feel like friendship. The way his chest tightened with relief to know that he had someone that belonged to him was sharp enough to bring him to his knees. He wanted to hold her, but he worried that perhaps he was misreading it all. Perhaps he was building a fantasy that did not match their reality.

She started to answer him, but he clasped his palm over her mouth.

"I've changed my mind. I do not care what we were," he said.

If she said yes, they had been together, it would break him because that meant he had forgotten everything about her. If she said no, they had not been together, it would mean he had built up a false expectation of her, and that he truly was as alone as he suspected. He didn't want to be led by the ghosts of his past. He wanted to focus on his future, and he knew without a shadow of a doubt that this girl was his future.

"Will you please let my companions go?" she whispered.

His face shuttered, and he drew back from her. He was the leader of the Silver Cross, or at least of the Wallachia brotherhood. Salvatore intended to have the brotherhood set up across Venice and the neighboring states. He could not with good conscience let them go. It defeated the purpose of his mission: to erase all vampir from this world.

"I will make it quick," he promised. "We will not wait till sunrise. We will send them back to God now."

"No," she said stubbornly. "You will release them for me."

He took out his blade and reached for the flaps of the tent. He would keep this promise. He would make it a quick death and not prolong their suffering. He would grant them mercy. For *her*.

"We need them, Ilyas," Aylin called. "My sister intends to fight a war against the Undying King, and we need to reach Hungary safely."

"We will fight this war with the hunters," he said. "We do not need them."

"Perhaps, but my sister will not forgive me. She is—" The words caught in her throat. "She is a vampir."

Ilyas squeezed his eyes shut tight.

"Your sister is an exception, but this party cannot be spared," he said. "I have given my vow to the brotherhood to erase the vampir from this earth."

He could not bear to look at her pleading eyes. For some odd reason, it made him weak in the knees.

"I know how you feel about duty," Aylin said. "You have never broken a vow in your life. You'd rather die than break your word. For once, Ilyas, I want to be put above your vows. I want to be the person you make sacrifices for. I want to be the person you serve."

Her voice cracked, and he wondered when he had ever made her feel second-best. He didn't turn around to face her. He stepped outside, letting the flaps slide shut. He could hear her broken sobs from out here. He inhaled the cold air, and he knew what he was going to do before he could fully think it through.

He tucked his blade back into its sheath.

"Release them," he said.

Borza frowned. "All of them?"

"Give them shelter until the sun sets," he replied.

"Do we pick and choose now which ones we slay and which ones we set free?" Teodor said. He was a forty-year-old man with loud opinions and a blinding hatred for the vampir. Borza had told him that his daughter had been killed by one and he had been a hunter ever since, driven by blind rage and the cold, faithful hands of vengeance.

Elijah, or perhaps he should now consider himself Ilyas, glared at him.

"I do not know how Salvatore did it, but under my leadership, refusal to follow a command is met with death." He withdrew his blade. "So, I ask again, will you do as I say?"

Teodor spat on the ground, but he didn't speak a word. And that was good enough for Ilyas. He nodded at Borza. "See to it they are guarded during the day."

He oversaw the men as they brought the vampir down. The dark-haired woman with the tail of braids had awoken. They had stuck blades into all their chests, close enough to their hearts to keep them pinned in place. They couldn't move without risking potential death.

"We will offer you safety until nightfall, and then we part ways," he said. "Consider this an act of mercy."

"What changed, hunter?" the woman with the braids asked.

She seemed to be their unspoken leader.

"Where is Aylin?" a young girl asked. "Is she harmed?"

"Aylin saved you," was all he said.

"Can I see her?" the girl asked. "*Please.*"

Ilyas thought it over before he nodded.

"I still have men in the trees if you decide to retaliate," he warned.

He opened the flap to find Aylin curled into a ball. He should have reassured her, but he didn't know what he would do until he stepped outside.

"Pariza." She gasped.

The girl was before Aylin in the blink of an eye and wrapped her arms around Aylin's small frame.

"I was worried you were hurt," Aylin said. "That you were dead."

"Thanks to you charming the hunter, we've been freed. We must wait out the day, but are free to go at nightfall."

She opened her mouth to speak some more, but Ilyas cut her off a bit sharply.

"That is enough," he said. "Return to your tent."

He didn't fully trust the vampir. And he certainly didn't trust them near Aylin.

"Is Aylin coming?" the girl, Pariza, asked. "To our tent?"

"She will remain here tonight."

"And tomorrow?" Pariza pressed.

"Good night," Ilyas said curtly.

She got the message and stood up, brushing past him. It wasn't until she was gone that Aylin finally spoke up, her brown eyes filled with gratitude.

"Thank you," Aylin said. "This means more to me than you can imagine. We will need their aid in the coming war."

He unwound the ropes around her wrists and was surprised when she wrapped her arms around his waist. She was small, barely coming to the middle of his chest. He tentatively touched her waist and wasn't sure if he should bend down to accommodate her or bring her up to accommodate him. He settled on the latter, pressing his hands to her hips and raising her so she could wrap her legs around him.

"I missed you so much," she whispered. "I could barely breathe without you."

"Is that so?" he asked.

"Still as arrogant as I remember." She chuckled. "And here I thought you were a more mature version of my Ilyas."

His lips lifted in a smile. It felt odd. He hadn't had much to be grateful for when he woke up. And for a moment, he'd believed that the brotherhood was all he would ever have. He had never dreamed that he could have someone. That he could have *her*. It filled a void in his chest. His hand stroked her back while his other palm lay flat on her thigh.

"Will you stay with me?" he asked. At the same time, she asked. "Will you come with us?"

Aylin chuckled.

Ilyas sat down but he didn't let go of her. He was worried that if he blinked, she'd be gone. She was the missing piece he had been looking for since the moment he woke up. And he had a bone-deep fear that this was all a terrible dream, and she wasn't real.

"We are hiring mercenaries to kill the Undying King; he is the king of the vampir," she explained. "Maybe we should band together. An allegiance of sorts. You lot can kill some vampir, and we can destroy the Undying King."

"That's an interesting proposal," he said. "But I don't know how the men will feel about playing nice. Even if we share the same goal."

They could barely handle him sparing vampir lives. They wouldn't be able to survive traveling and fighting alongside them. It would be a mess.

"Perhaps I can talk them into it," she said. "I can be rather charming."

He scoffed. "You are more brutal than charming."

"How have I conveyed that in such a short amount of time?"

"It isn't an observation. More like a feeling."

Her face softened, and he frowned.

"Don't pity me, Aylin."

"I can't help but feel as though I ruined your life," she said. "You were satisfied in Constantinople; you had your infantry and the sultan and your faith. I tore you away from that, and for weeks you felt as though you had nothing and no one. And I wasn't there to tell you otherwise."

"I do not long for a life I do not remember," he said. "I don't want you to blame yourself for anything."

Aylin nodded, but he could tell she was not finished berating herself. Her eyes were haunted, and he worried that she would not recover from it. She leaned down and surprised him when she kissed just below his blind eye. When she pulled away, there were tears in her eyes, and he hated it.

"I wish it was me," she whispered. "I wish I was the one who was hurt."

He felt the hot spike of anger at her words.

"There is some rabbit stew," he said, changing the topic. His voice was a bit rougher than expected. "You must be hungry."

He placed her down on the floor and gave her the bowl that was brought for him.

"I do not think you are weak, Ilyas," she said. Her words were a rushed whisper, as if she had not fully formed her thoughts before she spoke. "I could never think that. I just hate myself for failing you."

She smiled at him a bit weakly, as if she hoped he understood why she felt that way, but he didn't and he wouldn't pretend that he did. Ilyas stared at her, and she sighed before she picked up her spoon and ate in silence, taking quick little gulps.

She was so small and fragile.

It frightened him to think she had ever left his side and ventured out on her own. Any number of harm could befall her. Ilyas knew that he had to protect her. She had been brought to him for a reason.

And he would never let her leave his sight again.

XVIII

Eldar left the Grand Hall earlier than usual. Now that he knew Yara had unknowingly opened herself up to their sire bond, he had every intention of taking advantage of the situation. The sire bond worked both ways. Both parties had to have forged a strong emotional connection for it to snap into place. And there was nothing in the world stronger than pure hate.

He felt a flare of irritation at the sight of Vissarion and Tiger, who intercepted him. No doubt they were here to plead on Nikolina's behalf.

"I've told your fathers that we will speak upon Alexandru's return," Eldar said to them both. "Leave before I have you both hung from the rafters."

"We need to speak about Nikolina," Tiger said.

"And Maxim," Vissarion echoed in his soft voice.

"Last I recall, you are not the heads of your family, which means we should not even be speaking right now," Eldar said. He nodded at his guard to get rid of them both when Tiger spoke between clenched teeth.

"Name your price," he said. "You want to wed someone off. Pick me. Leave Nikolina alone."

"You have nothing to bargain with," Eldar said.

His irritation burned down to a dull enjoyment at their distraught nature. It was clear to see he had gotten under Tiger's skin, but Vissarion was a bit harder to read. "I can simply take anything I want." Eldar tilted his head, staring at Vissarion. "Now that I think of it, you would get a lot of interest from the trueborn. Next in line to the Kuznetsov empire. A favorite of the women. Perhaps I should find you someone, and you can have a joint celebration with Nikolina and Alexandru."

Vissarion stiffened. "On second thought, Maxim will get over it. And Nikolina can fight her own battles."

"Coward," Tiger snarled.

"I am not being chained with some cold trueborn woman," Vissarion said. His eyes filled with disgust. "Your sister. Your problem."

Vissarion spun on his heels and was gone before Tiger could insult him some more. So much for their friendship.

Eldar almost smiled. One down. One to go.

Tiger rolled his tongue in his mouth. If Eldar were anyone else but the Undying King, he would have beaten him to within an inch of his life, simply for delaying him from playing with his favorite nemesis: Yara.

"If I were you, I would be spending as much time with my sister as possible," Eldar said. "Knowing Alexandru, he's going to lock her away in that dreary castle of his in Moldovia like a trinket. Perhaps he will permit you to visit her once a decade."

Tiger gritted his teeth, but he did not speak, which was wise of him.

"If you leave now, I may allow you to attend the signing of the betrothal papers to say your goodbyes," Eldar said. "But only if you walk away now."

"We are your cousins. Our mothers are sisters," he spat. "Nikolina and I are your family."

"That is the reason I am not tearing out your throat as we speak," Eldar said. "Do not push me, Tiberius."

Tiger sulked away, casting him a dark, murderous look. He was lucky Eldar had more pressing matters to attend to than teaching him a painful lesson.

He had a conversation to have with his little mouse.

———

He had waited hours for her to sleep.

Some days it felt like all he did was wait for *her*. He waited for his soldiers to capture her, he waited for her to accept his offer and return home. And now he waited for her mind to silence so he would have better luck reaching out to her. He hated that she had this effect on him. She had made him desperate for her, wound him up so miserably that his days were now meaningless until he saw her. It had been a while since he had wanted something with a hunger that could rival a starved wolf. It reminded him of when he'd go to bed as a young boy, dreaming of the blood of his cruel father on his hands, and he'd wake up with a smile on his face. It was simply another obsession for him to conquer, another mountain for him to climb, another throne for him to claim.

And Eldar *never* failed.

She stood in the middle of the meadows. Moonlight fell over her silhouette, slipping over her like warm honey. Her dark hair was twisted in a long braid, and she wore a milk-colored nightgown. She didn't know that she had equal control of their surroundings. This was both of their minds, and they could construct it as they pleased. So, he tended to dress her as he pleased. In garments that tickled his fancy.

"You again," Yara said bitterly. "How do I sever this connection?"

"It takes two people to build a strong sire bond," he said. "You would have to *want* to see me for it to work."

Eldar closed the distance between them, enjoying how slight her frame was before him. How she tilted her neck so far back it was a miracle her head did not snap off, simply to glare at him.

He wished she were here. In Poenari. To glare at him, to curse at him, to fight him. He wanted to feel the sharpness of her new claws on his skin, her newfound strength when he pinned her to the wall. He wanted to feel her as his equal. To feel her as a *vampir*.

"I want to see you as a vampir," he said.

Her teeth were retracted, as were her claws.

"You are going to have to pay for that pleasure," she said.

Eldar placed his hand on her hip. It sunk into her soft flesh as if it belonged there, like she was welcoming him home.

"How do you want me to pay?"

She hesitated. "I wasn't serious."

"I'm serious," Eldar said, drawing her closer. He felt the weight of her leaning against his frame.

"Teach me how to use the voice of command," she said, staring at him under her lashes. Flirting with him to get her way, using him as she saw fit. She was getting better at being manipulative. It pleased him to see her progress. "I don't understand it, and nobody can teach me because they don't understand it either."

Finally. She was hungry to learn his power. To learn what he had made her. Perhaps this meant she was open to returning home to rule by his side, that she still ached for power.

"Will you come home?"

"To kill you, yes," she said.

His lips twitched. He liked that answer.

But it was not his favorite one.

"Then I will teach you," Eldar said. "The voice of command requires both intent and specificity. I cannot command someone to carry out an entire plot or anything complicated. But simple single commands are easy to do. The more you use it, the more it will tire you, and you will need to feed."

"That day you made Aylin and Ilyas stop," she said. "Can it be done to more than one person?"

"Yes, but that is more advanced. You must understand, my

power has been building since my first kill. I have been practicing in secret for some time now," Eldar said.

His father had been the first person whose heart he had devoured. His first taste of power. Vlad had claimed that to partake in cannibalism would drive one to madness, but that was simply his fear talking. He did not want anyone to overpower him someday. "It will not work on the vampir who sired you, but with anyone else, it should be effective. You know the trueborn will not like the thought of you with power. Sired vampir are meant to serve."

"I know," she said. "Mircea looked at me strangely the day I first used it, as did everyone else."

She clamped her lips shut, as if she had said too much. It reinforced what he had suspected: that Mircea was being sheltered by allies, and they were not alone.

"I'm going to kill him and anyone who stands by him. You understand this, right, little mouse?" he asked.

"No more threats, just lessons," she said, clapping her hand over his mouth to silence him. Her skin was the same temperature as his, devoid of that mortal warmth. He liked it. She frowned and withdrew her hand, surprised that she had willingly touched him. She took several steps away from him, as if the distance would protect her.

"*Sing for me*," he said. His voice echoed with power. He hadn't warned her that he'd use the voice of command on her, and her eyes widened as she sang a little song about a cursed monster who had haunted a village and been killed for it. In the end, none had mourned the monster except it's mother. She glared at him as she sang. It was clear to see the song had been chosen with him in mind.

"*Stop*," he said. "*Crawl to me*."

She dropped to her knees, and he watched the sway of her hips as she made her way over to him. He lifted his hand to his mouth, furiously rubbing his skin as he watched her.

Her eyes were narrowed in a glare. "Is there a lesson here?"

"Yes," he said. "Only if you pay attention."

She stopped by his boots, tilting her neck back to look at him.

"How did you do that?" she asked. "Teach me."

He sat down, stretching his long legs before him.

"Sit on my lap."

He leaned back on his arms, watching her darkly as she sat on his lap, swinging her legs around his hips.

"Touch me."

"Eldar," she snapped. "I want to learn how to use it, not to be toyed with."

But her hand still obeyed him, caressing his jaw. If he ignored the burn of her glare, he could almost pretend that she wanted him. There had been a time when he had not been the villain of her story. When she had looked to him to bring her home, to save her. He wondered if he should have played the role of hero longer. If it would have made a difference. If it would have made her stay.

"Kiss me," he said.

Yara lowered her head, and he felt her sweet mouth on his. It was sweeter knowing that his last words had not been a command. She had chosen this. Perhaps the belief that it was a command eased her guilt, but Eldar didn't care either way. His hand coiled around her braid, and he harshly yanked her head back, opening her up to him so he could devour her more thoroughly. He kissed her roughly, tongue swiping her mouth with both anger and desperation.

He hated that he wanted this. That he was controlled by something as foolish as desire. Desire was a weakness. He shouldn't let someone have this much control over him. He had killed any softness that had once existed in him a very, long time ago, dug his hand through his chest and torn it out. But he was also selfish, and he couldn't let her go. Kissing her was better now that he did not need to pause for her to catch her breath. He could simply drown in her for minutes at a time. Hours, if he pleased, and if she let him. He bit her lip and pulled her hips closer.

"I hate you," she said when he broke away from her. "How could you?"

"It was not a command, little mouse. Much like our sire bond, you wanted this, and so you did as you pleased."

"Liar," she said, but her words lacked conviction. They were heavy with doubt. "I don't believe a word from your mouth."

"You want me," he said. "You cannot hide it from me."

She never could. Just as he couldn't hide how much he wanted her. They were both cursed to want someone whom they despised.

"I wanted to learn what I am capable of," she said, scrambling off his lap. She lifted her hand to wipe him off her lips, and his brow quirked in amusement. But inside his chest, her little gesture upset him. "Don't mistake that for something it is not."

"Do you know why I made you a vampir?" Eldar asked.

"I don't care to understand the logic of a monster," she said.

"I didn't want you to die," he admitted.

It was the closest he'd ever come to a confession. To letting someone know that he cared in his own, twisted way. He'd seen a girl during the battle, a corpse who looked like her. With brown skin and a face covered by dark, curly hair. He'd fallen to his knees before her, feeling an ache in his chest. A tightening sensation, like someone had shoved a blade through his heart. Like he had survived the battle with Vlad for nothing. He'd scooped her up, her name a whisper on his lips. His voice was raw and strangled as he repeated her name. And when he peeled back her hair, he felt a relief so intense it blinded him.

"I didn't want to exist without you," Eldar said.

"Liar," she said again, in that same doubt-filled tone. And he could tell it was too much for her. Her form was fading like she was struggling to wake up. To run away from him.

"I'll teach you," he rushed. He needed to see her again, and he could not risk her severing their sire bond. "I will teach you to have it as a weapon in your arsenal, but you must never use it against my soldiers, little mouse. Promise me?"

"You have my word," she said.

It was a terrible thing that he could not hear her heartbeat. He could not tell if she lied or spoke the truth.

"I'll wait for you tomorrow."

I'll wait for you every day and night until you return to me.

XIX

Even when she was awake Eldar haunted her.

Eldar.

She didn't know what to feel about their sire bond, or what it meant that they were tied together in this manner. Mircea had told her that he had sired over five hundred vampir and never had a sire bond with anyone. Not even Zuri, and she was his right hand.

She squeezed her eyes shut, attempting to erase everything that had happened. The commands, the kiss, the promise to teach her, the explanation of why he had turned her. Everything he said was a lie. That much she was certain of. Nothing that passed his perfect lips could be trusted.

I didn't want to exist without you.

Why did she continue to hear the echo of his words in her mind? Spoken in his darkly melodious voice? And that kiss. It was pure manipulation. He claimed it wasn't a command, but she didn't believe a word that Eldar said.

She never would.

Yara reminded herself that she was using him, and she would not give him the chance to use her. She would learn his secrets to become stronger. Just as she intended to train her body physically, she would hone her power into a sharp blade so when the time came, she could cut him open with it.

———

She could feel the eyes of a few courtiers on her as she made her way to the courtyard. She'd never worn trousers before, but Volkan had insisted upon them for her training. They were snug on her hips, far too snug for comfort, and she had to fold the ends of the hem to accommodate her stature. Judging by the length, he'd given her his own pair, and she wore his tunic on top. It smelled like him.

The walls outside were dimly lit by sconces, and she could make out the white smear of his hair, billowing in the breeze. Her chest tightened at the sight of his dark silhouette and jarringly white hair. She couldn't resist sneaking up on him. She slowly made her way to him before she leaped onto his back, wrapping her legs around his hips and her fingers around his neck, unsheathing her claws as she did so.

"You should be more aware of your surroundings," she whispered in his ear.

His hand reached back to hold her legs in place. "Is that so?"

"Yes."

"What will you do to me?" Volkan asked, tilting his head back.

"I'll bite you," she said. "My teeth are sharper now."

"You say that as if I won't enjoy it," he said, his lips raised in a sharp grin. "Or that I won't bite you back."

He shifted her so she hung on to his torso rather than his back, gazing deep into her eyes. For a moment, she thought about confessing her sire bond with Eldar, about his games and lies. Because despite what Eldar had said, he *had* commanded her to kiss him, and she would not believe otherwise. But there were ears everywhere; guards patrolled the gates not too far from them, and she couldn't risk anybody discovering that she shared a bond with

Eldar. It would ruin her credibility along with any standing she had as Mircea's ally. It would destroy her future before it began. And Eldar had already cost her her life. She would not let him rob her of this.

"Ready to become a ruthless hunter?" he asked. "To learn to kill and maim?"

"I am," she said.

He pressed a soft kiss to her neck, just below her ear, before he put her down.

"Fight me," he said.

"I don't want to hurt you," she said.

He chuckled, amused, but there was a hollow look in his eyes. "I'm not afraid of pain."

"Volkan…"

"Come." He curled his fingers before she could address his words. It sickened her how, long after Pomona died, the torment he'd suffered under the Maleinos still existed like a scab that would not fall off.

It made her wish to have them brought back to life only so she could kill them again.

Yara charged at Volkan, struggling to fold her hands into fists. It was difficult to do so because of the length of her claws. Volkan caught her wrist before she could strike his chest, and he opened her fist.

"We fight with our claws, not our fists," he said. "Use them to cut and tear. They will be your strongest asset."

She aimed at him again, but before she could touch him, he was gone. She looked around until she heard a soft thud behind her. He had done a flip in the air, landing stunningly on his feet, as lithe as a panther.

"You're fast," she said.

"The fastest," he said arrogantly.

"And you are awfully humble," Yara said.

Volkan smirked. "Again."

———

Her back thudded against the ground, colliding with the grass and snow. A shock wave of pain traveled down her spine in a sharp line. Volkan pinned her with his boot to her chest, and when she tried to rise, he applied the slightest pressure. He had a victorious smile on his face.

"You are enjoying this," she snapped.

"I like it when you stomp and snarl," he said. "It is positively charming."

"How do you know how to fight so well?" she asked, peeved. "I thought you were too pretty and spoiled to know how to fight."

"My father forced me to take lessons," he said. "Not that I particularly enjoyed them. Besides, I am a rather *terrible* fighter compared to other vampir. Which says a lot about your lack of skills." He eased his boot off her chest. "You should run now."

"Why?" she asked warily. His teeth had begun to lengthen, scraping past his lips.

"Because if I catch you, I'll devour you," he promised.

Her skin burned, and a thrill shot down her back at the dark look in his eyes. It was the way he looked at her when she'd first arrived as a mortal. Like he would ruin her, and he'd enjoy every moment of it.

She scrambled to her feet, running through the empty courtyard and flinging herself over the gates, landing clumsily on her knees. She shot forward, struggling to navigate the tall trees. She heard him, but just barely.

He was fast, so incredibly fast.

And when he collided with her, she knew she'd failed.

"I hate this," she said. "I do not enjoy it one bit."

She despised fighting. It was uncouth and tiresome. She wondered how Aylin could stand it. She'd much rather be in the cool chambers of Lugrezia's council room, plotting their attack against the Undying King, than outside fighting with Volkan.

"My poor little girl," Volkan said, cooing in a sarcastic voice. He tossed a fistful of snow at her face, and her eyes narrowed at the whistling sound of his laugh. He was gone. *Again*. He simply disappeared into the night like a phantom.

"You have to fight harder if you hope to defeat my brother," Volkan said.

And when she looked up, he was dangling from a silver fir tree, hair swaying beautifully down like a threaded quilt.

"I know," she said. "But that doesn't mean I don't hate this. And you. I hate you."

Her words were weak, tainted by the struggle of the past three hours.

"That is good enough for today," he said, flipping off the branch and landing solidly on his two feet. "We shall pick it up tomorrow. We will train every night until I'm satisfied with your progress."

Yara looked up at the dark sky, sending a silent prayer that she be given the strength to survive this ordeal.

XX

Ilyas was different. Changed. He was still the blue-eyed devil, who was more beautiful than any man deserved to be. He had a faint scar on his jaw, almost impossible to see beneath his facial hair. It suited him and made him appear more rugged and darkly handsome. She supposed it made sense that he would become a different person when all the traces of his past were erased. He had to learn who he was all over again.

"The Janissaries were not allowed to grow out a beard," she said. "I've never seen you like that before."

"Hmm," he mused. He touched his jaw self-consciously, scratching the faint brown hair. "Do you like it?"

"I do," she said.

Ilyas slipped off his shirt and cleaned his chest with a wet cloth. The old Ilyas would have stepped outside for privacy, but this Ilyas was generous and let her drink in her fill. His trousers hung low on his toned hips, and each swipe of the cloth across his chest made her shiver.

"You are shameless," he said.

"What?" she asked defensively.

His lips were tilted in a crooked grin. "You didn't even pretend to look away."

"I am *not* looking at you."

"Of course, it was my mistake."

"You are the one desperate for attention," she said, folding her arms across her chest. "It is like you *want* me to watch."

"Maybe I do." He shrugged.

"I..." Aylin huffed and turned her back to him. She was the flirt. Not him. She didn't like this change. She didn't like being the one whose cheeks burned and whose tongue tangled with each word.

"Will you sleep?" she asked.

"I'm not on the vampir's schedule yet. I do not sleep during the day," he said. "But you should get some rest. I will look after you."

Her chest swelled. It was something the old Ilyas would say.

I will look after you.

There were still parts of him that she didn't recognize, but other parts were, without a doubt, her Ilyas.

———

Ilyas convinced his men to join their fight against the Undying King. And while Aylin knew a few men found it blasphemous to be working alongside their enemy, others didn't mind so long as they were promised that they would kill the vampir king in the end. They had packed their belongings and, between the brotherhood, their guards, and the blood slaves, they were a party of over one hundred and fifty people, with the hunters making up about eighty percent of the group.

"We missed you," Borza said, nudging Aylin's shoulder. "What happened to that fool Domenico?"

"His mother is some noble vampir, and Domenico unsurprisingly enjoys scheming, so he's by her side," she said.

His eyes widened. "Don Cristifano said his wife was dead."

"She faked her death," Aylin said. "There's also another secret to share. Now that Salvatore is no longer in charge of you scoundrels and I've found my sister, there is no need to hide it."

"Let me guess you are wed to a vampir," he said, with a chuckle.

"What are you two gossiping about?" Pietro asked, draping his arm over her shoulder. "We missed you, Aydin. Have you gotten prettier since I last saw you?"

"Why, thank you, Pietro," she said. "Now that you are here, I can tell you both my secret."

Borza and Pietro had always been her favorite men among the hunters. "My name is Aylin, and I am a girl."

Borza's mouth dropped open, while Pietro's eyes narrowed in mistrust.

"Do you jest?" Pietro asked. "Because if you speak the truth, then you will raise your tunic and show us."

Pietro released a howl of pain when Ilyas thumped him behind the head.

"Is that any way to speak to a lady?" he asked in a dark tone.

Aylin snickered. "We are also not related."

Ilyas coiled his hand around her waist, pulling her away from the men.

"I always knew there were secrets you hid," Borza called. "But this is the mother of all secrets."

She was a bit disappointed that nobody had fainted in surprise at her news. Some of the men bowed their heads in respect, while a few others seemed suspicious, and the rest had a shell-shocked expression on their faces, but nobody swooned, which was unfortunate.

Ilyas's frightful presence made them all swallow back the words that danced in their eyes.

"You will ride with me, yes?" Ilyas asked. "Or do you prefer the carriage?"

"You," she said.

He lifted her onto his horse. Her body tensed when he

climbed up behind her. He grabbed the reins with his leather-clad fingers and held her hip with the other palm.

"Pariza, good evening," she said, as the raven-haired girl made her way to the front. Half the men looked at her warily, while the other half could not conceal their desire. Pariza was beautiful beyond compare. It made sense that they ached for her.

"Hello, darling," she said. She looked at Ilyas with a mix of respect and wariness. "Hunter."

Ilyas gave her a curt nod and whistled to his men, and they resumed their path.

—————

Aylin stirred, feeling the rumble of Ilyas's chest as he spoke. She hadn't realized she'd dozed off. She felt the palm of his hand holding her head to his chest, so she didn't jolt from the horse's swift pace. That explained why it had taken her so long to rouse: she was far too comfortable. That, and she was also probably exhausted from the journey.

"You love her," Borza said. "It reminds me of me and my old lady."

"Why do you say that?" Ilyas asked.

"You've had an eye on the road and one eye on her this entire trip. You protect her head so she's more comfortable. When the branches rustled and you suspected a threat, you didn't hesitate to cover her first," Borza recounted. "You seem more enlivened in the last two days than you have since you awakened."

Ilyas was silent as he processed this information. Did he love her?

She was almost afraid to hear his answer.

"Have you told her how you feel about her?" Borza asked. "You were celibate, you know. And you swore that you would die celibate. I don't think you ever confessed how you felt."

"I don't want to be celibate," he said. "I don't *feel* celibate. I do not understand how a man can live a life with nothing but his fist for company."

Borza laughed, and Aylin couldn't pretend to be asleep anymore. She giggled under her breath.

"Were you eavesdropping?" Ilyas asked. "You are a troublesome one."

"I didn't know you were so frustrated," she said, poking his hard chest.

"I do not see why you are so bothered," he said. "Unless you are offering to help?"

Her mouth grew dry, and she looked up at him. His lips were tilted in a smug smile, and his gaze stared straight ahead. She could see the ripple of his throat as he swallowed.

"Have I found an effective way to silence you?" he asked.

"You surprise me," she confessed.

He seemed happier and lighter since she'd found him. His humor was different too. He had always had a dry sense of humor, but now it was sharper and bolder.

She hadn't known it then, but joining the sultan's army at such a young age and being robbed of his youth had put a weight on his shoulders that she could not begin to understand. Every decision he had ever made had been predetermined for him. His future had long been molded by the careful hands of the empire, and without that burden, he could simply exist.

"In a good way or a bad way?" he asked hesitantly.

"Good way," she whispered. "I feel as though I am meeting Ilyas if he had grown up in his childhood home with his family on a small farm in Transylvania, and not the boy who held a blade and joined a war that was not his to fight."

"Vincenzo thinks I may remember someday, but he could not give me a definitive answer," he replied. "What if I become *him* again? Did you like him?"

"I want you to be *you*," she said. "And to answer your question, yes, I loved him. Even if he could not be mine, and he'd always belong to the sultan. A part of me would always love him."

It was easier to speak of it in the past and to pretend as if she no longer loved him, even though feelings as big as hers did not fade with time.

Aylin didn't tell him she *still* loved him. It was terrifying to speak of it, and to risk being rejected. For so long, she had worn her heart on her sleeve, and Ilyas had given her nothing. She wondered if Domenico had been right when he said he would never appreciate her. If maybe he would never love her, and she would be cursed to exist in this place where she could not live without him, but she could not survive with him, because it hurt too much. All while she drowned in the crippling fear that maybe he didn't feel the same. And that maybe he never had.

She took a deep breath. He needed to know who he had been, what his vow to the sultan and his faith meant to him. Both were intricately tied to the person he was, or rather, who he had been. Even if it meant he would always be far from her reach. Even if it felt unfair to give him back to his oath. It was the right thing to do.

"Borza is right," she said. "All the Janissaries took a vow of celibacy. The sultan put it in place to ensure that they had no descendants. While the Janissaries were salaried and could grow to hold a high rank based on their accomplishments, they were still, for lack of a better word, slaves to the empire. After the initial adjustment period, you excelled at your role. You were a natural-born leader and led your own cavalry. You were also faithful, far more so than I, and devoted to the Empire. The sultan was as important to you as God."

"I do want to learn my faith," he said. "If it is as important to me as you say it was, I will seek to learn more, but..."

"But what?"

"I do not serve the Ottoman Empire," he said. "Any vow I said to the sultan no longer concerns me."

"You don't under—"

"I won't spend my life following orders given to me by a man who tore me from my family," Ilyas said sharply. His eyes were cold, and she could see his fists tighten around the reins. He wasn't angry at her, but he *was* angry. "Do you not see how unjust it is for him to tear us from our families and force us to take a vow that we will never have another family of our own? No wife. No kids. *Nothing.*"

"I know," she said. "But it never seemed like it bothered you. I don't want you to make decisions you do not understand. If your memories return, you will resent me for not trying hard enough to maintain your vows."

"I don't want to be who I was," Ilyas said. "I want to carve my own path forward. And if you care about me as you say you do, you will respect that."

"I didn't mean to upset you."

"I know," Ilyas said softly. "I...have been feeling a lot. Trying to connect who I am, with who I was. It's frustrating, and it's not your fault. I want to learn everything you have to teach me so I can make the right decision."

"I will do my best," Aylin promised.

"Ah, it is so nice to be with women again," Pariza said as Aylin and Zuri unfolded their bedrolls. "Half these men stink, and the other half have been leering at me. I feel like I need to bathe after that trip."

The three of them were sharing a tent together.

"We are almost there," Zuri said. "It was smart to work with them. They provide us with protection during the day and boost our numbers. Mircea will be pleased."

"I did this for my sister, not your prince," Aylin said.

"They fight the same war," Zuri said, "so it does not matter."

"No arguing, you two. I've suffered enough for one day," Pariza said. "God, I despise traveling. There is no water to bathe in. And their terrible leader refused to stop when we passed that stream. No offense, Aylin. I know you have some weird tension with him."

"May I enter?" a young man asked.

One of the servants who traveled with them brought some cooked meat and a tin of water. He also carried some spare blankets.

"Don Ilyas asked if you require more blankets," he said, staring at Aylin. "He also sent out some men to fetch you water if you wish to bathe or perform your prayers."

"Oh, I absolutely loathe him," Pariza fumed. "He treats you like a princess while the rest of us rot."

"I will share my water," Aylin said.

"Thank you," Pariza said. Just as the young soldier lifted the flaps to step outside, Pariza called out, "And tell Ilyas that we hate him!"

Aylin had rubbed some snow on herself earlier to wash for prayer, but the thought of warm water to bathe made her hum in delight.

"Good night, ladies," Pariza said. "Or rather, good day."

"Good day," Aylin said, ignoring the strangeness of sleeping during the day.

Before she knew it, she was drawn into a deep slumber.

———

They reached the Kingdom of Hungary late that night. The mercenary dealer they were to meet was called Dorjan. Alexandru had said he had thousands of sired vampir to hire, and even mortal men trained alongside the vampir to kill and maim their enemies. Dorjan lived in a gated castle with a ring of sentries patrolling the front ward, who came at them with weapons raised upon their arrival. Aylin spotted almost twenty men walking the length of the ramparts with bows drawn and arrows nocked in preparation.

Aylin reached in her pocket for the letter written by Prince Mircea.

"We were sent here by Mircea Dracul," Aylin said.

The guard snatched the note quickly, peering over his words. For a moment, Aylin wondered if Alexandru had intended to betray them and Mircea's letter would be burned, their bodies hung from the rafters for trespassing. She had forgotten the note until this moment. Yara had given it to her the night before she left with clear instructions that she had to show it to Dorjan. It was proof of where they could pick up their funds once Mircea was provided with the soldiers he needed for his war.

"Two of you may come to Dorjan," the guard said. "The rest of you will wait by the gates."

Naturally, Ilyas stepped forward for the men, and Aylin frowned when Zuri joined him.

"I say this with no ill intent, but perhaps we should let someone more politically inclined lead this conversation," Aylin said. "Pariza can be charming."

"Are you implying that I am not?" Zuri asked.

Aylin was silent, and Pariza simply giggled.

"I am not going inside without Aylin," Ilyas said. His eyes narrowed at Dorjan's guards. "I don't trust these men to keep her safe."

"This is bigger than her," Zuri said sharply. "This is Prince Mircea's war, and I will be included in this conversation."

"This is not up for discussion," he said firmly, in that commanding voice that sent a row of shivers down her back. "Aylin, come here."

She took a step forward, and he caught her hand. He didn't look back when he stormed away, and Aylin gave the fuming Zuri an apologetic smile.

"I can't keep defending you," Aylin said. "You make more enemies than there are hours in the day. Most of the vampir hate you, or at the very least greatly dislike you, you know."

"I don't care," he replied. "They are still our enemies. This is a temporary truce."

"People will hate me by association," she added.

"Nobody could hate you." He playfully chucked her chin with his fist. "That is impossible."

Aylin shook her head, an unwilling smile pulling at her lips.

"This feels familiar," he whispered, trailing a hand along the walls.

"The architecture is loosely inspired by traditional Transylvanian designs," Aylin said. "Does it remind you of home?"

"I suppose," he said. "It is more of a feeling than a memory."

She was hopeful that he'd recover his memories. He just needed time.

He stared at a landscape portrait of the Aegean Sea during a storm.

"Blue is my favorite color," he said.

"No," Aylin said. "It is my favorite color. Your favorite color is brown."

"Brown?" he asked, pleasantly surprised. "That's different."

"I said the same when you told me," she said.

"I know why," he said, his voice ringing with certainty.

"And why is that?"

"It is the eye color of my favorite person," Ilyas said.

"Your mother had brown eyes?"

"No," he whispered. "But you do."

"Oh," Aylin said.

Her heart thudded like someone had torn their fist through her chest and squeezed as hard as possible. Something hit her then. A strange, familiar echo of pain. She wondered how much longer she could lose herself to a man who had only ever given her crumbs. At what point did she sever this poisoned limb before the rot ate away at her heart?

The guard who led them cleared his throat, noticing that they had stopped walking. Her cheeks burned when Ilyas turned away to follow his lead, hand still caught tight in hers. Aylin discreetly pulled her hand away. Ilyas shot her a questioning look, but she glanced away before he could meet her eyes.

The oak doors were pulled back for them to enter, and they were led into a private dining area where a man with a thick beard and a shock of bright red hair sat. Blood stained his mouth, and he ran his tongue over his lips at the sight of them. He put down his chalice slowly, lazily, as if he had all the time in the world.

"New blood slaves?" he asked.

"No, friends of Mircea's," Aylin said. "He sends a note. You have been instructed to provide us with mercenaries and, in return, the sum of the expenses will be added to your account."

The man frowned. "Mircea has truly fallen if he is conspiring with mortals."

"And hunters," the guard said. "They carry the Christian brand. The Silver Cross."

Dorjan's lips peeled in disgust.

"I'm not a hunter," Aylin said, pulling out the chair across for him. "Well, at least not anymore. I've retired my services. I am more of an independent party."

"And you are?" he asked Ilyas.

"I'm the leader of the hunters," he said, drawing back the chair on her left.

"That makes it easy to know who to kill."

"That is not what Mircea said," Aylin said. "He said you had twenty thousand good men for us."

"I beg to ask what this is for," Dorjan said, leaning forward with clasped hands. "I've heard rumors of an uprising in Wallachia. It is said that we have a new, young Undying King."

"I am not in a position to say," Aylin said. The less he knew, the better. She was naturally suspicious of all the vampir. Even the ones being paid to help them. "We require discretion and a good path to travel back to Wallachia without raising civilian attention."

"You won't give me anything?" he asked. He raised his hand, his claws dancing an inch apart. "Not even a little bit?"

"No," she said, "though I request a day of rest. We've been on the road for some time."

"How do I know one of your zealots won't cut out my heart in my sleep?" he asked. His dark gaze turned to Ilyas.

"You have my word," Aylin said.

Dorjan still looked to Ilyas for reassurance. "What is her word worth to you?"

"Everything."

———

Dorjan allowed them to rest for a few days with the promise of providing them with twenty thousand men before their departure. Pariza had been delighted at the mention of a bed and warm water.

"Ah," she said, dramatically sighing as she sunk into the bath. Dorjan had a splendid bathhouse in his castle with a range of oils and bath salts. The edges of the tub were trimmed in moonstones, and the candles on the sconces created an air of warmth.

Aylin sighed at the feeling of the warm water lapping her naked skin.

"I could stay here forever," she said.

"I cannot say the same. Immortality is a *very* long time," Pariza said with a giggle.

"What is it like being immortal?" Aylin asked, resting her head behind her.

Her smile dropped. "It is fun at first, and then I presume it's lonely and then dreadful and then fun again. I'm young in comparison to most, so I am still exploring who I am without restriction. There are no rules or societal pressures to mold you into a little soldier. You are completely and utterly free."

"That must be nice," Aylin said.

"I think you would like being a vampir," Pariza said. "Yara is too sweet and scared to accept it, but you are more vicious. You would fit in well."

"The thought of drinking blood disgusts me," Aylin said, scrunching her face. "Besides, I'd hate to have my loyalty tied to the vampir who made me."

"It is not bad. Not if it is the right person," Pariza said.

"I would not want to be controlled by my hunger either," Aylin added.

"That is a myth," she said. "We have self-control."

Aylin raised a brow. "You're telling me if I cut my palm, you wouldn't lunge at me."

"I would not react," she said with a shrug.

Aylin grabbed her blade and soaked it in the water.

"What are you doing?" Pariza asked, staring at her as if she were insane.

"Proving a point," she said. She cut a thin slice on her neck and watched as almost instantly, Pariza's face transformed. Her canines elongated and her nails lengthened into sharp claws.

"See!" Aylin said. "You are driven by your hunger."

"Your mouth would salivate if you came before a meal, would it not?" she asked. She was closer than she had been before, sealing the space between them in the blink of an eye.

"Now that you've wasted perfectly good blood, may I have a taste?" she asked with an innocent bat of her lashes that would have been far more effective if she didn't look so monstrous just then.

"If you do, that means I've won this argument," Aylin said.

"Fine, you've won, little brat," she said, playfully shoving her.

Aylin could barely gloat before Pariza's teeth were sunk deep into her skin. She felt the warm wash of pleasure tingle her limbs, and a soft sigh escaped her. Her eyes fluttered shut. She understood why the blood slaves had that cloudy look in their eyes. Why they sat up straight when it was time for them to service the vampir, and the eagerness with which they extended their necks.

She felt her teeth release her and her tongue heal the bite wound, but Aylin was so dazed she couldn't move. Pariza lightly tapped her cheek, and her eyes shot open.

"That was nice," Aylin mused.

"I agree," Pariza purred. "Thank you, darling."

She affectionately kissed her cheek, and they finished up their bath. Aylin moved a bit sluggishly, and Pariza promised her she'd feel better in an hour and that some vampir had more potent venom than others to subdue their prey.

She said hers was *very* effective in a prideful tone.

Aylin laughed, and they returned to their bedroom to prepare for dinner.

XXI

"Yara, do you like this coat?" Volkan asked. It had been difficult finding a seamstress in this court, but he'd found one whose hands didn't tremble and who had far better vision than the last one he'd hired. The poor thing had kept calling him Thaddeus and said his *red* hair would look lovely with a verdant coat.

"Perfection," Yara said.

"And what of this one?"

"Anything you wear is splendid, Volkan," she said, staring at him in that adoring manner that made his chest warm. "You are the most beautiful man I've ever seen."

Volkan smiled. It was nice to have someone who enjoyed the things that made him happy. Yara loved helping him look pretty. She had done his kohl that morning, even though she said he did it far better than her, while he had played with the end of her braids, stroking them along his cheek. He liked it when she touched him. When her entire attention was on him. She was his devoted little kitten. So beautiful and wide-eyed and innocent and vicious. She was, put simply, a multitude of so many things. He felt like every day he learned something new about her.

He heard a knock on his door, and Mircea didn't wait a second before he entered.

"Council room," he said gruffly to Yara, refusing to meet Volkan's eyes. He liked to pretend that Volkan didn't exist, which did not work for Volkan.

"In an hour," Volkan said. "Yara is helping me with an important task."

Mircea's eyes were overflowing with disgust when he looked at him. "Does it not shame you that while everyone is busy, you spend your days preening like a peacock? And worse, you waste her valuable time."

"I am not the one who will lose to Eldar," Volkan said with a cruel smile.

Mircea charged at him, and Yara was between them before he could reach him. She was getting quicker with her reflexes. Stronger with her training, which, despite her pleas and protests, he had not eased. In fact, he'd found new and perverse ways to make her miserable.

He needed her to be the strongest version of herself. It was the only way she'd survive his world.

"One day I will knock your teeth out," Mircea promised.

Volkan rested his head on her chin. "I'd like to see you get past my *very* dangerous girl."

"Nobody hurts him, Mircea," Yara echoed. "You know the rules. I'll meet you there."

The door slammed shut behind him, and Volkan was pleased to have brought such a childish reaction out of him.

Yara spun around, gripping his jaw. "You know, I won't always be here to protect you. One day someone will tear out your tongue for your disrespect."

"That implies that I am a smartass when you are not around, which I am not," he said. "I am fully aware that there are vampir older and stronger than me who would wipe me on the ground any day of the week."

"Well, I am no Aylin. I do not thrive off of chaos," she said. "So, don't get me in trouble."

"I won't," he said.

She turned to leave, and he caught her wrist, drawing her back to him. He held her to his chest, feeling her small frame wrap around him. He had kept his promise to move slowly with her, but he ached to kiss her. To show her what true pleasure was like. To map out her body with his kisses. Some days, the thought of being with her so intimately made him tremble.

"I know that you came here for me, but are you happy?" she asked. "I know the entertainment is poor and you do not have your retinue to laugh at your terrible jokes and compliment you day and night, but is it bearable?"

"You think my jokes are terrible?"

Yara smiled as if she had known he'd react to that. But then she was serious once more, peering into his eyes as if she could pluck his every secret. "Are you happy, Volkan?"

"I don't know," he said. "It's strange to not be in his shadow. I think that for so long, Eldar and I had been hurt by everyone closest to us, so we refused to open ourselves up to more hurt. We trusted each other for protection. And a part of me feels guilty. A part of me hates myself for leaving him. A part of me is worried that if you hurt me, I'd have lost him for nothing. Because everyone always hurts me, except for Eldar."

"You think that I'd hurt you?" she whispered.

Volkan *knew* she would hurt him. It was merely a matter of time.

"No, of course not," he lied.

"Don't lie," Yara said. "Not to me."

Volkan despised being weak. For so long, he had been a weak son, a weak brother, a weak lover.

"Volkan?" she asked. Her soft hand touched his cheek.

She was tearing down his walls. Erasing the person he had once been, and making way for someone new. Someone different.

Volkan could feel it. It was why he did everything in his power to make her strong. To make her feed from mortals and give in to her strength. Because if he didn't change her, she would change him.

"Mircea is waiting. You don't want to upset the prince," he said.

Her face dropped, and she stepped away from him. "I see."

Volkan turned to the mirror, pretending to fix the buttons of his coat until the door clicked shut. He sunk into the chair, grabbing a chalice of wine. Vampir could not get drunk, but if he were blood starved, alcohol could have an effect, if he drank gallons within a short amount of time. He poured several cups until his mind felt muddled and his troubles floated away.

"What are we celebrating?" Thaddeus asked, entering the room with a flourish. "Pariza being gone, I presume."

Volkan snorted, leaning his head back.

"You should have your portrait commissioned just like that," Thaddeus said. "It will make the women faint."

"This is exactly why I made you a vampir," Volkan said. "I needed to hear that."

"Bored of your little trinket already?" Thaddeus asked. Thaddeus, much like Volkan, had never been in a relationship. They went through lovers the way they went through clothes. And this was perhaps the longest Volkan had gone without being in bed with someone.

"I feel too much," Volkan confessed. "It frightens me."

"I cannot relate," Thaddeus said. "I just had a servant girl bent over a barrel of wine."

Volkan wrinkled his nose. "Not the wine I'm drinking, I hope."

Thaddeus only grinned, and Volkan placed his cup down slowly.

"I think we should have a celebration," Thaddeus said. "Maybe we can say it is for the returning soldiers."

Thaddeus knew just the thing to say to distract him. Volkan

adored hosting parties. When his father, Cetin Demirci, died, he had thrown a three-day celebration. A bit crass, but it had been a long time coming. He'd hired naked performers covered in powdered sugar, a treat for all his guests, and brought in a famed flame dancer from Arberia. It had been city gossip for weeks.

"That is a good excuse for a revel," Volkan said. "See what you can put together on such short notice. I dare say we don't have many options."

"Will do."

"I've been thinking about Mircea," Volkan said. "If he overthrows Eldar, he will kill us both. Yara is too trusting to see it; she thinks he will spare me, but he won't, and he certainly won't spare Eldar."

"I thought you were fine with Eldar fighting his own battles," Thaddeus said. "He would be offended that you doubt his skill."

"It is not Mircea who concerns me," he said. "It is Yara. She is Eldar's true enemy; Mircea is merely the vessel for her ambition. She is the one who convinced Alexandru to back them. She is the one strong enough to destroy a hundred men. I think she has a fair shot to take Eldar down, and if not him, then certainly his army."

Yara trained twice every night. An hour with him, and an hour with Mircea and Lugrezia's men. Yesterday, he had seen her take down twenty men without breaking a sweat. The moment those dark veins trailed her skin, she was invincible. Ever since he had weened her off that stale mortal blood and introduced her to fresh blood, her strength had grown twofold. And while he was pleased that she was growing stronger, a part of him worried that he was strengthening the blade that would someday pierce his brother's heart.

"They are going to kill each other," Volkan said. "She won't bend for him, and he has never bent for anyone before."

"What do you reckon we do?" Thaddeus asked.

Volkan was torn. If he did nothing, then there was a chance that Eldar could get fatally hurt, but if he interfered, Yara would never forgive him. Especially since she had gone against everyone to keep him by her. It would break her. He could see the fear in her eyes when she looked at him sometimes. The same fear she probably saw in him. The fear that one day they would hurt each other so viciously that nothing would heal the cracks of their mutual destruction.

"What would Eldar do?" Volkan mused.

"He would kill Yara's sister or threaten her to stop her from aiding Mircea. He'd then convince the new men to turn against Mircea and, because they were bought with coin, he would offer them a higher price to turn in his favor. Once they agreed, he would kill Mircea and anyone who stood by him, return home and bed Yara."

Volkan frowned. "That was almost scary. You know my brother far too well."

Thaddeus smiled, pleased with himself. "He's used me to do his dirty work before. I picked up a thing or two."

But then his smile dropped, and when he spoke next, Volkan simply felt dread.

"You have to choose, Volkan," Thaddeus said. "Him or her."

Volkan didn't like this. He liked being the person who didn't have to think or plot. He hadn't come here for Eldar, he had come here for himself. Yet the thought of Mircea cutting down his brother made him feel ill. There did not exist a world where Volkan lived without Eldar. Even if he was blinded by power and falling down a dark path, Eldar was his brother.

He would *always* be his brother.

He remembered a conversation long ago with his mother. She often retreated to the library in the evening with her seven maids and a tray of steaming *kahve*, but that day she had invited him to join her. Volkan sat by the foot of her chair, and she absently stroked his head as he read a book of Turkish fairy tales. It was hidden behind a book of Roman war strategies and torture methods, in case his father caught him consuming mindless rubbish, as he tended to say.

"Do you love Eldar?" Volkan had asked his mother. He had noticed at a young age that she treated them differently. She was softer toward him, and more stern and curt with Eldar.

Her long, delicate fingers were stitching a blanket for him. It was a beautiful shade of green with brown robins flittering around the leafy vines. He would give it to Eldar. He always gave her gifts to Eldar. Because his brother deserved to feel loved and cherished. Sometimes he lied and said their mother made it for him, but Eldar didn't believe him. He was observant, even back then.

"When you were born, you came into the world red-faced and wailing, but Eldar came in a whisper. The nurse proclaimed him dead, and I couldn't mourn him because I had you. My little white-haired angel. But then the most terrible thing happened, and you refused to breathe. Your face grew red and blotchy, and we could not do a thing to help you. But then Eldar cried, and something in his voice made you breathe. It was like you were frightened to live in a world without him."

His mother shook her head. Her long, silvery hair, the color of all the Danesti women's, danced in the candlelight. "I knew then that he would be just like his father, cruel and selfish and controlling. Even then, he had his fist around your heart, and I don't think he will ever let go."

"I love Eldar," he whispered, "more than anyone in this world."

"I know, my sweet boy," she said. "But Eldar only loves himself. And you must never forget that."

Volkan had nearly died because he couldn't exist in a world without Eldar. All these years later, and that hadn't changed.

"We will let it unfold," Volkan said to Thaddeus. "If we sense that there is a chance that they have the upper hand, we will sabotage them."

Thaddeus picked up his drink. "To the Demircis."

Volkan raised an invisible drink because he refused to take a sip from the barrel, which his friend had potentially corrupted. "The Demircis."

———

He was drunk and shirtless. Volkan could feel the press of bodies around him, and a spike of panic shot down his chest. He found himself on his knees, crawling beneath the table where they had a blood slave laid on the flat surface as an unholy sacrifice. He let the flap of the velvet tablecloth hang down, shrouding him in darkness.

"Where is he?" he heard a soft, feminine voice ask above him.

It reminded him of another voice. Harder and rougher. He tried hard not to think about it, but sitting here under the table, he couldn't stop the memory from pulling him under.

"Where is he?" His father bellowed, his hard steps thundering into the dining hall. Servants moved around him, setting down the platters of food as, unbeknownst to them, the Demirci heir hid beneath the table. His arms coiled around his long legs, while he tucked his chin into his bony knees.

"We do not know, my lord," the servants echoed.

He heard his mother's delicate footsteps and, behind her, the near-silent steps of Eldar.

"Where is the boy?" Cetin barked, likely at his mother or Eldar, he could not tell. He spoke in that same harsh tone to them all.

"I don't know, Cetin," his mother said in a shaky voice. She was just as afraid of him as Volkan was. Eldar was the only one who hid his fear.

"He is sick," Eldar lied. "He has a fever."

"Weak," Cetin said. And Volkan could envision the curl of his lips as he spoke with a heavy dose of disgust. Volkan sat under the table, feeling his stomach tighten with hunger. It felt like hours until he heard their chairs scrape back and their footsteps disappear around the corner. All but one.

The tablecloth was swiftly raised, and he watched as Eldar crawled under the table. He had a plate of rice with lamb in his hand and placed it silently before him.

"I'm not hungry," Volkan said, pushing it away.

"Eat," Eldar ordered. "Or I'll shove it down your throat."

Volkan felt his lips pull in a wry smile. Eldar's words were rough, but his eyes were concerned and perhaps a bit sad.

"You know it makes him angrier when you hide," Eldar said. He tucked his dark hair behind his ear, sitting cross-legged before him.

"I wish I could run away," he confessed.

"Without me?" Eldar asked.

"With you and Mother," Volkan said.

Eldar frowned, not pleased that he'd included their mother. Eldar had grown to resent her as the years passed. It made him sad that she didn't love Eldar as she did Volkan.

Eldar deserved all the love in the world.

"I'm going to kill him one day," Eldar said darkly.

"Don't say that," Volkan said. His stomach tightened with fear. If someone heard Eldar and told their father, he would punish them with no mercy. All the servants feared him and wouldn't hesitate to gain his favor by betraying their secrets.

"I will," his brother echoed. "I swear it."

Volkan flinched, tightening his arms around his knees. He dug his nails into his skin, feeling the biting pain and then the hot rush of blood. He needed wine to drown the heaviness of his thoughts. He'd been twelve then, far too young to become a drunkard, but it helped him forget how much he despised being Volkan Demirci.

He was older now, far too old to be drunk and hiding from the shadows of his past. He watched as the tablecloth rose up and for a moment, he thought it was Eldar come to slay his demons as he always did.

But it was a girl—a beautiful girl, but just a girl.

"I'm taken," he said coldly.

"Did you rehearse that in the mirror?" she teased.

"Go away," he said.

Her smile dropped. "How drunk are you?"

He lost track of how much he drank. It had taken him three hours of drinking to get like this. And he knew he would be clearheaded in an hour. It would fade just as quickly as it came on.

"It's me," she said. "Yara."

He blinked a few times before he saw her stunning brown eyes and skin. Her hair was coiled on her head, soft tendrils surrounding her face.

"Yara?" he whispered. He stretched out his legs and pulled her into his arms, burying his face in her neck and inhaling her scent. She smelled like fresh jasmine mixed with a fragrant oil. He felt her fingers run through his long hair, the delicious scrape of her claws on his scalp making him shiver.

"Why are you hiding?" she asked.

"It is what I do best," he said.

"You don't have to hide anymore," Yara said. "I'll never let anything happen to you."

"My little warrior," he said. "My fierce slayer."

"Why are you half-naked?" she asked.

"Because I am too beautiful to cover myself."

She laughed, and he realized then that he loved the sound of it. She didn't laugh much. Not that she'd had a reason to, back at court. He'd been cruel to her, as he was to all mortals. But he wanted to make her laugh more.

"I'm sorry that I hurt you," he said. "In Vlad's court."

"I know," she said. "I forgave you for that."

The guilt still haunted him. It was one of the rare times where he felt true regret.

"Come," she whispered. "Let me take you to bed."

He crawled out, bumping into the leg of the table. He could barely stand straight, and the noise was deafening. People were tangled together, dancing or kissing or coupling. Yara draped her hand around his waist, carrying most of his weight as she led him past the sitting room. Thaddeus was gyrating his hips on a pair of girls, and he winked at them from across the room. Volkan gave him a lazy salute. He felt like a proud father anytime he witnessed Thaddeus partaking in some debauchery or the other.

Yara dropped him on the bed, and he began to fumble with his trouser button. He needed to feel the sheets on his naked flesh. He couldn't sleep fully clothed. It was unnatural.

"What are you doing?" Yara asked, swatting his hand away.

"Undressing for bed," he said.

"I am still in the room," she said.

"And?"

She bit her lip, staring at the ceiling. "You have to remain clothed if you want me to stay."

"You'll stay?" Volkan asked hopefully.

"I will," she promised.

He tried to hide his smile, but he couldn't control it. He couldn't control much around her. And he watched as her lips pulled back in a matching grin. They probably looked like idiots, but he didn't care a damn bit.

"I'm going to prepare for bed," Yara said. "Give me a few minutes."

He nodded, feeling his eyes grow heavy. He closed them for a few minutes, and when he opened them, he felt his chest tighten. She was pulling on his tunic to wear as a nightgown, and while she was tucked away in a corner filled with shadows, his vision was stronger than mortals', and he watched, entranced, as the fabric fell over her naked spine.

He quickly closed his eyes before she turned around, feeling a bit guilty. But he hadn't known she was changing, and admitting that he was not in fact asleep as she assumed would only embarrass her. He heard her gently climb onto the bed and place a soft kiss on his cheek.

"Sweet dreams, Volkan," she whispered.

Volkan felt his chest ache with her words, something overwhelming cutting through him like a blade. Something that he hadn't felt since his mother had died at the hands of raiders. Not since he'd been sentenced to be imprisoned by Dracul and lost a piece of himself to his tormentors. Not since he'd returned to court, a shell of the person he had once been.

It was overwhelming and vivid.

And it drew him into the arms of a sweet slumber.

XXII

BUDA, HUNGARY

Ilyas waited at the foot of the stairs for her. The men had gone inside to feast, and he could hear their boisterous laughter and rough voices from outside. It wasn't long before he heard Aylin and Pariza's girlish giggles before they turned the corner. Ever since their conversation the night they met Dorjan, Aylin had been distant, and he didn't know how to fix it.

It wasn't obvious at first; she still acknowledged him and smiled, but that feeling that when she looked at him, he was the only person in the world had dimmed. His fear had given way to a terrible panic earlier, and he'd gripped the basin he used to rinse for prayer as Aylin had taught him. He was scared that she would abandon him. He was scared that he'd lose her. He didn't want to be alone again.

Ilyas wondered if perhaps it had been when he said her eyes were his favorite color. His words had both softened and frightened her. But now he wondered if he had been too forward. Maybe it was the wrong thing to say.

His breath caught in his throat at the sight of her. She wore a long, gathered, Hungarian-style skirt and a bodice with soft embroidery. Her short hair was brushed back, and her eyes were decorated in kohl. She was too busy in conversation to notice him. And when she reached him, his hand rose to touch hers, their fingers grazing delicately.

"Ilyas," she said. "What do you think?" She twirled for him. "Aunt Sevda would be pleased. A lady at last."

"You look beautiful," Ilyas said. His throat was tight with some unnamed feeling. "You always do."

She smiled shyly, looking at the ground for a bit.

"Come along," Pariza said, yanking her. "Let us see the rest of the men react to you."

Ilyas frowned as they both burst through the double doors. He could hear their wolf whistles from out here and shouts of her name. Ilyas was quick on their heels, prepared to shield her from their lecherous stares. Pietro pulled her into an embrace, drunkenly and foolishly asking her why she hadn't told him her secret.

"This is why," she said. "Because you are an idiot."

"I've undressed before you," he said. "More times than I can count." He spun around to face the room. "Raise your hand if Aylin saw you naked!"

Several hands shot to the sky, and Ilyas chuckled at the sheepish look on Aylin's face.

Ilyas found an empty spot by Dorjan, who eyed him warily, pale fingers stroking his red beard in contemplation.

"Never thought I'd see the day where I accepted hunters in my home," he said. "It sounds like the start of a terrible joke."

"It is as strange for you as it is for them," Ilyas said. "We appreciate your hospitality."

"Eat, then," he said. "And drink if you will. Lord knows your men have drunk enough of my wine. They guzzle it like it is cheap ale, but it is the finest of sweet wines. I export shipments several times a year to the Russian and French courts. The mortal kings and queens adore it."

Music began in a corner of the hall, and the men grabbed the servant woman and broke into dance. Ilyas sat back, cutting into his bread and dipping it into his fish soup. There was stuffed cabbage and venison mixed with salt and horseradish across the table. He stuck to water to keep his mind clear and because his fingers hesitated when he reached for the jug. It didn't feel like he was a heavy drinker. So, he did not drink. He made a note to ask Aylin about it.

"I presume this war has to do with unseating the new Undying King, Eldar Demirci," Dorjan said conversationally.

"I don't know what you speak of," Ilyas said.

"Still being secretive, are you?" he asked.

Ilyas merely grunted. He was not here to gossip. He had a job to do. His back stiffened when he heard Aylin shriek, but it was only Pietro, that idiot, pulling her into a dance and spinning her like a doll. His fingers tightened around his chalice, and he gritted his teeth at the sight of the other man's hand resting on the small of her back.

"What are you sulking about?" Pariza asked, grabbing a grape from his bowl. He attempted to stab her with his fork, but she was too fast to catch.

"Leave," he said. His head shot up, but Pietro no longer danced with Aylin. She had been spun into the arms of Marcello, a younger boy in his troop, closer to her age.

"Oh, I see," Pariza said with a knowing grin. "You stare at our jewel."

"Is she mad at me?" he asked, turning his attention to her at last. "Did I say something?"

"It is not what you say but rather what you *don't* say," she said.

"Do not speak in riddles," he said. His brows creased in irritation. Must she always be so insufferable?

"Why would I give you the answer to her heart?" she asked. "I don't think you deserve her."

"You don't even know me," Ilyas said gruffly. He hardly knew himself. His past was a blank canvas. All he saw now was Aylin. Her beautiful face and mischievous smile and unending kindness.

He knew without a shadow of a doubt that she was his other half. That she was made for him.

"I know that she has loved you for years, and you always reminded her that she was not a part of your future," Pariza said. "For so long, she has wanted nothing more than to know that you loved her, but you do not, Ilyas. You are poisonous to her. Anytime she builds the courage to leave you, you pull her back to you, and you feed her just enough lies to believe that you are changing, that you are ready to put her first. But you are not, and you *never* do."

Ilyas felt guilt twist in his stomach. He didn't want to move too fast. He didn't want to frighten her. So, he had held his tongue. He hadn't considered that everything was so new and fresh to him alone, and not to Aylin.

"I need to speak to her," he said, prepared to rise. But Pariza grabbed his wrist, her claws pinching his skin.

"If you do not make a choice, she will," she said. "And my bet is on Domenico."

"What is he to her?" Ilyas demanded.

He had heard Salvatore mention him vaguely, but no picture came to mind of this individual. And he once more cursed his abandoned memories for leaving him lost and confused.

"A man not afraid to confess how much he wants her," Pariza said. "He waits for her in Wallachia. He keeps their bed warm until she returns."

Ilyas felt his stomach burn in anger. He knew what she was doing. She was meddling in their affairs, attempting to get a rise out of him, and it was working. The thought of another man stealing Aylin away from him made him see red and his fists clenched so tight, he could feel the stinging bite of the marks that were left behind by his brutal touch.

He had to speak to Aylin.

He had to fix everything that was wrong.

XXIII

Yara hadn't slept that morning. It felt wrong to speak to *him* when she lay beside Volkan. And he only seemed to be able to reach her when she was asleep, so she'd stayed awake, staring at the ceiling without blinking, wondering what it would feel like to live for centuries. She assumed it would be much like reading a book with no end in sight, just countless pages of a story that was eternally unfolding. It would feel like being turned on a spindle. An unraveling silk to be made into the trail of a deathless gown.

At some point Volkan had awoken and curled between her legs like a cat, resting his cheek on her chest, pale hair sprawled along her torso like a veil. His frost-colored lashes were still on his cheekbones. He had a silver ring dangling from each of his nipples. She'd never paid much attention to it before, but now that she did, she realized it was odd but pretty. She'd never seen such a thing before, and she wondered if it hurt.

She stroked his hair absently, feeling a strange warmth in her chest, like she was losing herself to him. He was easy to care for and impossible to resist.

"You're awake," he said.

"You know our kind don't move in their sleep," Yara said. "We sleep like the dead."

"Strange," he mused, scratching his jaw. "How did I get over here then?"

Yara giggled at his mock confusion. He laid his head back down and tilted ever so slightly so he stared at her eyes.

"Like it here," he murmured, pressing a kiss to her collarbone. "Want to stay here forever."

"You'd get bored," she said.

"Never," he said. "We haven't gotten to the fun part yet."

"The fun part?"

"When I corrupt you." He smiled wickedly.

"Volkan," she said. Her words were shaky when she spoke next. "Behave."

"Make me," he said. A bit arrogant, a bit hopeful, like he wanted her to do something untoward.

She tilted his chin up and kissed him, feeling his body twist to reach her better. His hand slid behind her nape, slightly raising her, and she felt his tongue twist with hers, a soft groan slipping past his lips.

A knock sounded on the door, and Volkan cursed under his breath, making her chuckle.

"Come in," he grumbled.

"My lady, Mircea has summoned you to the hall," the servant girl said, looking down at the floor.

"Now?" she asked.

"Immediately," she echoed.

"Tell Mircea she is not his to summon," Volkan said. "Tell him she is occupied."

Yara sat up, slipping out from under him.

"I'll be there in ten minutes," she said.

Volkan pouted when the door shut. "Stay here and play with me."

"Later," she promised.

"What will I do until you return?" Volkan said.

"Sit here and look pretty," Yara said.

"You underestimate my ability to do just that," he said with a confident smile. "Be quick."

"I will."

———

The hall was empty, save for Lugrezia and Mircea sitting on the dais and four chained men before them. They wore black breast-plates with the silver twin scorpions, and they had the hard look of men who'd survived a brutal training regimen in their eyes. It was the look of seasoned warriors. Vampir who would kill without any hesitation. The old Yara would have flinched at the sight of their cold gazes, but the Yara she was now simply steeled back her shoulders and stood inches away from the one in the middle.

"Is this...?"

"We found them about three hours from our location," Mircea said. "Demirci trackers."

"Kill them," Lugrezia said.

"Wait." Yara held up her hand. It wasn't the best plan she'd thought of. There was a chance it could ruin everything. But the thought of taking advantage of the situation was too tempting to ignore. "I want to send him a message."

Mircea frowned. "What message?"

"One that implies I am coming for him," she said. And then she remembered that this was not simply her war, as she had begun to think of it. It was Mircea's war. "*We* are coming for him."

"As you wish," Mircea said, amused.

"When they are dead, put their heads in a box, and I want my note in one of their mouths," she said. She pointed at the one in the middle. She could tell by his powerful gaze that he led this sorry lot. "Put my note in his mouth."

The guard nodded, drawing out his blade. Their mouths were

bound so they could not scream, but their eyes widened. Yara stared at them, refusing to turn away.

You are strong.

You will stomach it.

It is a war. Men die in wars.

She heard the wet sound of the blade striking their chests and watched the way their bodies wrinkled like raisins and their skin turned a mottled grey. Mircea had told her if you plucked a sired vampir's heart out without injuring the organ, they could live. Unlike trueborn vampir, the sired vampir were a bit tricky to kill. He said a long time ago, some trueborn would hold their sired vampir's hearts hostage, to further maintain their control over them. He said it was an outdated practice that was no longer done, except by certain families like the Ramose, the Maleinos, and the Kuznetsov, whom he said were the crueler trueborn families.

She watched as the guard severed their heads as she'd instructed. The screeching sound of iron cutting through bone grated on her nerves. Finally, they fell to the ground with a soft thud. A crate was brought forward, and their heads were packed like cargo as Yara scrawled her note. She wished she could see Eldar's reaction when he received her package.

"I want the messenger to be provided with a vial of poison," Yara said. "If they are caught, they will die before they spill our secrets."

It was a risk, and she worried that her arrogance would bring about their downfall. All she could do was pray that the messenger was not captured and that she had not started a battle that would lead them into a losing war. All because of her desperate need to prove to Eldar that she had changed. That she was ruthless and cruel. That she would not hesitate to kill him when the time came, just as she'd killed his men.

"Is this wise?" Lugrezia asked.

No.

"Yes," Yara said. "He needs to know we will destroy him."

I will destroy him.

The guard nodded. "As you wish, my lady."

"What did you write to him?" Mircea asked.

"Something he said to me a long time ago," she said.

Only Eldar, the Undying King, would know what it meant.

It would infuriate him, and her lips lifted in a ghost of a smile at the thought of spoiling his night.

It was the least of what he deserved.

And the first attack of many to come.

XXIV

"You cheat!" Pietro accused.

Aylin flipped through her set of cards, an innocent look on her face.

"I am a proper lady," she said, raising her chin. "How dare you!"

"I agree with Pietro. It is impossible for you to have won so many rounds," Borza said with narrowed eyes.

Before she could defend her honor, Pietro grabbed her wrist and pulled up her sleeve, revealing the hidden card she had tucked there. For one long moment, it was silent before the men broke out in laughter. They were far too drunk to care that she had swindled them out of their hard-earned coin.

"May we speak?" Ilyas asked.

His deep voice warmed her, and she frowned. She had been avoiding him since the night they had arrived together. She had told Pariza earlier that she could not continue to be friends with him, not when she felt so strongly about him. It felt like the right time to draw these boundaries. It wouldn't hurt him because he hardly remembered her. It would only be her who suffered the outcome of that decision.

But she was prepared to do what she must to protect her stupid, foolish heart.

"I suppose," she said. "I don't think the men will ever let me play cards with them again."

"Did they catch you cheating?"

Her eyes narrowed. "How do you know about that?"

He had arrived *after* Pietro had exposed her, so he could not have known about her little sleeve trick.

"I was watching you shovel cards up your sleeve half the night," he said. "They must have been drunk."

"Or you simply have a soldier's eye."

Ilyas led her out of the hall and toward an empty room. Aylin had just slid the doors shut and spun around when she felt his mouth on hers. Her back slammed against the door, and his big fist coiled in her hair, tilting her head as far back as it could go. Her limbs were locked in shock, and it took her a minute before her hand tangled in the fabric of his tunic. He kissed her like she was the air he needed to breathe, his tongue swiping her mouth with a hunger that drowned her. Her shaky hand drifted along his jaw, feeling the prickle of hair that had grown in the past few days, nails slightly scraping his flesh. Her knees knocked together, limbs turning weak from his rough caresses.

Aylin was dazed when he pulled back. For once, she was at a loss for words.

"Have I broken you?" he asked with a faint smile. His thumb traced her swollen lips. "I never thought there would be a day where you ran out of words."

Aylin blinked. "I don't understand."

"I need you, Aylin," he said.

His fist tightened in her hair, desperate fingers clutching her like he was a dying man. "I do not know what I've done to hurt you, but I promise never to do it again. I promise that I will remind you every day that you matter to me. I know in my heart that you mean the world to me. I haven't fully grasped why, but I would be a fool to lose you."

"Your memories will return, Ilyas, and you will resent me for breaking your vow," she whispered. "You will hate me, and I can't bear it."

"I do not care for the sultan or the empire or my oaths. I care about *you*."

As much as his words made her melt, they were not as impactful as they would have been if he had his memories. If this were the old Ilyas, she would have been floating in a cloud of happiness. But his words now felt hollow, like she was taking advantage of him. And she didn't like that.

"It does not feel right, Ilyas. It does not feel like you chose me," she said. "You don't remember anything. And...and what if it is too late for us?"

He pulled away from her. His eyes were distant and cold when he spoke next. "So, you will punish me then because I am not your old Ilyas. You said it the other night, but I didn't listen. You loved him, and you've made it abundantly clear that I am *not* him. You do not love who I am. Or who I've become."

"I didn't say that, Ilyas," she said. "I'm struggling to match you to the old you, but that doesn't mean I dislike you. I'm just scared that your memories will return, and it will go back to the way it was and this side of you will be gone."

In truth, she loved this version of him so much more. She could lose herself in the man he was now. The man she had always dreamed and hoped he would become. He looked at her as if she were his salvation.

"I like this side of you," she whispered. "But until your memories return and you can fully decide your future, I don't think we should make a decision that could ruin us."

He looked stricken and miserable, so terribly miserable it made her chest ache. He didn't look at her when he left, and that hurt most of all. It was strange to be the one to hurt him and not the other way around. Strange to have power over him when, for so long, he'd held the strings of her heart in his unyielding fist.

Aylin hoped that she was making the right decision for them both, and she prayed that she was strong enough to stick by it.

————

Aylin felt empty after her conversation with Ilyas last night. She couldn't help but feel that she had made a mistake. Ilyas had no memories, and all he knew was her. She was his safety, and she had torn that away from him. She had pushed him away because she didn't trust his intentions. But the way he had looked at her last night had been nothing short of adoration and a bone-deep need that made her shudder. He had been so protective and doting this entire trip. He put her above everyone else in a way that he never had before.

She hadn't given him a chance, and she regretted that.

She snuck to his room that night and was surprised to find it jarringly empty. She found a note by the tabletop.

Aylin frowned as she unfolded the letter.

Aylin,

I apologize for my reaction last night. The truth is you do not owe me anything, not even your heart. From what I understand, the person I was before hurt you, and the person I am now is a stranger. The hunters and I have left to set up our new stronghold in Wallachia. You have your men, and I've left behind Borza to keep you safe. If you ever need to send word to me, Borza knows our address, and he will reach out to me. If you still require our assistance to defeat the Undying King, we will heed your call when the time comes. I wish you a life of happiness and love.

Even if it is not with me.

Ilyas

It was curt and to the point. It didn't begin or end with any endearments. And it brought an ache to her chest. He had left to protect his heart, and while she had been the one to push him away, it didn't lessen the pain she felt at his absence.

This was not how their story ended.

Aylin didn't want it to end at all.

XXV

They brought the crate to him in the Grand Hall. Eldar sat alone on his throne in the dark. Most of the courtiers had retired for the day, and he was annoyed that she hadn't found him yesterday. She hadn't slept at all. If she had, he'd have been able to reach her, which meant she was avoiding him. He'd have to work harder to reach out to her. He couldn't risk their sire bond growing weak. It was his only means of speaking to her.

He wouldn't allow *anything* to ruin it.

"It was at the front gate," the guard said. "The messenger was gone before we caught sight of them."

"Open it," Eldar said.

The crate was pried open to reveal several decapitated heads. They smelled of rot and sour vampir blood. He could make out the white of a scroll tucked into the open mouth of the man in the middle.

"It is our missing trackers," Rahim said, entering the Hall. "What does the note say?"

Eldar unfurled the note, staring at the pretty, curling letters.

Three down and one hundred and forty-six thousand to go.

Yara

His lips twitched. She'd changed. She was merciless. She was ruthless. She used the same words he had when he tricked her into thinking he'd mutilated her father.

She intended to kill his entire army, it seemed.

"What does it say?" Rahim pressed.

Eldar folded it, tucking it into his pocket. It felt secret, private, like the words had been written for him alone. It felt like a love letter.

"Burn the heads," Eldar said. "Punish the commander of their infantry for training such weak soldiers."

Rahim looked like he wanted to protest.

"Do as I say," Eldar said. "I won't repeat myself."

Rahim nodded. "As you wish, my lord."

He waited until the door clicked shut before he tossed his head back and closed his eyes. He enjoyed a strange sense of relief when he felt her, and their secret world unspooled behind his eyes. She sat on a bed in the woods, the tall grass sweeping the mahogany legs of the bed frame. She held a blade of grass in her hand, stroking it absently along her delicate collarbones. Her gaze was thoughtful. He'd dressed her in a black nightgown with silver scorpions intertwined. When she looked at him, her eyes were bright and eager.

She sat on her heels, back ramrod straight. She had such perfect posture and graceful manners, an indicator of her high upbringing.

"Did you get my gift?" Yara asked coyly.

"I did," he said.

He stood at the foot of the bed, raising his arms to grip the wood that supported the canopy, feeling his tunic unravel from his trousers. He watched her eyes dart to the sliver of skin before they quickly shot up to meet his. Eldar ran his tongue along his lips, delighted by that little reaction.

"And?" she asked.

"You've been a bad girl," Eldar said.

"I wish I could have seen your face when that box arrived," Yara said wistfully. "I wish I could soak in your anger."

"Do you think I care so much about the lives of some useless foot soldiers?" he asked. "They are all ants to me. If a few get struck by someone's boot, there will always be more. They are replaceable."

Her smile fell. "You are a monster."

Eldar smiled a sharp, cold smile. "It takes one to know one. Tell me, did you enjoy taking their lives?"

"Just as much as you enjoyed hurting my father," she spat.

"It wasn't him," Eldar said.

Another confession for her. Another secret passed from his lips to her ears.

"What?"

"The fingers were someone else's," he said. Doubt clouded her eyes at his words. "I only made you think they were his."

Yara frowned. "You are lying."

"Not about this," Eldar said.

She was silent. He didn't know whether it was her little gift that had made him want her more, or if he had always wanted her this much but had been too afraid to pursue her. But he didn't want her to hate him. Not anymore.

"I missed you," he said, tearing the truth from his chest like a splinter from a wound. It was difficult to say it aloud, and he clenched his teeth hard after. "I waited for you all day."

I think of you every second of every day.

"Stop it," she said. "Just stop it."

I am losing my mind, and it is all because of you.

"I want you to know the truth," Eldar said.

It was all a game.

It was all a lie.

It was all to protect my foolish heart.

"We are enemies," Yara said, raising her chin. "And we'll never be anything more. Stop trying to manipulate me. I am not that naive girl anymore. I will not fall for your lies."

"I want you to come home," Eldar said. "I don't care if you hate me or curse me or if you try to kill me every day. I just want *you*. All of you."

She sat back, stretching her short legs. She was looking above him, not quite meeting his eyes.

"Can we start our lesson?" she whispered. Her voice was desperate. Fingers strangling the fabric of her nightgown. "*Please.*"

"You forgave him," he said. His voice grew harder with each word he spoke. "You forgave him, but you refuse to forgive me."

Why was he so much easier to love than him? Why did everyone always choose Volkan?

"Volkan did not kill me," she said sharply. "He did not nearly kill Ilyas and throw my sister out after she spent months looking for me. He did not turn his back on me when I needed protection from Augustus Maleinos, and he saved me from Pomona, who nearly killed me. He saved me again and again and again."

"I killed Pomona," he said. "I killed her. For what she did to Volkan, and for daring to touch you. Do you think I would let Augustus hurt you? Do you think I didn't have a plan for him? And your sister arrived with *hunters*. That boy was a hunter; I couldn't risk them hurting you when I intended to turn you. They are trained to kill us. It doesn't matter if they are related to you. If you are a vampir, you are as good as dead. They would kill their own kin if they were vampir."

"Aylin would not hurt me, nor would Ilyas," she said. "They would *never* hurt me."

"I didn't know that," Eldar said.

"It is too late, Eldar," she said. "I am with your brother. And your throne belongs to Mircea. Our fate cannot be rewritten."

His fists clenched along the canopy, feeling the wood crack beneath his palm.

How many more ways could he say that he wanted her, that he wouldn't hurt her again, before she believed him? Would she ever believe him?

"It is easier in the beginning to make eye contact with the person you wish to command," Eldar said, falling into their lesson. It was the only thing that kept her coming back to him, so he would feed it to her in bits and pieces. So long as he held her attention. So long as she returned.

He coiled two of his fingers. "Come here."

His chest spiked in pleasure when she listened to him without complaint. She crawled to the end of the bed, and he knew she did not intend to tease him, but the way her hips swayed was maddening. He wondered if she knew that he could stare at her forever. He remembered the night he'd asked her to be his spy, when he had been suspended on her ceiling and captivated by her beauty. It had been the first time in his life he'd appreciated someone else. The first time he'd been struck silent by the beauty of another.

He crouched down, so they were at eye level, falling onto his knees on the dirt. If he sat on the bed, his mind would spin with ideas and scenarios and darkness and lust. And she was not his. Not yet, at least.

"Try it," he said.

"It won't work," she said.

"I know," he said. "But I need to hear how you enunciate your words. It must be clear and simple. Try it."

"Stand up," she said.

"Slower," he said. "Let each word stand alone, like this. *Stand. Up.*"

She stood up, and he tilted his neck to look at her.

"You look good on your knees," she said, surprising him.

His lips lifted in a wry smile. "Do I?"

His hand reached for her bare ankle, and before she could protest, he pressed a kiss to her skin. She trembled beneath his lips, and when he looked up at her, she pretended as if that had not not just happened. As if he hadn't simply given in to his urges, to prove to her that he could be soft. He wasn't always rough. He could be different to her. He could be cruel to everyone but her. He could be their monster and simply be *her* Eldar.

"Speak slowly, keep eye contact." She counted on her fingers. "What else?"

"Single-word commands, or double-word if you must, but start off in singles," he said. "Practice on the mortals. Once you perfect that, you can try it on the vampir."

"I don't understand it," she said. "How can we command the mortals because of our venom, but you and I can do it with our voices?"

Eldar turned his back to her, sitting on the grass. It was his silent command for her to come off the bed and sit by him. She was a curious little thing, and his lips twitched when she slipped off the bed and sat beside him, small and perfect.

His little mouse.

"I think when you eat a vampir heart, you become something else. Not just a vampir but—"

"A monster," she whispered.

Eldar scoffed. "How original. I was going to say it connects one to bloodlines of vampir. Especially Vlad's heart. Everything changed when I consumed him."

Yara glared at him. "Of course, you don't care. You were born a monster. You do not need poisoned veins and void eyes to prove it."

"You sound like my mother," he said with a dry laugh.

He remembered his mother doting on Volkan. He remembered how she loved to comb his hair, to run her claws through the snow-white strands and mention his similarities to her, as if she was proud he'd taken her hair and beauty. Yet she flinched when she touched Eldar. As if he were cursed.

"You didn't get along with her?" Yara asked.

"I used to tell myself that she never had room in her heart to love us both, and that if she were to pick one of us, I was glad it was Volkan. I could exist with nothing, but Volkan craved love and attention. He could not survive a world where he was devoid of both. He would wilt and die," Eldar said. "I didn't understand it at first. I'd wait for her to pick me up as she did Volkan, or kiss me at night, but she simply didn't. She was superstitious. Volkan had her pale hair, while I had my father's, and to her, that meant I was like him. That I was all the worst parts of my father, while Volkan was the best parts of her."

He didn't know why he was telling her this. He didn't lose sleep over his father or his mother. The truth that he had hidden even from Volkan was that he'd killed her too. It hadn't been intentional. After he'd killed his father, she had found him eating his raw heart, strengthening himself on his power. And she'd stared at him with horror and disgust. As much as she hated Cetin, she hated Eldar more, and he knew she wouldn't protect him. She would expose him to Vlad, so he charged at her and plunged his hand into her chest.

"I wish you loved me," he'd whispered to his mother, staring at her wide eyes as he held her life in the palm of his hands. He felt a wave of sadness so intense it almost undid him as he looked into the eyes of the woman who should have loved him unconditionally. "I wish I was enough for you."

"Look at you," she spat. "Who can love a monster?"

"You would never leave Cetin," Eldar said. "Volkan would never leave you. And I would never leave Volkan. He would rule us for the rest of our immortal lives and break us under his thumb. I did this for all of us!"

"You did this for yourself," she said, eyes filled with loathing. "You are no son of mine. Nobody will ever love you. Nobody will ever want you."

Somehow, her words had always been able to cut him, more so than his father's. Cetin hated everyone, so Eldar did not care for him, but his mother *only* hated him. Her words echoed in his mind as he tore her heart out. And ate it too.

Nobody will ever love you.

He felt a small hand tilt his face to the right, and Yara looked at him, brows creased in worry, mouth tightened in a firm line.

"You didn't deserve that," she said.

Eldar gripped her wrist, pulling her hand away from his face. He felt far too vulnerable looking into her wide, beautiful eyes. They were filled with sadness, and it was all for him. A part of him was pleased that she cared about him, but he didn't want her pity. He didn't deserve it. If she knew what he had done to his parents, she would shrink away from him, and he didn't want that. There had been a time when he had craved her fear, but now it only made him feel empty.

"It made me stronger," Eldar said. "I only regret that Volkan had to endure that miserable childhood. He deserved better."

"You were a child too, Eldar," Yara said. "Volkan is not the only one worthy of love and happiness."

Eldar didn't know what to say to that. He'd learned, perhaps from his mother, that Volkan should come first. *Always.* He had never done anything without thinking about his brother first and foremost. Except now, when he was stealing the attention of the girl he knew his brother cared about. It was the first time he'd wanted to be selfish to have something for himself. He wanted someone to love him more than they did Volkan, someone to choose him for once. As his father had picked Volkan to be his heir, as his mother had doted on him and called him her precious son. He wanted to be loved by someone who valued him alone.

His hand was still curled around her wrist, and he lowered it to her palm, feeling something odd lurch in his chest when her fingers willingly tangled around his own.

"I didn't mean it when I said you were born a monster," she said. "Monsters are not born, they are made."

"And you?" he asked, tracing his thumb over her claws. "Are you not a monster?"

"Maybe," she whispered. "I thought I wanted to go home to the Ottoman court, that it was where I belonged. For so long, it felt like I was untethered, uncertain of where I was meant to be. But I think everything that happened was meant to happen. I was meant to be here. To find a new home. To make a new family. I could never be more than a wife and a mother in Constantinople, and while I still want that life, I can also be strong and ruthless and powerful. I do not have to pick one or the other. I can be soft and hard. I can be nurturing and merciless. I do not have to pick. I can simply *be*."

"I knew you were meant for this," Eldar said, enjoying the feel of her hand in his. It fit perfectly. "I saw it in your eyes when you pinned Augustus's death on me. When you chose to betray me and stand with Mircea. I could see you had the potential to be more terrible than anyone thought possible."

We could be terrible together.

She was silent, and when she spoke next, her words were a gentle flutter by his ear, and Eldar felt a fear so deep it undid him. It was the realization that this small girl had a piece of him unknowingly caught in her snare, and she could destroy him more thoroughly than he ever thought possible.

"I must leave," she said.

And before he could convince her to stay, she was gone.

XXVI

They packed their belongings late that afternoon. Once the sun had set, they would make their way back home, seeking immediate cover in the forest. With such a big party, it was easier to travel through the thicket of the trees than through the villages. The night would shelter them from any prying eyes. Borza had left a few hours before sunrise to go after Ilyas as she had bid him to do. In a few hours, they would be on their path back to Wallachia, and the thought of leaving before Ilyas returned made her sick to her stomach.

Aylin recalled how she'd walked with numb steps to Borza, fingers clutching the letter in a death grip. It had taken her a while of prying open doors only to find them empty. He'd taken all the hunters. He'd left her, and that hurt.

"Aylin?" Borza had asked, wiping the sleep from his eyes. He had his blade in his hand before the door had fully cracked open.

"Borza, please go after Ilyas," Aylin said. "He cannot be far ahead."

"Who?"

"Elijah!"

Borza frowned. "And say what?"

"Tell him that I need him," she said.

Borza nodded. "I'll ride out with haste."

He hadn't yet returned, and it had been several hours. If they left, he'd never be able to find her, and she wouldn't find him. He had mentioned that Salvatore had gotten them a new stronghold in Wallachia, but she did not know the location.

"Why are they in such a rush?" Pariza groaned. "I cannot believe we have to travel all the way back with *more* stinky men."

"You are such a princess," Aylin teased. Pariza had little tolerance for hardship. "You are a lot like my sister."

"Makes sense why you and I get along so well," she said. "I remind you of your sister."

Aylin smiled. It was strange to have a friend so different yet so similar to her.

"I'm glad that Volkan let you come," Aylin said. "It would have been rather unbearable without your company."

"I suppose he is not always an idiot," she said with a fond smile. It was clear to see that she considered him a brother. If Yara *and* Pariza saw some good in him, perhaps Aylin could let down her guard a bit around him. When she returned, she would make an effort to be cordial with him.

Aylin made her way downstairs to the front door. She saw all of Dorjan's stern-faced soldiers dressed in unmarked livery and carrying the finest blades on the market. These were high-quality mercenaries––both trained and effective. Aylin had expected a ragtag group of men much like the hunters, with nothing in common but their rage. But these men were different, tougher and trained in the art of destruction.

Aylin paced the foyer. Her shoes were scuffing the delicate carpet. Aunt Sevda would have had words to say about idle hands. Aylin missed the old woman and her father. She hoped that Aunt Sevda looked after him, and his duty to the sultan eased his heartache and provided him with a sufficient distraction.

"You'll be leaving shortly, yes?" Dorjan asked, descending the stairs.

"Yes, once Ilyas has returned," she said.

"He left here like the devil was on his tail," Dorjan said. He sat by the base of the stairs. "You remind me of my daughter."

"Your daughter cut her hair and joined a cabal of hunters to track her sister and save her from a court of bloodthirsty vampir?"

He smiled. "Not exactly. But she's like you in the sense that she has blood of steel."

"Thank you," Aylin said. "But I'm still not telling you why we need your men."

His lips lifted in a sharp grin. "Smart girl, but I've already deduced you intend to unseat a certain king and reinstate the Draculesti line again."

"Nonsense," Aylin said.

"I do not have a vested interest in politics, but war is good for business," Dorjan said. He sounded *exactly* like Alexandru. Men and their greed. "If you are ever interested in work, I can introduce you to my daughter, who runs my weapons operations."

"I'll let you know once it is all over," she said. "My sister is here now, and there is nothing for me in Constantinople. I may need a job when the war ends."

He offered her his hand, and Aylin shook it, feeling the firm grip of his shake. Dorjan left, and Aylin continued her mindless pacing. They would have to leave soon. Since they did most of their traveling at night, they couldn't afford to waste any time. It would be an hour before everyone was prepared and ready to depart. They had stepped outside to prepare their belongings and horses, and still she caught no sight of Borza and Ilyas.

"We need to leave soon," Zuri said. "Are you ready?"

"I'm waiting for Ilyas," she said. "He made a mistake, but he's coming back."

"Mircea needs his men," she said. "We do not have time for this."

"He's coming," Aylin said. "I know he is."

"Five minutes," Zuri snapped. "If we don't leave soon, we're leaving you behind."

"God, she's unbearable," Pariza said under her breath.

"I heard that," Zuri said.

"I hoped you did."

Aylin elbowed her. "She already dislikes us. Don't give her a reason to kill us in our sleep."

The gates were pulled open, and a sigh of relief escaped her at the sight of Ilyas. His brown hair fell torturously over his face like he was a hero from a fairy tale, and the rain smeared the kohl drawn around his eyes. He didn't bring his horse to a halt before he jumped down mere feet away from her and swallowed the last bit of distance with his long legs.

"Are you hurt?" he demanded, gripping her arm tight. His eyes scanned her, hunting for some invisible harm. "Borza said you needed me."

Each word he said was a layered gasp, as if he could not quite catch his breath.

"Aylin," he said, cupping her cheeks. "Speak to me."

Her throat was dry. She was distracted by how beautiful he looked, gasping and sputtering before her. His face was red from having ridden so hard to come for her. It didn't matter if he had his memories or not. He would *always* come for her. Even if death tore them apart, Ilyas would always find his way back to her.

"You came," she said.

Ilyas frowned. "I would come to you on my deathbed. I would fight an army and the sultan and any empire that took me from you. I would sink warships if it helped me cross oceans to get to you. There is nothing in my power I would not do to come to you. There is no force strong enough to keep me away from you."

"I know," she whispered. "I made a mistake."

"I didn't leave to force your hand, Aylin," Ilyas said. "I did what I assume I've been far too weak to do for a very long time, which was to set you free."

"I want this. I want *you*," she said. A part of her was glad that the rain was picking up and nobody could see her tears. Aylin stood on her toes and drew him down to her. His mouth was warm and soft, and she heard the hunters cheering as she smiled against his lips.

Ilyas pulled away from her. "Let's not give these depraved men a show."

"If you are done, can we be on our way now?" Zuri asked, tapping her foot impatiently.

Ilyas nodded, folding Aylin's hand in his own. Aylin followed him. She would follow him anywhere he asked.

He lifted her onto his horse.

"You're welcome," Borza said, looking severely out of breath. "I think I punctured a lung."

"Thank you," Aylin said, "for bringing him back to me."

"Let us go then," Ilyas said. "To kill the king!"

Cheers broke out among the men, and they rode back to Wallachia.

———

Ilyas gripped her waist and pulled her down from the horse. Aylin stretched her stiff muscles, feeling the weight of his hands on her hips. It made her tremble ever so slightly.

"This is it?" he asked.

Aylin nodded at Lugrezia's dark castle, with its pointed spires and hollow balconies. The guards had let them pass with their large party. She had barely settled into the realization that they were back before the doors were thrown open and Mircea's pale face shone down at them with satisfaction. Yara flew down the stairs, reaching her in the blink of an eye.

She wrapped her arms around her in a tight hug.

"Look who I brought," Aylin said in a pleased manner. She waved at the tall man behind her, and it took Yara a moment to recognize him. When she did, she ran to hug him, but Ilyas frowned deeply, pressing a harsh hand to her shoulder to keep her at bay.

"Don't touch me," he said stiffly.

"Ilyas, that's my sister, whom I told you of," Aylin said with a small gasp at his rude reaction.

"Your sister, not mine," he replied. "We can exchange pleasantries from afar."

Ilyas stood behind Aylin, placing a hand on her shoulder and using her as a shield against Yara.

"I'm sorry," Aylin said. "He suffered a head injury. He doesn't remember anything. I've been helping fill in the gaps. He can be rather curt to strangers."

Yara stared at him with a sad expression. "I suppose you don't remember that it was my fault that you were hurt. I owe you everything, both of you, for coming for me. Just know that you are our family, Ilyas. And you are loved."

He nodded. "I appreciate it. Thank you."

"He needs time," Aylin said.

Ilyas had become suspicious of everyone. And he was a lot more guarded and distant now than he'd been before. He needed patience and understanding.

"You're alive," Domenico said, staring bitterly at Ilyas.

His pale hair danced in the breeze, and Aylin was shocked by the venom in his tone. She had known he disliked Ilyas, but she hadn't known just how much. Ilyas pulled her behind him, sensing his hostility. But it wasn't her that Domenico despised.

"Move," Domenico said.

"It's fine," Aylin said, patting Ilyas's back. "He's harmless."

"He's anything but," Ilyas said cautiously. "Don't come near her."

"He's a friend," she assured. "Trust me."

Domenico brushed past him, digging his shoulder into him. The old Ilyas would have tolerated it, always the peacekeeper. But this Ilyas grabbed him by the neck and punched him. Domenico was quick to recover and punched him so hard, she winced. Ilyas tackled him to the ground, knocking some terrible blows at his face.

"Stop them," Aylin hissed at the guards.

They were slow to move into action, finally catching on to their stray limbs and untangling them. The boys panted heavily, glaring at each other, while sweat lined their brows. Ilyas had a dark bloom unraveling on his jaw. Aylin stared at them both with a mix of disappointment and annoyance.

"You are both idiots," she said.

"He doesn't deserve to live," Domenico snarled. "He should be dead."

"Was it you?" Ilyas snapped. "Did you send those vampir assassins? You are a hunter, you would have known where the brotherhood resided and you seem surprised that I'm alive."

"I don't hire people to do my dirty work," he replied.

"If I find out if it was you, I'll cut your throat out," Ilyas promised darkly. "And stay away from Aylin. You don't look at her. You don't speak to her. You don't breathe near her."

Ilyas snatched her wrist, tugging her to his side.

"We will speak tomorrow," Aylin said to Domenico. "We've been riding all night long."

She owed him an explanation. She owed him *something*. He had helped her find Yara. For that, she owed him the world, but the only thing he wanted was the one piece of her that she could not give. If she could love him, she would have. The weeks she'd believed Ilyas was dead or captured, she would have accepted his desire for them to become more. But Aylin had waited for Ilyas, and she knew that even if a hundred years passed, she would still wait for him.

And he was hers now, unafraid to claim her. Blinded by need and desire, as she had only ever dreamed of. Even now, his hand had snuck beneath her short hair to grip her nape, squeezing tightly as if to remind himself she was still here. That she was his.

Domenico had murder in his eyes, and she was worried when he spun on his heels and disappeared back upstairs.

"I'll have someone keep an eye on him," Yara said, looking at them both with concern. "If he did send those assassins, I'll get to the bottom of it."

"Domenico wouldn't do that," Aylin said. "He has his limits. He knows I would never forgive him for it."

"I'll find out for you," Yara promised.

Domenico would not send assassins to hurt Ilyas while he was recovering from an attack. It was too cruel, too sickening to think that he could hurt her in that way. To attempt to erase the boy she loved from this world so he could win her. The thought made her want to vomit.

"Stay close by me," she whispered to Ilyas.

"Always."

XXVII

"What do you think?" Mircea asked.

Yara sat on his wardrobe, legs dangling off the side. Now that she was a vampir, she liked sitting in high places. It gave her a good view of her surroundings. She didn't know when she'd become so paranoid, but it was a vampir thing. Even when they were relaxed, they were alert.

"What does *she* think?" Yara said.

"She said she'll think about it," he said.

Mircea had revealed to her that he intended to wed Lugrezia and unite their families. A part of her was envious that she was not his true family. Someday he would have a child that he loved more than her, and that made her sick. A part of her wanted to advise him against it, but that was selfish and foolish. They were preparing for war, and now was the time to make allies.

And betrothals were the strongest alliances there were.

"With great risk comes great reward," Yara said. "If she accepts your offer, would you make her the Undying Queen?"

Her throat burned as she spoke the words. It felt like the title belonged to her ever since Eldar had voiced it. He didn't usually make false promises, but he had that day. Or perhaps a *trick* was a better word. He'd tricked her. And now someone else would sit on what felt like *her* throne.

"No," he said. "It is foolish to share power. Especially as an immortal. You never know if the person will betray you or if your affections will sour."

"Do you think Eldar would ever make his wife the Undying Queen?" she asked absently.

"Men like Eldar are incapable of love," Mircea said, a silent warning in his eyes. "And to believe otherwise makes you a fool."

"I don't care for him," she said a bit defensively.

"Let us keep it that way," he said. "Do not believe his honeyed lies. Do not forget that you wore the same chains as me in that prison. You shared the same fate that I did."

"I know," she said softly. "I will never forget."

"Good," he said. "If you want someone to raise your station, you should seriously consider Dante. The truth is you do not have many options, Yara, not because of a lack of beauty or wit, but because you are a sired vampir. To wed a sired is no different than marrying a mortal: useless and unnecessary. We wed to continue our lineage and secure power. Neither can be done with a sired, but Dante can be convinced if you prove to be an asset."

"I do not love him," she said. "And I told you, Volkan and I are together."

"Volkan will never wed you," Mircea said. "And I can see in your eyes that is what you want."

Yara wrapped her arms around her chest. She hated being so easy to read. For believing in silly ideals like marriage and true love.

"You don't know us," she said.

Volkan had been through a lot. It would take him time to heal from it. And she would be patient and wait for him to be ready. He would want more than what they had someday. He would want forever.

Mircea stood up and stretched his arm to pat her knee.

"Just think about it, child," he said. "You can be wed and have lovers."

Yara was silent. She believed in the kind of love that men wrote sonnets about, and women wept alongside the banks of rivers for. The love that was simply magic in disguise.

Mircea left, and it took Yara a while before she jumped from her position and landed lightly on the balls of her feet. She had just cracked the door open when she heard a pair of voices outside.

"Deliver it with haste," Dante said sharply.

"Yes, my lord," a low, obedient voice said.

Yara frowned, stepping out of the bedroom and just barely catching the flutter of Dante's cloak. She turned in the opposite direction, tracking down his messenger. Something about his tone raised her hackles. Yara didn't quite trust Dante. Since Volkan had shared his distaste for the Carrara heir, Yara had been cautious around him. And whatever was in this note, she knew it could not be good.

It wasn't hard to intercept the servant. He walked quickly, but it was no match for her speed. She placed her hand on his chest, pausing him in his tracks.

"I apologize for this," she said quickly before she twisted his neck.

The vampir fell in a heap at her feet. Yara dug through his coat pocket till she found the letter. Dante was quiet and watchful, and she didn't trust men like that. Besides, he didn't like Volkan, which was strange since Volkan was so charming and easy to love, which meant there was something terribly wrong with Dante.

She unraveled the letter, scanning the words before her.

What you are looking for resides at my home.
I will name my price once you've found your traitor.
Dante Carrara

Her fingers tightened, the paper crinkling under her touch. Dante was going to tell the Undying King where Mircea was. It made sense. He would become the head of the Carrara family when Lugrezia was hanged for her crimes. He would have his own power to wield, and Eldar would owe him a favor. He had likely grown nervous with Domenico's presence. Perhaps he thought that Lugrezia would turn him and name him her heir. Or perhaps he was too impatient to wait for Lugrezia to pass the torch to him.

It seemed that everyone was playing their own game.

And nobody could be trusted.

She tucked the letter in her bodice and then she swiftly tore the sired vampir's heart out, cutting it to shreds in the process as Mircea had advised her to always do when it came to the sired. Her fingers were wet and bloody, and she looked around before she tossed the heart off the adjacent balcony. She picked him up by his legs and flung him off the balcony as well before she leaped off after him. She barely made the landing, falling painfully on her side. Rocks scraped against her hips, tearing the fabric of her dress. She clenched her teeth in pain. How did Volkan make that look so easy?

She dragged the corpse along until she bumped into someone. She looked up at Volkan who stared at her with thinly veiled amusement.

"Is that a dead person?" Volkan asked, lips peeling up in a sharp grin. "Have you been a naughty girl?"

"Oh, thank God," Yara said. "Will you help me bury him?"

"Who is that, even?" He wrinkled his nose. "I don't want to touch *it*."

"Volkan!" she said. "Not now, please."

He sighed and bent down to pick up the legs.

"Is this how you spend your free time?"

"It was necessary," she said. And in the dark, she could almost believe her words. "I had no choice."

"What did he do to you?" Volkan asked.

"It was for political reasons," she said with an apologetic

smile. "I can't say any more than that."

"Not even a little bit?" he said with a little pout that she found rather charming. "I am helping you bury this unfortunate soul, after all."

"I can't say," she repeated.

As much as she trusted Volkan, she did not want to risk being betrayed again. If he knew that Dante supported his brother, perhaps he would aid him in some manner. And she still hadn't decided how best to navigate the issue of Dante's betrayal. Her first thought was to tell Mircea and Lugrezia, but a part of her wanted to handle it herself. To prove that she had what it took to survive in this cutthroat world.

"I think we should bury him here under the snow," she said. "Will the sun turn him to ash if he's already dead?"

"I believe so," Volkan said. "Can't say I've ever tested it out, but our skin can't handle it now, so it is safe to assume the same also applies after death."

"Good," she said. Yara sunk to her knees and dug out a heap of snow and dirt with her claws. By the time Volkan had rolled up his sleeves and tied his hair back to help her, she'd already finished marking out the grave.

Volkan dumped him in none too gently and wiped his fingers along his coat with a grimace.

"I haven't done such hard labor before in my life," he said. "Positively filthy, and not the kind of filthy I like."

"What kind of filthy do you like?" she asked absently, consumed with the task at hand.

"Ones that involve a bathhouse with sixty naked people, dozens of bottles of oil, and a few toys."

"Volkan!"

"You asked!"

Yara shoved him playfully when she stood up. He wrapped his arm around her neck, pulling her to him as they walked back.

"When did you become so vicious?" he asked curiously.

"When I died," she said. "A part of me died. My innocence,

mainly. And I haven't been able to find it since."

"There is nothing wrong with change, my darling pet," he said. "Nobody is meant to be the same person their entire life."

"Do you like me like this?" she asked, indicating the blood that splattered her forearm.

"I like you in anything," he said, squeezing her shoulder. "Even another man's blood."

Yara leaned her head on his shoulder, feeling a deep pit in her stomach. She should have *felt* something. She'd cut a man's life short, but all she could think about was making Dante suffer for forcing her hand. All she could think about was more death and bloodshed.

Maybe Eldar was right.

Maybe she was a monster.

———

"Waiting for me?" Eldar asked.

Yara felt a burst of irritation. She'd been sitting on the grass, waiting for him for what felt like hours. Normally, she'd feel a single tug on her mind, like he was calling her before this world sprang behind her vision. But today it had been her who'd called his name into the dark echo of her mind. It was Yara who unspooled this nameless place for them both.

"Where were you?" she snapped.

"Busy," he said coyly, his hands tucked deep into his trouser pocket. The sleeves of his tunic were rolled up, revealing his pale forearms and those inky veins that traveled like rivers of poison beneath his skin. His dark hair sat in a tangled loop that he'd hastily piled and contained under a leather strap.

"You kept me waiting," she said.

His lips twitched. "I did. Am I in trouble?"

It was strange to see him like this, like a barrier had been pulled back to reveal a different person. It was hard to compare the person he was when they were locked in their secret world to the person he'd been at court. She remembered how cold and aloof he'd been. How he'd look at her with thinly veiled disgust, like she was unworthy of his time.

But then she remembered the other day when he'd told her that his mother had never loved him. She'd already known that their father hurt them, and her heart had broken for him.

"I need your advice on a situation," she said.

His eyes brightened. It was harder to read his new eyes that were simply pools of shadows, but she could tell, if ever so slightly what emotion, he felt.

"You care for my opinion?" he asked.

"No," she said. "I simply don't know many ruthless and manipulative people like you."

Eldar sat beside her, stretching his long legs. She felt him bend his knee, so it touched hers. It didn't escape her that he did these little things, so they were in constant contact. She thought of the feeling of his hand tangled with hers. How his thumb had stroked her knuckles while he spoke. Her stomach lurched. She didn't know what she was doing here.

Why are you here?

He had nothing more to teach her. She'd been practicing her voice of command last night on unsuspecting guests at Lugrezia's court. After ten tries, one of them had stuck, and she was eager to practice again tonight.

He had offered the other night to teach her hand-to-hand combat, even though she trained with several guards for an hour every night, and then with Volkan for another hour. Now he was simply looking for excuses to keep her coming, and it felt like she was indulging him. To consort with him in this manner went against everything she fought for. If discovered, it could ruin all that she was trying to build. It could fracture Volkan's and Mircea's trust in her—the two most important people in her life besides her sister. In fact, Aylin would hate her for it as well.

She could lose everyone.

"I shouldn't be here," she said aloud.

"I am the only person who understands you, Yara," he said in that silky voice of his. "The only person who knows how you truly feel."

"You are trying to manipulate me," she said because it was easier to believe this side of him was a facade than to accept the fact that she truly did not know him as well as she thought she did. "What do you get from it?"

"Am I?" he asked. "I hadn't realized."

"Stop answering my question with a question," she snapped.

"Should I?" he asked.

Her nostrils flared, and he tilted his head back to the sky, biting hard on his lower lip to control his smile. He didn't intend for it to be so, but it looked rather sensual. And she shifted, a bit uncomfortable with the thought. He had Volkan's face, and that made her feel suddenly uneasy. Was it Volkan's face that attracted her to Eldar? Or was she attracted to Eldar's face on Volkan?

The questions made her head spin, and she tucked them away to ponder over another time.

"Why do you never smile?" she asked suddenly.

"I do," Eldar said.

"Not that evil smile," she said. "Not the one that gives me chills."

"I give you chills?"

"Stop focusing on the wrong sentence," she said. "Answer me."

"You don't make demands, little mouse," he said. "Say please, and I'll tell you."

"Please," she said between gritted teeth, but only because the more of his secrets she gathered, the easier it'd be to destroy him.

"I don't have many reasons to smile," he said. "I feel different when we're here, like we're in our own secret place. Do you feel it too?

Yara lifted her knees, wrapping her arms around herself.

"Our interactions change nothing," she said. "I will kill you, one day."

"I can't wait for the day you come for me," Eldar said.

"I came to you for a reason," she said, shaking her head to erase the vision of his dark, monstrous eyes staring at her with that intense look.

"How may I be of assistance to you?" he asked.

"There is someone who intends to betray me," she said.

It was important that she kept it vague and that she not give him any hint of where she was or who their allies were. "But I can't kill them, not without permission from Mircea. So how shall I hurt them?"

Eldar stared at her. For a long moment, he said nothing, just stared at her as if her words had drawn her closer to him. As if her monstrosity spoke to his.

"Can you blackmail them with this information?" he asked.

"I could," she said.

If she told Lugrezia he intended to betray her to secure his own position, Dante could be killed or imprisoned. She held all the cards in the palms of her hand, and a rush ran through her at the thought of using Dante's ruination to heighten her own power.

Eldar's eyes darkened, as if he knew exactly how she felt.

"Let us say somehow Mircea wins this war. How does that benefit *you*?" he asked.

"He will give me anything I want," she said.

"Anything within reason," Eldar corrected. "You will still be a sired vampir. You will have no house to lead. You will have no birthright home, or vampir loyal to you alone. Your position at court will be weak and tremulous. If you fall out of Mircea's favor, nobody will think about you twice. Nobody will care about you."

"So, what shall I do?" she asked, even though she knew he was attempting to drive a wedge between her and Mircea.

"Is this person whom you mentioned a trueborn?" he asked.

"I can't say."

"If they are, tell them to give you five thousand sired vampir to command. Make sure that he makes them take an oath to be loyal to you first and foremost," Eldar continued. "You can have them sent to one of my houses. A safe house, in case you ever need to get away. You'll have protection and a place that's yours alone."

"It's yours," she corrected him. "A place where you can find me. A place where you have access to me."

"Is that such a bad thing?" he asked. His claw stroked down her cheek. "Is it so wretched to be the object of my affection? To be the single thought that infects my mind in a never-ending loop? To be the wreckage that robs me of my senses, my madness and misery and hope?"

"I want to be your enemy alone," Yara said.

"Liar," he whispered. "You are as drawn to me as I am to you."

"It is one-sided," she said. But she felt her mouth grow dry as his claw lifted her chin, dancing along her flesh like it belonged to him alone.

"Say it again," he breathed, his words a gust of air along her lips. "And this time try to mean it."

"The house will be mine?" she asked.

"For a price," he added.

"Of course," she said, unimpressed. "Would you like my soul?"

"Don't silence our bond," he said. "Don't ignore my call."

Yara opened her mouth, but he pressed his finger to her lips.

"I've been alone all my life. I was born with someone, yet I've always felt alone," Eldar said. "I don't want to feel empty anymore."

"I can't be what you need me to be," she said. "I can't..."

"You can and you will," Eldar said. "I will survive on the scraps of your attention until then, but I will *never* let you go, Yara."

A small, frail part of her was pleased by the intensity of his obsession. It was consuming and overwhelming, and she wanted to soak in the darkness. To wrap herself in the cocoon of his attention. But another part of her was so afraid she trembled.

"You are incapable of love," she said. "And you know that, Eldar."

"What is this, then?" he asked. "Why is it that I've never wanted another woman before? Why is it that you are all I think about? Why is it that I am losing my mind now that you're gone?"

"It is an obsession," Yara said. "It will fade and wither with time. Until there is nothing left but rot."

"You misunderstand," Eldar said. "I do not tire of what is mine. If you are mine, Yara, my attention will never waver, and my gaze will never stray. I will give you everything I am, and in return, you will do the same."

"And if I don't?" Yara asked. "Will you kill me?"

"No," Eldar said. "I made you a vampir so you'd never die. Why would I rob you of that?"

"Because we are enemies," she said tightly. "Nothing else matters but that. I will kill you. And that is a promise."

She looked at him, waiting to see his pretty face twist with rage, but he seemed flattered by the thought that she intended to kill him. A startled laugh escaped her. He was utterly mad.

"I'll have the house written under your name," he promised. "It is in Wallachia. Two hours away from court." He snatched a stick and began to inscribe the directions to her on the dirt, highlighting the surroundings. "Once the papers are done, I'll notify the guards to vacate."

"Thank you," she said.

"Anything for my little mouse," Eldar said.

Yara frowned. "I don't want you to be kind to me."

His perfectly arched brow rose slightly, complimenting the kohl that lined his eyes. "Do you want me to call you names? Is that what arouses you?"

Her skin burned, which was impossible because she was *undead*, but she felt the echo of her old responses, the heat of a flush climbing her neck that never appeared on her skin because she was not alive.

"Do you want me to treat you unkindly?" he asked. And the

fingers that had stroked her chin earlier tightened around her neck in an unbreakable hold. He drew her close enough that she could count each feathery lash that surrounded his eyes and feel the cold draft of his breath. "I can be your monster if you'd like."

"Good," she breathed. "Because I will always be *your* monster."

"I want you to be my Undying Queen," he said. His words were a dark whisper that tangled around her heart, shredding her with its phantom limbs. "I want you to be mine."

Fear crawled up her chest. He must have seen it in her eyes, because his hand dropped, and she felt the pressure in her chest ease.

It was hard to yearn for power when the pursuit of it would mean hurting every single person she cared about. Eldar could offer her so much more than Mircea could. But Eldar could not be trusted, not after everything that had happened. Even now she did not believe that he truly cared for her. He had made that promise to her before, then had her chained shortly after. Still, it would be a lie to say she was not tempted by the idea of becoming the Undying Queen, of ruling over the vampir. For so long she had craved power, and it was hard to resist when it was offered to her on a silver platter.

"I must go work on my plans," he said.

She narrowed her eyes. "What plans?"

"My plans to bring you home," he said.

Yara sighed. "Good luck."

Eldar's lips lifted in that corrupt smile of his. "I don't need luck. If all goes well, you'll be in my arms within the fortnight."

She stiffened. He spoke so confidently it frightened her. She could tell he was plotting something, and Eldar was the master of plots. The throne he occupied was proof of that.

She could not underestimate him.

Not for a single moment.

XXVIII

Yara knocked on the door and patiently waited for an answer. She could barely hide the smile that tilted her lips. She had forgotten how delicious it was to be the one in power. To look upon someone and know that you dealt the cards of their fate. That their life and existence now belonged to you alone. She could understand why men became monsters, why they fought over thrones and riches, playing with the lives of lesser men to stoke the flames of their ambition.

It took a few minutes for Dante to answer. And when he did, his brow quirked in pleasant surprise. His dark hair was wet, as if he had just bathed, and droplets of water soaked the collar of his tunic.

"Yara," he said. "To what do I owe this pleasure?"

"Hello, Dante," she said, brushing past him.

He spun around, clicking the door shut. His dark hair flared around him as he turned to face her.

"Is now a good time to speak?" she asked.

"You smell nice," he said with a wry smile.

"Volkan thinks so," she said, watching his smile drop.

Dante folded his arms across his chest. "So, what are you here for, if you're still with that idiot?"

"Say another word about him and I'll cut out your tongue before you can finish the sentence," she warned.

His jaw tightened, but blessedly he didn't say another word.

"I found an interesting letter the other night," she said.

He quirked a brow but said nothing. He was not a man of many words, it seemed. Yara walked around the room, her finger lazily trailing across his belongings.

"One intended for the Undying King," she continued. "The man whom your aunt and Mircea are plotting against. The man whom you intended to betray your aunt for."

"Do you have proof?" Dante asked. "Or simply hearsay?"

"Am I foolish enough to bring it with me?" she asked.

His knee bent slightly, as if he intended to charge at her.

"Let's not do that." She *tsk*ed. "If anything happens to me, I have someone prepared to send the letter to Lugrezia."

"What do you want?" he spat. "If you were going to tell her, you already would have."

"How many sired do you command?" she asked.

"Fifty or sixty," he said.

"That is it?"

"Fifty or sixty *thousand*," he snarled.

"I want forty-five," she said. "You will command them to serve me."

"That is more than half," Dante snapped, lips peeled back in a vicious snarl. "You are a fool to think I'd give you that many. Do you think it is easy work to make a vampir? To train one?"

Yara ignored his impassioned speech and simply continued her demands. "I will also need one of your homes in Wallachia to be signed under my name," she said. "You will send my vampir there."

While Eldar had promised her a house, Yara realized it was safer to sell that property once he had it signed in her name and keep the coin. If she housed her new vampir at Eldar's house, he could discover whom her new vampir had belonged to and realize she was allied with the Carrara.

"You think you are so wise," Dante said with a sneer, "but you are a child playing a dangerous game."

Yara left her spot in the corner to stand before him. She was far too close for comfort. It was Eldar's favorite intimidation tactic, and she saw no harm in stealing it. She let her eyes darken and the veins spread down her skin.

"I am stronger than you," she said. "Stronger than all of you. I could kill you if I wanted to, or better yet, I could let Lugrezia kill you. Did you think you could get rid of her and become the leader of the Carrara family? Did you think you could gain *his* favor by betraying your own family?"

"How do I know you won't go to her the moment I give you what you want?" he asked.

"You don't," she said. "You have no power. Remember that."

Yara patted his chest and turned to leave. "I will be expecting you to complete your side of our deal within the week."

His voice was cloaked in anger when he spoke. "That is too soon."

"You will find a way," Yara said. "Your fate is in my hands. Never forget it."

———

"May I ask why you are so pleased?" Volkan asked. "You are losing this game."

Yara was not quite paying attention to the card game they played. Her mind was stuck on her encounter with Dante. She could vividly recall the heady sensation of having complete and utter control over someone else's life. It was spectacular.

Volkan and Thaddeus sat on either side of her as they played a card game, she could not wrap her mind around. Thaddeus was cheating, which she did not care enough about to call out, and Volkan was a lot more intelligent than he let on because even with Thaddeus cheating, he seemed to win every round.

"I successfully blackmailed someone," she said. "I can't say who," she rushed when Thaddeus opened his mouth. "We keep politics separate, remember."

"Was it Dante?" Volkan asked.

Her eyes narrowed. "Are you spying on me?"

"No, he was simply glaring at you during dinner," he said. "I'm glad that you are making him miserable. I hate that smug bastard."

"I told him I'd cut his tongue out if he spoke ill of you," Yara said. "And I meant it."

"My vicious girl," he said with a wide grin.

"Shall we play a game?" Thaddeus asked. "The winner of the round can pick a loser to answer a question of their choosing."

"I haven't won a round yet." Yara pointed out. "How shall that be any fun for me?"

Thaddeus shrugged. "Use it as your motivation to win."

"Fine," she said. "Let us play your little game."

Thaddeus, surprisingly, triumphed. She stared at him suspiciously; it was easy to see that he had pitched that idea knowing that he would likely win that round.

The cheat.

She opened her mouth to call him out when his question shot out quicker than she could speak.

"Yara," he said, "have you ever kissed Eldar?"

"What?" she asked, turning to face him. She could tell by the glint in his mismatched eyes that he was gaining some perverse enjoyment from making her uncomfortable.

"Do you still have your mortal hearing, or do you intend to play deaf?" he asked. "Answer the question."

Yara sighed. "At the betrothal party, I thought he was Volkan because he was masked and I kissed him. That was the first time."

"There were more?" Thaddeus asked.

She couldn't quite look at Volkan. "I tried to manipulate him when he turned me into a vampir in the hopes that I could use it against him. It was a strategy. Nothing more."

"Interesting," Thaddeus drawled. "What do you say to that, Volkan?"

Yara struck up the courage to look at him. It was strange to see him irritated, worse that it was directed at her. He looked so much like Eldar when he was serious. It was jarring.

"It didn't mean anything," she said weakly. "The first was a mistake. I wanted to kiss you!"

"And the second time?" Volkan asked.

In the corner of her eye, she could see Thaddeus's head volleying between them both, amused by the chaos he'd caused. She wanted to strangle him. It was not that she wanted to hide it from Volkan. It was that they had barely defined what they were then. And it hadn't seemed important at the time.

"It was a strategy," she repeated. "It was politics."

Just like their sire bond was a tool for her to pick apart his secrets. The kiss had been intended to seduce him. To convince him that she was to be trusted just so he wouldn't see the blade she'd thrust into his chest when the time came.

"So, we can kiss other people in the name of politics?" Volkan tilted his head. "Did you kiss Dante?"

"No!" she said. "I would never do that."

"No, only my brother is the exception," he said sharply. "Do you like him?"

"Do you think I would ever want to be with someone as unpredictable and monstrous as him?" Yara asked, surprised that he would even think such a thing. That he believed that somebody could survive a relationship with Eldar.

"I didn't ask if you wanted to be with him. I asked if you *liked* him," he said. "It is a simple question."

"I hate him," she said. "I am leading a war against him. Do you think I do that to people I like?"

"Maybe you are as twisted as him," Volkan snapped. "Maybe your darkness calls to his."

"Is that what you think of me?" she whispered. "You think I am just like him."

"I think you are callous and power-hungry," Volkan said. His eyes stung with hurt. "I think that you only think about yourself, and everyone else is just a stepping stool to the top, where you believe you are destined to be. I think you would damn us all if it meant you won."

When he stood up, his chair screeched loudly behind him, making her flinch. She could not find the words to make him stay. It would be a lie if she said his words did not slice her. That they did not make her bleed. Her heart ached as she watched him walk away from her.

"Well, that was eventful," Thaddeus said, stretching his legs out.

"What did you accomplish from hurting us?" she snapped. The chair handle cracked beneath her tight grip, cutting a seam down the middle.

"Volkan deserves to know whatever is going on between you and Eldar," Thaddeus said. "It isn't fair to blindside him with it."

"And what exactly is going on between Eldar and me?" she asked. "Since you seem to know everything."

"I know that Eldar's dead heart yearns for you. I know that once he realizes that he feels more than hate toward you, he will pursue you to the ends of the world and beyond. I know that Eldar will win because he never loses, and he fights harder than anyone I know," Thaddeus said. "I know that you will never be satisfied being a connoisseur of life and enjoying all it has to offer, as Volkan and his sired tend to do. You will always be drawn to court and politics and power and death."

Thaddeus leaned forward, resting his chin in his palm.

"As much as I would love for you to pick Volkan, you will pick Eldar," he said. "Because he can give you the life you desire, and you will give him the love he has never had. You did not see Eldar's face when you left. He was devastated."

He was devastated.

Yara wanted to cut out his tongue just to stop him from talking. His words drowned her, pulling her deep into an ocean of despair against tides that she could not fight.

It was easier to draw lines. On the one side, it was her and Volkan, and on the other side was her and Eldar. One was the boy she cared for and the other her bitter enemy. But she had never stopped to wonder what would happen if those lines blurred. If Eldar wanted her for himself and their carefully crafted role as enemies became something more.

She would be lying if she said she did not enjoy their secret world. She had felt so close to him the other day, plotting how best to hurt Dante. As though she could be herself and he would never judge her. She liked that he stared at her with that intensity that would make anyone but her flinch. She liked that he found small ways to touch her, so they were always in contact.

She also hated him for hurting her worse than anyone ever had. She hated him for hurting her loved ones. She hated him because she didn't know if he was simply manipulating her as he had before or if it was real. And she hated that she would never really know.

"Pick one of them before you ruin them both," Thaddeus said. "Don't be selfish."

He was gone before she could say another word.

XXIX

It had been three days since the card game with Volkan and Thaddeus. And Volkan had made it no secret that he was ignoring her. Yara felt terrible for hurting him. For causing this rift between them both. He had condemned her for the sins he knew of, but not the ones that were hidden. Not this sire bond that she had nurtured. She could not help but fear that if he knew that, he would *never* forgive her.

She loved Volkan, and Yara did not love easily. In the Ottoman courts, she'd always thought of marriage as a strategic endeavor to improve her station. As much as she ached for an unforgettable love, she'd learned early on that men did not love as women did. And it would be a miracle to find someone who saw her as a person with a working mind rather than a soft body to sink into and a breeding horse to provide them with sufficient heirs. It was different with the vampir. Men and women were equals. She was not a commodity, and they could love freely without the constraints of inequality.

She cracked open the door to her bedroom, shocked by the state of her space. Someone had torn apart her room. Her mattress was covered in claw marks, and feathers poured forth like blood from a wound. Glass was sprayed on the ground from the broken vase and baubles. The armoire door hung crookedly, ripped from its hinges by a terrible force.

She didn't see the attack or catch sight of the intruder.

All she heard was the terrible crack of her neck being twisted before darkness poured down her vision like a blanket.

And then there was nothing.

———

Pain blinded her, and a scream tore out of her throat. Her eyes adjusted quickly to the dark. In the shadows, Yara could make out the lean form of Dante resting against the wall, picking under the base of his sharp claws in a leisurely manner.

"Took you long enough," he said, rolling up his sleeves.

There were wooden stakes dug into her palms and thighs. Her kneecaps were broken, and blood trickled from the open wounds. There was a scarlet pool beneath her, and she wondered how long she'd been suspended in the air by the stakes in her flesh.

"I'm going to ask you nicely," Dante said slowly. "Where. Is. The. Letter?"

"I told you, a trusted—"

"You see I don't believe you," he said. "I've been watching you, and you have no friends. Even your precious Volkan cannot bear the thought of being with you anymore. He hardly glanced at you twice the last few days. And your sister spends more time in the barracks with the soldiers than by your side."

She flinched, watching his lips peel back in a terrible smile.

"Did I strike a nerve?"

"Mircea will wonder where I am," she said. "You can't hurt me."

"He will just think you ran away after Volkan rejected you. He will think you are a silly girl and nothing more once I pitch the idea that you were moping about recently after your lovers' spat," he said.

"Volkan will come for me," she continued. "He won't fall for your lies.

"He is too busy getting drunk to care for you," Dante said. "He cannot take a step without tripping over his own feet. Besides, from the looks of it, he's already forgotten you."

His words hurt her far more than she cared to admit, digging into her chest like daggers.

Yara looked around, studying the empty cellar. There were old barrels of wine covered in cobwebs, as if the space had once been used for storage. It was damp and dark. The perfect place to drown out her screams. It brought back terrible memories of when she'd been trapped in the bowels of Poenari. Memories that struck a chord of fear in her heart. She had sworn that she would never be left at the mercy of another man, that she would never be hurt again. Yet here she was, tortured, abused, and once again in the dark. Fear wrapped its icy claws around her throat, strangling her till she felt as though she would crumble.

"Where are you going?"

"Dinner. And when I return, you will tell me where the letter is," he said. "I assume from your broken whimpers that you've never been tortured before, so I know you'll be squealing within the hour."

He changed course and came back to her. A broken cry escaped her when he twisted the stake in her left leg hard enough to bring tears to her eyes. She could feel the sharp cut of the shattered bone slicing her from the inside out, and when he didn't let go, a sob tangled in a plea escaped her lips. His mouth curled in satisfaction when she begged him to stop. She hated that the words had slipped past her numb mouth. She hated that she was weak.

"*YARA.*"

For a moment she worried that the pain had fractured her mind. That the rage-filled voice that sounded like Eldar was a phantom of her misery.

"*WHO TOUCHED YOU?*"

"*Eldar?*" Yara asked softly, cautiously within her mind. He had never spoken to her like this. Inside her mind. It felt strange and intimate.

Dante disappeared around the corner, and her limbs twitched, struggling to uphold her pinned body. The more she moved, the more a sharp line of pain spread through her limbs like wildfire.

"*It's me. I'm here,*" Eldar said. "*Who touched you? Who hurt you?*"

"*He's angry that I blackmailed him,*" she said. "*He wants the letter I found, or he will torture me.*"

"*Where are you?*" Eldar asked darkly. "*I'll cut out his worthless heart.*"

"*I can't tell you. You know that,*" she said, closing her eyes and gritting her teeth to withstand the pain. "*I'm scared.*"

"*You are not scared. You are my brave girl who fears nothing and no one,*" he said. "*Tell me everything in your vicinity. Are you chained?*"

"*There are two wooden stakes in my shoulders and two in my thighs, and my knees are broken, but it's healing,*" she said. "*I'm in a cellar and it's dark. There is nothing near me.*"

"*Can you move?*" he asked.

"*It hurts,*" she said.

"*I know,*" he said softly. "*But you'll have to try. Start with one shoulder. You just need to have one arm free and then you can pull out the rest.*"

"*I can't,*" she said, a bit hopelessly.

Even the smallest movement made her want to cry out in pain. There was no way she could drag her torso forward and free herself. She could not shift when a line of pain struck her nerves each time she moved.

"*Yara, you are the fiercest person I know, and you must not shy away from a little pain,*" Eldar said. "*Think of the pain you'll inflict on him when you're free.*"

Yara tried to move, encouraged by his words, but the pain was nearly unbearable, and a scream ripped out her throat. To free herself, she'd have to fold her torso in half, digging the stake through her burning shoulders, and then free her legs next. It was impossible to do it one at a time.

"*You can do it, my little mouse,*" Eldar said in a strangely gentle voice. "*You can do anything you set your mind to. You are the strongest person I know.*"

"*I can't,*" she said. A soft sob escaped her lips. "*I can't do it.*"

"*You can do it,*" he said. "*Because I said you can.*"

A choked laugh escaped her. "*You are so stubborn.*"

"*And you are changing the topic,*" he said. "*Is your arm free?*"

"*I'll try,*" she said.

"*Do it,*" he said. "*For me.*"

It hurt, but she bit her lip hard enough to bleed and kept going. Every push forward made her aching knees tremble, and a spark of pain lit up her nerves. Tears soaked her eyes, but she could feel his presence in her mind, and for some odd reason, she wanted to please him. She wanted to prove that she was strong.

"*I got a few inches forward,*" she said.

"*Good girl,*" Eldar said. "*I'm here. I'm not going to leave you. I will never leave you.*"

His words spurred her onward. He'd called her his brave girl, his perfect girl, his unbreakable girl.

The last inch hurt the most, where the blade was sharpest. She was tilted forward uncomfortably and couldn't stay long in that position. She forced herself forward, and the stake left her skin with a squelching sound. She reached for the stake in her legs and ripped it out as fast as she could. It hurt, and she could feel the broken bone tingle as it began to heal itself. At least she was a vampir who could heal. It was her only consolation.

"*I did it,*" she said, crumbling to the floor and waiting for her body to heal.

"*Good girl,*" he purred. "*I told you. You can do anything.*"

"*Can I see you?*" she whispered, sealing her eyes shut.

She felt strangely vulnerable, as if she had never truly considered the fact that she could die. Being a vampir had made her believe she was invincible and that nothing could touch or hurt her anymore, but she was wrong. She could be broken. She could be killed. And Dante had almost won.

"*Always*," Eldar said.

She watched as their dark meadow unfurled before her. He was standing a few feet away from her, dark hair billowing in the breeze. Before she could talk herself out of it, she found herself running toward him, flinging herself into his open arms. He lifted her, long fingers circling her heavy thighs.

"I was so scared," she confessed.

"You have nothing to fear," he said. "Our bond is stronger now. We can speak through our minds. You will always have me."

A spike of fear struck her chest. It was getting too deep, too tangled, and she didn't know what to do to stop it.

"We are still enemies," she said. Even as their foreheads lay on each other, their noses grazed, and their breaths intermingled. Even as his hands tightened around her thighs and her arms around his shoulder were interlocked so fiercely it must have hurt him. Even as she pretended that she didn't see the desire in his eyes.

"I will be anything you want," Eldar said. "So long as I am yours."

Thaddeus's words haunted her mind, and all she could think about was what if she was lying to herself? What if there was more to this than just blind hatred? What if she was drawn to the wrong person?

"You need to kill him," Eldar said. "Whoever hurt you must die. There is no other option."

"I'll get in trouble," she said.

Lugrezia would lose her mind. She liked Dante, and he was her heir. For his crimes, he would likely be imprisoned since Mircea had said that trueborn vampir were rarely sentenced to death. It didn't make sense to cut an immortal life short. Not when they could continue the bloodline.

"If he survives and is imprisoned, he will come after you. He will hunger for vengeance, and you will be his prey," Eldar said. "Kill him now and claim that it was self-defense."

"What if nobody believes me?" she asked.

"Then kill them as well and come to me," Eldar said as if that were a perfectly sensible idea. "I'll take care of you."

Yara felt her resolve grow stronger. She had to kill Dante. Eldar was right. If she didn't kill him, he would come after her one day for ruining his life. Lugrezia would likely disinherit him for betraying her, and he would have nothing to lose. He would satiate himself with her death. She had to protect herself. Just as she had against Augustus Maleinos.

She had to erase Dante Carrara from this world.

"I need to wake up," she said.

"Find me when it is done," Eldar said.

Yara nodded. "Goodbye."

"Stay safe, my little mouse."

———

It took an hour before Dante returned. He walked with confidence, as if he knew he would win this battle. Yara crouched low in the corner, waiting for her moment, and when it presented itself, she struck. Her claws cut his throat, blood gushing on her palm like a scarlet river. He spun around and caught her throat in a painful hold.

"You filthy whore," he snarled, eyes wide with rage. "I will end you."

"What a clever insult," she said, just as she slammed her elbow down on his arm, feeling the bone snap in two.

She'd been diligently training with Mircea and Volkan the past few weeks, and was skilled enough to hold her own in a fight. It had been almost three months since the war at Poenari. Three months of honing her weakness into a strength. She would never be overpowered again. "How long did it take you to come up with that?"

Dante charged at her, using his weight to knock her down. She fell hard enough to feel a painful crack down her back. Her legs felt numb, and she knew he'd injured her spine. His fingers wrapped around her neck, prepared to snap her neck again. Yara screamed in rage before she pushed her fist through his chest, feeling the bone break under the force of the impact. She felt the heavy wet slab that made his heart and grasped it in her delicate fingers.

"Lugrezia will kill you," he bellowed.

Yet his eyes widened ever so slightly in fear.

Yara's lips lifted in a cold smile. "I'd like to see her try."

"Please," Dante whispered. "Please, don't—"

Before he could finish, she'd ripped out his heart and tossed it away. It hit the wall viciously and she watched as his face grew grey and empty. She wiped the blood on her ruined shirt and lay there for twenty minutes, waiting for her spine to heal. Once she could wiggle her toes, she stood upright and left the room, her head held high, shoulders braced.

"*It is done*," she whispered.

Yara could feel him. She couldn't explain it, but it felt as though there was a shadow in the corner of her mind.

A thing that did not belong, but also somehow felt safe.

He didn't say anything, but she could feel his approval surround her like a warm blanket.

XXX

Yara made her way from the dark cellar to the main hall. She had come out into the servants' quarters covered in blood and, to her surprise, the servants had barely flinched at the sight of her, which made her wonder what horrors they'd seen during their service. She saw Volkan down the hall and she straightened, feeling a pinch of sorrow in her stomach. She'd hurt him, but she hated that he hadn't given her the chance to apologize. Instead of working out their troubles, he would rather pretend as if she didn't exist. His absence had forced her in some inexplicable way to turn to her vicious monster—Eldar Demirci.

"Why are you covered in blood?" Volkan asked.

A small crease lined his brow. His bone-white hair was messy, and he had a faraway look in his eyes, like he did that night she'd found him under the table. Like the ghosts that tormented his mind were haunting him again.

It was clear to see his mind was clouded with substances, and he smelled of herbal smoke and wine.

"You are speaking to me now?" she asked sharply.

It had been three days since they'd last spoken. She had tried to be patient to give him time to come to her, but she wondered if he even cared to fight for her or if he simply sought to erase her from his life. And that thought scared her. She loved him. Even when she was confused and afraid, she had never stopped loving him. But she had always wondered if perhaps she loved him a bit too much, if everything she felt was heightened by their connection as his sired and if he could ever feel half as much as she did. It frightened her to think he did not feel as she did.

She would not survive the loss of him.

"What happened to you?" he asked, gripping her elbow.

"As if you care," Yara snapped. "If you did, you would have looked for me. I've been gone for over eight hours, and you didn't even look for me."

Her voice cracked at the last sentence. She could have died, but he had been too busy drinking his problems away to notice. Dante had been right. Volkan simply did not care.

"I would have looked for you," she whispered. "If anything had happened to you, I'd burn this place down for you. But you weren't there. You weren't there when I needed you most!"

Eldar was there. Eldar had come.

"Yara, speak to me," he said gently. "What happened?"

"Dante kidnapped me," she said, unable to meet his eyes. She felt raw, like someone had stripped her naked and she couldn't find a way to conceal herself. "He took me to a dark cellar and pinned me with wooden stakes. There were two in my thighs and two in my shoulders, and I was stuck."

His jaw clenched. "Where is he?"

"Dead," she said.

He placed his palms on her shoulders, a sad look in his eyes. "You must have been so frightened. Yara, I'm sorry."

He pulled her to his chest, and she felt his arms wrap around her. She leaned her head on his chest, inhaling his soothing scent.

"I don't want to fight anymore," he said. "But I need to know the truth: do you like Eldar?"

"I am confused," she whispered. "We have a sire bond."

The words slipped past her lips, despite how badly she wanted to swallow them. She had to be honest with him. For them to work, she had to tell him the truth.

His jaw clenched. "Since when?"

"Since I turned," she said. "I wanted to learn how to use my voice of command, so I tolerated him, but then he would find ways to keep me coming back. There was always one lesson or another he wished to teach me."

"You never said anything," he said.

"I didn't want you to feel like he had leverage over you. I only have one with him, because it is incredibly rare to have one sire bond, and unheard of to have two. You are bonded with Thaddeus. You couldn't be bonded to me as well," she said. "It doesn't mean Eldar is more important than you."

"So, you've been spending time with him," Volkan said, rolling his tongue in his mouth as if he tasted something sour. "Since the day you turned."

"It was a mutually beneficial relationship," she said.

"He must be so smug," Volkan said with a dry laugh. "He has his throne and realized that all that power means nothing without a person to share it with."

"Maybe," she said. "Or maybe it's another one of his games. It changes nothing. I will not stop my war for him. We are destined to kill each other."

"You've said a lot without answering my question," Volkan said, staring at her in an intense manner that was unlike him. "Do. You. Like. Eldar."

It had been purely hatred at first, and Yara liked to think it still was. She knew that at the fundamental core of her heart, that hatred still lingered like a stain, but it did not bloom and unravel as fiercely as it once had. She hated him for hurting her and the people she cared about, for holding her in his arms on that grim throne and promising her the dark future she longed for, only to tear it away from her in the next breath. But there was a small part of her that was drawn to him, to his brutality, along with his cruelty and monstrousness. Just as she was drawn to his odd kindness and tenderness that he'd never shown her before. That he'd never shown *anyone*.

Eldar had never looked twice at any woman. It was as though they did not exist. And to be the focus of his attention was both flattering and terrifying.

"I don't know." Yara sighed. "I wish I knew, Volkan. It would make everything easier."

"Do you like me?" he asked.

"Far more than you know," she whispered. "I love you, Volkan. I don't want to lose you."

"Sever your sire bond," Volkan said, holding her chin. "End it, Yara, and you won't lose me."

She felt his arms wrap around her, and she felt so unbearably sad. The ache inside her grew tenfold, spiraling into a web of misery. He was right: she had to end this bond with Eldar. It only hurt Volkan and confused her.

And in the end, she could not change her destiny.

She was made to destroy Eldar Demirci.

––––––––

"He is dead," Mircea whispered harshly. "How?"

Yara shifted nervously on her feet. His heavy brows were twisted into a menacing stare. She'd waited until he'd left the hall before she pulled him into the adjacent library.

"I had to defend myself," she said. "It was him or me. He intended to betray Lugrezia." She handed him the letter she'd found. "And when I confronted him, he attacked me."

Yara didn't tell him that she had attempted to blackmail him. Mircea wouldn't like *that*.

"Lugrezia will be devastated," he said, scanning the contents of the letter. "You couldn't break his neck? You couldn't immobilize him in a manner that wasn't permanent?"

The veins in his throat stretched across his skin with every raised word.

"It is not my fault!" Yara said. "He was going to kill me. Look at me. He tortured me. This is *my* blood."

Something in her words made him soften, but only slightly.

"I am sorry that you were hurt, child," he said. "But you must see that this reflects badly on us both. Your allies are not supposed to kill your family. He was the heir to the Carrara line. Forget Lugrezia his aunt, what will his mother say to this? What will his siblings say to this? Do you understand the political magnitude of what this could cost us?"

"He almost killed me," she said for the millionth time. "Does that count for anything?"

"You are a sired vampir, Yara," he said. "Nobody would care if a servant killed you. And I do not say this to be harsh, but this is the reality of our world. Some of us were born into power, and others were simply made in our image. If you die, another vampir will be made to take your place. We are limited in number, and you are limitless."

Yara felt a rush of anger at his words. She had already been treated like nothing when she'd been a mortal, and she would not tolerate it now that she was a vampir. She did not care that they were trueborn and she was not. She did not need to be born a vampir to wield power, and she would prove it.

"If you trueborn are so powerful, why did I kill two of you?" Yara demanded.

Mircea's eyes widened before they narrowed in suspicion. "Who else did you kill?"

Augustus Maleinos.

"It doesn't matter," she said. "But I will not be underestimated or spoken down to. I have the power to make all of you tear out your own hearts. I have the power to bring down the entire Carrara line if they make a move against me. You are lucky to have me on your side. Not the other way around."

"There is nothing wrong with having a sense of self-worth, but do not trick yourself into thinking you are invincible," Mircea said. "Many young vampir die every day because their hubris becomes their downfall. See to it that the same fate does not befall you. There is a reason a sired vampir is never in power. You cannot become your own person if you are controlled by another. And you are controlled by two vampir, which makes you far weaker than the rest of your kind."

She wished she could tell him that she *chose* whom she served and wasn't forced to do anything she did not want. Unlike sired vampir who were loyal to one, she was sired by two vampir, which meant that neither had full control of her. If they did, Eldar would have forced her to return to him months ago. It had been three months since the battle at Poenari, and she was still here by Mircea's side. But she would keep her secrets tucked close to her chest. The less anyone knew about her, the better.

Let them underestimate her.

One day she would prove them wrong.

"Lugrezia will lose her mind," he said. "I hope you are prepared to face the consequences of your actions. We'll have a meeting privately to discuss how to proceed."

Mircea summoned Lugrezia to the library while Yara made herself comfortable on one of the high-backed chairs at the head of the table. Mircea looked like he was going to chide her for sitting at what was clearly intended to be Lugrezia's seat in their conversation, but then the doors opened and Lugrezia arrived with her advisors and Domenico. She didn't know what angle Domenico played, but he was sticking close to his mother. Perhaps to get in her good graces or to win a sum of her fortunes.

"Fetch Dante," Lugrezia said.

"About that..." Yara began, but Mircea swiftly cut her off.

"There was an incident," he said calmly. "An unfortunate one."

Lugrezia sat down on Yara's left side. Her advisors did not seem pleased that they had to sit around Yara. But the other chair at the opposite end was missing, so Lugrezia was forced to sit among her three advisors. Stefano eyed her with displeasure, and Yara simply smiled sharply at him.

I am not afraid, her smile said. *I am not afraid of any of you.*

After her altercation with Dante, she refused to let that old fear trickle in. There was no room for doubt and terror. Only a cold rage that had morphed into fearlessness. One driven by Eldar's unwavering belief in her. He had known she would defeat Dante. And for some odd reason, his certainty strengthened her.

"It seems Dante intended to betray us both," Mircea said, sliding the letter her way. Lugrezia read it before she placed it down, folding her palms on top of it. She seemed disappointed but not surprised.

"Never liked him," Domenico chimed. "Can we kill him now?"

"Has he fled?" Lugrezia asked.

"Yara found out the truth, and he tried to kill her," Mircea said. "They fought and ,well, he didn't survive the altercation. You must understand that Yara was tortured and barely survived herself."

"He is dead," Lugrezia whispered. Her head snapped to Yara. "You killed him."

"Unintentionally," she said. The lie was smooth on her tongue. "I had no choice."

"Why couldn't you simply disengage him and flee?" Lugrezia demanded. Her fingers clutched the letter, and her teeth and claws elongated, making her look unbearably vicious. "Or break his neck?"

"I tried," she said. "He attacked me first. He pinned me to the wall with wooden stakes and sought to kill me for learning of his deception."

"You do not kill my family!" Lugrezia roared. "You are a guest in my home."

"Lugrezia," Mircea said gently.

"I want her gone," she snapped. "I want her gone from my sight."

"He was going to tell Eldar that you stood with Mircea. Eldar would have killed you, and your precious Dante would sit upon your family throne," Yara said. "You are pathetic, losing your mind over someone who would dance on top of your grave."

"How dare you insult me in my own home?" she yelled. Her eyes were wild, and she looked mere seconds away from lunging at Yara. "Dante was a child, barely a century old. He was a fool whom I would have taught a severe lesson to, but he did not deserve to die. He is a Carrara, and we protect our own."

"Lugrezia," Mircea said. "She is a child as well, younger than hi—"

"She is not a trueborn," Lugrezia said harshly. "Her life means nothing."

"If I will not be respected, I will leave," Yara said, standing up. "I would rather stand with Eldar than be spoken to as if I am a worthless soldier."

She stood up, palms flat on the table. In truth, she was merely bluffing; she had no intention of running back to Eldar with her tail tucked between her legs, and she owed Mircea her life. But they had to believe that she could leave if she wished it. That she did not rely on anybody.

"Can we all calm down?" Mircea asked. "This is getting out of hand."

"Your little stray is lashing out at the hand that feeds her," Lugrezia said, staring at her with a heavy dose of disgust. "You need to gain better control of your vampir, Mircea."

Yara felt her teeth and claws lengthen. Anger coiled in her stomach, and she had the terrible urge to kill them all. To reduce them to ashes.

"Should I force you to tear out your heart?" Yara whispered.

"Yara!" Mircea bellowed. "Do not dare say another word."

Lugrezia and Yara glared at each other. The room filled with tension. From the corner of her eye, she could see her soldiers straighten and slowly begin to inch closer to her, as if they intended to subdue her.

"*Stop*," she called, letting her voice of command fill the room with its unspoken grip. The men came to a sharp halt, as if their feet were stuck to the ground. Surprise danced across Lugrezia's and Mircea's faces. Nobody had known she had been practicing her power. Nobody knew how much stronger she had gotten since the first day she arrived.

"I will kill everyone," she warned, pointing at the guards. "Get your men in order, before I end them all."

"This is getting out of hand," Mircea said again. "If we cause a rift between ourselves, we won't survive this war. We need Yara. And we need you, Lugrezia. It is an unfortunate accident that Dante did not survive, but he was going to get us both killed, and we should not lose sleep over a traitor."

"I don't like this, Mircea," Lugrezia said warily. "None of this is acceptable. She threatened me, she threatened my soldiers, she killed my nephew, and we are to pretend that it is all fine?"

"We are to work together to destroy our true enemy, the usurper," Mircea said. "We need to work together, not against one another."

"I will stand down if she does," Yara said in an amiable tone.

It was silent for a long while.

"To be fair, she did us a favor," Domenico said. "And Aylin won't like it if she is turned away or punished for this."

"Please, Domenico," Lugrezia said, rubbing her forehead. "Don't even start with me."

Domenico smirked as if he was pleased he was being a nuisance. Yara was glad that, because of Aylin, someone besides Mircea had her back. She still was trying to figure out if Domenico had been the one to send those assassins after Ilyas, but the few servants she'd questioned were deeply loyal to the Carrara, and they unfortunately now considered Domenico to be part of the family.

"Fine," Lugrezia said. "For you, Mircea."

Yara felt the tension leave her shoulders, and she sat back in her chair just as Lugrezia waved at the soldiers who were no longer stuck in place to return to their posts.

"Where is his body?" Lugrezia asked, eyes tight with sorrow.

"In the cellar," she said. "Beneath the servants quarters."

Lugrezia stood up and left the room. Mircea looked displeased, and she knew he intended to lecture her on her behavior, but she didn't want to hear it, so she disappeared before he could say a word.

It had been a long night, and her mind was spinning with all that had occurred. She knew she couldn't see Eldar when she slept; she needed to keep her distance.

She needed to protect what she had with Volkan and not tangle the carefully drawn lines between her and Eldar.

XXXI

Eldar toyed with his family ring, staring out at his court. It was strangely fulfilling to see the Demirci flag on either side of his throne. He hoped Cetin Demirci was watching him from the bowels of hell and seeing him accomplish everything Cetin had dreamed of. His father had always been driven by power.

The festivities of dinner had long since ended, but he liked sitting here in the darkness long after the courtiers were gone. The scorpions on the cloth danced in the darkness, interlocked in their eternal embrace. The Demircis had come from a long line of twins. Every decade, there was at least one pair of twins born to the family. So, it had made sense to have two scorpions to honor the twinned.

Eldar felt a ghost of a smile cross his lips when he thought of her. Sitting before him with her big, brown eyes locked on his, asking him for his advice on how to destroy her foes. He felt something strange and warm in his chest because she'd come to him in her moment of need.

And then when someone had hurt her, he'd felt the pain of her torment echo sharply through their bond. He had felt the terrible fear that he could lose her and there was nothing he could do to stop it. That same powerless feeling he'd felt during the battle at Poenari when he'd come upon the corpse he'd believed to be her.

"My lord," Rahim said. "They've returned."

Eldar sat upright, a pleased smile crossing his face.

"Bring him in," he said.

Rahim hesitated. "They could not find the man you described, but they have confirmed the death of the imperial prince and the sultana. They did not survive the fire. It consumed the entirety of the east wing."

Eldar leaned forward, his fists clenched tight. The screech of his claws echoed terribly around them.

"They had one objective," Eldar said. "Retrieve Beşir Ağa alive."

They were to bring him Yara's father. He was tired of this game of push and pull between them. He needed her here by his side. And if he had to play dirty to capture her, he would do so.

"They found someone else of use," Rahim said. "I will let Commander Grozav explain the mission failure."

The door opened, and Grozav entered with his stern face and dutifully clasped arms. He was an old sired vampir of his grandfather's. Most of the Demirci vampir were made by his grandfather and father. Volkan and he were too young to have many under them. So, he had to make use of the older sired Demirci vampir.

There was a short, old Turkish woman behind him. A *very* angry woman.

"Where is she?" she snapped. "Where is my little girl?"

"Who is this dreadful woman?" Eldar demanded. "Someone better have answers, or I swear on my life heads will roll. Starting with yours, Grozav."

Grozav didn't waver under his threats. "He was not at the palace. He was deployed on a diplomatic mission to West Africa before we arrived. But the old woman said she knew what we were, and we were to return the girl, Yara, back home. I believe she will be a good hostage to bring her back to your side, my lord."

"Yara is not here?" the woman asked. She looked around the hall as if she would magically appear before them. "What of Aylin? And Ilyas?"

"What are you to Yara?" Eldar asked.

"My name is Sevda Ghulam, and I raised those girls," she said, raising her chin proudly. "If any harm has befallen them, I will tear your eyes out."

"Shall I cut her tongue out, my lord?" Grozav asked.

Eldar ignored him. "Does Yara care for you?"

"I will not be used as a ploy to lure her back to your side," she said. "I have looked upon the eyes of monsters who desired her before. Do you think you are the worst man who has hungered for her?"

"Leave us," Eldar said. "Punish your men, Grozav. I will not tolerate incompetence."

Eldar nodded at Rahim to ensure that his orders were followed, then turned his eyes back to the old woman.

"I had a nursemaid once," Eldar said. "Never liked her much. Frankly, I found her intolerable. You remind me of her."

Sevda must have been suffering an ailment of the mind, because she crossed the room with her weak knees and climbed the dais, stopping before him as if she could fight him. Her brown eyes burned with a hatred that reminded him of a certain little mouse.

"What do you want with her?" she asked boldly. "If it is her life you wish to take, then take mine instead."

"I do not want her dead. In fact, I turned her into a vampir to keep her alive for as long as possible."

Eldar barely caught her wrists when she lunged at him, prepared to claw out his eyes.

"How dare you taint her with your curse, with your blasphemy and monstrosity?" she roared, revealing the expanse of her crooked teeth.

"Stand down before I break your arm," he snapped. He was

already angry at her implying that Yara was anything less than perfect. If she was a monster, then she was *his* monster.

She was blinded by her rage and refused to listen to his command.

Eldar did not hesitate to snap her hand. He did not make false threats. The crack of her weak bones filled him with some measure of satisfaction as her howl of pain pierced his ear and she fell to her knee.

Eldar crouched beside her.

"When Yara returns, you will welcome her with open arms. If I get a hint of disgust from you about her nature, I will tear your miserable heart out and feast on your flesh," he promised.

She shuddered beneath him, and Eldar stepped over her.

"She will never love you," she spat, cradling her broken arm to her chest.

He felt the ghost of a smile cross his lips.

She was falling for him.

He could feel it. Just as he was falling for her.

"We will see," he said.

———

Eldar was becoming *very* fond of their secret interactions. He knew a part of her craved him. He had made her, filled her with his blood, and stitched her with the essence of his darkness. She would always return to him. He hadn't been able to reach her in two nights, and he was slowly losing his mind without her. He had been patient, waiting for her to come to him, as she had that night when she'd run into his arms. But she was avoiding him, and with each hour that passed, his patience grew thinner.

"*I need to see you.*" He spoke in her mind.

"*I am busy.*"

"*Liar,*" he said. "*If you don't see me, I'll just keep talking in your mind.*"

"*You don't talk much,*" she said. "*Good luck pulling that off.*"

"*Don't test me,*" he said.

"*One hour,*" she said. "*To end this for good.*"

It was the longest hour of his life.

"Why am I always in this silly nightgown?" she asked, spinning in the meadows.

She liked being outside, so he always made sure they were out in an empty field, *and* he liked her in nightgowns. So delicate and airy, like a forest spirit. All she was missing was her wings.

"You have equal control of this place. It is merely a fusion of our minds," he said.

Yara looked at him doubtfully. "So, anything I think can happen."

Eldar folded his arms. "Try it."

Yara closed her eyes, dark brows creased in concentration.

"Do not strain yourself," he said, lips tilting in amusement.

Her eyes shot open just as Eldar felt the air lick his skin. He didn't have to look down to know he was utterly naked. He could feel his long, dark hair tickling his hipbone.

"Oh, God," she whispered. "I didn't think it would *truly* work."

Eldar walked toward her, watching her struggle to keep her gaze fixed on his eyes, but it lowered slightly. He could have himself dressed in a split second, but he liked having her eyes on him. For her to see every naked inch of him. Nobody had ever seen him this undone. Nobody had ever feasted their eyes on him with equal parts horror and desire. Or he hoped that the burning glint in her eyes was desire.

"I...I'll fix it," she said, squeezing her eyes shut again.

Eldar felt his clothes again, and relief flooded her eyes when she reopened them.

"I tell you that you have control of this world and the first thing you do is undress me," Eldar said, lifting his hand to wrap around her throat, feeling her smooth skin beneath his fingers. "I think it's only fair that I do the same."

"I didn't think it would happen!" she said in a hoarse voice.

"And I didn't see anything."

"Liar," he whispered.

She whimpered when he placed his hand on her hip, fisting her nightgown. Her head lowered to look down at his hand, revealing the smooth expanse of her leg. His pale hand looked sickly against her pretty, brown skin.

"I will give you something else in return," she blurted. "It will be far better."

"Is that so?" he asked.

With every inch he raised her nightgown, she seemed to grow more disoriented. Interesting that she did not push him away or fight him. She submitted to his touch like she was *his*. He had long suspected that she harbored the same attraction that he felt for her, long before he had ruined it and caused this rift between them. But if he had not made her into a vampir, then he would not have this tether between them, and she would still be a mortal, weak and susceptible to the call of death. They were linked together now, for better or worse.

"Yes, I'll give you a secret," she said.

He paused. "Speak then."

"There is a traitor among you," she said. "Someone who supports Mircea, but I presume also pretends to support you."

Eldar didn't react to her words. He knew what she was doing. Yara was a smart girl. She knew feeding him this information would put him in a tailspin. He'd be so busy hunting for the traitor he wouldn't be prepared for her attack.

"And I suppose I won't get a name," he said.

"I do not know who it is. Mircea does not share everything with me. I think he is threatened by my power," she whispered. "You are the only one who doesn't fear me."

He loved it when she manipulated him with her soft little voice and wide-eyed stare. Even if Mircea feared her, she probably loved it. She was not as saddened by it as she pretended to be. He let her nightgown fall back in place and reached up to grip her jaw, tilting her head back.

"You believe me then when I say nobody will ever have your best interests at heart like I do," he said. "Nobody will understand you the way I do."

Yara danced away from him and lay on the grass, staring at the night sky, a strange, wistful look on her face.

"I miss the sun," she whispered.

Eldar lay down beside her. "Then walk outside."

"Funny," she said dryly. "You need to improve your attempts at killing me if that is your best try."

"I've been building my tolerance," he said. "It isn't simply my strength that has improved, but the endurance of my flesh. It is no longer poisoned by the sun. It is still highly sensitive and uncomfortable, but I presume in a few years I may be able to tolerate a few hours."

"Truly?" she whispered. "Do you think I can do that?"

"I'm not certain," he said. "We both sired you, which is to say that you may not possess all of my strengths."

He watched the hope bleed from her eyes, and she turned her head to the sky, that hopeless look in her eyes again. She pretended to rub her cheek, but he knew she was subtly brushing away her tears. Eldar didn't know what to say or do. His skin tightened at the sight of her tears, like he had grown two sizes too big.

"Put your hand by the window during the day. If it is a painful tingle that you can handle, then perhaps you share my affinity, but if your flesh grows charred and blackens rapidly, then you do not share my tolerance."

Yara nodded. He felt a strange sense of relief at the hope that returned to her face.

"I came here tonight to say goodbye," she said. "We must end this. Whatever this is."

"I have a surprise for you," he said, ignoring her pathetic attempt at a farewell.

"Is it a dead body? Oh, or perhaps a new colorful threat. How long did this one take for you to think of?"

"No, it is a gift," Eldar promised. "But you have to come home first."

"I will," she said. "To kill you."

Eldar leaned his chin on the palm of his hand. He stared at her with an intensity that tended to make her uncomfortable and, as expected, she squirmed under his gaze.

"I don't like when you look at me like that," she whispered.

"Like what?"

"Like a black-hearted wolf who seeks to devour me."

"Have you heard of a Sevda Ghulam?" he asked abruptly. The thought that she could be by his side within the fortnight brought glee to his chest. And it took much to hide the smile that ached to pull apart his lips.

Oh, she was getting better at playing the great game. She barely reacted, brushing a strand of hair from her eyes with an indifference that would have surprised him if it were not for the small tremble of her fingers. Such a mortal reaction. Vampir did not have muscle spasms. Yet she still clung to her old habits.

"Who is that?" she asked, feigning curiosity.

"My gift to you," he said. "She is excited for your return. She misses you dearly. I heard her crying an hour ago just thinking of you."

Eldar was trying a different approach, presenting the illusion of a peace offering wrapped in a threat. He stroked her hair, feeling the looping strands tangle between his fingers. His claw soothingly scraped her scalp.

"No threats, my little mouse. Just a gift. She is a guest in my court not to be touched or harmed," he said. "She waits for you."

"And how did you get her? By sending a letter or tearing her from her home?" she snapped. "Was it an act of violence or as innocent as you make it seem?"

"My methods are not worthy of discussion," he replied. "Are you turning your nose up at my gift?"

"And what happens to your *gift* if I refuse to claim it?" she asked.

"It will be discarded and another one will be procured. And if that one isn't enough, then I will find another," he said. "I will not stop until you have returned to me."

She shuddered and pulled away from his touch.

"That is not a threat," Eldar clarified.

"How is that anything but?" she hissed.

"It is what you make of it," he said with a shrug. "But until you arrive, she is a guest at my court."

"You pretend as if you have changed," she said, fingers digging so deep into the earth, it was as if she were one with nature. Her fingers the roots of a tree. "As if you intend to make me your equal, but the truth is you will never see me as anything less than an object made for your pleasure."

"Have I cut her fingers or pulled her teeth out or torn her eyes from their sockets?" Eldar demanded. He didn't mention that he had broken Sevda's arm, but she had disobeyed him and had only herself to blame. It would hopefully heal before Yara arrived. "She sleeps on a feathered bed and is provided three meals a day. So, tell me then, Yara, who has power over whom."

I am losing my mind over you.

"You do," she said. "You won't stop punishing me for choosing Mircea, but you pushed me to him when you hurt me. You wonder why my loyalty is with him, but he has never used my family against me. He has never manipulated me to get what he wants. We are equals. And it doesn't matter if I come or not; you'll kill her if you see fit. You will do whatever you please. As you have always done."

She didn't give him space to speak, just barreled on to her heart's content. "The only time I will return to you is to tear your miserable heart out. And that is my oath. Let God be my witness."

He had almost forgotten how marvelous she looked when she was angry. How her nostrils flared, and her hands balled into little fists and her dark hair fluttered behind her like shadows.

She would belong to him soon.

And that was *his* oath.

XXXII

Yara carried the secret of Aunt Sevda's capture deep in her chest. She had thought to unburden her troubles to Aylin yesterday, but she knew Aylin would run headfirst into danger, and then Eldar would have two people she cared about in his clutches. She could not allow that. She had already lost so much. She could not afford to lose any more.

It was clear she could not fall for Eldar's bait. As much as it tore her apart to leave Aunt Sevda in his clutches, she knew that Eldar was unpredictable. He would likely kill her the moment Yara returned, as punishment. And everything she had worked so hard on would have been in vain. She had been so foolish to think he had changed. That a few honest conversations had made her believe that he was more complex than she believed. That he was a broken beast who would only ever lick the heel of her palm and shred anyone that was not her to pieces.

She had fallen for his lies *again*.

And it was exactly what she deserved.

———

Magno and Tobias stood at the helm of the map sprawled on the table. There were wooden pawns to depict their men assembled by the red X mark that signified the gates of Poenari.

"Magno and Tobias have won my ancestors' many victories," Lugrezia said. "I am confident in their ability to turn this war in our favor."

Mircea leaned over the table, staring at the map of Poenari. "It is safe to assume after our escape that the tunnels are blocked. I had Zuri map out the tunnels on the parchment. The red lines are the underground veins."

Yara stared at the thin lines that ran like cracks beneath the castle.

"We have to assume he's increased security measures as well," Yara said. "We should not underestimate him. He knows Prince Mircea will strike back. He also knows we escaped through the tunnels."

Yara did not want to rush this attack. Everything had to be perfectly aligned. Mircea was eager to go in with torches blazing, but Yara was more cautious. They would only have one chance to make a bid for the throne. If they failed, they'd never get a chance like this again, and that was assuming they survived the aftermath.

"Poenari has the advantage of height," Magno said. "And the villagers are loyal to the Undying King. The hunters had the upper hand last time due to their small numbers, but we will be seen coming. It takes but one hasty letter or an unforeseen messenger to flag our arrival for him to assemble his forces."

"We estimate roughly one hundred and fifty thousand soldiers serve him," Tobias said. "Between the armies of his trueborn allies, the orphaned Dracul vampir army and the Demirci army, that is far more men than we possess."

"So, we lack the numbers and the advantage of terrain," Lugrezia said. "What *do* we have?"

"The element of surprise, if we plan it right," Magno said. "But that is assuming we can pay off the villagers in advance and that they do not betray us, because if they do, we may lose the war before it begins."

"Perhaps we should reach out to our trueborn allies," Stefano said. "See if we can gain further support."

"It has been a little over three months since the fall of House Dracul," Mircea said. "I worry if we wait any longer, he will simply strengthen his rule."

"Men have waited years to unseat usurpers," Yara said. "We must be patient. Tobias, what do you estimate our chances of winning this war are?"

Tobias was excellent with numbers. He thought of things by percentage and probability. So, she was not surprised when he began to scratch on the sheet of paper before him, dark brows creasing in concentration.

"Thirty percent chance," he said. "I reckon a forty-five percent chance is the highest."

"That does not reek of confidence," Lugrezia said.

Mircea sighed. "It is hard to tell who truly supported my brother and who simply wished to be in his good graces. Besides you, Lugrezia, I'm afraid I do not have many allies to convince."

"The Carrara were always close with the Yamazaki," Lugrezia said. "And they've always respected the House of Dracul."

"The Yamazaki have always been neutral when it comes to family wars," Mircea said. "They do not condone violence and won't risk the wrath of Eldar."

"What of Nezhka Kuznetsova?" Lugrezia asked. "She has not been seen at court for some years and is far from the lies and deceit of the usurper."

"Nezhka was wed to Luan Osakwe," Mircea replied. "The Osakwe have always been close with the Demirci. Cetin even intended to have the boys wed to Osakwe's little princess, Nikolina. It is a conflict of interest."

"Nezhka is strong-minded," Lugrezia said. "And Luan is a gentle soul. Even if they refuse us their support, they will not tell

Eldar that we approached them, nor will Nezhka tell her father. And if Nezhka offers her support, we will have forty thousand more men. Let me invite them to dinner. We will test the waters."

"I think it is worth a try," Yara said. "Forty thousand more men would give us a fighting chance. Run us the numbers, Tobias."

It took a few seconds for him to do his calculations before he said. "Sixty percent success rate."

Yara gave Mircea a look that said they had to at least try this angle in the hopes that they offered them their support.

"We will invite them and see," Mircea said.

Lugrezia nodded at them in dismissal. Chairs screeched as everyone left the room. Yara was a bit worried by Domenico's absence. He hadn't been pleased by Ilyas's return, and she worried that he was plotting something. She had wanted to warn Aylin yesterday, but it had slipped her mind. In learning that Aunt Sevda was in the hands of their enemy, she hadn't had time for a visit. Not since Aylin had begun to sleep in the barracks. Her sister had said she wanted to stay close to the soldiers and continue to train alongside them in preparation for the war. Yara also suspected that she wanted to be near Ilyas.

She heard Thaddeus's and Volkan's laughter before they appeared around the corner. Her heart raced at the sight of him.

"I'll see you in the dining hall," he said, squeezing Thaddeus's shoulder. Thaddeus's eyes were narrowed in warning at her. They said, *Hurt him and you will have me to deal with.*

"Well?" Volkan asked.

"It is over," she said. "I'm sorry. It was a mistake."

Volkan wrapped his arms around her, and a soft sob escaped her. She hated herself for hurting him, for thinking that she could outsmart Eldar. He was far more intelligent than she gave him credit for, and while she had been busy trying to manipulate him, he had been the one playing her like a puppet. She had once again fallen for his charm and lies.

"Do you forgive me?" Yara asked.

"I don't want to lose you, Yara," Volkan said. "You are the only thing that makes sense to me."

Yara pulled away, resting her hand on his cheek. It felt good to be with someone who did not fill her with doubt and pain. Volkan felt like home.

He bent down and kissed her fiercely, tongue tangling desperately with hers. She felt her body slacken, and his strong arms held her upright as she lost herself in him. She knew then that if the world was tilting, Volkan would straighten it for her. He was her safety. He was *hers*. And she regretted doubting it for even a moment. She hated herself for hurting him, but she had the clarity she required to know that Volkan was the right choice. Volkan was the *only* choice.

A wolf whistle made her break apart from him.

Aylin was grinning widely, and even Ilyas's lips were pulled in a reluctant smile. Pariza was with them, arms tangled with Aylin's. Yara felt a spark of envy that Aylin had a friend that was not her, and because Aylin now existed in a world that did not collide with hers. Yara stayed in Lugrezia's home, while Aylin had moved to the soldiers' barracks to be with Ilyas and the hunters. She missed sharing a bedroom with her sister.

"You are insufferable," Yara said.

Aylin tucked her arm in hers and led her to the Main Hall. Yara decided to sit with Aylin and Ilyas instead of on the dais. Seeing them all together made her realize she didn't spend enough time with the people in her life. She had been so busy plotting this war and colluding with Eldar to strengthen her power that she hadn't enjoyed a night of carefree joy.

Yara sat on one side with Volkan between her and Thaddeus. At the same time, Aylin sat between Ilyas and Pariza.

"What did you do to make her befriend you?" Thaddeus asked Pariza, looking between her and Aylin. "Did you hold a blade to her heart?"

"You know you are not as funny as Volkan pretends you are," Aylin said.

Pariza snickered and Aylin smirked when Thaddeus's smile dropped.

"How about we both tell our best joke and the table votes on the winner?" Thaddeus asked, staring challengingly at her sister.

"Excellent idea," she said. "You, first."

Thaddeus clapped his hand, sitting up enthusiastically.

"There was once a man who was rather superbly well-endowed—"

"Is this about Volkan?" Aylin asked. "If so, I would like to keep my food down."

"No, interrupting," Volkan said. "I don't think I heard this one before."

"Thank you!" Thaddeus said. "As I was saying this man was called Giant Gavius and all the women were rather fond of him. Except for this one bitter, witch you see Gavius had scorned her, and she had plans—"

"Really? A scorned woman how predictable." Aylin said.

"You are ruining my flow," Thaddeus said. "If you are so amusing you tell yours first."

Aylin straightened with a wide smile. "My pleasure. So, there was a village fool whom everyone knew by his eyes. They were different colors you see which is a fact that has nothing to do with the joke, but I would just like to point it out for awareness. His name was Maddeus."

Ilyas snorted and Yara and Pariza chuckled. Thaddeus was frowning so deeply, that Volkan had to reach over to smooth his brow.

"I won!" Aylin said. "I didn't even need to finish my joke for people to laugh."

"I didn't even say mine." Thaddeus pouted. "And you have more friends at the table, so it wasn't a fair reaction."

It wasn't long before everyone was bickering and teasing. Yara felt a smile tug at her mouth. For the first time in a long while, she felt the warmth of being surrounded by the people she loved. Even though the fate of Aunt Sevda loomed over her like a dark cloud at this moment, all she felt was happiness.

She felt foolish for almost losing everything to Eldar.

She would never make that mistake again.

XXXIII

It was late afternoon when Ilyas arose from his sleep. All the hunters had found themselves following the vampir schedule. It was easier to train and plan that way. He'd carried Aylin from the roof earlier. She liked to watch the sunrise most days and sit in quiet contemplation, but when he'd pushed open the heavy door, he had found her asleep on her prayer mat, curled like a cat. Her body had adapted to the new schedule just as much as his had.

Ilyas had shook his head fondly before carrying her to her bedroom and tucking her under the covers.

He had trouble sleeping due to the blinding headaches he tended to get. He could close his eyes and feel the pain ebb away when he was near her, when he felt the firm beat of her heart against his chest and smelled her lovely scent of oranges and lilies. He missed when they were traveling and shared a tent. He missed her closeness and often looked forward to her religion lessons. His faith had been important to him, so he was starting from scratch.

Aylin was very good at narrating tales about the prophets and their lives. And he looked forward to those evenings, sitting with her at the dining room table and reciting prayers. It felt familiar, like an echo of his beating heart.

Ilyas made his way to the bathhouse. It was empty and he slid the lock into place, pulling his tunic from his chest.

"You must think you've won."

Ilyas spun around, lips curled in a snarl. It was the pale-haired mutt that had been sniffing around Aylin when they first arrived. He'd been keeping to himself upon their return, attempting to maintain a false sense of civility, but Ilyas knew a rabid dog when he saw one.

And it seemed Domenico was done playing nice.

"I see my assassins failed," Domenico said. His fist tightened around a cord of rope. "It is a pity. If you want something done, you have to do it yourself."

Ilyas recalled the vampir who had attacked him when he'd returned with Salvatore to Venice. How it had always struck him as odd that they had found the location of the brotherhood. How it had not made sense that they had not come with an army and that there were only two of them. As if their mission had been personal. As if they had come simply to kill him. Even after Salvatore had one of the men torture the female, she had refused to speak.

His eyes darted to the rope in Domenico's hands.

"Let me guess: you intend to hang me from the walls and play it off like I was so miserable that I killed myself," Ilyas said. "Do you think she'll want you if I'm gone?

"We'll see," Domenico said.

Ilyas ducked just as the glint of a sharp blade whizzed past his head.

Domenico lunged for him, tangling the rope around his neck. Ilyas slid his hand beneath the rope, feeling the burning slash of the thread cutting into his fingers. Ilyas kicked his legs out from under him, knocking him off-balance. He tore his blade from his hip and slashed at his throat, but Domenico twisted out of the way, and it nicked his cheek instead. Ilyas smiled in satisfaction at the sight of his blood smearing his skin.

Domenico lunged at him, kicking the blade from his fingers.

It fell a few feet away from them. They both lunged for the blade, and Domenico grabbed it before he could. Ilyas had barely risen when he felt the wet slide of the blade digging between his ribs. The pain made him clench his teeth.

"You are a worthless piece of shit," Domenico snarled. His face was red with exertion. "You do not deserve to take another breath. You do not deserve her."

He pulled out the blade, and Ilyas stared down at the wound. A thin slit that resembled a smiling mouth was engraved in his side. It dripped into the lining of his trousers, soaking the fabric. Ilyas did not have long before he passed out and left his fate in Domenico's hands. He tackled him with everything he had and dug his fist into his face. Ilyas was bigger than him, and with each blow of his fist, he could see Domenico's eyes roll back in his head. Ilyas gripped his head and slammed it down onto the marble, hearing the satisfying crunch of bone. And then there was only silence. His blank green eyes looked at the ceiling, empty and lifeless.

Ilyas crawled away from him, pressing hard into the wound to stanch the bleeding. He was losing too much blood and needed to be treated soon.

Ilyas walked to the door and found Marcello waiting for him outside, one of the younger hunters who tended to follow him around to ask a dozen questions about training and combat. It didn't shock him in the least that he had come to disturb his bath. For once he was relieved at the sight of him.

"Make sure nobody goes in there," Ilyas said, gripping his shoulder. "Guard it with your life."

"Are you well, Don Elijah?" he asked. His face had whitened like a sheet. "That doesn't look too good."

"Borza will stitch me up," Ilyas said, patting the boy's chest.

He winced at the gesture, which had strained his wound. Borza was good at patching up the hunters. For a large man, he had surprisingly steady fingers. And Ilyas could not risk being caught by any of Lugrezia's men or using her healers. Vincenzo, their healer, was resting at the main home, and to summon him at this hour would raise suspicion. Domenico was Lugrezia's child. If she discovered that Ilyas had killed him, she would call for his head.

Borza was not pleased to be awakened when he rapped thrice on his door. Some of them had trouble following the new schedule, and Borza was one of the prime complainers.

His eyes widened at the sight of his wound. Ilyas's fingers gripped the doorframe, chest heaving and sweat dripping down his face.

"Fix me," he said, just as the world blackened and he collapsed.

———

Ilyas felt a blinding pain in his side and hissed when he moved. His entire body ached as if someone had dragged him behind a horse.

"Easy," Borza said. "You need to rest for a few days. No training, no walking, no fucking."

The door burst open, and he winced at the loud sound. Aylin's fingers gripped the doorframe. She had an ashen look on her face, and her bottom lip trembled. He flinched at the sight of her visible distress.

"You told her," Ilyas asked accusingly.

"You didn't tell me not to," he said, with an indifferent shrug.

"It was implied," Ilyas said.

"I will let you both speak," Borza said. "Your girl deserves answers."

"How could you keep this from me?" Aylin asked. "Who did this?"

Ilyas wasn't prepared for her questions. In an ideal world, he would discretely dispose of Domenico's corpse and recover in Borza's care until he was better. He wasn't ready to tell her that he killed someone she may or may not have cared for. He didn't know what her history was with him, and a part of him was afraid to find out. Pariza had hinted that they shared something that night in Hungary. Something that frightened him.

He couldn't bear the thought of her looking at him with mistrust.

Aylin sat on the bed, fingers hovering above the angry red stitches that covered his left side.

"Who did this?" she repeated. Her jaws clenched tight. "I will kill them."

"They are dead," he said, in a detached manner. He couldn't lie to her. Not when she looked at him with so much worry and rage it made his heart race. He couldn't describe what it felt like to have someone who believed in him and wanted him unconditionally. Someone whom he would burn the world for just to keep them warm.

"He is dead. Domenico. I killed him," he continued. "I had no choice."

Her hand pulled away, and she stared at him with a stricken look, as if he had just slapped her. He flinched again.

"He was our friend," she said in a small voice. "That can't be."

"He was not *our* friend," Ilyas said tightly. "Certainly not mine. He confessed that he was the one who sent the assassins to Venice to kill me. And he had come to finish the job. He attacked me. He injured me."

"He wasn't a monster, Ilyas," she said, furiously wiping the tears from her cheek. "He was young, and he had a bad life. His father—"

"I don't care," Ilyas said sharply. "I don't care about his story. He is dead. And he does not deserve to be mourned."

Domenico was a vile man, undeserving of her tears. A manipulative bastard who intended to play his death off as self-inflicted while Domenico remained to pick up the pieces of her heart. He would have killed someone she loved just to be the victor. What kind of man did that make him?

"Where is he, Ilyas?" she asked.

Ilyas turned his cheek away from her. How could she speak of the man who intended to murder him with so much gentleness, as if he hadn't nearly bled to death because of his assault? How could she care more about him than Ilyas? Did she love him more? Domenico had to have believed so to be driven to such lengths.

"Ilyas, this is not about you," she snapped. "He was my friend. He took care of me when you were not there. I never got to say goodbye or explain my decision or even speak to him, and now he's gone."

Ilyas clenched his jaw. Jealousy, anger, and madness twisted his gut. Every tear she shed was a tear that was not for him. He wondered if she regretted that he was the one who survived, if she would look a little less broken if it were *him* sitting before her.

"Where is he?" Aylin asked again.

"In the bathhouse," he said. "If he is not disposed of, his mother will come for my head."

He wondered if she even cared that this would come back to bite him in the arse. She seemed dazed and sad, as if he were not there. She stood up and left, whispering a few words to Borza that he could not make out.

"Take it she wasn't too pleased you've gone off and got yourself hurt," Borza said, the bed creaking under his weight.

"She doesn't care," Ilyas said, staring out the window. All of the vampir mercenaries slept in the bunkers that ran below the barracks, far from the windows and terraces, but the humans remained up top. He stared at the skeletal branches scraping the glass with their barren fingers.

"She was choked with emotion when she told me to look after you," Borza said. "That girl loves you with everything in her."

Ilyas hoped she still felt that way and she forgave him for Domenico's death. He could feel her absence, and it tore him apart that she was with him now instead of Ilyas.

He had every intention of waiting for her, but exhaustion pulled at his limbs, and he fell into a deep, empty sleep.

XXXIV

Aylin walked to the bathhouse. Her heart was full of pain. She hadn't loved Domenico, not the way she loved Ilyas, but she had cared for him. He had found her sister for her and protected her with everything he had.

She had always known there was something darkly disturbing about Domenico. The fact that Ilyas had been hurt in Domenico's pursuit of her was proof of that. Domenico was dangerous and, while she was upset he was dead, she still believed that he deserved to be mourned. Lugrezia could *never* find out about his death. That meant that Aylin would be the only person who would mourn him. And the thought saddened her.

"Ilyas sent me," she told Marcello, who guarded the door with a serious expression that was more endearing than frightening. "Can you summon my sister and ensure that she comes alone?"

Her fingers trembled when she turned the doorknob, and she swiftly locked it behind her.

Domenico lay on the marble floor. His face was pale, and his green eyes were wide open. A sob split her chest open, and she fell to her knees beside him. His hand was cold when she clutched it tightly between her own.

"I'm sorry. I'm so sorry, Domenico," she whispered. "I wish I had done more to seek you out. To explain why I picked him and to not leave it up to fate. You didn't deserve this. I wanted you to be happy, even if it was not with me. I wanted you to live, even if I wasn't the reason your heart beat."

Aylin fell onto his chest and mourned the life he'd lost. To see someone so young cut down so cruelly was wretched. She didn't blame Ilyas, not fully, but she did blame him for his reaction. For staring at her like she was a fool for being sad, for dismissing her feelings because he had no love for Domenico.

"Aylin?" she heard Yara ask cautiously from outside the bathhouse. "Marcello said you needed me."

Aylin wiped away the tears and stood up on weak legs. She unlocked the door, and Yara gasped. If there was someone who could erase this mess and protect Ilyas, it was Yara. Aylin would have never involved the old Yara. Her sweet, innocent younger sister would not have known what to do. But the Yara who had survived ordeals she could not begin to fathom assessed the situation swiftly, taking stock of the damage.

"Is that Lugrezia's son?"

Aylin pulled her inside, locking the door behind her.

"He and Ilyas had a fight that took a terrible turn," Aylin said.

"Lugrezia will have Ilyas executed for this. The vampir have their own law, and this is her home."

"I know," Aylin said. "But he was provoked. Domenico attacked him. Ilyas is injured, and I'm afraid for him."

"Domenico has been missing for a few days. That can work in our favor," Yara said. "We will bury him. Grab me the cloth over there."

Aylin pulled as much cloth as she could. It was stacked on a wooden rack, intended for those who bathed to dry themselves. Yara piled it on him till his entire body was covered in cotton.

"Get Marcello to ensure a clear path out for me, free of any eyes," Yara ordered.

"How will we carry him?"

"I'm a vampir. I'm stronger than I look," she said. "I'll do it."

Aylin nodded and relayed her orders to Marcello.

"How are you so good at this?" Aylin asked.

"I killed a vampir and set up a scene to pin it on Eldar," she said. "I imagine it is easier cleaning one up than setting it up."

Aylin realized there was so much she did not know about Yara. About the things she suffered when she was kidnapped, about this person she had become whom she scarcely recognized, but at times was shockingly predictable. It was Yara, but she was changed.

"We are good," Marcello whispered.

Yara hefted his body over her shoulders, looking surprisingly small under his weight.

"You should stay behind," Yara said. "Clean up the blood. Marcello and I will handle the rest. You trust the boy, right?"

Aylin stared at the wide-eyed boy and nodded. "He is loyal to Ilyas. And we are doing this for him."

"I'll do anything to keep him safe," Marcello echoed. "Just say the word."

Yara nodded. "I'll find you when it's done."

"Thank you," Aylin said.

Aylin had just finished cleaning the floors to a shine and making sure not a drop of blood remained when Borza came to her with a grim look on his face.

"What?" Aylin asked.

"I've brought a healer to him even though he refused. He has a fever, and Vincenzo thinks it's an infection. It's not looking too good," he said.

Aylin felt like she was about to be sick. It seemed like everyone she cared for was being taken from her.

Borza rubbed her shoulder in a gentle, almost fatherly gesture and guided her to his bedroom, where Ilyas rested.

Vincenzo, the old healer, looked wary when he stepped out.

"Can't say the boy doesn't keep me busy," he murmured. "Gave him some herbs to fight the infection. The next six to eight hours will determine if he survives. If the fever breaks, he will live to tell the tale. If not…"

He did not need to elaborate. From his pursed lips, she could tell what fate awaited him.

"Send for me if his condition worsens," Vincenzo said. "Make sure he is comfortable and drinks water every hour."

"Thank you both," Aylin said. "I'll look after him."

Aylin cracked the door open. Her heart clenched at the sight of him. He looked terrible. His skin was a horrid pale grey in the candlelight. His hair was plastered to his forehead, damp with sweat, and his lips were dry and colorless. His eyes were closed, and he mumbled under his breath, speaking Hungarian words she did not understand.

Aylin curled beside him, pressing her fingers to his forehead. His skin was so warm, he felt like a fire pit. He released a small groan at the touch of her cold flesh. She brushed away the damp strands of his hair, stroking his brows.

"Shh," she said softly. "Everything is fine."

He sounded distressed, mumbling under his breath in tangled words she could not understand. She occasionally heard him whisper her name. Ilyas twisted, resting his head on her chest and leaning into her absent touch. His hand gripped her ribs so tight they ached.

"Don't leave," he whispered against her skin. His words were a frantic prayer. "Please, don't leave me."

His eyes opened. He looked feverish and disoriented, staring at her in confusion before relief flooded his features. Aylin opened her mouth to ask how he was feeling, but she felt the warm press of his lips on hers, desperately stroking her skin. His tongue didn't hesitate to explore her mouth. The weight of his body pushed her deeper into the bed, and she felt her fingers tangle in his dark hair. It was difficult to be angry with him when he was so clearly upset, and she needed him to focus on healing, not their argument. Despite it all, she would be here by his side. She would *always* be by his side.

"Ilyas, you need to rest," she murmured against his lips. "Vincenzo is worried you won't make it to nightfall."

"Let me worry about myself," he mused. "I'm a hard man to kill."

His lips were on hers again, punishing and hot. He was kissing her like he was angry at her.

"I won't let you leave me," he breathed. "I won't lose you. I'll *never* let you go. If you walk away from me again, Aylin, I will not survive it."

He was panting hard, like he couldn't quite catch his breath, and she frowned, pushing him back down.

"Stop kissing me, Ilyas," she said sternly. "You need to focus on healing."

Aylin brought a cup of water to him and forced him to drink more. Then she pulled the blankets over him and left his side to sit in the chair in the corner. He clearly had no interest in resting when she was nearby.

"Come back," he said hoarsely.

"No. Sleep," she said. "I won't let you exert yourself needlessly."

Ilyas groaned, but within moments he was asleep again. Her heart clenched in fear that he might not awaken again. Hours passed, and she watched him, refusing to close her eyes in fear that she'd lose him if she took her eyes off him. Once she was satisfied that he was asleep, she returned to his side to watch over him more closely.

He awakened a few hours later, falling into her arms during his twists and turns, always seeking her like he was tethered to her. When he spoke, his words were a soft confession whispered into the crook of her neck, as if he were afraid to look into her eyes.

"I am madly in love with you, Aylin," he said. "I cannot exist in a world without you. I am nothing without you. Even when I lost my memories I could feel your absence, as if someone had torn out my own heart. You are the light that guides me. You are my reason for existing. You give me purpose. I will follow you in life and death. I will follow you for as long as my legs can carry me. And if they fail me, I will crawl to you."

"Ilyas," she whispered.

Her heart felt full, as if everything she had ever longed for had been given to her wrapped in the breath of his words. As if she had achieved the greatest feat by simply being worthy of his love.

He leaned forward, and she felt his warm mouth on hers again. His words were a tangled mess between them. Her heart raced, pounding like a fist in her chest. His big hand lay flat on her chest, as if he knew just how chaotic her heart was. She could feel the gentle pressure of his fingers, absorbing the sound.

"You need to heal," she said, drawing back. "And rest."

Another dramatic groan escaped him, but when she rolled him over with a stern look, he'd fallen back to sleep.

A soft knock sounded, and Aylin rose to find Yara outside. She had changed into fresh clothes and her hair was braided in a loose tail.

"It is done," she whispered.

Aylin nodded. "Thank you."

"How is he?" she asked.

"He has a fever, but he is the strongest person I know," Aylin said, staring at him fondly.

"I will pray for him," Yara said.

"You pray?" Aylin teased.

Yara chuckled. "We can't all be as pious as you."

Aylin reached for her, surprising herself, and Yara held her tight. It was impossible to imagine life without her sister. Even when her world was crumbling around her, the sight of Yara eased her troubles.

Much like when they were young, they were two halves of one whole.

And she never wanted to lose her again.

XXXV

It had been a week since he last saw her, and Eldar could feel himself falling into the darkness. It was like the light had been sucked from his world. As if a giant hand had smothered the flames of the candle to wisps of smoke.

"Was this what it felt like?" He wondered. "To miss someone."

He stood above the map in the war room. He had sent Rahim to get an updated list of all the lands and property owned by the trueborn to see who could be sheltering Mircea. There were only three families who had sent a lower family member as a delegate to confirm that they supported his reign. The Kuznetsov, the Carrara, and the Yamazaki were more private and less inclined to visit court for months at a time, whereas the remaining six families enjoyed the splendor and politics of court.

"You have been staring at this all day," Rahim said. "Perhaps some distance will clear your mind."

"He is amassing an army," Eldar said. "I can *feel* it."

Eldar could not let him get the chance to strike. It would destabilize his rule. People believed that Mircea was dead, or at the very least, a lone wolf with no power or support. If he arrived at Eldar's doorstep with an army, it would prove that the Draculesti were alive and stronger than ever before.

He was not foolish enough to think the vampir adored him. He was harsh and cruel. Not only had he put himself in charge of their betrothals, which had caused much displeasure, but he had also punished anyone who had objected by cutting off their worthless tongues. As far as everyone knew, he was inciting unwanted attention with the mortals by attacking the Great Palace at Constantinople. And while his initial intent was to find Yara's father, it wasn't the only motive he had for the attack. Eldar's moves were never uncalculated and certainly not foolish.

He had heard intel from his spies that a Venetian diplomat and an ambassador of the Church were going to Constantinople to raise a matter of grave importance to the sultan. It was evident that the thorn in his side known as Salvatore Di Mazi intended to seek an alliance with the Turks against their common enemy, the vampir. And while the vampir were stronger than the mortals, they did not have the numbers the mortals possessed. If the Romans and the Ottoman Empire banded against them, they'd be extinct within the century.

So, he had plotted the attack suspiciously during their visit. The Ottomans were already wary of the Venetians, and this attack did not help smooth over tensions. The sultana and the imperial prince had both perished in the fire. And there was an investigation going on, which Eldar had ensured would lead to suspicions falling on the Venetians. So long as the mortals fought their petty wars, it meant he and his kind were safe.

"I want delegates sent to these three families tonight," he said. "Do not send a letter or notice in advance. I need to know if there is anything suspicious going on. If they are sheltering the traitor."

"I'll see to it that it is done," Rahim said. His eyes drifted to the door. "Uh, what do you want to be done with the old lady?"

"Who do you call old?" Sevda snapped. "You are no younger than me. Your curse merely prevents it from showing on your skin."

Eldar sighed deeply. "Who was in charge of guarding you?"

"I pretended to faint, and he went for a healer. Fool!" she spat.

"May I ask why you are disturbing me while I work?" Eldar asked.

"I am losing my mind, trapped in that room. Breaking an old woman's bones and locking her up like a prisoner. What has the world come to?" she said. "Boys your age are supposed to be helping their elders, not torturing them."

She had the audacity to slap his shoulder and peer down at his map in curiosity. It seemed, much like Yara, she was one of the rare people who were not frightened of him.

"Is this the hunt for my girls?" she asked.

"Your precious Yara knows you are trapped here, but she refuses to come and save you. She must find you just as insufferable as I do," he said.

He felt some measure of delight at the crestfallen look on her face.

"Then she has become a lot wiser than I remember," she said. "I am old and dying, while she has much to live for. No use saving an old, dying woman."

"So, it seems I'm stuck with you," Eldar said, glaring at her. It was clearly *her* fault that Yara didn't even find her worthy of saving. Now he wasn't quite sure what to do with her. The obvious choice would be to snap her neck and permanently silence her. But he was trying to prove a point to Yara that he would not hurt her anymore.

And he knew that if he ever hoped to win her heart, he would have to show it.

———

Eldar was surprised she found him that night. They were in his old bedroom. It was strange and intimate, and he supposed that's why she chose it: to intimidate him. Now that she knew she had control of their world, she hadn't hesitated to use her imagination to build it from the ground up. She was cloaked in the shadows, and he had awoken resting on the bed, dozens of pillows behind his back.

Eldar raised his knee, draping his wrist over it.

"You've been causing me a lot of trouble," she said.

"Have I?" he asked, tilting his head.

He liked to pop into her mind unannounced, often with a sarcastic comment on his tongue. She ignored him, but it was clear to see his persistence was being rewarded with a visit.

Her claws drifted along the smooth mahogany of his armoire, tearing the glossy finish like it was paint. She had a dagger in the other hand, hidden between the folds of her nightgown. Interesting. She thought she could hurt him, but this was not real, it did not exist outside their minds. Hence, she could not cause any bodily harm.

Eldar leaned back, watching her darkly. Her vicious and cunning mind would belong to him one day. They would plot *together* instead of against each other.

And they would be unstoppable.

She was close enough to touch, and he couldn't resist tangling his fist in her dark hair. He coiled it along the length of his wrist till his claws scraped her scalp and he yanked her close to him.

He felt the phantom touch of her blade sinking into his flesh. It felt like a faint sting and then nothing. There was no blood and no scar. And the frown that crossed her face delighted him. The last time she had tried it, it had been ineffectual due to their bond. But it was impossible to understand the complexity of their bond because she was also sired by Volkan. Perhaps she could hurt him, or maybe she had known in her heart that it would not faze him.

"I hoped..." she whispered.

"You hoped it would kill me," he said.

Her jaw clenched, and she caught his wrist. "Release me."

Eldar tugged on her hair until she fell on his chest.

"I'm going to enjoy watching Mircea unseat you. He is the true Undying King. He is the one that I will bend the knee to, whom I will serve with loyalty and grace," she said. By the venomous nature of her words, it seemed she was trying to provoke him, to get a reaction from him. "You are an imposter, a usurper and a traitor."

Eldar felt the steady thrum of anger. His teeth ground together, and his claws lengthened.

Bend, serve, loyal.

The words tangled in his mind in a poisonous loop.

"You would rather be his servant than my equal," he said tightly. "You would rather be nobody than be my queen."

"Exactly," she snarled.

His fist tightened, and he pulled her to him. His palm lay flat on her jaw, and he kissed her roughly, swallowing the little squeak of surprise that escaped her. He felt the burning rush of rage and desire twist his insides. Nobody drove him as crazy as she did. Nobody provoked him, angered him, delighted him and tormented him as she did. It was like she had a fist inside his chest with the power to kill him or save him. He licked every corner of her mouth before he lowered his head pressing biting kisses to her neck, inhaling her sweet scent of jasmine.

"You're ruining me," he said.

"And you are destroying me," she said, pulling away from him before he could devour her some more.

He licked the taste of her off his lips, and she shuddered. Her eyes were soaked with guilt.

"I should have never come," she said. "Do not speak to me in my mind. Do not call me to this place. Just leave me alone. I have chosen Volkan. I love him. I want to be with him."

The words cut him like a blade. It was the reaction she had likely intended when she'd stabbed him with that dagger, except this hurt ten times worse.

"What did you think, Eldar?" she asked coldly. "That I would go against everyone I love for the boy who betrayed me? The boy who *continues* to betray me?"

He had always known he would have to fight tooth and nail to gain her interest. Volkan was a worthy rival. Volkan had been luring girls to him from a young age. He knew how to flirt, and to seduce. Eldar often felt painfully out of place with Yara. Killing, maiming and usurping a throne: those were his fields of expertise, not making a girl smile, not making a girl happy.

It did not surprise him that she'd picked Volkan, but it did hurt, more than he thought it would.

"What if I released her as a gesture of goodwill?" Eldar asked.

He regretted the offer as soon as he said it. His father was probably rolling in his unmarked grave at the thought that he would utter words so unbearably weak. Cetin had been a ruthless man. Eldar had sworn that he would be twice as ruthless as him when he grew up, and that he would accomplish everything Cetin had failed to. So he knew then he would have to find a way for this to benefit him. He would have to find his best tracker and ensure that she followed the old lady directly to their hideout. Where Yara was, Mircea was. Once Mircea was gone, he would have better luck drawing her back to him.

Yara stared at him suspiciously. "Release her where?"

"Somewhere neutral," he said. "You can send someone to retrieve her."

"How do I know this is not a trap?" she asked. "That you won't simply kidnap whomever I send?"

"It is an exercise of trust," Eldar said. "You must trust that I will keep my word, and I will trust that you will return to me once I have proven that I am willing to concede to you and you *alone*."

"Truly?" she whispered. "You will free her?"

"If you promise to return to me soon after," he said. "As you know, this is not my preferred method of gaining results. So, I need to know I can trust you."

"You can trust me," she said eagerly.

Eldar felt her arms wrap around his lean shoulders in a tight embrace. He felt a strange warmth in his chest, like someone had lit a fire within him. When had been the last time she had touched him so willingly and so earnestly?

It felt different.

It felt good.

But would she forgive him when she learned it was just another trick?

———

Eldar's claws clicked impatiently against his armrest until his guest swept into the room.

He had called back the messengers he had sent to visit the missing trueborn families. There was no need for investigating. The old nursemaid would lead him straight to his little mouse.

Bahiti Ramose stared at him with unimpressed eyes. It was clear to see she was still sour about his broken engagement. If she had it her way, her daughter would be the Undying Queen, whom she would manipulate to further her goals. But he did not want the demure Akila. He never had. He had intended to tolerate her for power, but now the thought of ever being trapped with her when his vicious, magnetic Yara existed was a sickening thought. Yara was his equal. Yara was his forever.

"How may I be of service, my lord?" Bahiti asked.

"I know you are upset by the events that occurred after I overthrew Dracul. But I do not wish for us to be estranged. I think Akila would be well suited for Volkan," he said. "I can arrange a new betrothal."

Volkan would need a distraction once he stole Yara. While Eldar felt no enjoyment at the thought of hurting his brother, he wanted her with a blind focus, and any obstacle in his path would be carefully removed.

"Your drunk and silly brother?" Bahiti asked, wrinkling her nose.

His nails dug so deep into his armrest a crack appeared like a seam.

"You insult my brother," Eldar said. "You forget yourself."

Volkan was the best version of him. To insult Volkan was to insult Eldar.

Bahiti looked wary. "Apologies, my lord, but I'm not sure this is the best match for her."

"You may have heard, but I oversee matches now, and this is what I decree."

It would be nearly impossible to get Volkan to do it, but he'd make him. This push and pull that they both had with Yara would not last long. And he did not want any rivalry with his brother.

"I see," Bahiti said.

"This will benefit us both," Eldar said. "You will still be family. You will still be an ally. The Demirci name is worth something. Our family will be the next line of rulers."

Bahiti folded her hands on her chest. "My daughter will not be slighted by your family again. If Volkan does not accept her, then we will retire from the court. You will lose the support of the Ramose."

"I will make sure he accepts," he said.

Bahiti nodded. "What did you need from me?"

"You are the best tracker I know. I need you to follow a woman from a distance. I have cause to believe she will lead us to the hole Mircea is crouched in."

"I'll make sure I am not sensed," she assured him. "I will find you the traitor."

"I bid you good fortune," he said.

"As you wish, my lord."

XXXVI

Yara had been thinking about it constantly. Her conversation with Eldar. It was stuck on her mind, caught like a thorn snagging on flesh.

Eldar thought she was so blinded by Aunt Sevda's return that she would not see the careful trap he was laying for her under the guise of building "trust", but Eldar never did anything selflessly. If it did not directly benefit him, then it was a waste of his time and resources. There was nothing *good* about Eldar. He was all rot and ruin.

She knew him almost as well as she knew herself. It was what she would have done if she were him.

Eldar and Yara were two sides of the same coin.

And so she knew then *exactly* what she had to do.

———

"You speak with him in private?" Mircea roared.

"You are missing the point," Yara said, feeling the weight of the council watching her with suspicious eyes. "He will send a spy with her. A spy that will lead him straight to us."

"You say that like it is a good thing," Lugrezia said.

"It is," Yara said. "We were worried about the terrain and all those unaccounted variables, but if he comes to us, that eliminates half our problems. We won't have to risk reaching out to Nezhka or any other trueborn. Eldar will leave half his army behind to protect Poenari, underestimating our numbers. He will know our location, but not the strength of our army. We will have the upper hand, not him. It is in our best interest to lure him to us."

"There is some merit to this plan," Magno said. "If we know that he is coming, we can begin fortifying the compound. It has walls strong enough to keep them out should they beat our first line of defense. The hill outside leading to the walls is small, but if we know they're coming it will give us an advantage."

They had been fortifying the walls of Lugrezia's stronghold since Mircea and her arrived. It could hold back Eldar's troops.

"And we have yet to send a messenger to Nezkha and Luan," Lugrezia said. "We wouldn't have to risk them turning against us."

"We will line archers on the walls."

Yara's head snapped to the door, where Ilyas stood. He looked terrible. His face was ashen, and he seemed to favor his right side when he placed the weight of his leg on it. She had spoken to him earlier and asked him to join their war strategy meeting. He had been vital in leading the battle in Poenari, not to mention several small-scale battles on behalf of the sultan.

"We will use oil and douse it in flames. The smoke will cloud their sight," Ilyas said. "We will use the hunters as archers, as we've been trained in most weaponry, and use the vampir as foot soldiers lining the trees. I've already had the men split into nine infantries and assigned a leader for each. The second line of defense will slip out the back gates and split into teams of three. They will convene at the center and create a fortified shield, with the stronger soldiers in the back to breach their front line. Once we've contained them, we will send out the majority of the men from our cavalry, with a remaining ten thousand left behind to protect the compound."

"You are young. What experience do you have leading a war?" Mircea demanded.

"I served the sultan's army since I was a child," he said.

"It is a good strategy, my lord," Tobias said. "The boy knows what he is speaking about."

Ilyas folded his arms across his chest smugly.

"You look terrible," Mircea said. "Go rest."

"Will do," Ilyas said, pushing his weight from the doorframe he leaned against. "You are welcome."

"Arrogant bastard," Tobias said, with a hint of respect.

"Wait, Ilyas," Yara called.

She stepped out, stomach twisting with nerves.

"Aylin doesn't know that Aunt Sevda was captured by El—the Undying King," she said. She didn't know how long he had been standing there and if he had overheard that piece of the war council. "I would like to speak to her first."

"Don't prolong it," Ilyas warned. "There are no secrets between Aylin and I."

Yara sighed. "I will. I promise."

Yara returned to the war room just as Lugrezia asked, "Has anyone seen Domenico lately? It has been two weeks since he disappeared."

Yara blinked, staring around the room as if someone would advise them of his whereabouts. She was grateful she was a vampir and her heart rate did not pick up. It was also good that Ilyas was long gone so his heart rate could not be heard.

"No, my lady," Stefano said. "I can put together a search party."

"Please do," she said, worry creasing her brows. "This is not like him."

Everyone left until it was just her and Mircea.

"You've done well, my child," he said, lips stretching in a fond smile. Her heart swelled with pride. He didn't seem as upset that she had a sire bond with Eldar as she had expected. It seemed it wasn't an issue when it was used in his favor.

"It is almost over," Yara said.

She hadn't thought of what she'd do when the war ended. Perhaps she would take Volkan up on his offer to travel the world. There were so many places to see, so many cultures and experiences to be had. Maybe she would remain at court and help Mircea strengthen his rule. She didn't know, but for once there was something to look forward to beyond the horizon of war. Something she could hold on to.

"I will give you Eldar's head," she vowed.

She tried not to think of him. Especially not how, for a small moment, she had melted in his arms.

She wished things were different. She wished he wasn't so terrible and wretched and conniving. But their ending had long been spun by the fingers of fate. One of them would kill the other in the end, and Yara had to make sure it was she who wielded the blade and not the one who was left bleeding.

"I know," Mircea said. "You have served me loyally. Despite being sired by him, you would destroy him and see me rightfully crowned. When we've returned, I will gift you with whatever choice of land you desire and a flock of servants to aid you. You will have a seat at my council table as well."

"Thank you," she said. "It has been difficult the past few months, but I know we will come out victorious."

This plan would work. It simply had to.

Now they only needed to wait for Aunt Sevda.

And Eldar's army would follow.

———

"How could you keep this from me?" Aylin demanded.

Yara flinched at her raised voice. It was never fun being on the receiving end of her sister's temper.

"I knew that you would run to her if you knew he had her," Yara said. "I couldn't risk him holding my true weakness in his grasp. You are the only person I would come for. The only person I would lose everything for."

"Weakness?" Aylin spat. "Is that all I am to you?"

Yara was silent. Nothing she said would be well received. Aylin would go on to her heart's content, and she just had to let her get it off her chest.

"If it didn't benefit your war, would you even make a trade for Aunt Sevda?" Aylin asked.

"Eldar is strong because he doesn't let his emotions get the best of him. If I want to win this war, I must do the same," Yara said. "Besides, Aunt Sevda has lived a long, fulfilling life, and she would not want us both to risk ourselves in a misguided attempt to save her."

Aylin's anger vanished, replaced with a frightened look.

"I hardly recognize you anymore," Aylin whispered. "You are becoming everything you despised."

Yara felt a stray tear roll down her cheek.

"You are lucky, Aylin," she said sharply, "that you can retain your innocence. But if I do not become like them, then I will not survive."

"You do this for power. Nobody is forcing you to fight this war," Aylin snapped. "I asked you to walk away, Volkan asked you to walk away, but you cannot. You are just as obsessed with the Undying King as he is with you."

Aylin turned her back, but just before she left, she could not resist cutting her wide open.

"You are both perfect for each other," Aylin said, chin raised high. "I am afraid you picked the wrong brother, Yara."

———

Borza returned with Aunt Sevda a week after their council meeting. Aylin had been adamant that Borza go retrieve her since she trusted him most, and Ilyas was still recovering from his injury.

"I don't trust your men," she had snapped at Yara when she offered to send someone herself. It was clear to see Aylin still had not forgiven her.

Aylin sat by the windows in the alcove, staring wistfully outside, when Yara placed her hand on her shoulder. Aylin jolted, staring up at her with a wary look. It was strange for her to not smile or delight in her presence. It hurt Yara more than she cared to admit.

"You need to start wearing a bell around your neck so we can hear you coming," Aylin grumbled.

"You're just jealous I can now lay you flat on the mat without breaking a sweat," Yara said.

Sometimes they sparred, but it was never an even match, since Yara was stronger than most vampir, which meant she was leagues away from mortals. Aylin was a stubborn fighter, and her sister was always pleased when she got in a jab or two. Most days Yara let her, just to see her victorious smile.

Aylin scoffed. "I take it easy on you."

It felt good that she was speaking to her. Even during their nastiest squabbles, Aylin always forgot about their troubles the next day, while Yara would cling to her anger for weeks until her father begged her to forgive her sister.

"Do you forgive me, then?" Yara asked. "For everything?"

Yara sat down beside her and reached for her hand, feeling the rough pad of her thumb, calloused from all her training.

"Aunt Sevda is being released to us," Aylin said. "I know you did what you thought was right, but..."

"But?" Yara asked.

"But I feel as though my sister is gone," Aylin said, looking at her sadly. "I wonder if some part of you died that night in Poenari."

Yara felt her chest tighten at her words. A burning need to snap back at her and tell her that she did not know what she had suffered consumed her. Aylin had never been a blood slave. She had never had her agency robbed from her. She had never been tortured and hurt and broken. She did not know what it was like to not know if you'd survive to see the next day.

"Oh, look, I see two figures approaching," Aylin said, sitting upright, ignoring the turmoil that Yara faced.

Yara's vision was far superior, so she knew it was Borza's big frame, and the dainty figure covered in a thick velvet cloak was Aunt Sevda.

"See you outside," Yara said, disappearing before her sister even stood up.

Air rushed past her as she flew down the stairs. Yara miscalculated her speed and nearly knocked Aunt Sevda down when she wrapped her arms around her. For a moment, Yara felt such shame it choked her, for being prepared to sacrifice her, for only accepting Eldar's offer in order to outsmart him.

"I'm so sorry," she whispered.

"My little Yara," Aunt Sevda said. Her warm, buttery voice slipped over her like a soft blanket "You are not as I remember. You've become hardened, and not just your skin," she said, giving her a light pinch as if to test the strength of her skin. "But here." She placed a palm flat to her heart.

From the sad look in her eyes, Yara wondered if Eldar had told her that she'd abandoned her, and she flinched at the thought. He was cruel enough to do such a thing.

Aylin pushed her aside, stealing Aunt Sevda from her.

"As unruly as I remember," Sevda said. "What has become of your hair, you little monster?"

"Didn't have you to comb it, so I shucked it off," Aylin said with a wicked smile.

"You terrible girl," Aunt Sevda said, but there were tears in her eyes, and she held Aylin so tightly it must have hurt. "And where is your boy?"

"Ilyas is here, but he had an injury, so his memories are lost. He won't know who you are, so he may be a bit prickly," Aylin warned.

"Prickly? He is as sharp as a thorn," Yara said. Ilyas was rather neutral to her, but he was not pleased that she'd upset Aylin. He hadn't hidden his displeasure anytime she had come to visit to check on his health, and she wasn't quite certain how to handle it.

"He'll remember me well enough when I scold him for letting you cut your hair," Aunt Sevda said.

Aylin shot her a look, and they snickered.

"Take me to the boy!"

———

"Who is this woman?" Ilyas demanded.

Yara and Aylin stood mischievously by the door as Aunt Sevda marched in like a general. Her face was stern, but her eyes were fond when she looked at him. She had always liked Ilyas because he was pious and well-mannered.

"Who are you calling a woman?" she demanded. "I am Aunt Sevda to you."

She came to his side and pressed a palm to his forehead, swiping his dark hair aside.

"Once you are well, I will trim your hair," she said. "It is wild and unruly."

"Aylin likes it," he said defensively.

"What do you know of Aylin? You've made a vow to the sultan, or have you forgotten?"

"I don't care about the sultan," he murmured. "Not anymore. I care about Aylin."

"Is that so?" Sevda asked. "What are your intentions for her? Her father isn't here, but that doesn't mean you can sample the goods without purchase."

Aylin choked on her spit, and Yara slapped her back heartily, struggling to control her laughter.

"I assure you I've sampled nothing, as you imply," he said.

"Lies," Sevda said, smacking his hand. "I saw how you looked at her when we arrived. I am old, not blind."

"You are also not my mother," Ilyas said, glaring at her the way he seemed to glare at everyone these days except for her sister. "I will do as I please with Aylin."

Yara's jaw dropped. Oh, this was better than she expected. Between the dark blush spreading on Aylin's face and the scandalized horror on Aunt Sevda's face, it took everything in her not to laugh aloud.

"He jests, Aunt Sevda," Aylin said in a rush. "We have been courting in a proper manner. Ilyas has been nothing short of a gentleman."

"Only because I am bedridden and cannot kiss—"

"Shall we take you to your chambers?" Aylin said, guiding Sevda away from Ilyas. "You must be exhausted."

"He is ruined," Aunt Sevda said, the moment the door clicked shut. "Our pious boy is gone, and there is a wicked devil in his place. You must bring him back to the light of God," she continued. "This is unacceptable."

Yara shot Aylin a look that said, *Good luck*. Aylin sighed as she led Aunt Sevda to bed, her familiar lecture about men and wolves slipping past her lips in a steady hum. It felt like they were children again, young girls being chided by the woman who loved them.

It felt like home.

XXXVII

Volkan didn't know when he decided it, but he knew he had to do *something*. His brother was walking into an ambush, and he couldn't let him die. Not at the hands of Mircea. Yara would hate him for this, but it was the price he had to pay for his brother's life.

"I'll need you to distract the guards at the gate," Volkan said. "Also, if Yara asks for me, make up a creative lie, and don't tell Pariza about my whereabouts. She is a bit too close to Aylin for comfort."

"Where are you going?" Thaddeus asked.

"To warn my brother," Volkan said.

They anticipated Eldar would arrive in the next ten hours. Lugrezia's home had been transformed into a war camp in the past week. Everywhere he looked were men in the Carrara livery and the hunters of the Silver Cross with their shields painted with the crucifix. The tension was high, and while Volkan usually loved the taste of chaos, knowing that some harm could befall his brother was more than he could bear.

"Well, I'll go and distract the guards," Thaddeus said. "I'll whistle when it's clear to go."

Volkan nodded. Thaddeus took a step forward before he returned and pulled Volkan into a hard embrace.

"Don't let him push you around," he said. "Be safe."

"He won't hurt me," Volkan said.

"I never said he'll physically hurt you," Thaddeus said. "He's a manipulative bastard who cares about no one but himself."

Volkan trusted Eldar. A part of him worried that Yara would never forgive him for this. But he could not let Eldar fall. He could not let Mircea win.

Volkan left the castle and made his way outside. He swiftly climbed up the snow-stained arms of a cypress tree. His long limbs clung to the thinning branches, hoping that they were strong enough to hold his weight. The smallest branch hovered close to the top of the wall. It was several minutes before he heard the sharp sound of a whistle. He leaped onto the wall and scaled down the other side.

Eldar's camp was about an hour's walk. He could see the faint outline of the black tents they'd pitched. There was a storm brewing, and the wind wailed like a mournful lover.

Volkan was about ten feet away from their camp when he came to a skidding halt. His leather boots raised a flurry of snow around him. Every weapon in sight was withdrawn from multiple hooks and belts with a hiss. They all wore the Demirci livery, and it was strange to see the pale-faced Wallachian men who supported Dracul stand alongside the olive-skinned Turks who made up House Demirci. All of them wore the livery of his house, and he was shocked by the force of his brother's army.

Volkan drew down the hood of his kaftan, revealing his pale hair.

"Stand down," Volkan called. "You hoist my family sigil, yet you point your blades at me."

They wavered in uncertainty.

"Down," Rahim called.

Rahim had been a close advisor to his father. Volkan was surprised Eldar had summoned him from their family home to help with his reign. Eldar had always thought anybody sired by their father was a stain upon this earth.

Volkan's lips rose in a wolfish grin. "Rahim, my dearest uncle."

Rahim wasn't *truly* his uncle. Volkan simply called him that out of respect.

"My favorite nephew," Rahim said, patting him heartily on the back. "You've returned. To stand by House Demirci."

"Could not stay far away from my better half," he said. "Or should I say my worse half?"

Rahim led him to the big, pointed tent. Two mirrored flags of the Demirci sigil were crossed at the entrance and guarded by four men.

It was warm inside. A fire burned in the hearth, which was merely decorative as the winter did not chill their skin. It was fancy, with a feather bed placed upon a makeshift platform and covered in fox furs. Eldar stood atop a table overlooking a map. His dark hair was stark against his pale face. It wasn't long before his black eyes shot up to face Volkan.

"We have a spy in our midst, it seems," Eldar said with little emotion in his voice.

"Spies are selected based on who blends into a room best. And you, my dear brother, know full well that I shine like a jewel," Volkan said. "Did you miss me?"

"As a whore misses the pox," he spat.

Volkan chuckled. "Your insults are cleverer. Well, I, for one, missed *you*."

Volkan's head appraised the high ceilings.

"You've done well for yourself."

"No thanks to you," Eldar said behind clenched teeth. "Give us the room, Rahim."

"As you wish, my lord," he said, closing the flaps behind him.

"Give me one good reason why I should not tear your heart out and eat it," Eldar said.

"Such vicious threats," Volkan said. "How utterly unoriginal."

A thrill slithered down his spine when he glimpsed the poisonous rage that covered his brother's face like a veil. He did so enjoy poking him, and much like a slumbering beast who'd caught a whiff of its prey, Eldar was quick to react. Volkan felt the shudder of the wooden post behind him as his back slammed into it and Eldar's tight fist coiled around his neck.

"You betrayed me," Eldar snarled. "Betrayed everything we fought for."

"*You* fought for," he clarified. "I did not want a throne. I just wanted Pomona and her cursed family slain."

"And how would we accomplish that without backlash? If I did not claim power for us, we'd be dead or imprisoned for killing them both."

"We are not one person, Eldar. I do not want this life you've built," Volkan said. "I am free to live my own life. I am not your shadow."

"That is unacceptable. We have duties to upkeep, even you," Eldar said. "Bahiti was slighted by my broken betrothal, and I've paired you with Akila. You will wed her before spring arrives. You will do your duty for your family, for your king."

Volkan laughed, throwing his head back. He lifted his hand to wipe the tears that came to his eyes.

"I almost forgot how funny you were."

Eldar shook him roughly. "I do not jest. You will wed Akila in a fortnight. There will be no extended engagement. We cannot shun the Ramose again. We cannot afford to have any more enemies than we already do."

"And let me guess: you will wed Yara," Volkan snapped.

He could feel the anger coiling in his gut. How dare Eldar try to force him into an unwanted marriage, simply so he could steal *his* girl? "She does not love you. She will *never* love you. Look in the mirror, Eldar. You are a monster. You are the spitting image of our father. You are all rot on the inside."

He felt the pain in his jaw as Eldar punched him. Volkan tackled him to the ground, punching blindly, feeling satisfaction anytime he clipped him.

Eldar had never lost control before. He had never struck out at him. A deep voice in his mind told him that he liked Yara more than he let on. That what his brother felt had grown and twisted into a creature far too big for him to slay. It meant that Eldar would win her, as he had won his throne, as he had won everything he had ever set his sights on.

And the fear that he could steal her made Volkan's chest tighten.

"You are weak," Eldar said, spitting a wad of blood on the floor. "You would be dead if it were not for me. I became strong so you could survive, you ungrateful bastard."

"You would never survive what I have," Volkan hissed. "You would break and fall into a hollow shell of yourself. You do not know what true strength is. You never have."

"I'll show you what strength is," Eldar growled.

Volkan watched as those dreadful black veins crawled up his face and his teeth grew in length. He didn't feel so much as hear the resounding crack of his neck.

And then there was only darkness.

XXXVIII

Eldar tossed Volkan's unconscious body off of him.

He stood up and kicked him in the ribs for good measure. As if his brother could best him in a fight. Even before he had gotten so powerful, Volkan had never been a match for him. He methodically removed Volkan's clothes till he was down to his undergarments. He thought about shackling him for a moment, but he was sensitive about chains and being tied down. So, he let him be. He would have his guards ensure that he did not escape.

Eldar donned Volkan's clothes and found the wig he had asked Bahiti for. The Egyptians were known for their wigs, and Bahiti had found him a decent one to match his brother's pale hair. It wasn't perfect. Nothing man-made could ever replicate the glorious white of his brother's hair, but it was a close imitation.

He found a tin of powder to erase the veins that darkened his skin, and he retracted his claws and made sure his eyes appeared normal. It was difficult to control his eyes, to pull back the darkness that spread along their shells. But he had practiced for days, ever since they had received word from Bahiti that Yara's nursemaid had gone to Lugrezia Carrara's house, and that the traitorous family had been aiding Mircea. Eldar had been plotting his scheme.

A quick glance in the mirror told Eldar that he looked quite like his brother. Eldar practiced his carefree smile, but it felt and looked painfully forced.

Very well then, he'd have to fake it.

He hadn't expected Volkan to reach out, but he had planned for it just in case he had a change of heart. Eldar was a meticulous planner, so he had been prepared for all the possible scenarios o ensure he won the war...and the heart of Yara.

Volkan had abandoned him when he needed him most, and he felt little guilt about using him to further his own agenda.

He unlocked the small chest on his table, pulled out the papers he had drawn up a few weeks ago and hid them in the folds of his kaftan.

Everything was going exactly as he had planned.

"Rahim," he barked, stepping out.

Rahim's face lit up, but when he didn't return his good-natured smile, it slowly dropped into a frown.

"It is you, isn't it?"

"I'm going to infiltrate them from within," Eldar said. "Kill as many as I can. When you hear the chaos, then you attack."

"Where is Volkan?" Rahim asked.

"Sleeping," Eldar said evenly. "Have four guards watch over him. He is not to leave until my return. You are in charge, Rahim. Do not fail me."

He nodded. "Never, my lord."

"Do not let your softness for Volkan weaken you," he added sharply.

Rahim preferred Volkan to him. But, after years of witnessing the world bend to fill his brother with adoration, it no longer hurt to be second-best. Eldar had accepted it. But the only person whom he could not tolerate losing was *her*. It did not matter if the world despised him. So long as she didn't, Eldar could survive the rest.

"It is time to kill the traitors," Eldar said.
And bring his *little mouse* home.

XXXIX

Yara fixed her breastplate and tied her hair into a thick braid. She reached for her necklace with the intertwined scorpions, a reminder that she was a Demirci now, and she had the blood of the scorpions inside her. Volkan would be pleased.

It was time to face her demons. To slaughter all of them and come out victorious. They had received word early yesterday morning from their scout that Eldar's army was marching toward them.

Their plan had succeeded. Eldar was coming to her.

The door to her bedroom swung open, and she stared at Volkan. His expression was serious, and she immediately wondered if something was wrong. Volkan was rarely serious about anything. Perhaps he was upset that today they would kill his brother.

"Come," Yara said, reaching out a hand for him. He approached and sat down, stretching his long legs. "I know you're scared, but I won't let anything happen to you."

She could not promise the same for his brother.

"I have something for you. For us," he said.

He tucked his hand in his pocket and offered her a sheet of

paper. Yara unfolded it, her chest tightening at the words. She knew what this was: a *nikah* agreement. A marriage contract.

"I know you are faithful and wanted to follow your religion," he said. "So, I've had the papers drawn up as per Islamic law. I've listed out your dowry and had two witnesses oversee my signature."

"I can see that," she whispered, fingers shaking as her eyes scanned the words. He had been *very* generous with the dowry. Her mind spun at the sheer thought of owning so much wealth. He was offering her a seaside house in Marrakech, a villa near the Balkans, and an unnamed castle in Wallachia. This didn't include the staggering sum of coin, solid gold, and a dozen thoroughbred Arabian horses being offered. Along with the two hundred servants who would be at her disposal and a treasure chest that belonged to Myriam Demirci, his great-grandmother, that was estimated to be worth a fortune.

"I didn't know you were so wealthy," she said. "Or that you were ever interested in being wed. You always said you did not need a piece of paper to prove you loved someone."

"You once told me it was your dream to be wed when you lived in the Ottoman courts," he said. "Is this not what you want?"

Yara stared at the paper, surprised and perhaps a bit excited. She had never had a chance to think of the future. And while Volkan had promised her a life filled with adventure, he had never promised her anything more. A part of her longed for marriage. It was all she had dreamed of for so long. The trueborn often wed for marriage alliances and to continue their lineage, but it seemed the sired vampir did not bother with the tradition. She hated that sometimes she felt like she was lesser than the trueborn, and thus not worthy of being treasured and respected as they were.

"Is this what you want?" she asked.

He was so serious, not a single smile in sight, and it worried her that maybe he was doing this only to please her. Volkan placed his palm on her cheek, staring at her so intensely and darkly it made her shiver. It was unlike any way he had looked at her before, like he'd swallow her whole if he could.

His words were a dark purr when he spoke. "All I want is you."

He stood up and walked around the room till he found an inkpot and quill. He stepped outside and called two of the guards who lined the hallway.

"Your witnesses," he said.

"You haven't made a grand declaration of love," Yara said, fondly stroking his hair when he returned to his seat by her. It felt different, dry and not as luscious as usual. He caught her hand, pressing a hard kiss to the inside of her palm and folding it on his lap.

"I am not a man of many words. I am a man of action," he said.

"You? Not a man of many words?" she teased. "I simply cannot tell who speaks more, you or Thaddeus."

"There are no words to describe what I feel for you. It is consuming and frightening and poisonous. I am completely and utterly spellbound by you. Ever since the day you arrived and looked at me with those magnificent brown eyes, I couldn't think of anything else but you. I have tried to erase you from my mind, but you haunt me, and I know now that you will haunt me for the rest of my days. If you are my curse to bear, I will happily bear it for as long as I live. I do not want to be immortal without you by my side. I do not want power without you there to share it with."

It was an odd speech, not flowery or spun with garlands as she'd expect from him. It was harsh and overwhelming and intense, and when he looked at her it felt as though he looked into her soul. As if he saw every version of her, past, present and future, and he loved them all.

He pressed the quill into her hand.

"Sign the letters, my little—" He paused. "Yara."

"I want Aylin to be here and, oh, how could you not think of

Thaddeus! If Aylin is here, then Ilyas will be here too. And I'd love it if Mircea could give me away. I know he is not my father, but I love him as one."

He frowned as if the thought of all those people were disturbing.

"Sign first, celebrate after," he said.

"I never knew you were so impatient to be mine," Yara said, absently stroking his cheek. She was pleased by this turn of events. If she won her war today, then she would consider herself truly blessed. She would have victory *and* she would have Volkan.

Volkan brought the sheet closer to her, and she stared above the line next to his. He signed it with his surname and Yara signed it with her maiden name. She had thought for a second of signing it with his surname to please him, but she did not want it to be considered invalid.

She looked at him, and the relief in his eyes made her insides twist. Her cheeks ached when she smiled, and she threw her arms around him. He waved away the guards, and she tightened her hold the moment the guards stepped outside. It was over. A simple signature and they were husband and wife. There was no ceremony, no flourish, just them. It was not the marriage she expected, but they could throw a grand celebration after. All that mattered now was that he was hers. Volkan, a beautiful, thoughtful, and occasionally foolish boy, was now her husband.

"I will be the best wife in the entire world," she whispered. "I have so many plans for the wedding celebration. I want peonies and lilies everywhere. There must be lilies, and, oh, performers and acrobats. And I want to wear a red dress with crystals and beading that weighs more than a king's ransom."

"Anything you wish shall be done," he promised. "My little mouse."

A shiver rolled down her back.

"What did you call me?" Yara whispered.

"My little mouse, my Yara, my wife."

A troubling thought ran through her mind, and she pulled

away from him. She looked at him, truly looked at him. His eyes were not expressive, they were terribly dead. She should have noticed it sooner, and she cursed herself for it. His lips were firm and didn't have the smooth flow of Volkan's, who was used to smiling often.

My little mouse.

"How?" she asked in a choked voice.

"I needed to see you," he said. His claws descended, long and menacing. More deadly and vicious than Volkan's. He stroked her cheek, and she watched his eyes darken into pools of onyx. "I needed to touch you."

"Where's Volkan?" she asked warily. "Does he know you are getting married to people under the guise of his good name?"

"No, don't think he'd like that," Eldar said.

Because he *was* Eldar, and if she hadn't been so blinded by joy and desperation, she would have known that. Of course Volkan hadn't done this. He had never spoken of marriage or even hinted that he had an interest in the act. Volkan had never made such a heartfelt confession to her. He was still afraid of sharing his true emotions. Now that she truly thought about it, it had been Eldar to whom she'd confessed and told that she had craved marriage that terrible night on his throne.

"Every word I spoke was the truth. I want forever with you, Yara. You can become the Undying Queen," he whispered in that sensual voice, ripping off the harsh wig to reveal the silky black strands of his hair. He held out his hand for her, and she stared at the delicate black veins she could see now that he'd pulled off his leather gloves. "Stand by me. And I will reward you."

"You expect me to betray the only person who ever helped me at court. Who took me under their wing when you tormented and threatened and hurt me?" she whispered. "I won't betray Mircea, the rightful king."

"Pick me as I have picked you, and I will spare your loved ones. But stand against me, and I will burn everything to the ground," Eldar promised. "Nobody will be spared from my wrath."

Yara clutched her dagger. Her fingers had slipped to her sheath as he spoke, and the handle was cold beneath her finger. She had one chance to end him. But something coiled in her chest. The sire bond was restraining her. It made her fingers stiff and clunky. Her teeth clenched as she struggled to pull her hand free; it felt like it weighed a hundred pounds. She was sired by them both, which meant that she was not fully loyal to one or the other. Perhaps she could kill him.

It took everything in her to unsheathe the dagger and plunge it into his chest. It squelched terribly as blood sprung from the wound, and he stumbled forward, clutching his chest. Pain laced his face, twisting his beautiful features, and she felt the barest flicker of sorrow. Blood spilled out his mouth, an inky black stain pooling on the ornate carpet.

"Eldar," she whispered. Her voice was thick with regret, and she stepped toward him, fingers unknowingly skirting the bleeding wound as if she could contain his lifeblood. Tears sprang to her eyes.

"Eldar," she repeated, this time a bit more stricken.

His fingers clutched the dagger, and he yanked it out of the torn fabric of his kaftan. It clattered to the floor, the ringing sound making her flinch.

"That was the wrong choice," he said between clenched teeth.

She watched in horror as his skin stitched back together, and she drew back her fingers in shock. It should have been fatal. But besides a bit of coughing and blood, he seemed fine.

"You're not dead," she whispered.

"You missed," he said, rising on shaky knees.

The attack had weakened him, but only barely.

"If I were you, I'd run."

She didn't have to be told twice.

Yara ran.

XL

The tail of her braid flew behind her. Her mind spun with all that had happened. He could have used his disguise as Volkan to cause mayhem, but instead, he had used it to deceive her. To lure her into a false marriage agreement. In Eldar's twisted mind, he likely thought he had won her. That a piece of paper would ensure that she was his alone.

"Keep him contained," she instructed the guards. "That man is a threat. He is the—"

She could not finish her words before the door caved in. The guards didn't have a chance to react. His fist tore through both their chests and swiftly ripped out the bloody pulp that was their hearts. They collapsed in a pile behind her. Eldar smiled at her, licking his fingers clean of the blood. Somehow the gesture appeared vulgar, his eyes locked on her as if he were tasting her. Her eyes widened slightly, tripping a bit over her own feet in a graceless manner and nearly crashing down to her knees.

"Run," he mouthed.

Yara hated that she was forced to flee him. He walked behind her while she ran as fast as she could. It was demeaning. But she could not fight him. He was more powerful than she had thought.

"He is here!" she screamed. "The Undying King is here!"

In every hall she passed, she shook the guards into action with her loud bellows.

For each guard that she roused, another was quick to fall to Eldar's cursed hands. All she heard behind her were screams and the heavy thud of bodies dropping to the floor. They were no match for him. They'd need to find a way to contain him. To surround him so he could not escape. With Eldar here, perhaps their army had a chance to defeat his soldiers.

Yara leaped off the top stair, falling into a crouch at the bottom. The chaos from upstairs had brought the guards who protected the first floor to attention. Lugrezia stood among sixty men in the foyer. Their eyes widened at the sight of her frantic form, and she quickly stood to face them.

"What is the matter?" Lugrezia asked.

"Eldar Demirci is here," she said. "We must call the guards to protect this area. It is the only way down. We cannot let him descend. We cannot let him escape."

Lugrezia opened the front doors, and the soldiers who'd been guarding the front yard poured in by the dozens.

Yara prayed that it was enough.

"Where's Mircea?" she asked.

"The main hall," she said.

"Half of you, guard the hall," Yara said. "Half, the foyer."

"Almost missed the fun," Aylin said, swinging her blade around. "Ilyas said they are marching forward. I think the Undying King is just a distraction for what is to come."

"Either way, he dies tonight," Yara said firmly.

And this time she would strike true.

She fell into a crouch, unsheathing her claws. She preferred to fight with blades, but this was the way of the vampir. It was quicker, more straightforward and less messy. There was no need for weapons when her body was a weapon.

Everyone stood at attention. They outnumbered him. Even if

they could not kill him, they could capture him. They could immobilize him. They could imprison him.

Someone stumbled forward from the hallway as if they had been pushed, and Thaddeus stared at them with his hands raised. Water dripped down his chest, and he had a cloth loosely wrapped around his hips as if he had been interrupted during his bath.

"I was enjoying my bath when I was attacked," he grumbled. "It is like nobody respects me. It is like I do not even mat—"

Thaddeus looked to the corner before he nodded firmly. "He says if I don't get to the point, he will cut out my tongue. He says to bring him Prince Mircea, and he'll imprison everyone to be sentenced at court. If not, then only death awaits the traitors."

"Tell him to stop being a coward and come out," Yara said. "We have him surrounded."

Thaddeus looked at the wall.

"Oh, he says that..." Thaddeus paused dramatically. "That I look delicious enough to ravish. And oh, he's going to kill you all."

Something barreled into them with such force, it took out a half a dozen men. Yara stared at the severed head of a dead woman. Her vacant eyes stared up at the ceiling. Several more heads were volleyed in such rapid succession the men had to duck to escape them. Those who didn't were swiftly injured. One of them was hit so hard in the face, she saw the fluid of his shattered eyes slip down his cheek and heard the miserable crack of his facial bones. Yara fell to her knees, pulling Aylin down with her. The carpet was drenched with blood and gore, and the innards of the soldiers spilled from the gruesome holes in their torsos. The severed heads Eldar had volleyed towards them had cut through the men like glass.

"How many bloody heads does he have?" Aylin grumbled. She cried out when someone fell atop her legs.

"You're hurt," Yara said, pulling her out swiftly.

"Just a small twist," Aylin said, but her eyes were shuttered in pain. "I'll be fine."

Dread slithered down her spine. Eldar was too strong. They had to vacate the castle and take the battle outside. They didn't have the numbers to fight him, not inside the castle at least. They'd have better luck outside.

Yara gripped the shoulder of the closest soldier. "Lure him outside."

He nodded pushing forward to pass along her command.

"We need to get to Mircea. The castle is compromised," she said. "Shall I carry you?"

Aylin shook her head. "I can walk."

Yara wrapped her arm around Aylin's neck and pulled her in the direction of the double doors. There were three rows of guards standing with their weapons drawn. They created a narrow path for them to pass. Yara heard the shattering screams of the soldiers they'd left behind, and she looked back to find that Eldar had long since descended the stairs. He cut and tore with a grace that could almost be described as beautiful.

She watched with her heart in her throat as he caught Lugrezia by the neck. He had cut through her shield of men like they were nothing. It felt like time stilled when he held her high above him, dangling her like she was a doll. His face was covered in blood. His black hair was tangled and wet with gore. His teeth descended past his lips in an animalistic snarl.

"No, no, no," Yara said. Her voice was a broken whisper.

Her fears unraveled before her eyes as he dug his hand into her chest and cut out her heart.

Then, just as she had anticipated, he took a bite of it. Another trueborn for him to devour. Another person's power and lifeblood to steal.

For a moment it felt like the world paused, and it was only the two of them. His eyes locked on hers, and then his lips peeled back in a wicked smile, blood coating his white teeth. Those monstrous veins multiplied like a disease. He moved so fast that it was almost like he had disappeared for a moment. She didn't see it happen, only the end result. Bodies fell in limp piles, and their torn hearts plopped down on top of them like grave markers.

"That can't be good," Aylin said.

"We need to get to Mircea," Yara said.

"I need to find Ilyas," Aylin said.

Yara grabbed her elbow. "It's too dangerous to go out there. We need to find Mircea and regroup. Mircea is the priority."

"And what of Ilyas? He is fighting a losing battle."

"He is a soldier. He knew the risks."

Yara said this in a factual manner, but Aylin reacted as if she had just confessed to his murder. She stared at her like she was a stranger.

"How could you say that? He gave up everything to save you when you were taken. He sacrificed so much for you," she said. "You would rather save a vampir than Ilyas."

Yara opened her mouth to tell her that everything he had done was for Aylin, not her. If Aylin asked him to help her find a white stone in the ocean, he would be the first person to drain the water and start searching. Nothing had ever been done for Yara. And now that he didn't have the memories of their history, he didn't have to pretend to like her. The Ilyas he was now would not blink if she were killed before him. But there was no time for arguments and indecision.

"Mircea is the face of this war. Without him there is nothing," Yara said. She reached for Aylin's shoulders and shook her. "Mircea is all that matters."

"To you," Aylin snapped. "He is all that matters to you."

She dove under Yara's arms and crawled under the legs of the guards, attempting to evade her. Yara cursed under her breath. She didn't have the time to chase her stubborn sister. She'd figure out Mircea's escape route and ensure his safety and then come back for them both. She pushed forward.

"Keep the door locked. Guard it with your life," she said to the sentries.

It sealed shut behind her. Zuri lunged at her, blade to her throat.

"What is going on out there? How did they breach the gates so soon?"

Mircea was behind her, staring at her suspiciously.

"Eldar pretended to be Volkan," she said. "He's inside and he's fed on Lugrezia, so he's stronger than ever. We need to escape and reconvene."

"Of course, your little partner ran off to confide in his brother and gave him access to our stronghold," Mircea barked. "This is all your fault. You and your foolish heart! Lugrezia was our only ally, and she is dead because of you."

"Mircea, I—"

He pushed past Zuri, and she felt the cold grasp of his hand around her throat. His nails sliced deep into her neck, and a whimper escaped her lips.

"You are sired by them. I thought you could be trusted, but you cannot. For all I know, you let him in with open arms," he said. "You let the snake inside to inject us with its venom."

Yara looked around the room. There were no doors or windows. It was fortified. They were trapped.

"What are you doing?" she asked, wincing from the pain when he pulled her closer. His nails were so deep in her skin that she could not pry him off, and when she tried, he simply banded his other arm over her chest, containing her flailing arms.

She opened her mouth to use her voice of command, but Zuri pried her mouth open and stuffed a rag deep down her throat, forcing her to choke on her words.

"*Leverage,*" Mircea whispered just as the doors were torn open.

And the Undying King came to destroy them all.

XLI

Eldar was covered in so much blood. It trailed behind him in a crimson puddle. His hair was matted in a long black tangle, and he had discarded his kaftan and tunic. His chest was bare. Rivulets of blood slithered down his collarbone and chest, staining his dark trousers that hung loosely on his slim hips. He raised his hand and licked his fingers clean again.

"I'm aroused," Thaddeus said behind him, dressed in the stolen garb of a fallen soldier. "Oh, I'm not allied with him. I'm not a political person. You can say I am unaffiliated. Just here to watch."

He drew out a dinner chair in the corner and sat down, crossing his ankles and watching them with rapt attention.

"What is that you have over there?" Eldar asked Mircea. He didn't have to speak it for her to hear him say, *I told you so*.

"Your obsession," Mircea said. "You are fast, but I can tear out her heart before you take another step."

Eldar stared at him passively. "You are threatening me with someone who is loyal to House Dracul. Killing her would be in my favor."

"You think I don't know what is going on? I knew the moment she said you had a sire bond that you cared for her,"

Mircea said. "Sire bonds are incredibly rare. One in every thousand trueborn shares such a bond with their sired vampir. Do you know when a sire bond snaps into place? It is not when a sired vampir feels an unbearable attachment to their master. If it were, then all vampir would have a sire bond with their sired. It is when the *master* feels an undeniable connection to their sired. It means you care for her. More than you dare to admit."

Eldar folded his arms across his naked chest. "You would kill someone loyal to your family based on suspicion? I may be a monster, but even I don't kill those under House Demirci. Why do you think that idiot is sitting in the corner?"

"That is terribly sweet of you, Eldar," Thaddeus called.

Yara would have laughed if she was not in so much pain. Every minor twitch of her muscles brought a shooting pain down her neck where his claws dug in, cutting through flesh and muscle and scraping her bone. Blood trickled down her throat in thin strips, and she was beginning to grow weak as she lost more blood.

"We will leave, and once we are gone, I'll release the girl," Mircea said. "Those are my terms."

She felt terribly betrayed by Mircea. She had sacrificed so much for him. Her bond with her sister was cracked, and she had almost let Aunt Sevda to die to further *his* goals. Eldar had been right when he said there would be no reward for her when Mircea was crowned. She would not be his equal. She would be nothing.

A part of her wanted to believe this was a ploy, that he was doing this to trick Eldar. But Mircea was not that intelligent. He was headstrong and commanding, but strategy was not his strength. And he would have warned her before this if it were a ploy. He wouldn't have looked at her like all their misfortune was her fault. He wouldn't have accused her of sabotage and deception.

No, he believed she was in league with Eldar, and he would use her as his scapegoat. He would survive while she would be left at the mercy of Eldar Demirci.

Her body shook, both from the lack of blood and the

ravaging hunger that clawed at her stomach. She needed to feed and replenish her strength. Her mind grew foggy with each minute that passed. Her limbs were weak and dangling as she was painfully held upright by Mircea's callous grip.

"I can't let that happen," Eldar said. "It is over, Mircea. And this last attempt at salvation is rather pathetic and desperate."

Yara screamed when she felt the blinding pain of his hand tearing through her chest. The cloth inside her mouth slipped out, falling to the floor and letting the echo of her pain surround them. She could feel it, the painful grip of his hand around her heart. It felt like being torn in half. Blood spilled from her open chest cavity, soaking the marble floor, blooming like a dark flower. It was a pain unlike anything she had ever imagined. Far worse than Dante's torture.

A wailing sob tore from her throat.

"No!" Eldar roared.

His voice echoed terribly along the high ceilings. His rage was a sound so raw it made her tremble. It felt like her chest was on fire, and she did not know why, but her eyes locked on his, seeking him as she had in Dante's torture chamber. It was like a tether, and for the first time since she met him, she saw his eyes drowning in fear alongside an emotion she could not describe. Something deeper, bottomless, much like the ocean.

"If you are thinking about using the voice of command on me, just know that her heart will be on the floor before you can finish the words." Mircea warned.

"Fine. Run, you coward," Eldar spat. "There is no hole you can squat in that I won't find. There is nowhere you can go to escape me."

"I've changed my mind," Mircea said with a cruel smile. "Beg me. On your knees. Beg me to spare her."

When Eldar didn't react, Mircea shook his hand in her chest, making her body rattle and tearing a cry from her lips.

"Beg me," Mircea repeated. "Now."

Eldar's eyes were locked on hers when he slid to his knees. He refused to look at Mircea, as if he wanted her to know he would only ever bend for her and no one else. As if his pain and misery and humiliation belonged to her alone. It was strange to see him so vulnerable, so undone.

"Crawl to us, you pathetic usurper," Mircea snarled, getting some perverse enjoyment from breaking his pride.

Eldar glared at him. His teeth pulled back in a snarl. "Let her go."

"You have two seconds to do it before I tear my hand out, along with her heart," Mircea warned. "Do not test me, Eldar. A man with nothing to lose is a dangerous man indeed."

How could Mircea hurt her like this after everything? How could he stare ahead so coldly, not acknowledging the pain he was subjecting her to?

Eldar dragged his knees forward, his beautiful face a mask of rage. His dark hair swept the ground, and her heart ached at the sight of him suffering for her. His fists were clenched so tightly that his claws had shredded his flesh. Slivers of his tainted blood ran between his closed fingers, dripping slowly onto the marble ground, leaving behind a trail of despair.

"*I'm sorry,*" she whispered. Her words slipped through their minds, tugging on their sire bond. It was like the wall that had once separated their minds had collapsed, and she could feel the bitterness of his rage and the choking fingers of his fear. She wondered if he could feel her too. From the way his hand tightened and the blood flowed more freely to the ground, she knew that he felt her pain, just like the night Dante had tortured her.

"*It is my fault,*" he said. "*I pushed you to him. I am to blame for it all. You could have been mine if I were not so afraid.*"

"*He's hurting you because of me,*" Yara said. "*He is breaking you because of me.*"

She was a fool for putting her trust in another man. For giving Mircea her loyalty and her kindness. How many more times would she be betrayed before she learned her lesson? How many more times until she realized that the men in her life would *never* put her first?

"*And he is hurting you because of me,*" Eldar said. "*Because you are my weakness, and my enemies have learned the truth. They see what I hid so well before, even from myself.*"

"I knew you were weak," Mircea spat. "Being led by the balls by a woman. Not even a trueborn one at that. A pitiful sired who, not too long ago, was a mortal and who still behaves and thinks and acts like a mortal. You should be ashamed of yourself."

"You dare insult her before me," Eldar said. His words were a mere rumble in his chest.

"How far would you go for her?" Mircea asked with a sharp grin. "Put your hand through your chest. Hold your heart in your palm."

"Eldar, don't—"

Her words were cut off when Mircea loosened his grip on her heart for a split second, and relief flooded her at the absence of his painful hold. But it was merely a trick. A chance for her to relax before he gripped her heart again, twice as hard, making her cry out in pain.

"Stop," Eldar yelled. "I'll do it."

It felt as though the world paused when he unsheathed his claws. She heard the painful splinter of bone as he tore his hand through his chest and gripped his heart. Blood spilled from the wound, gushing forth like a river and soaking the floor in a pool of red. His eyes were twisted in pain, teeth pulled back in a grimace. She wondered how much courage it took for one to harm themselves so viciously. It must have been much like severing one's own limb.

"You're hurting him," she said. Tears slipped down her cheek. "He's in pain."

"*Eldar, please stop,*" she whispered in his mind. "*Do not fall for his manipulations.*"

"*I've just found you. I won't lose you,*" he said. "*Mark my words, Yara. I will die for you. You are my wife. You are my everything."*

His words spun in her mind in a loop. She'd almost forgotten his little trick earlier. How he had pretended to be Volkan to wed her. It had felt like decades had passed since he had spoken his beautiful, cursed vow to her. It had felt like ages ago when he declared his frightening attention and twisted love to her.

You are my wife. You are my everything.

"You know what to do next," Mircea said viciously. "If you want her to survive, you will tear your heart out."

Eldar looked down for a moment. When he looked up at her, his eyes were resigned.

"ELDAR," she yelled in his mind. *"ELDAR, DON'T LISTEN TO HIM."*

His lips lifted in a sad smile.

"I wish I had more time with you," he said. *"I wish I had learned all your smiles and traced my mouth along your body. I wish I had been your happiness as much as I was your sadness and anger. I wish there were a world where you loved me. I wish there were a world where I was deserving of it."*

His face twisted in anguish as his hand traveled forth to rip out his heart. He wasn't as invincible as he made himself seem. He was strong, but even the strong could fall. She knew from his hopeless eyes that this would mark his end.

A painful wail tore out of her throat. She didn't want him to die. She didn't want to lose him. And it had taken this moment to realize that she could love him. She could love him so hard it would ruin them both. It would unravel them till there was nothing left behind but the fragments of their dark love.

It happened so fast. If she blinked, she would have missed it. A blade whizzed in the air and, while Mircea caught it before it hit his eye, the surprise of the attack made his grip loosen.

Yara twisted out his arms taking advantage of the distraction.

From across the room Thaddeus nodded at her. He still sat on his chair; feet kicked up on the table. She felt a good dose of relief mingled with the strange urge to laugh at his relaxed demeanor.

Eldar tore across the room, just as Mircea spun on his heels to capture her again. But Eldar was quicker, and he pulled her harshly behind him and caught on to Mircea's arm, twisting mercilessly, his bones cracking miserably in several places.

Eldar tore at his cheek, yanking off a pound of flesh, revealing muscle and blood and sinew. Mircea's ravaged face didn't have a chance to heal before Eldar tore out another fistful. They were a mere blur of hair and claws and the tendrils of their clothing as they grew more tangled in their battle for dominance.

Yara fell to her knees and crawled away from their fight. She felt a tight hand in her hair and a blade to her throat.

"You're not getting away so easily," Zuri snarled.

Yara elbowed her, enjoying the crunching sound of her broken nose. She twisted around just as Zuri lunged for her. Zuri's claws scratched her cheek, and Yara gritted her teeth against the pain. She had narrowly missed having her eye gouged out. Yara landed an effective punch to her jaw that made her stumble back several paces.

Yara's moves were slow and sluggish. She had lost too much blood. Yet she felt a rush of determination, a need to come out of this battle victorious. It felt like all her months of training had been preparing her for this.

In the corner, she saw Mircea and Eldar circling each other like predators.

"How could he do this to me?" Yara demanded. "After everything I've done."

"You've outgrown your usefulness," Zuri said. "Don't take it personally. You simply cannot be trusted."

"I've been loyal," Yara said. "It is him who betrayed me."

"You are sired by him, by Eldar Demirci," she said. "You will never be anything less than his servant, just as I serve Mircea. It was foolish to think you could be anything more than a being born to serve her betters."

Yara took advantage of her distraction to tackle her to the floor and grab the blade in her boot. Each time she got in a good angle, Zuri would swiftly evade her, throwing her off balance. They rolled on the ground like a pair of wild dogs fighting for dominance. Yara used all her strength to pin her to the ground and raised her blade high above her.

"Then you can die with him," Yara snarled.

She plunged the blade deep into her chest, watching her dark skin wrinkle with age and her dead eyes stare hauntingly at the ceiling. For a moment, she felt a hint of sadness before it was quickly erased by the luminous taste of victory. She had defeated a vampir decades older than her. She had taken someone from Mircea, as he intended to take Eldar from her. Even when she had begged him to spare him, he had callously tried to force Eldar to kill himself.

Eldar had been willing to sacrifice himself while her supposed allies watched from the sidelines.

Yara felt a painful grasp on her hair. Mircea ripped her away from Zuri's body with blinding strength. She screamed, feeling the root of her hair untether from her scalp. He held a mass of it in his fist like it were nothing. The door cracked open, and dozens of Lugrezia's soldiers flooded inside, charging at Eldar like a swarm of bees.

"You ungrateful girl," Mircea snapped. "I should have left you to rot in that prison."

"I gave you everything," she cried. "I put your cause above everyone else. I would have seen you crowned. I would have seen you the victor."

"You let his brother in when we advised you not to, and Lugrezia's death is on your hands," he growled. "Zuri was following you ever since you killed Dante. She saw you dispose of Lugrezia's boy's body. You killed Dante and Domenico. You have been plotting against us since the moment you arrived. You sought to make an enemy of Lugrezia and thus leave me in a weakened position. You have been a spy for Eldar since the moment you arrived."

His eyes were wild and filled with a rage that could not be quenched.

"Domenico's death was an unfortunate accident," Yara said. "And I got rid of him to keep the peace. If I had confessed his death, that would have truly spoiled your alliance."

"You murdered several of our ally's kin. If Lugrezia were alive, she'd tear out your heart herself."

She spoke between clenched teeth. "It. Was. An. Accident."

"And what of Volkan? You insisted he was trustworthy. He ran to his brother the second he had the chance, and shared our plans with him? How else would Eldar be able to disguise himself and breech our defenses?"

"I didn't kn—"

Mircea swiftly cut her off. "The truth is that you are weak, and you are no child of mine."

Eldar watched them both, jaw clenched tight, but he made no move to get involved, as if he wanted her see his true colors. As if he wanted her to see that nobody would ever care about her.

Anger burst from her veins, burning her like liquid fire. She twisted and scratched at his face blindly, much like a wild beast. She would never confess that his words hurt. That it was the worst thing he could have said to her. She had done everything in her power to be strong, to be ruthless, to be cruel, but it wasn't enough. Nothing would ever be enough except for full carnage.

He fought valiantly. He was older and wiser. He knew fighting tactics that she had never known existed. But unlike him, she had the flames of a burning sun tearing her apart from the inside out. She was more monster than girl at that moment. Her steps were fluid. Her eyes were covered in the darkness of her sire. Veins crawled along her forearms like poison. His power rushed through her blood in a frenzy, like a wildfire. It consumed her.

His step faltered, and she took the opportunity to reach for his unprotected chest. She was covered in cuts, and the more she fought, the more her head spun, weakened and hungry for mortal blood. Her vision grew foggy, but she pushed away her weakness and focused with a single-mindedness that Eldar would admire. All she needed was to reach for his heart. The prize that would end this dance of death.

Yara didn't flinch when she saw his eyes widen in horror, when he realized that she had won. One of her vicious reaches had hooked into his skin, and it didn't take long for her claws to burrow between his bones and feel the dead pulp that was his heart. Mircea stared at her with a haunted look. It was the realization that the girl he had underestimated and betrayed had erased him from this world like he was nothing. The moment she ripped his worthless heart out, he fell to his knees, his mouth gaping open in surprise.

Yara lunged over his fallen corpse and clawed his chest again, and again, and again, cutting through bone, and muscle, and mass. A scream built in her chest, ravaging her from the inside out. Blood dripped down her wrist, sinking into the crevice of her arm like a curling river. It stained her skin, leaving behind the essence of the man she had once seen as a father, a friend, an ally. Only to come to the bitter realization that she would always be hurt. She would always be alone. She would always be left wanting.

You hurt me.

You betrayed me.

You broke me.

XLII

She felt a pair of strong arms pull her back, and she sunk into the embrace. Yara could smell his scent of midnight and steel. His arm banded across her chest like a leather strap, containing her fury as if he knew she would come undone at any moment. As if he knew just how far gone she was. Like he could see the ghosts dancing in her eyes.

"You've done beautifully," Eldar whispered. "It is over. We have won."

She felt the weakness she had been fighting off assault her senses till she stumbled into his arms, accepting the strength of his hold. Eldar sank to the floor with her, grabbing a discarded chalice from the table. She greedily drank the blood offered, feeling the budding headache fade away to nothing. The burn that scratched her throat eased, and her vision was clear once more. He wiped the trickle of blood that slipped down her chin and licked his thumb clean.

"You have won," she said in an empty voice. "*Congratulations.*"

Eldar tilted her chin, the sharp point of his claw scraping her sensitive skin. Her gaze fell to his chest, unsurprised that there was no scar, no reminder of the torment he had experienced for her.

Her fingers drifted absently along his pale skin, feeling the flute-thin bones underneath. For someone so vicious, he was built so delicately––all slim lines and feather-soft skin.

"*We* have won," he corrected. "You are my wife. Everything that is mine is yours."

Yara laughed, a cold, withering sound. "That marriage is not valid under any law. You pretended to be your brother."

"And? What of it?" he asked. "It was signed E. Demirci. The E was tangled so deeply with the D, you must have missed it."

"I do not even know how this marriage benefits you," she murmured. "I do not understand you."

I wish there were a world where you loved me.

I wish there were a world where I was deserving of it.

His words haunted her, filling her with this strange burning need to erase his pain. To be his salvation. To simply be *his*.

But she belonged to another, to Volkan. It was hard to feel loyal to Volkan after he'd betrayed her. He had promised that he would not get involved, that he would remain neutral. But in the end, he had chosen Eldar.

And Eldar had chosen her.

"I can show you," Eldar said.

His gaze drifted down to her lips, and she felt his arms tighten around her waist before he kissed her. It was different than their usual rough and lustful kisses. It was slow and lingering, filled with the pain of what they had endured. The fear that they could have lost each other. And while she had been prepared to kill him, she would never let anyone else kill him. He was hers, in a strange way that rang of finality. Her fingers tangled between his blood-soaked hair strands with an obsessive and desperate need.

It was as if their sire bond had strengthened. She could feel his desire wash over her like a white-hot flame, and his hunger became her own. He sunk his teeth into her neck. Even though her blood did not fulfill him, he feasted on her like she was still mortal. Her back arched, feeling his slim fingers race across her torso, dancing along her ribs.

"What are you doing to me?" she asked dazed.

Everything was heightened, but not by the venom of his teeth — that no longer affected her—but by the overwhelming strength of their sire bond. She could not tell where he ended and she began. It was like a cord ran between their hearts. He pulled away from her flesh with a wet, squelching sound. Sharp teeth stained with her blood.

"You want this," he said, almost viciously, kissing her neck and collarbone, scraping his long teeth along her skin, as if in warning. "You want the throne, *and* you want me. You are simply too stubborn to accept it."

"I want you dead, Eldar. I want the crows feasting on your corpse, that is what I truly want," she lied.

She knew she was betraying everyone and everything for this taste of power and desire. But she was too tangled now to rip herself from him without hurting herself in the process. She knew then with a dawning certainty that he had claimed another piece of her for himself, and that maybe he had far too many pieces for her to ever be whole again.

His hand lifted, stroking her cheek back and forth. "Then hate me as you rule beside me. Curse me with every breath in your chest, so long as they all belong to me. So long as you are *mine*."

She had nothing. With Mircea gone, she had no one to lead the charge for the throne. As the Undying Queen, perhaps she could reclaim her lost power.

Volkan had betrayed her. He had ruined everything. If Eldar hadn't infiltrated them from within, they could have won. They could have been marching home as victors now, but he had robbed her of that. It was too late to salvage their relationship. All she could do was sever their final ties. It saddened her, because a part of her had loved him.

There was also a rift growing between Aylin and her, strengthening with every day that passed. Ever since she had hidden Aunt Sevda's captivity from her, she had been wary around Yara. They had never been similar, but ever since she had become a vampir she had changed, while Aylin was still the same person she had always been. She didn't know if she could even fix it. To pick Eldar would be to fracture their strained relationship further.

And of all the betrayals, Mircea's had hurt her worst.

She felt raw from it all. Everything she had once known had burned to ashes around her.

"Everyone has pretended to be something they are not, but I have always been myself. I am a liar, a manipulator, a villain and a thief, and I will never act as if I am anything less," Eldar said, as if he could read her thoughts. And perhaps, in some ways, he could, since she could feel his emotions. He was satisfied. He was pleased. And she was torn down the middle like a seam.

Eldar could never betray her because he had *always* been untrustworthy. From the moment she met him, he had always been a snake. And he had never pretended to be otherwise. In a world of deceit, he was the truth.

"Vlad had many wives, I heard, but none of them were titled," she said. "Being your wife is no guarantee of a title."

"Smart girl," Eldar said, pleased that she had figured it out. "I would need to announce you publicly as the Undying Queen. There is no formal ceremony nor papers to be drawn. Unlike your mortal kings, we are terribly informal."

"So, it all depends on your word," she said. "In that case, I am no longer interested."

Eldar smiled that bitingly sharp smile that brought a jolt of fear to her chest.

"You have so little faith in me."

She wasn't going to fall for this ploy again. He was going to simply drag her back to Poenari, dangling the promise of the title of Undying Queen like a carrot before a horse until she was trapped.

It was time to call for a ceasefire to end the war that brewed outside. Eldar had won and Mircea had fallen. There was no one to lead this war, so these men fought for nothing. Perhaps she could save some of them.

"So, you are picking him?" Thaddeus asked, twirling his cup. He didn't hide the accusation in his eyes or the disappointment in his words.

"Thaddeus, go call a ceasefire. Tell the soldiers to stand down," she said, unable to meet his eyes, so she turned to Eldar. "Per the command of the Undying King, the traitor has been slain."

Thaddeus folded his arms across his chest like a petulant child.

"I am not your messenger," he said. "Go do it yourself."

"Go. *Now*," Eldar said sharply.

He stood up swiftly. "Yes, sir."

"Why does he listen to you and not me?" Yara asked.

"Because I know how to wield my power. Perhaps I shall teach you one day how to evoke true fear, little mouse," he said. His claw stroked her cheek gently, fondly.

"I am your queen, or I am nothing," she whispered. "You decide."

"I will announce you as the Undying Queen before my soldiers. Let them bear witness until we reach home," he said. Eldar removed the iron ring with his family sigil and placed it on her thumb. It was loose and ill fitting, so he removed a smaller ring from her other finger to hold it in place. The ring was cold and heavy. It weighed down her hand.

Eldar pinned her to the ground. A shiver ran down her back when she felt the blood on the floor, soaking her back. It was disgusting, and she opened her mouth to say as much when she felt the hard pressure of his mouth on hers again and the heavy weight of his hips pining her beneath him.

It is all a part of the plan to become the Undying Queen, she told herself as she tangled her fingers in his thick hair, feeling the hard strands of dry blood.

He bit her lip and soothed the sting with his tongue. His hand slid beneath her dress, grazing her bare skin.

"I need you," he said against her mouth. "Now." He licked her jaw, and she shuddered.

"Anyone can come in," she whispered, feeling his hand stroking the inside of her thigh. "I need to speak to Volkan."

The lust in his eyes faded, replaced by a somber look. "Be gentle with him."

Yara felt guilt and dread twist her stomach. Her throat tightened at the thought of breaking his heart. She felt like the worst person alive.

"I must go speak to Mircea's soldiers as well," she said. "Let them know we are standing down."

Eldar nodded. "I'll come with you."

"Perhaps I should do it alone," she said. "They don't trust you."

"We will do it together," he said, reaching for her hand. His long fingers wrapped around her own before he pulled her to his side.

"You are half-naked," she said. "Will you put something on?"

"No."

"People will think you are shameless," Yara said. She lifted her hand, rubbing away the dried blood on his chin, attempting to make him look like anything besides the crazed, bloodthirsty, vampir king that he was.

"My doting wife," he said with a wry smile.

"You never told me how this benefits you. How does having me as your wife and queen accomplish your goals? How does it feed into your quest for power?"

"Maybe this has nothing to do with power," he said, staring at her beneath his thick lashes.

"Then what?"

She looked into his dark eyes and wondered if he truly did love her. He had almost died for her. It should have been her proof that he did, but she could not quite wrap her mind around it. If it were not for the fact that she'd witnessed his love for his brother, she would not believe that he was capable of it.

"You know why," he said softly. And then he tugged her hand, pulling her out the doors as if he did not wish to speak on it anymore. They stepped over the dead bodies, and Yara kept her eyes straight ahead. She could not look down at the familiar faces of Lugrezia's men. Nobody would understand why she had switched sides so fast, why she was dishonoring the dead lady of the castle by standing with the man who slayed Lugrezia, who had slain hundreds with his bare hands and teeth.

A monster. A killer. A destroyer.

To stand by Eldar was to turn against everyone she loved. It meant turning her heart cold and accepting his wretchedness.

They will hate me.

They will never forgive me.

XLIII

Death surrounded her like a cloak. Aylin whispered a prayer to her blade before she cut through the men like thread. She couldn't see Ilyas in the tangled bodies. All around her was a savagery she could not find the words to describe. It was difficult to make out the vampir. They moved with a speed and grace that was a mere blur of color to the mortal eye. She swung her blade in an arc, cutting the throat of a vampir. It was easier to maim them than to kill them. They were careful about protecting their chests. Their breastplates were so thick they were almost impenetrable, so Aylin aimed for the unprotected parts. Their eyes, their throats, their hands. The plan was for the hunters to maim them, and the vampir soldiers would kill them once they came across them in their weakened state.

Her hands were wet with blood and the fluid of their shattered eyes. Her throat was raw from her rage-filled screams. She needed to find Ilyas. Nothing mattered but him. She had checked to see if he was at the top of the gates with the archers, but he wasn't. It was hard to see anything from down here. The field was covered in smoke and ashes.

"Borza," she called, making out his big form. "Where's Elijah?"

"Somewhere. I lost him," he said.

Tears were streaming down her face, the smoke irritating her eyes. Fear tightened her chest; she couldn't lose him not again. Not after everything.

"Ilyas," she cried. "Ilyas!"

"Aylin," he called.

She saw him cutting through two vampir. Aylin was quick to slide her blade into one of them while Ilyas finished off the other. He wrapped his arm around her in a quick embrace, his eyes alert.

"It's getting bad, Aylin," he said. "I need to get you out of here."

"What about the hunters?" she asked. Some of them were in the middle of the thick of the battle while others were on the gates. It would be hell trying to find all of them, and the smoke didn't help.

Ilyas's bloodstained fingers cupped her cheek. "You're my first priority."

Aylin smiled when he brushed his lips across her forehead.

"We can't fall back," Aylin said. "Yara is relying on us to hold back his forces. We must keep going."

It was looking rather bleak for them. Eldar's vampir were better trained than theirs. Some of them had the hardened eyes of vampir who had survived more wars than she could imagine. It would be a miracle if Mircea's forces survived the bloodbath. She looked at Ilyas, who didn't seem to like the idea of fighting on when their odds were so low. It struck her then that the old Ilyas would have fought on. All he had ever known was the life of a soldier. But the Ilyas he was now would choose her over his men, over his own life. It meant everything to her that he would do that for her. All she had ever wanted was to be put before the sultan, before the army, before the empire.

Ilyas shoved her forcefully down, digging his blade into the open mouth of a vampir. Blood poured from the gaping wound that cut through his head as he stared at them with a hollow look.

His arms still moved, and Ilyas was swift to sever them, cutting through bone and mass like it was nothing.

"Oh," Ilyas said, wiping the specks of blood from his face with his elbow. The gesture only smeared it on his face some more. "And I love you."

Aylin chuckled. "I love you too."

————

Aylin had known that fighting a war without casualties was impossible. But still, it hurt to see her fellow hunters' corpses around her.

Borza had a grim look on his face. He was carrying someone, and it took her a long moment to realize it was Marcello. He was two years younger than her, making him the youngest member on the team. He adored Ilyas and looked up to him like he hung the stars in the sky.

"Marcello," she called.

He was bleeding from his temple, and his torso was all wrong, like someone had snapped him in half. Aylin touched his flushed cheeks. Ilyas protected them, cutting at anyone who dared to come close.

"Marcello," she said. She tapped his cheek. "Look at me."

"It hurts, Aylin," he whimpered. His brown hair clung to his forehead in wet streaks.

"I know," she said. "I know, but I need you to be strong for me."

"I can't feel my legs," he whispered.

"It's fine," she lied. "You're fine, I promise."

She looked at Ilyas helplessly. His mouth tightened, but he didn't offer any words of comfort. She could tell he was upset, but he hid it well. Ilyas was not the type to crumble. He kept moving, even when he was in pain.

"Borza, take him somewhere safe and don't leave his side," Ilyas said.

Fear struck her chest like an arrow. She could lose some of them. Pietro and Borza were her closest friends among the hunters, and Aylin knew that Ilyas adored Marcello like he were a younger brother. Despite their differences, these hunters were their family, and she couldn't bear to lose her family.

XLIV

It was chaos outside. The Demirci soldiers had breached the gates, and the mercenaries they hired were struggling to hold them back. The archers were efficient, but their arrows only injured the vampir, not killing them entirely. Thaddeus ran up the stairs to where she stood with Eldar watching the war unfold before them, a bloody scar healing on his cheek.

"They won't listen to anyone but you," Thaddeus said. "Is my face okay?"

"Give them the command, Eldar," Yara said. "Now, before anyone else gets hurt."

"I don't think I will," Eldar said. He surveyed the wreckage before him with a dark gleam in his eyes. "We will watch it unfold."

"Why did you send Thaddeus with the message then?"

"I was hoping someone would kill him while he accomplished the task," he said. "Rahim only takes orders from me. It was a fool's errand."

Yara could see Ilyas cutting through men like water. A short figure fought alongside him, moving like his shadow, protecting his left side. Her heart clenched at the sight of her sister caught between such sharp swords, and sharper teeth. Aylin had barely dodged the attack of one of the Demirci vampir, her head nearly cut off by his choking grip. How much longer until one of them or *both* got hurt? Or worse. Yara couldn't stand by and watch her sister get killed. She bent her knees to run into the carnage, but Eldar caught her wrist before she could disappear.

"My family is out there," she said sharply. "I can see Aylin and Ilyas."

"I am your family, little mouse," Eldar said.

"Then do as I say, or you will only be my enemy."

He gritted his teeth, and for a moment, she was certain he'd refuse her.

"Stand down," he bellowed.

Yara watched in both dread and fascination as his men abruptly ceased their assault. All of them were covered in blood and sweat and the cloying scent of war. Many lay dead in piles of limbs, several of them mutilated and howling in pain, tears trapped behind their sorrowful eyes.

"Stand down," Yara echoed to her soldiers, who appeared uncertain as to whether they should continue attacking the frozen soldiers or stand down as well.

"Our enemies are dead, and all those who stood with Mircea the coward and Lugrezia the traitor will be sentenced once we return to court," he said. "Flee now and you will be hunted and killed."

"That was not what we decided," Yara said.

"You wanted your family spared, and they are spared. But everyone else will pay," Eldar said softly, then spoke louder, "Round them up. All of them."

Some of them attempted to flee but were quickly killed for their insubordination, their hearts torn out mercilessly by Eldar's soldiers and their limp bodies falling with a dull thud. She watched as a flock of soldiers whose breastplates were stamped with the twin scorpions surrounded her and Eldar in a suffocating display of protection.

"Protect her," Eldar commanded them.

They shuffled closer, four of them in front of her and four behind her, and three each on her right and left side, enclosing her in a shield of protection. "She is the Undying Queen, the Great Lady of the Vampir, and you are sworn from this moment forth to protect and serve her."

The force of his words brought forth an intense wave of satisfaction that warmed her bones. When she marched forward to retrieve her sister, they followed quickly on her tail, stern faces staring straight ahead.

She could see a glimpse of her sister between their heavy shoulders.

"Aylin," she called.

"Yara!"

Aylin limped toward her, and Ilyas was quick to sweep her off her feet with a single arm, his blade readied in his other arm. He raised it at Yara and the guards.

"Step back," he growled. His eyes were wild and feral.

"It is me," she said, slipping past the guards.

"Is that supposed to assure me?" he asked. "You stand with the enemy."

"Mircea is dead. We lost the second Eldar infiltrated the compound," Yara said. "I accepted his offer to rule by his side, and in return we will be spared from his punishment."

"So, you will wed him?" Aylin frowned. "Or serve on his council?"

"We are wed," she said. "The papers are signed."

Aylin's mouth dropped in shock.

"And what of my men? Will they be spared?" Ilyas interrupted. "They are good men."

"He is not killing them outright," Yara said. "They will be tried and sentenced. I will ensure that it is done in a fair manner. But we are all absolved, we are safe."

"And what of Borza, Pietro and the other men?" Aylin asked. "They are like family to us. What if they are condemned?"

"They are hunters. Killers of vampir," Yara said. "They have served their purpose, and their deaths are of no concern to me."

"If my men are to pay for aiding *you* in *your* war, then I will stand with them," Ilyas said, with his chin raised.

"Me too," Aylin echoed.

"You are both so stubborn," Yara said, annoyed by their misguided display of loyalty. What one did, the other swiftly copied. It was impossible to rationalize with them. The hunters were made to kill people like her. They stood against her very existence. If they released the hunters now, they would come after the vampir twice as hard. They no longer shared a common enemy and were therefore no longer allies.

"Maybe you should tell your *husband* to let us all go," Aylin said. She said the word *husband* like it was a curse.

"Her husband makes his own decisions," Eldar said, wrapping his arm around Yara's waist, fingers settling possessively over her stomach. "If you want to hang with them, it is no issue to me." He circled his finger and guards surrounded them, carrying weighted chains. They rounded up the hunters, snapping the chains on them. It was a length of chain that ran between the men. Ilyas lifted his head when they did the same to him, staring at her with his icy eyes.

"Not my sister," Yara whispered when they took a step toward Aylin. The guards stood down, to her surprise. They truly did serve her now. She looked at Eldar, who looked back with a cocked eyebrow as if to say, *Do you trust me now?*

"No," Aylin said. "I'm not leaving him. I swear, Yara. I will hate you forever if you separate us."

Aylin huddled close to Ilyas. Her sister trembled at the thought of being parted from him, and Ilyas hunched over her as if he could protect her. Even with his hands bound and severely outnumbered, he would die for Aylin.

"Let them be together," Yara said. "For now."

It felt like her chest was cracking in half, as she watched Aylin be shackled along with Ilyas and the rest of the hunters. The click of the lock sealing shut echoed with finality. Aylin stared at her with a betrayed look that made her chest ache.

It took an hour to round the mercenaries up in chains. Their dirt-stained faces were hollow as they stood in a circle of misery.

"Kill them all," Eldar said.

"You said you would see them sentenced," Yara said, tugging his sleeve.

Aylin and the hunters watched in horror, as his soldiers ripped the hearts of the mercenaries who had surrendered. There was something sickening about seeing men who were incapable of fighting back being murdered. It felt inhumane. She heard the brutal sound of their ribs crashing inwards and the wet sound of their heart being ripped from their shocked forms. "You said it would be fair."

"There is no reprieve but death for the guilty," Eldar said coldly. "Kill the servants, and the blood slaves, and all who served House Carrara."

In the distance, she saw his soldiers yanking out wide-eyed servants and forcing them to their knees beside young girls and boys with haunted looks in their eyes. Their coltish limbs shivered in the cold. She saw Aunt Sevda among the humans, her old bones pressed to the ground.

"Aunt Sevda," Aylin yelled. "Yara, stop them. Stop them, please!"

"You must make difficult choices to become the Undying Queen," Eldar said, stroking a dark claw along her cheek. "Prove to me that you have what it takes. Prove to me that you are mine."

He placed a dagger in her hand. It was heavy. The handle was made of a glossy black enamel. Between the dagger and his ring, it felt like she was slowly being marked by him, covered in his most valued possessions.

Her head tilted. "And then you make me the Undying Queen before the trueborn."

"And then I make you the Undying Queen before all."

"We can use the mortals as blood slaves," she said. "They are not loyal to any house. It is foolish to cut them down."

"Mm-hmm," Eldar murmured. "You have a point."

She felt a bone-deep relief that she'd swayed him. She could not stomach the thought of killing innocent women and children.

"Kill the traitors," he said. "Kill them for me."

Yara stared at the sky. It rumbled, and rain fell as if it sought to erase her sins.

"Do not fall for his deceit, Yara," Aunt Sevda yelled from across the field. "Do not fall for his spell. Be brave. Be steady. Be my Yara."

"Listen to her, Yara," Aylin echoed. "These men fought *your* war. They were loyal to your cause. They have surrendered. They have laid down their arms."

Yara hesitated. On one side, she had her sister and the woman who raised her, and on the other side, she had her monstrous husband.

"Yara, do this for me," Eldar whispered, "and I will give you the world. I swear it."

"He is lying," Aylin yelled. "It is all he knows."

"I don't trust you," she said.

He had swiftly turned against the men whom he had offered a fair trial. He was slaughtering people who had willingly surrendered to his false words. What if all of this was a carefully built lie to destroy her? Yara was his enemy, and what if he had not forgiven her for plotting his demise, for standing with Mircea? What if he intended to turn her against all the people she loved until she had no allies or friends left? What if this was the beginning of the end?

"I never want to lose you again," Eldar said. "There is no trick or deception. Only one final test to prove that I can trust you and that you won't be my undoing."

Yara looked at Aylin. She hoped she could forgive her in the end. She hoped she understood that Yara had nothing anymore, but this last grasp at power. It was the only thing that would fix her. It was the only thing that would make her whole.

"Your Yara is dead," she whispered.

Yara was before the mercenaries within seconds. She didn't blink when she dug the blade into the first man's heart and twisted, watching his face grow ashen and grey. It got easier after the first one, and she could stomach the horrible, squelching sound of her blade tearing out their flesh. She did not linger to watch them fall like uprooted trees. She just moved to the next and the next. Blood soaked her hand and dripped down her wrist like a gruesome bracelet. It was never-ending, and their deaths tainted her soul with invisible marks. But each death was her climb to power and brought her one step closer to gaining Eldar's trust.

"Please," one begged, eyes wide with fear. "Please, do—"

Her blade was in his chest before he could finish his pleas.

Eldar's men worked alongside her, killing them efficiently until there was a mountain of corpses around them and she was drowning in blood. Her claws and teeth had lengthened, and she knew her veins and eyes were just like *his*.

Aylin shivered when she met her eyes, and Aunt Sevda had tears staining her cheeks. She knew then that she had lost them.

She had lost her family.

Yara looked away from them as she returned to Eldar, who gripped her jaw harshly, and she felt his mouth crash down on hers in a bruising kiss.

It was painful.

It was delicious.

It was dreadful.

It was the start of something ruinous and darkly beautiful.

———

A great pyre had been lit for the corpses; they were being tossed into the hungry flames by the dozens. The few who were still alive howled in pain, their mournful sounds echoing miserably in the night. It was only when they had been burned to a crisp that their hearts were torn out from their chests. Eldar had left her side to watch them burn, enjoying their deaths as one would a theatre performance. He stood behind he now, resting his chin on her head, draping his tall form over her in a protective stance.

"I could not picture a better wedding day," Eldar said. "Your God smiles down at us."

"Only you would consider men burning to death a blessing," she said.

Yara stared at him, not fully certain of what she was doing. Only that everything ached. The pain of the past few hours tore through her with the force of a hurricane, leaving behind nothing but ruins. How could she ever trust anyone again? The only person worth trusting was the man behind her, the only person who had never pretended to be anything other than a monster. He could give her power. He could make her strong. He could make her a queen. And so, what if he were her husband? Women had married for status and power for ages. From this moment forward, nothing mattered but her climb to power. Nothing mattered but her ascent to glory. Once her position as queen was secured, she would worry about the rest.

"We will need to stay the day," he said. "Dawn is close."

"Where is Volkan?" she asked. She hadn't seen him since the battle started, and she worried that some harm had befallen him. She couldn't describe all the feelings she was feeling just then. Only that they threatened to knock her over.

"He is confined to my tent," Eldar said, pointing in the distance. "Be gentle but firm when you break his heart."

But it was Volkan who had broken her heart. Torn his fist into her chest cavity and yanked it free. Yara might have stoked the flames of the fire, but Volkan had struck the match. For all she knew he could have been a spy this entire time. And she hated him for it, just as she hated that a part of her understood why he had done it. If she hadn't had Aylin in her life she might have never understood, but she did.

Despite it all, she had loved him. She had felt safe and nurtured in his arms, and when she had thought he'd proposed, she'd been ecstatic. But the truth was that Volkan had never given her his entire heart. A part of him was trapped in the past, in the memories and torment that haunted his mind. He had never fully given himself over to her. He had never promised her a future besides the faint mention of travels and revels. He had never confessed his love. He had never understood why she craved power. Perhaps he had in a superficial manner, but nothing deep or thoughtful. He didn't understand her the way Eldar did.

"I will wait for you when it ends," Eldar said, pressing a cold kiss to her forehead. "I will *always* wait for you."

She leaned against him, feeling his strong frame support her weight. It was easy to get lost in him. His darkness was a comfort. His monstrosity reflected her own.

I could fall in love with him.

And the thought terrified her far more than the war they'd survived.

It was time to cut the last thread that remained of the girl she had been.

It was time for the old Yara to finally die.

XLV

It was strange that her world was falling to ashes around her, and all she felt was numb. She could hear his curses and threats before she lifted the flap of the oily black tent and slipped inside. He kept charging at the four men who surrounded him, but he was simply knocked back off his feet with each attempt at escape.

"Do you worthless mutts know who I am? I am—"

The words caught in his throat at the sight of her. He staggered forward, and she realized she was covered in blood: hers, Mircea's, Zuri's, the men she'd slain. Drenched in the blood of her allies and old friends. All because of Volkan. The anger she'd felt at his betrayal sprung to her chest, lighting her aflame.

"Leave us," she said curtly to the guards.

"We do not take orders from you," the young guard said.

Anger coiled down her spine like a serpent, and she raised her hand to show Eldar's ring. If they failed to see the answer right before them then she would cut out their hearts for it.

"You do now," she said.

"My apologies, my lady," the older, wiser one said. He wrangled the others out of the tent, securing the flaps shut behind him.

"Eldar gave you his ring? He gets defensive when I touch it,"

Volkan said, brushing back a loose strand of his silvery hair. "Like he's earned it. Suppose he has, since he killed our father for it. He thinks I don't know, but I do."

"We lost," she said, in an empty voice. "But you know that already."

"Yara—"

"Did you let him sneak past the gates as you? Offer him your kaftan, so he could destabilize us from within?" she asked. "Did you always know you would betray me?"

"My sweet pet, I—"

"No," she snapped. "No more endearments or pretense. I just want the truth."

He sighed. "I never intended to tell him if there was no chance you would win. I'd let it unfold as it was. Eldar would win, and I would be there to lick your wounds. But if there was the smallest chance that I would be burying my brother at the end of the night, I would find a way to save him," Volkan whispered. "You do not understand, but we came into this world together and we promised that in the end, we would leave together. I would die for him. I would die *with* him."

She felt the wet slide of a tear burn her cheek, and she furiously rubbed it away. Volkan crossed the space between them, daring to put his traitorous hands on her face.

"I'm sorry, Yara," he said, cupping her cheeks. "I'm sorry that saving him came at the cost of hurting you. You are my entire world."

"I don't believe that," she said. "Mircea tried to kill me because he thought I betrayed him. I almost died because of you."

She said that to hurt him, and it brought her some sense of satisfaction when he reared back in shock. His hands trembled when they ran down her body, as if he could feel the evidence of her near death.

"He tore his hand through my chest. I can still feel his fist around my heart. The way he squeezed, and the pain that rippled through my frame," she said. "It is not something I will ever forget. You do not know what it is like to watch someone you trusted hurt you so wretchedly. I had to kill him because he would never stop trying to kill me. He saved my life once, and I was forced to take his. And now there is nothing but this raw ache inside me. Like I will never be whole again."

She didn't tell him of how her sister despised her, and Ilyas looked at her like she was rotten, and Aunt Sevda, who'd been the strongest person she knew, had cried for her as if she too knew she was beyond saving. How everyone she loved hated her, and soon he would hate her too.

"I'm sorry, Yara," Volkan said, staring at her with those big, sad eyes that nearly unraveled the last of her will to stay angry at him. "Tell me how to fix it. I'll do anything."

"It is too late," she whispered. "You broke us."

"No," he said with a firm shake of his head. "We'll leave it all behind. He will never come between us again."

"He has already come between us," she said. "He pretended to be you when he came to me. And that was not all. He also came with a marriage proposal in hand."

"You fell for it?" he asked warily. "Do you not know me well enough by now to tell the difference between my brother and me? I've told you what I thought of marriages, how they're outdated and unfashionable."

"And you know what I thought of marriage, how I dreamed of one as a little girl. I thought the man I loved was giving me what I wanted," she said. "I'm sorry if I didn't analyze every little cue in detail. I was blinded by joy."

"Well, it doesn't matter because it is not valid," he said. "I cannot believe Eldar would— actually, I quite believe he would do something so despicable and conniving."

"He said I could be the Undying Queen," she said. "I have nothing left but this."

Volkan frowned. "You have me. Who cares about ruling a bunch of immortal brats and listening to their petty squabbles?"

"I don't have you, Volkan," Yara said. "I cannot risk being

hurt again. I hate how I feel. I hate all of this. But most of all I hate how much it hurts. *Everything* hurts."

"So, you will give up on us for a shot at power with my unpredictable brother?" he asked between clenched teeth. "And what shall you do when you return to court, and he locks you in a cage as he did before? When he breaks you? Because that is all Eldar is capable of. He does not know how to love. He never has and he never will."

"He almost died for me," she said. "He will make me his queen."

Volkan laughed, a strange, bitter sound. "You are obsessed with him."

"No, I am not," she said.

"You are," Volkan said, his eyes empty and devoid of feeling. "And he is obsessed with you."

"That is not true," she said.

"If you would rather spend your life being miserable with Eldar, then be my guest. It is only a matter of time till one of you kills the other," he said. "I will not beg you to stay with me."

His words were harsh, and he turned his back to her, just as a stray tear trickled down his high cheekbone.

"Volkan," she whispered, reaching for him rather desperately. How did she tell him that this alliance with Eldar was only temporary until she found a way to permanently secure power? That she didn't trust Eldar and she didn't know if she ever could? Even though he had almost died for her, it was not enough to erase this seed of doubt. "It is not as it se—"

"Leave," he snapped. "I never want to see you again."

Out of all the blows she had received today, that one hurt the most. It cut her like glass, shattered her from the inside out, creating a wound she knew might never heal. A strangled sob escaped her lips. She felt small and frightened and weak, and she wanted to be strong again.

She wanted to be unbreakable.

He didn't reach to comfort her. He didn't look at her. It was as if she did not exist.

Yara left just as the sun began to rise from the horizon. Her skin prickled in discomfort, but she ran as fast as she could till she was back in Lugrezia's destroyed manor. Blood stained the floor and corpses lay flat in every corner, limbs twisted and empty eyes staring at the ceiling. She climbed upstairs in a dazed manner to her old guest bedroom. She found a small corner where she could disappear into the shadows and let all the grief of the day assault her at once. She did not deserve the comfort of her bed. Not when she'd had her sister chained and taken to the cellars below. Not when she'd killed so many people who had pleaded for her to spare them. Not when she'd hurt the boy who loved her.

She cried for the dead, the dying and the forgotten.

She cried for Volkan, for her sister and for herself.

She cried until she felt she could not cry anymore.

She felt him before she saw him. Her skin prickled with awareness because of their strengthened sire bond. He crouched down in front of her, his hand absently brushing away her tears.

"I have to go see him," she said, her words a painful hiccup. "I...I made the wrong choice. I...I need to fi–"

"Look at me, Yara," Eldar said, tilting her chin. "You made the right choice. I will lay the world at your feet. I will give you everything your heart desires. I will give you more power than you can imagine. I will give you my soul if you let me."

"How do I know that?" she whispered.

"Because I hated when you left," he said, his brows descending in anger. His voice was slightly raw, like it half killed him to say this. "I hated the silence and the emptiness of the court. I wanted your barbed words and sharp tongue and your beautifully infuriating face. I wanted your plots and schemes and betrayal because it was mine. And they were the only things I had of you. I would have died for you. I would have erased myself from existence if it meant you were whole and safe."

Yara stared into his unreadable black eyes filled with an

unnamed emotion that she did not dare attempt to understand. It tugged at her, and she could feel herself soften at his words. She could feel a bit of her icy heart melt as he claimed a bit of her, snatching the pieces of her soul like a thief.

"Everyone always chose him. My father chose him as his heir to spite me, and my mother loved him in a way she never did me. She thought I was like our father that there was the same rot in me as there was in him. So, she nurtured Volkan, held him and kissed him, and I just stood there and watched. It felt like I was doomed to watch everyone who should have loved me, love him instead. I want you to choose me because no one else ever has. I want you to be mine in a way that no one ever dared to before."

Yara hesitated for a second before she laid her palm flat on his cheek. "Tell me more. I want to understand you."

"I don't want you to think I am weak," he said softly.

"You are the strongest person I know," she said. Her lips pulled up wryly. "Not any person could defeat Vlad, the first vampir."

"You make an excellent point," he said.

He drew her hand from his cheek, clasping it tightly in his palm. It was easier to touch him in the dark, and probably easier for him to speak as well. "He hurt Volkan more because it hurt me. He used him to get to me, and my mother hated that I was the catalyst of his anger. She blamed me for his temper, said that my eyes challenged him. But it wasn't intentional. I hated him so much. I could never quite hide it. So, I'd pretend I didn't care about Volkan and that I hated him. Volkan knew that I was pretending, but my mother didn't. So, she hated me more. She told me she wished I hadn't been born."

"I'm sorry," Yara said, tightening her hold on his hand. "She should have never said such a vile thing. You did not deserve that. Neither of you deserved that. You've shouldered a heavy burden. More than most."

It didn't excuse his actions, but she could understand why someone who had been filled with so much hate had never learned to love. He was cruel because it was all he'd ever known. A harsh mother and a despicable father. At least Volkan had his mother's love, but Eldar had nothing.

He stared at her with those black, void eyes of his, waiting for her to reject him, to turn him away like everyone else.

"When I first arrived at court, I wanted you to save me," she said. "I don't know what it was, but it felt like you had done it before. Saved someone, that is. I know now that you saved Volkan. In every way that counted, you saved your brother. I had thought you would be the reluctant, dark prince who would bring me home," she whispered. "I chose you, Eldar. But you didn't choose me. You *never* chose me."

"I didn't know what it was I felt, and it frightened me. I don't even know what it is now. I don't think there are words for it, and if there are, they escape me," Eldar said. "I know that it consumes me, that it eats away at me like rot in your absence. That the only way to fix it is to have you by my side."

Yara bit her lip, uncertain of how to respond. It was a lot. This entire night had been a lot. A lot of emotions, a lot of death, a lot of confusion. But something inside her was drawn to him. And when she wrapped her arms around him, pulling him into a tight embrace and feeling him rest his head in the crook of her neck like she was his home, Yara had a desperate need to become his home. To become the person he turned to when he had nothing left.

Because they both had nothing anymore. Their family and friends despised them.

All they had now was each other.

XLVI

They were locked in a dark cellar, chained together in one long, silver length and pressed shoulder to shoulder. It should have hurt that her sister had turned on her so swiftly and saw the hunters who had served *her* as a threat, but all she felt was numb. Aylin had trained and fought alongside these men for months on end and saw them as her brothers in arms. She could smell the sharp scents of blood and sweat and decay that created a dank odor. Several of the men were injured. Her own leg shot up a twinge of pain with every step she took.

"Sorry," she whispered when she reached for Ilyas's arm for support. The chains were loose giving her enough room to touch him.

"Come, let me carry you," he said. The guard looked annoyed when he swept her up, but didn't retaliate, possibly following her sister's orders to leave her untouched.

They barely fit in the dark cellar. They were huddled together like lambs to the slaughter. It was strange to see the men look so grim. She looked at Marcello's pain lanced face. She felt a strange sadness that he would never walk again. It didn't take a trained healer to see that his spine was broken. Beside him was Pietro, whose temple was wet with blood. His eyes were glazed, and he was blinking very slowly.

"Are you well, Pietro?" she whispered.

"I'll survive," he said, lips lifting in a hollow smile before dropping abruptly, as if he could not muster up the courage to keep it fixed. Pain lined his face, tension bracketing his pale mouth. "How's your leg?"

A strangled laugh escaped her. Her injury was not bad, compared to the other men. Some of their wounds were so deep and bloody they made her nauseous.

"I'm good," she said, even though the ache made her want to curl up in a ball. "You know how dramatic this one is." She nodded at Ilyas.

"Love makes fools of us all," Pietro said.

Ilyas sat down, cradling her on his lap. He tucked her head beneath his chin.

"Do you need water?" he whispered. "Does your ankle hurt? Are you comfortable? Can I see it? Roll your trousers."

Aylin exchanged an amused look with Pietro.

"I'm injured too," Pietro said with a pout. "I don't see you fussing over me."

Some of the men chuckled and then groaned, as if the action had caused them some pain. Ilyas looked up to the ceiling, and his lips moved as he recited a prayer trying to gather his patience. One of the many she had taught him. He rolled up the leg of her trousers, brushing his fingers over the blooming bruise. It was a starling blue-purple that glowed against her brown skin.

"You shouldn't be here," Ilyas said. "The men and I can handle ourselves. You need a healer."

"No," she said, shaking her head. "She'll hurt you if I leave your side."

Strange that her own sister was now their biggest threat. Aylin had never thought there was a world where she and Yara were fighting a battle from opposite sides. It made her chest ache to think of how cold her sister's eyes had been when she made her decree. How stiff her shoulders. How she'd leaned into him ever so slightly, as if his corruption was leaking into her.

"I can handle myself, Aylin," he said. "But I need you to take care of yourself."

"I'm not leaving you," she said fiercely. "I will *never* leave you."

He sighed, but then he placed his forehead on hers, resigned. Her fingers brushed the sharp bristles of hair that lined his jaw. They were like that for what felt like hours, simply drowning in each other's eyes. The world could be burning to ashes around her, but she knew if she looked into his eyes, she'd only ever feel peace.

"Shall we give you some privacy?" Pietro asked. "I've never seen anyone make love with their eyes."

Pietro made a strangled sound beside them, and she looked at him, alarmed.

"Did you punch him?" she whispered. It had happened so fast she hadn't even registered it.

"In the throat," Ilyas said.

"He's injured. Leave him be," she said in a chiding tone.

Ilyas's lips twitched. "As you wish, my lady."

She felt a yawn split her mouth open, and he tucked her head back onto his chest.

"Get some rest," Ilyas said. "I'll look after you."

His arms tightened around her as the exhaustion of the past few days caught up to her and she fell into a deep, dreamless sleep.

———

"Aylin." Ilyas shook her gently. "Wake up."

"In ten minutes," she promised.

"Now, my love," he whispered. "You have a visitor."

She begrudgingly opened her eyes. When she moved her lower legs, she noticed that someone, likely Ilyas, had bandaged her injured ankle with the scraps of a tunic. Her eyes rose to the person before them, and her mouth pulled into a wide grin.

"Pariza?" she asked. "Have you been imprisoned as well?"

"I've come to save you lot," she said with a pleased impression. "The guards outside are unconscious, and I've stolen the key to your chains."

Aylin wrapped her arms around her friend. Someone had pulled the heavy chains off her wrist without rousing her, which was a miracle.

"Thank you," she said. "I don't know what we'd have done without you."

"It is morning," she said. "Now is your best chance to leave. They cannot follow you until nightfall. Go to the stables. There should be a few horses, enough for you lot."

"Do you know where Sevda is?" Aylin asked.

"The mortals have escaped," Pariza said. "I fear she fled with them."

"Or your sister likely killed her," Ilyas said, his words coated in venom. It sounded so unlike him that her head snapped up to look at him, and then she regretted that she had. He had a murderous look in his eyes that made her stomach lurch with unease. But she did not have time to pick it apart, so she turned back to Pariza.

"Will you come with us?" Aylin asked. "We can wrap you with some blankets against the sun. We'll protect you, won't we, Ilyas?"

"With our lives," Ilyas echoed.

"As much as I'd love to, I cannot abandon Volkan. Not now," she said. "Perhaps, when all this mayhem subsides, we can find a way to see each other."

"I'd like that very much," Aylin said. She kissed her on both cheeks. "Be safe, for me."

"You as well, my sister," she said. She squeezed her hand tight. "Now off you go, before your tyrant sister gets wind of our schemes."

Ilyas stood up, lifting her and gesturing with his fingers for his men to follow. They poured out the doorway, stealing the weapons of the sleeping guards. Pariza took care of the ones by the front door, and Ilyas nodded at her.

"We are in your debt," he said.

"Consider it fulfilled. You could have killed us the day we met," she said. "Take care of her."

"Always," he said.

They made their way to the stables and paired off, since there were not enough horses to ride individually. Ilyas quickly placed her on a stallion and gestured at his men to ride out ahead of them. Ilyas usually led the charge, but she supposed her weakened state made him fall back to the middle, where they were surrounded by the men.

"Where will we go?" she asked, leaning against him.

"Rome," he said. "I will not stop until *he* is dead."

From the venom that coated his voice, she knew exactly who Ilyas spoke of.

"I will assemble an army," he said. "He dared to have his men put their hands on you, and he will lose his life for it."

"What of Yara?" she asked.

Ilyas was silent, and she didn't like how heavy it was. How he didn't reassure her that her sister's life would be spared. While she was beginning to feel something suspiciously like hatred toward Yara, Aylin didn't think she could ever kill her. Or remain sane if she did.

"Ilyas," she said sharply. "Answer me."

"Anyone who stands with him will fall," he said.

"Ilyas!" she said. "If you hurt my sister, there will not be an *us*. Do you understand that?"

"She chained you in a cellar while you were injured," he said. A vein ticked in his jaw. "She has hurt you again and again. Yet you defend her."

"She is my only sister and what she's done is unforgivable, but she will not die at my hands or the hands of man I love," Aylin said. "Do you understand?"

"I like when you yell at me," he said with a soft smile.

"Ilyas Çorbaci!"

"I won't hurt your sister," Ilyas promised.

"Promise me," Aylin said.

"I promise."

She relaxed back into him. Her anger melted as quickly as it arrived; she couldn't be angry at him. Not for long, at least.

Her gaze turned to the sycamore trees before them. The air was still brittle and menacing, leaving behind its frosty touch. The land was weeping tears of melted snow as winter turned over to spring.

"Back to Salvatore then," she said. "He won't like that I lied about being a boy."

"I'll punch him if he says anything," Ilyas said.

Aylin laughed, tilting her head back to look at him.

"Even though you get on my nerves sometimes, I love you," she said. It sounded effortless, but her heart raced so fast she worried it would leap from her skin. It would never get easier speaking those words. For so long she had swallowed them, burying the feeling so deep inside her that giving it life was frightening. They had spoken it earlier on the battlefield, but it was different now. Silent and sweet.

He kissed her forehead. "Love you more. You are my light. You always have been, and you always will be."

His words sank into her chest like a soft lullaby, drawing her deeper into the safety of his arms. With Ilyas, her fears melted away, her insecurities vanished and all that was left was this warm feeling of contentment. She did not want to exist in a world without him.

"And stop distracting me with those big brown eyes of yours," Ilyas said, almost sternly. "I don't want to lose control of the beast."

She chuckled and looked at the path ahead. Surrounded by

the men she trusted most, and safe in the arms of the man she loved, she felt a strange sense of belonging.

But she wouldn't feel entirely satisfied until she killed the Undying King.

And saved Yara from his ruination.

XLVII

Yara stared out the window from inside the carriage. Rain slammed down on the curved roof and dripped down the window. Her claw trailed the glass, following the footprint of the grimy water to the ledge. Aylin had left her, and she'd be lying if she said it didn't hurt. It shouldn't have affected her so much, since she'd known what would happen when she stood with Eldar. She knew she'd have to lose all the people she loved. Not to mention that the loss of Volkan had cut her deeper than she expected.

She felt Eldar's claw scrape her cheek. She hadn't even felt the tear slip past her eyes until he touched her.

"I will take care of you, little mouse," he whispered. "I will give you everything this world has to offer and more."

She looked at him, feeling sad and forlorn, wondering if power was worth this empty feeling in her chest. He lifted her, pulling her onto his lap, and she hated that his proximity soothed her.

"We've won, Yara," Eldar said. "The throne is ours. And we are together, as it was always meant to be. It was always supposed to be you and me in the end."

"How do you know that?" Yara whispered.

"Because I can't survive without you," Eldar said, fingers stroking down her spine. "And I know, despite it all, you feel the same about me."

Yara was silent, but she leaned her forehead against his shoulder. Several hours passed before the carriage came to a stop.

"This isn't Poenari," she said staring out the window. It was a small manor with a corpse of trees shrouding it. For a moment a spike of fear struck her. What if this was another prison? Yara quickly stepped out of the carriage. He followed her, folding his tall frame in half to step outside.

"Eldar?"

"It is one of the many houses I've put under your name," he said. "I thought we could spend a few days here and get to know each other better."

He had a nervous look in his eyes, and he tucked his hands awkwardly into his pockets as if he did not quite know what to do with them. It took her a second for his words to sink in, and her eyes widened. When she'd been in the Ottoman court, she'd spent time with the women in the harem, and they'd spoken much about consummating a marriage. She had gained enough information that Yara was familiar with the intimate details of the act. She wondered if that was what he wanted. If it would be anything like when he'd touched her in Lugrezia's Hall, raw and wild.

"Or we can return to court," he said a bit stiffly, like he regretted pitching the idea. He turned to the carriage, and she grabbed his forearm.

"Why are we here?" she whispered.

"I told you," Eldar said. "To learn about each other. I know a few things about you. I know that you like flowers, in particular lilies. I know that you don't read for leisure unless you are learning something from it. I know that you don't need a blade in your hand because your mind is the sharpest blade you have. I know that you like being outside rather than inside. I know that your favorite color is red. I know that you adjust your dress once every few hours because you are uncomfortable in your own skin, which is hard to believe since you are the most striking woman in every room you enter."

Yara felt herself soften at his words. He'd always watched her at court, she just hadn't known he'd been paying so much attention to her. She lifted her hand to touch his cheek, feeling an odd tightness in her chest.

"I'd like to learn more about you too," she said. He leaned his cheek into her palm. His eyes were slightly closed, long lashes fluttering against his high cheekbones. As if he were content to spend eternity locked in this moment.

When her hand dropped back to her side, Eldar grasped her palm and led her up the stone stairs into the foyer. Servants were lined on one side and blood slaves on the other side. The stone walls were dark, casting the room in shadows. Only the dim candles placed sporadically on the bone-white ledges illuminated the space. It was dark and soulless, reminding her a bit of her new husband.

He guided her up the wide stairs, and when he looked back at her with a sharp smile that was intended to be reassuring, all she could think was that she'd accepted the hand of the Devil.

And he would lead her straight to Hell.

Yara sat nervously on the edge of the bed. Her hair was plaited in a long, thick braid that hung down her back. The servants had bathed and dressed her, working in silence. Eldar had left to prepare in his bedroom, which was connected to her own by a pair of double doors. The bed sheets had been changed while she was dressed, a ring of maids tugging the fresh cotton sheets and flattening the bear fur.

She wore a long, flimsy nightgown the color of cherries. The ends of her gown stretched along the Turkish carpets, covering the fabric like a second skin. It was comforting to find little touches of home.

Her back was straight, and she toyed with her fingers as she waited for him. It felt like hours passed before he knocked. If she were still a mortal, she knew her heart at that moment would be beating a fierce rhythm. She felt oddly shy at the thought of seeing him. It was strange to not be fighting or actively hating each other. It made their truce feel intimate in a way she could not describe. As if now that they had seen the worst of each other and had not run off, it meant something.

"These cuffs are infuriating," he grumbled, fumbling with the buttons gracing his wrists that were far too small for his big hands.

"Did you frighten your servants away?" she asked. "Why didn't they fix it for you?"

"I don't let anyone touch me," he said. "*Ever.*"

"Come," she said standing. "Let me."

His head snapped up, and he saw her for the first time. He'd seen her in nightgowns plenty of times, but not one as grandiose and sensual as this. She watched his eyes darken, and a thrill ran down her stomach at how completely entranced he looked.

It took her a minute to fix his buttons. When she was done, she focused on separating the ends of his hair with her fingers. He hadn't bothered to comb it, and it lay in a dark tangle on his chest.

"Perfect," she said, smoothing a palm over his chest to fix the crinkles of his black coat. "I thought we were preparing for bed, not dinner."

"We can do what you please," he said politely.

"How accommodating," she said with a small twitch of her lips. "Will you always be this kind to me?"

"I will," Eldar said in a serious tone. "I have no reason to push you away anymore. I am done lying to myself about what I want."

"May we dance?" she asked. "Together."

"There is no music," he said. "And I don't like to dance."

"We will pretend that there is music," she said. "And you can pretend that you like to dance."

"You will sing for me," Eldar said. "And I will dance with you."

Yara bit her lip. "I don't want to sing."

She felt a timidness that she couldn't shake off. One that she'd never felt before. As if they were meeting for the first time. And perhaps, in some ways, they were. She had never seen this side of him before: quiet, sullen, thoughtful and kind. It was strange.

"You've performed before thousands," Eldar said. "You won't do it for your husband?"

She could tell he was pleased to call himself her husband. And more so when her eyes widened in shock.

"Fine," she whispered. She sang a song Aunt Sevda had taught her, of a girl who had loved a trickster whose final trick was stealing her heart. Eldar wrapped his hands around her waist. And he didn't really dance, he simply held her and watched her with his void eyes. She closed her eyes to escape the intensity of his stare as she sang.

"Did you like it?" she whispered when she was done.

"Am I your trickster?" he asked, leaning down to whisper in her ear. "Your wolf in disguise. Your black-hearted thief. Your monstrous villain."

"Yes," she said, feeling his teeth graze her ear. She shivered in his arms, unable to hide the echoes of her mortal habits from him.

"Did I tell you how beautiful you look?" Eldar asked.

"No," she said.

"Let me show you," he said.

His hand clasped her neck and drew her toward him till their mouths collided. He kissed her with a desperation that drowned her. Their tongues tangled in hunger as his palm ran up her side, fingers digging into her ribs like he intended to leave a mark. His fist wrapped around her braid, using it to keep her in place. As if she could run from him. As if she *wanted* to. At this moment, she realized that this cord between them was a lot stronger than she had thought. And it was slowly beginning to wrap around her heart like a stray vine, cutting her with all its thorns. There was a reason they shared a sire bond. There was a reason he'd fallen to his knees for her and crawled to Mircea to save her life.

It struck her then that he loved her, and a small part of her loved him too.

"How long did you want me?" she asked against his hungry mouth.

"I've wanted you since the day you crawled between my legs to run from my brother and looked at me with those big brown eyes," Eldar said. "I just didn't know it then."

She pressed her mouth to his again. Eldar drew back, staring at her in that intense manner of his.

"But I knew that it was far more than I could fathom when Mircea threatened to kill you," Eldar said. "I knew then that I would die for you, and it frightened me because I didn't think I was capable of caring for anyone."

"I'm scared," she whispered, "of falling in love with you."

His lips curved in a glorious smile that made her chest ache because she had never seen *that* smile before. She hadn't known it even existed.

He ran his thumb along her cheekbone before he lifted her with a single arm, laying her flat on the feather bed and pinning her with his body. His tongue tangled with hers with a burning need far more fervent than earlier. It was almost worshipful, and his fists clutched her hair like she was his salvation. Everything was so intense with Eldar: talking, kissing, fighting. It was like she was too big for her skin. Like she would unwind into nothing if she allowed herself to. His kisses were growing more intense, more wrecking, more destructive. And she felt a small kernel of panic.

"I hate you," she murmured when his mouth drifted to her jaw.

"Then hate me," he replied.

"Did you do this before?" she asked nervously, drowning in his dark gaze. He was on his knees above her, fingers slowly and delicately unraveling the golden buttons of his black velvet coat. He drew it back, revealing his pale torso.

"No."

"No?" She rested on her elbows, staring at him curiously. "Truly?"

Volkan had been with so many people, she had assumed Eldar had his fair share of lovers. His fingers undid the button of his trousers and she swallowed, eyes locked on the flash of skin.

"I don't like people."

"I'm people."

"You don't count."

Her lips lifted in a strangely triumphant smile.

"Do you trust me?" he asked.

"Not yet," she whispered. "But at this moment I do."

"I can live with that."

Eldar kissed her longer and slower. Desire knotted her stomach, and she was surprised by the sounds that escaped her as he kissed a path down her neck.

"Touch me," he breathed against her skin in a soft tone so unlike himself, she wanted to weep. She didn't want him to change for her. She was so scared of not hating him that it made her want to hide.

She did as he said and curled her fingers into his hair, feeling his cursed mouth bite and lick and torment. It was a wonder that the same mouth that had once spewed such vile words at her now sought to paint her with his devotion.

In the dark, she could hide from her sins and let her vicious husband worship her.

———

Yara stared up at him, head resting on his pale chest. His skin was smooth as marble. Eldar toyed with his ring on her thumb. His other hand stroked her spine, claws running along her flesh in a light caress. She hadn't expected him to be so gentle. To unravel her like she was the finest gift he had ever received. To whisper to her that he'd keep her safe *always*. It was getting easier to believe his words, to fall into them like a dream. But she still didn't know if it was the truth he spoke or just beautiful lies.

"Do you want it back?" she whispered.

"No," he said. "It belongs to you now. I'll have it resized when we get home."

Home.

The word had haunted her ever since she left the Ottoman court, trailing after her like a ghost and clinging to her hem with slippery fingers. She had wanted to return home so badly. It was an incessant ache inside her. When she had reunited with Aylin, for a second, it felt like she could go home, could erase the nightmare of the vampir court, scrubbing at it like a stain until it vanished. But that life was robbed from her, and she had learned to accept who she was. With Eldar's words, that old longing crept up inside her, a need for a place that belonged to her. A place that made her feel safe.

"Poenari is not my home," she said.

It was where she'd lost everything. It was where she had bled.

"It won't be like before," he said. "You won't be alone. You will *never* be alone again."

"What if you hurt me again?" Yara whispered. "What if it is all a lie?"

"None of this is a lie," Eldar said. His finger slid behind her nape. "Did my touch feel like a lie?"

"No," she said.

"What about my kiss?" he asked. He pressed his mouth to hers softly, but still hungrily. Even when he tried to be gentle, he could not hide that hunger. He could not hide the desperate press of his fingers sinking deep into her flesh, or the slide of his vicious canines that unraveled with desire and claws that lengthened to sharp points. He could not hide that he was a monster.

"No," she said against his mouth.

"I do not seduce my enemies, Yara," Eldar said. "I cannot stomach the thought of ever touching someone, let alone under the guise of politics. You are the only person whom I ache to touch. You are the only person who is strong and brilliant enough to be my equal. To be my queen."

"I will need a lot of reassurance," she said, "until I can learn to trust you."

He was a difficult person to read. It was like flipping through a book that had been written in a foreign language. All she had were his words, and those were not enough. She wondered if they would ever be enough. If it was possible to build something with someone she did not trust, or if their relationship would simply burn around them in ashes.

"Do you trust me?" she asked.

"No," Eldar said.

Yara laughed, the sound surprising her. "We are a miserable pair."

Eldar's lips quirked slightly, and she realized he and Volkan had different smiles, and that perhaps she liked his more. She didn't know what that meant, and she was too tired to pluck it apart. So, she tucked it away, somewhere deep inside her.

"Do you think he will ever forgive me?" he asked.

Yara stared at him, and he looked away, but not before she caught the glimmer of sadness that flickered across his face.

"I hope so," she whispered. "I hope they all forgive us."

Aylin, Ilyas and Aunt Sevda might never forgive her. Volkan might never forgive Yara or Eldar. It was a risk they took by choosing their ruthless ambition over the people who loved them. There was a deep abyss in her chest. An emptiness that could not be filled. Out of all the misery she had caused, the worst was the harm she'd inflicted on Aylin. Aylin, who had chased away her nightmares. Aylin, who had loved her even when she became the very creature she hunted. Aylin, who had sacrificed everything to fight her war and who had been rewarded with nothing in the end.

Eldar tightened his arms around her as if he could stop her from breaking.

It had to be worth it in the end. All this pain had to amount to something.

She clung tight to Eldar as if she could bury herself under his skin. As if they could become one person if she simply tried hard enough. She slid her eyes shut, hunting for sleep to pull her into its dark abyss. To flee the pain she'd caused and fall into a deep oblivion, a place where her sins no longer consumed her.

XLVIII

Yara awoke feeling Eldar's limbs tangled around her own. She felt different, changed, yet still somehow the same girl who had arrived in Poenari with her heart in her throat and her dreams clutched tight in her fist. She still had those echoes of longing for a love that destroyed, and lying here tangled in the arms of her enemy and husband, it felt as though perhaps those dreams had morphed into something that resembled a beautiful nightmare.

Eldar was a force that could sweep over villages and houses until there was nothing left behind but wreckage, and he had swept up Yara, plucking her from everything she had once known until there was only *him*. She felt the tight cord of their sire bond running between them, stronger than ever before. A trickle of fear slipped down her gut at the thought that, by giving herself to him, she had strengthened their sire bond. Her nostrils grazed his pale throat, inhaling his scent, and her teeth lengthened even though she had fed. It was a strange, primal need to sink under his skin. To be so utterly wrapped in him that nobody could unravel them both.

She had sunk her teeth into him earlier, and he had done the same to her. They drank each other's blood even though it did not keep them fed. An act layered in intimacy.

Yara stood up and snatched his discarded kaftan, tightening it around her body. She needed some space to think, distance to clear her mind.

The wood creaked under her feet, and she was surprised to find the front door was wide open. The wind whistled as it swept inside the foyer, bringing with it a dusting of snow. She could smell rotten blood. Vampir blood. And when she stepped outside, she saw the fallen forms of the dead sentries, their vacant eyes staring at the sky, their skin grey and mottled. Yara felt a cold hand wrap around her mouth, choking her cry of alarm. The grip was far too strong to be a mortal. It had to be a vampir.

A figure approached, tall and fair-haired. His robe was finely made and threaded by the finest Venetian dressmakers. She had seen him before, during the battle at Poenari. He was the leader of the vampir hunters.

"Do you know my name?" he asked.

Since her mouth was still bound by a forceful hand, she could not answer.

"My name is Salvatore Di Mazi," he continued.

Yara frowned, confused by his presence. How had he found them? How had he defeated Eldar's sentries so swiftly? Had he forced one of them to betray the others?

Yara tried to fight off the vampir behind her, but it was far stronger than most vampir. Mircea had told her the strongest vampir were newborns who had been freshly awakened. Their bodies were filled with so much fresh blood, it made them almost invincible. Her neck twisted to see who stood behind her.

Her mouth dropped open in shock.

It was *Domenico*.

Domenico, whom she had buried in an empty plot of land to protect Ilyas and her sister. Domenico, who had fallen by Ilyas's hand. Domenico, who should have been *dead*.

His skin was pale and ghostly, and his eyes were empty, as if what little humanity had once resided behind the green orbs had been sucked away.

"Surprise," he said with a cold smile.

Her thoughts tripped over themselves, buzzing in her head like a swarm of bees. How was he alive? How had he found them? How had he survived? Why was he working with the hunters if he was a vampir? Why had he brought their leader to their doorstep?

"I had Stefano waiting in the shadows of the bathhouse," Domenico explained. "He came to me with a vial of my mother's blood when that bastard left before Aylin arrived. I was awake, you see. I just pretended. Felt her pretty tears dripping on my chest. Felt the dirt fill my nose as you buried me."

Domenico's hand slipped a little, not far enough that she could get through a command, without him slamming it back down before the words slipped past her mouth. He was smarter than she had thought.

"Why are you working with the hunters?" she whispered. "Why are you working with *him*?"

"I never stopped working with Salvatore to kill the Undying King and all those who stand by him. I always served the hunters. But I didn't fully hatch my plan to sell you to Salvatore until *his* return, until I saw him take her from me. Aylin will feel what I felt when I lost her. The pain I felt knowing that she protected him, and I was left in an empty plot of land to rot. You will suffer for all her sins."

There was a madness that clouded his eyes that frightened her. It wasn't mere obsession that she was witnessing. It was destruction. It was pandemonium.

"Aylin should not have chosen him," Domenico whispered harshly in her ear. "I will break everything she has ever loved. I will not stop until there is nothing left behind but ashes."

"You will not survive the end of this tale," Salvatore said in his soft voice, such a contrast to the harsh look in his eyes.

Yara knew in that moment that she was going to experience an ordeal worse than she ever had before. It was written in his eyes.

Any hardship she had experienced in the vampir court as a mortal would be nothing compared to the pain the hunters would enact on her vampir flesh. "Your vampir husband had the chance to kill me, but he let his hubris get the best of him. He let me live, and that choice will cost him everything."

Her anger spiked, both that he dared to think he could break her, and because Eldar had spared him. She could not fathom the decision behind Eldar's choices, but she knew that he had been wrong. Salvatore and Domenico should have never been allowed to survive the battle at Poenari.

The enemy he had spared would be the one to doom them all.

"Sleep," Salvatore said.

Yara heard the jolting crack of her neck being broken.

And then there was only an abyss of darkness.

XLIX

Eldar jolted, feeling a sense of panic. It tugged at his chest, yanking him awake with a roughness that was unsettling. Vampir did not dream, so it could not have been a sour nightmare. The side of his bed was empty. He could smell Yara's floral scent still fresh on the sheets. She could not have been gone long. Fear slid down his nape with its ghostly fingers. Had she left him?

He had barely dragged on his trousers before he was out the room. He moved like the wind, flying down the stairs and walking out the abandoned doorway, his nostrils tinged with the smell of vampir blood. His men were dead. All of them. He knew then without a shadow of a doubt that she was gone.

Yara was gone.

A creak behind him made him shoot out his hand and catch the intruder. He stared at a blond-haired vampir who did not belong to his household. He did not wear the Demirci livery.

"Who are you?" Eldar snarled. "Where is she? Where is my *wife?*"

"She left you," he said. "She killed your men and left."

"Who are you?" His grip around his throat tightened.

"Domenico Carrara," he said. "My mother was the traitor you slain. I have come to serve you. And the girl you speak of has left."

Eldar frowned. "Where did she go?"

Why would she leave me?

He had given her everything he could possibly give. He had given her his title and his land and his dead, rotting heart. He would have given her anything she desired.

"It was a ploy," Domenico said. "All of it. She returned to her sister and the big idiot." A spark of anger crossed his eyes before it was gone. "She stands with the hunters. She stands with Salvatore Di Mazi. She intends to kill you."

"No," Eldar said, his voice hoarse and ravaged. The word was full of doubt. His chest clenched in pain. She had given herself to him. She had chosen him, and he refused to believe she would leave him. Not after he had proven himself.

"I am sorry, my lord," Domenico said. "She is not who she seems. She is a traitor like my mother, like her sister, like all of them. None of them can be trusted."

"I don't even know you," Eldar snarled.

"I know her sister Aylin," Domenico replied. "We were close, and she betrayed me. It is in their blood to be unfaithful, to betray."

His words were bitter. From the dark look in his eyes, he had indeed met Yara's sister and there was bad blood between them. But Yara was *nothing* like her sister. Yara was supposed to be *his* queen.

Domenico opened his hand, revealing the ring he had given Yara. It was cold when it fell in his palm. The iron ring glistened in the dark. His family sigil mocking him.

Nobody will ever love you.

Nobody will ever want you.

His mother's word spun in his mind like a broken lullaby, and for the first time in a long time, he felt his dead heart splinter. It wasn't enough. Nothing he did was enough. No trick, no manipulation, no raw truth would ever endear him to her. He had bared himself to her, softened himself to appeal to her, and erased all his harsh edges until he resembled a man worthy of her affection. He had ostracized and hurt his brother for nothing. He had pushed away the only person who loved him in this world for her.

And still it was not enough.

He would always be the monster in her story.

He would always be the villain.

He closed his eyes, feeling the invisible lines that made their sire bond. An invisible cord that traveled between their souls. He could still feel the echo of her panic, but nothing else, as if she had forged a shield to keep him out. She was likely worried that he would hunt her down, that he would reach out to her, but Eldar would not hunt her. Not when he could not feel her.

He was done giving his heart to a girl who would *never* love him. He was done trying to convince himself that he could be loved.

He severed their sire bond. It cut him in half, like he was cleaving his heart in two, like he was breaking and crumbling to pieces far too small for him to ever be whole again. The pain was enough to bring him to his knees. His hair swept his face in a curtain of despair.

He sealed his eyes shut.

And when they reopened, he felt the way he always had.

Empty.

Broken.

Alone.

Acknowledgments

Huge thank you to all the readers who read *The Court of the Undead* this sequel would be nothing without all of you. Thank you to my editor Lynsey for editing this beast of a book, and to all the professionals who collaborated on this project. I'd like to thank my alpha and beta readers who read this book, and whose enthusiasm reminded me why I wrote this book. I'd like to thank my parents for raising me to love books and nurturing my passion for writing. Lots of love to my best friends for praying for my success and for supporting me unconditionally and unwaveringly. You inspire me in every way that matters. Lastly, thank you to Damon Salvatore and Klaus Mikaelson who ignited my love for villains, and who inspired Eldar Demirci.

About the Author

F.M. Aden has been writing ever since she learned how to hold a pen. She grew up in Toronto, Canada, and is a lover of all things dark, gothic, and romantic. She likes to spend her free time drinking iced coffee and baking. When not reading or watching T.V, she can be found traveling across the globe and discovering new ways to make her characters suffer.